I0636519

"An invenetive, wildly entertaining novel, which revolves around the hazards of writing a memoir about one's family. What a cast of characters Brian Alessandro has brought to life, thorugh sparkling dialogue and vivid, often comical scenes. I enjoyed *Julian's Debut* immensely!" —Bill Hayes, author of *Insomniac City: New York, Oliver Sacks, and Me*

"Brian Alessandro has written a rollicking family story that follows a flawed and fascinating character through the ethical terrain of memoir writing. Funny, beautifully written and brimming with the best kind of big questions." —Lexi Freiman, author of *The Book of Ayn*

"Brian Alessandro's *Julian's Debut* is a masterful exploration of wit and emotional depth—a fearless, unapologetic examination of the fine line between truth and betrayal in storytelling. With raw vulnerability and sardonic humor, Alessandro vividly captures a protagonist navigating the delicate balance of baring familial scars to the world. This novel delves into the complexities of loyalty, identity, and the resilience that defines us, all while embracing our beautiful imperfections." —Emanuel Xavier, author of *Love(ly) Child*

"Julian Sorrento has had enough. Enough of being an underseen writer, enough of being used by his family, who have thrust him into the role of 'everyone's therapist, support coordinate, advocate, sounding board, and bank.' When he sits down to write a memoir about them, all brakes are off. One after another, they confront him after it's a success, but in the world of this novel, the greatest prize turns out to be liberation: where art begins. By turns comic, wrenching, appalling, bewildered, shrewd, never nice, and always alive, *Julian's Debut* is a powder keg of a book that explodes and explodes." —Paul Lisicky, author of *Song So Wild and Blue: A Life with the Music of Joni Mitchell*

JULIAN'S DEBUT

BRIAN ALESSANDRO

REBEL SATORI PRESS

New Orleans & New York

Published in the United States of America by
Rebel Satori Press
www.rebelsatoripress.com

Cover design: Brian Alessandro

Library of Congress Control Number: 2024952379

This book is dedicated to Annette Alaggia, Anthony "Tony" Vargas, Jr., and LeeAnn Passaro. Though you left us far too soon, your impressions remain. And for Edmund White and Michael Carroll, your friendship continues to nourish. I'm a braver writer because of you.

"To say the secret of another is a betrayal, to say yours is a stupidity."
— Voltaire

CHAPTER 1

If murder were legal, my family would have killed me. When my essay about them was published in *The New Yorker*, the Sorrentos, the Barthas, the Byrnes, and the Clints called incessantly, left hostile voicemails, and sent threatening texts with too many exclamation points and exploding head emojis, the ones with the censored expletives over the mouths. Those who lived nearby even showed up to complain about what I'd included and omitted. Fortunately, my pre-war one-bedroom was on the sixth floor of a Jackson Heights walkup and required an intercom buzz-in, which I ignored. Even my ex, Raul, who was not at all implicated in the piece, fired off furious, damning texts. It was his nature to excoriate.

Everyone challenged my account of events, expressed their displeasure with my admission, suggesting a betrayal of trust. Their suspicions were absurd, and the accusations were offensive. I have always prided myself on my integrity, even if I like a good fable well told. Life is often tedious or boring or too sad to bear, but I do not make things up whole cloth. I certainly did not lie in the article. *The New Yorker* has fact checkers anyway and a huge legal department, so they wouldn't publish anything that might come back to bite them on the ass. Maybe I tend to exaggerate a bit or to condense characters and events when writing, but even leading memoirists find that acceptable when writing an autobiography for the sake of readability. My Aunt Mary—my mother's "weird, bookish sister," according to my father—was generous with her guidance when I was in high school and thought I would become a writer. An abandoned pursuit until this essay. She would take time out of her busy academic career to read my short stories about sex robots, anarchistic mind readers, and pornographer clones to give me notes. Her feedback was always encouraging even when the stories lacked plausibility, and she especially complimented my "easy grace with verisimilitude." To her, I could make even the most unbelievable events seem believable. Or maybe she was just being encouraging because she saw my passion and didn't want to nip it in the bud.

My Mighty Meekness, the problematic article, really a mini memoir, raised the ire of not only my parents, but also my sister, brother, sister-in-law, brother-in-law, paternal grandfather, two nephews, Aunt Mary, her husband, my Uncle Monroe, and their son, Pegasus. I was surprised to learn that not everyone sought fame or to be written about. I thought they'd appreciate what I'd done. I thought they would have been flattered to be included.

My mother had rushed out to buy a copy of the issue the day it arrived at the Barnes & Noble in the mall near her house. Maybe the only time she's ever bought a copy of *The New Yorker*. She called multiple times as she read it. Couldn't even wait until she got to the end. When I tuned out her calls and didn't listen to her voicemail messages, she began texting. Something she abhorred. Her messages reiterated the same request:

> Mom: Julian, please call me. I hate texting. I am proud of you for getting yourself up there, but we need to talk about what you've done.

I could understand everyone's reluctance to share the family saga with readers. After all, our origin story was one of shame, humiliation, poverty, loss, and disgrace.

> Mom: Julian, call me right now! Stop making me text!

During the week of publication, my father buzzed my intercom every other day, as the drive from Bergen County wasn't too bad after rush hour: "You did what you had to do to get up there, right? The rest of us saps be damned! Look, I know you're home, you fucking ingrate! Open the goddamn

door and let me up! I just want to talk!"

By the second week it was once every three days and then once a week and then not at all. No one had my stamina. I could outlast them all.

The janitor in my building was a sweet, middle-aged man from Hermosillo named Arturo, and I would regal him with recollections of my Peace Corps work in Mexico City. I recounted the time I saved three children from a burning orphanage, rushing in through a broken back door to pull them away from the roof that I knew would collapse within minutes. Then there was the encounter with a defected mule from the Sinaloa cartel, who had stolen a bazooka. He and I would drive up to the Sonoran Desert to fire it off into the ink black sky in the middle of the night, prompting tarantulas, Gila monsters, and javelinas to scamper out of sight. Another episode centered on my Olympian swim from Mazatlán to Cabo San Lucas, outwitting sharks, heat stroke, and riptides. Maybe because my Spanish was as poor as his English, he seemed to believe me. Why would I make any of this up? I mean, of course, I did, and I've only ever been to Mexico once and that was when I was fifteen and went with a friend and his parents for a week to Puerto Vallarta. Maybe he knew I'd lied and was just being polite, humoring my demented tall tales. I am not sure why I was compelled to lie to Arturo. I guess I wanted to see how convincingly I could tell incredible stories. That said, my essay in *The New Yorker* is completely true.

In fact, I'd been told that my article offered a rare insight into self-sacrifice from someone within the social service industry. Some readers and my agent, the influential Caroline Herzer, said that I had offered a rarified look inside at a social condition and psychological predisposition not often accurately explored. Some would argue it was poverty porn or fetishistic in its compromising minutiae about my family. But the nature of the piece was always about exploitation itself, mine, that is. How my family had used me, leaned on me too heavily, and how their needs throughout my childhood and young adulthood led me to social work, where I would continue to go without, in this case an adequate salary and a desire to one day write fiction, in lieu of helping others.

Caroline had decided to represent me based solely on the popularity of the essay, but with the understandable promise that I would develop it into a book, something we'd both be able to monetize, which meant that I'd need to write even more about these people who were still angry with me. Mere paragraphs would swell to become entire chapters. One or two personal admissions would become dozens. Glossed over incidents would demand microscopic scrutiny. If the article was a tremor, a book would be a major seismic event.

My brother, James, his wife, Luz, and their son, Vaughan, took turns texting and calling me those first few days after the article was published. Their voicemail messages ranged from the moderately patient to the downright apoplectic.

> James: "What were you thinking, bro? I know you wanted to get yourself up there, but like this? Give me a call. We need to talk about this garbage."
>
> Luz: "I am a little embarrassed for you, Julian, if this is what you think you need to do to succeed as a writer."
>
> Vaughan: "Uncle Julian, I thought we were cool, man."
>
> James: "You're a fucking boneheaded pussy, Julian! You don't get to just write whatever crazy fucking shit pops into your sick head!"
>
> Luz: "You are lucky we don't sue your ass, Julian! You are a hateful, stupid hack!"
>
> Vaughan: "You're a traitor to your family and

to the gay community and I hope this eats you
up, you miserable wannabe."

My sister, Sophia (she and James were full siblings, unlike me, and were almost the same age), her husband, Doug, and their son, Arnold, surprised me by being at first the most congenial and understanding of the lot, though Arnold did eventually spook me with his threats. They called and I didn't answer, so they left voice mail messages and sent texts, of course.

Sophia: I guess you had your reasons to do
what you did to get up there, but you have to
live with it now, Julian.

Douglas: It was a scumbag thing to do, to
pulverize us like that, but I get it. You're
playing dirty like we all play dirty. Just
don't act like you're above any of it anymore.
You had to get yourself up there as much as
any other lowlife gold digger I've ever known.

Arnold: Uncle Julian, I always respected you
and it's cool that you got yourself up there
and even though you're gay I never let any of
my friends talk shit about you or other homos.
But now. I don't know no more. I may go fuck
up a faggot just to get back at you.

They all used the same expression, "up there," as though "up there" was this mythic place of better people with better lives and if I ascended, I'd be better, too, and entitled to do what I pleased with impunity, which maybe in their minds I already did.

The most interesting plots centered on Aunt Mary, Uncle Monroe, and Pegasus. Their stories, only a few pages in *My Mighty Meekness*, had caught the attention of the Darlington Brothers. They optioned the rights to the entire piece, but they were only interested in adapting the storylines about

Mary, Monroe, and Pegasus into a MAX series, all other family members would be excised, except for a cameo by my mother. Mary was a Columbia University anthropologist who had inadvertently caused a civil war in northeastern India due to her clumsy ethnographic methodologies. Her engineer husband, Monroe, built bombs for Raytheon in their New Jersey plant. Their radical poet son, Pegasus, protested both of their "immoral" behaviors by inviting homeless people to live with them, thereby testing their tolerances, or mercies. The Darlington Brothers renamed the story *The Touring Barbarism*. The title was poetic and apt.

They too texted.

> Mary: Julian, you know I always considered you the bright star in the family. A true thinker who would pull himself out of that peasant mentality, but with this essay, maybe I just don't think I was right about you. Please do not go forward with the book!

> Monroe: The temerity to accuse me of building bombs. That you would, first of all, reveal that information is legally suspect. And second, I am not a killer, you little twerp.

> Pegasus: Rock on, cousin. Burn it all down.

Sometimes I would strike up conversations with the teenagers playing basketball in the schoolyard down the block from my apartment. It was the location of the horrible murder of Julio Rivera, a gay man, in 1990. Three white skinheads wanted to "reclaim" their turf from the gays and the homeless and targeted him with a hammer and knife. All the kids I spoke with knew of Julio as his death had so disturbed the neighborhood that residents made sure to turn Jackson Heights into a haven for the LGBTQ community. I had told these boys that I was a police officer at the local precinct, the 115th, and was undercover, looking for members of the Latin Kings and MS13 wanted for human trafficking and murder. I even had phony cards printed with a bogus name, "Detective Jason Johnson," with a fake number. They looked real enough to convince the kids. I have no idea if they ever called the number on the card but whenever I would see them, on my way to the train or returning from food shopping or the gym, they would nod, knowingly, as though they thought of themselves as informants helping with an important operation.

By the time my article was released, all my grandparents had been dead except for Angelo, my father's father. He was an ornery eighty-five, still capable of carrying his own groceries and vacuuming his own apartment, cooking his own meals, and bedding myriad "mistresses" (since he'd never divorced my grandmother, any lover felt like an infidelity) in his undersized Bay Ridge studio.

I received a handwritten letter from Grandpa. It was thoughtful and poignant, if not wounding.

Julian,

You write well. Maybe you could have been Steinbeck. Or Mickey Spillane. But you decided to go and do a hit job on your family instead. And so now you don't have the soul to write about the everyman anymore. The poor man. The struggle. You have lost that right. The right to tell the world about desperation. You will not be a crime writer either because your tall tales are unbelievable. They will all see right through you. Life is short. It goes fast. Don't hurt the wrong people.

Love, Grandpa A.

In addition to getting a major literary agent to represent me and celebrated filmmakers to hire me for a screenwriting gig, the article also brought the author Edward Grey and his husband Kevin Tracy into my life.

Edward was well into his eighties and regarded as the godfather of queer literature and his husband Kevin, a full thirty years younger than him, was also a writer, but had given it up to, as he put it, "play dutiful housewife." Kevin had read my article in *The New Yorker* when it was first published over a year ago and then found me on Facebook a few days later. He'd sent me a message and we chatted for a week or two before he invited me over for one of their weekly dinners that were always well attended by New York luminaries and other, smaller writers or composers or socialites or scientists, sometimes even actors, and we have remained great friends ever since. Though I doubted my place at their table, the two things that made me feel instantly safe with Edward and Kevin were their lack of pretense and their kindness. They ordered pizza or Chinese food during these parties with important people probably accustomed to caviar, white truffles, and duck confit, and they seemed genuinely interested in me and my work, and never made me feel inadequate, even when I didn't get an Opera reference or a French phrase. I think everyone liked the way Ed and Kevin made them feel at home and appreciated, which is why they kept coming, a different set of guests every week on an ever-rotating carousel of outsized personalities.

My family, on the other hand, not nearly as cultured, successful, or famous, almost always made me feel insecure with their apathy or criticisms. With them, I'd assumed the roles of accommodator and doormat. They were unfortunate in their way. Not bad. Not intentionally bad. They were misguided, ignorant, maybe willfully. Uneducated, uncultured, uncouth, sure. But not bad. Because of their limitations, something of a handicap in managing life, I always felt as if I were responsible for them. They hated me for writing this in the essay, but they're inherently incapable people and woefully self-destructive. For most of my teenage years when other boys were having sex and getting into mischief, I was busy catering to them to the point of sickness and sacrifice, no less. I never had the chance to be a dumb kid, to create a life for myself. I became a hermit when they finally broke up and moved away. Even though I wrote and submitted novels that were rejected by publishers, I took a job in social services because I felt the need to continue helping people. Because of my family's special needs, I also became socially awkward. Even through college, at Columbia, miraculously, I availed myself to my family. Whatever they needed. Whenever they needed it.

> Mom: Well, now you're just being a real dick, Julian! Pick up the fucking phone and call me!

To be fair, my family were also loyal and looked out for each other. They provided for their children and spouses, or at least tried. They cared about each other's well-being. I hoped I'd captured those elements, too. Even if they all thought my account of their lives was full of lies and would doom them all.

CHAPTER 2

Before *My Mighty Meekness* changed my life for better (making writing financially sustainable through the partial adaptation of my eventual book by the great and daring Darlington Brothers) and worse (forging a wide wedge between me and my family), I made a living in mental health. More specifically, I worked for a care coordination company that helped homeless people secure funding from the government and organize their services. I had grown accustomed to the interminable days of solitude writing individual service plans, reviewing clinical notes, and helping to plan state-issued assessments meant to determine the severity of malady and thereby the monetary allocation our service recipients would receive.

Kathy Nian, my direct supervisor at The Dayton Organization, was an emotionless bureaucrat who obsessed over budgets and metrics and funding and testimonials from clients she could bandy about to the company's CEO and president and the state. The Dayton Organization was founded in 1983 in Dayton, Ohio and had locations in a dozen states. They worked closely with their host cities and states to receive funding. The homeless people in their shelters needed to prove that they were seeking jobs so that Dayton could provide them housing. The entire initiative was waiver based. The clients—the homeless people were called either clients or customers or service recipients—had to be entered into a tracking system, a company-wide database, to receive the services, which included temporary housing (in the shelters), meals, and employment training. I was a therapist who worked closely with the support coordinators who would manage the necessary employment and housing pursuits.

Some of the cases that I still can't stop thinking about include "Elise," a young woman who'd been squatting in a tenement in Fort Green, Brooklyn, and whose OCD had progressed to psychosis. She could no longer be in a bathroom alone for she required frequent reassurance from a monitor that she was not doing that most awful, vile thing in the world, at least, to her— licking the toilet bowl rim. She had no desire to lick the toilet bowl rim, but she could not be trusted to not do so, either. Her fear was one of a loss of control and of contamination.

Another case involved "Georgios," a young man from Astoria, Queens, with intermittent explosive disorder and paranoid schizophrenia. His mother, neurotic but responsible, infantilized him, and would cuddle him, though he was twenty-two years old, and playfully wrestle with him. He once took things too far and bit the tip of her nose clean off. The mother survived the hideous attack and the tip of her nose had been restored with only a faint line circling the point of severance, but her emotional trauma put a distance between her and her son, and he eventually left, preferring the solitude of the park beneath Hell's Gate Bridge to the cold stares of his mother in her row house.

A third case that I can't shake was that of "Peter," an old man from the East Village who moved into Tompkins Square Park after his landlord evicted him from his Bowery studio for failure to pay rent. He had been in arrears for seven months after losing his job at a nearby diner. "Peter" would wander around the park and eat dirt, rocks, and eventually roaches and rats. He kept a journal about the diet (he'd taken a rucksack full of notebooks, pens, and cutlery, but nothing else, when he was forced out by the marshal), detailing his procedure for selecting what he would ingest and how difficult some of the digestion was. He also chronicled people's reactions. Some would try to stop him, some would encourage him, many would record it with their phones, and a few called the cops. He also wrote about how everyone should live like this, with such basic needs met without money or "terrible jobs." He described it as a kind of power and ultimate freedom. The eating of rocks and dirt was a form of pica, a psychological disorder, called geophagy, consumption of the earth, and Peter's was caused in part by undiagnosed schizophrenia and a nutritional deficit (iron, zinc, and calcium).

I had kept a journal since I was twelve and instead of saying cruel things out loud, I wrote them down. You know, to avoid hurting people. When I became a social worker, the journal entries began including case notes. To ensure everything was HIPAA compliant I never wrote down any of my client's names and I kept the identifying biographical details minimal and vague. The observations, the frustrations, the experiences all became a years-long meditation on service, selflessness, and the abuses of such things.

It was Raul's idea to develop the journal into an essay about giving and the cost of altruism.

"It's too bad that you don't have an interest in becoming a writer," I said while bird watching with him in Fort Tryon Park, far enough from the Cloisters to avoid tourists.

"What, so I could be embraced by those ridiculous phonies you spend so much time with now?"

"They're good people, Raul."

"I'm sure they're very fine people, just like the sociopaths I work for."

"Anyway," I continued, "You'd get an agent and a book deal with your name alone."

Raul's grandfather was the legendary Mexican essayist and poet, Guadalupe Sandoval. His work was socially complex and provocative and his style labyrinthine and lilting. His mystique had only been enhanced by the many communist labor leaders in Central and South American countries who championed him as an icon and guide and the college professors who deepened the mysteries of his surreal, metaphysical stories. Despite his socialist leanings and the fact that he'd been dead for nearly thirty years, his books still sold well, and Raul's family still profited off his royalties. The language was Borgesian with storytelling chops on the level of Garcia Marquez, but the politics were Guevarra or Chavez. It made it even more ironic that Raul, Guadalupe's descendant, would earn a six-figure salary in big media, big tech, and big finance as a programmer and code writer for *RFN* (*Remington Financial News*), which he called "The Evil Empire," when he wasn't donating his time as a Muay Thai trainer for fun, and sublimation. The volunteerism was likely his way of acquitting himself for his day job.

"Maybe it'll be useful to people," Raul had said over a year ago.

His argument had been simple but effective. I began writing that night. I'd remind him of this conversation almost a year and half later in the middle of August, a few months after the release of *The New Yorker* article.

Raul began taking photos of cardinals as they alighted on a nearby maple, and I slid my hand over his bicep that was flexed as he framed the birds. He smirked at me. Warm days in early spring did something to us, turned sex into the one unavoidable topic that quieted all frustrations, anxieties, and intellectual discourse.

"I dreamt I firebombed *RFN*," he mumbled. Our erotic foreplay was almost always coupled with Raul's fantasies of large-scale violence.

In my apartment we ripped each other's clothes off and kissed frenetically. Neither of us wanted a relationship with each other outside of what we had. We felt lucky, even superior, to be gay and not feel pressured into cohabitating or marrying or adopting children, even approaching forty. We fancied ourselves old fashioned that way. We were in it for the magnetic tug toward bodies, not cultural significance, or markers of heteronormativity.

In the afterglow, Raul was my biggest fan. He'd repeat his interpretations of my essay while playing with my nipples or nibbling on my neck. We both lay on the floor, atop the plush Persian rug my friend Omar brought be back from Kabul, nude and semi-erect. Chiaroscuro lighting was made possible by my lone lamp in the corner that was set to a dim amber. Raul thumbed through a copy of *The Loser* by the German satirist Thomas Bernhard. I'd been reading it and kept it on my coffee table.

"You know, it feels like an achievement that would benefit people if they read it."

"The Bernhard?"

"Your New Yorker essay, silly."

"Caroline said The Darlington Brothers agreed to let me adapt it, but she also wants me to expand the article into a whole book. That's a lot of memoir. Scary prospect."

I'd been too responsible to quit my day job to write full time, but the series promised to be made in the same prestigious spirit as *The Sopranos* or *Six Feet Under* or *Euphoria* or *Succession*. Another Shakespearean epic about bizarre, broken families coping with each other and their lot in life.

"She is about to give you a career, so I'd listen to her," said Raul, biting my finger and smiling up at me to continue his thought. "Only cost you a family."

I looked at him sideways, considered smacking him in the head, but didn't because his expression suggested regret; he'd known he'd overstepped.

"Hey, Julian, sorry, man. That was stupid."

I pulled away from him. "It was stupid, yeah, but not wrong."

I walked across my living room until I reached a throw my mother had bought me for Christmas, which had been draped over the sofa, and covered myself before he could say anything else to hurt me. He stood, glorious in his unashamed nudity, and sat beside me on the sofa. His body was a reminder that sometimes nature did things right. Skin the color of hazelnut and nary a hair. Long, lithe muscles that indented and swelled in all the right places with veins that rose and crisscrossed and beat like a nest of feeding, interlocked snakes.

"I really didn't mean anything by it," he said, wrapping his arm around me, resting his head on my shoulder. His warm touch made me horny again, but I didn't engage.

"It's what happened," I said. "It's how things happened, so why be upset about it? It's their problem."

"But ... how the hell are you going to get them to open up again for a book?"

"I may have to invent some shit," I said, only half-joking.

Raul laughed. "Still not as immoral as working for an evil empire."

He then forced me onto my back, pulled away the throw, and began to make love to me again. As his tongue traveled my body, bringing me out of my head, a final thought occurred before succumbing to the corporeal delight of Raul's mouth. In *The Loser*, Bernhard did well by himself by denigrating his homeland of Austria and writing about real people, albeit often in fictive stories, and he became a villain to some but an astute cultural critic—maybe even a folk hero—to many others.

CHAPTER 3

My first meeting with Edward and Kevin had felt fantastical. During periods of self-doubt or uncertainty, I'd replay it to gird my will. Whenever I told Kevin about how impressive he and Ed and their coterie of celebrity friends were, Kevin would laugh, and say that they were no big deal and he was bored by all the "impressive" people, that they were "regular joes" with some public works and who sometimes knew esoteric things. Kevin and Ed themselves were not rich, but their apartment had been valued at three million dollars and they had plenty of nice things. The courtyard of their Chelsea condominium was small but stately. Sunken, with a tall, black wrought iron gate, cobblestone walkway, on either side of which were rows of emerald greens budding through a blanket of red mulch. The quality of the gardening and landscaping made it clear that someone had tended it regularly.

A woman with a savage fury of fire red hair and near translucent skin white as a cadaver had passed me as she entered. Her bloodshot eyes and nervy gait intimated that she'd not let me in. Indeed, she'd pulled the door closed behind her as I gestured to grab the handle. I'd recognized her from *People* magazine as Gay Cardigan, the former creative director at *Vogue*.

I looked back through the window into the lobby to steal another peek at the Celtic witch, but she was gone.

The intercom hissed. A voice warbled through static. I assumed it was Kevin's. I smiled bashfully, holding a raspberry souffle I'd bought at a bakery around the corner, knowing it was Edward's favorite dessert, at least based on interviews I'd read in *The Paris Review*.

The doorman in the lobby looked up from his book, nodded, and pointed to a nearby elevator.

When I first met him, Kevin Tracey had struck me with his distinct appearance, sort of debonair. He was short with a goat-tee and highly stylized hairdo—shaved around the sides and back with a tall, sculpted tuft on top. He wore a ratty smoker's jacket and jeans with colorful designer socks. He held a glass of whiskey and smiled warmly as he greeted me in the hallway before his front door. Though I'd read in *Electric Literature* that he was in his mid-fifties, he'd looked much younger.

"Jesus, you're tall, too?" Kevin had a Southern drawl; I'd read he was from Memphis. "First Jackson and then Chris, and now you. Is everyone taller than me?"

I'd had no idea who Jackson and Chris were, but Kevin exuded a casualness and hospitality that immediately set my mind at ease. I laughed and introduced myself. Kevin hugged me like a long-lost friend and for a long time before taking me by the arm and whisking me inside. I'd later learn that Jackson was the heir to a pharmaceutical company and Chris was a travel writer for *The New York Times*.

I had barely said two words and just smiled idiotically as Kevin led me to the dining room where Edward was seated at the head of a long oak table. On either side of him were a veritable who's who of living literati. Writers I'd grown up reading and mythologizing, made legends in my mind. And here they were, drinking wine, picking at dumplings and crab Rangoon, and smirking up at me like grandparents I'd not visited enough.

The dinner guests included Suliman Raj, Colin Trigg, Fanny Lowenstein, and Joan Cathy Grains, who practiced a kind of automatism, scribbling on a small note pad, waiting for the doodles to morph into words. No one seemed to mind that she was working during dinner as they'd become used to it and even come to expect it. Everyone had seemed relaxed, and the mood was casual.

Kevin snatched the souffle from me and examined it.

"Is that my souffle?" Edward asked.

I had turned to him and blushed. "It is!"

The apartment was a pre-war oddity that Joan Cathy Grains had described as "elegant" in *Vanity Fair*. It was elegant in its way, but also shabby. I'd decided it was shabby chic. The bookcase haphazardly slouched to a side with stacks of novels and biographies creating uneven towers. I hadn't noticed it the first time I'd been there, but on one wall was an assortment of paintings and busts of Edward and Kevin at various stages in their twenty-year relationship rendered by artists of varying skill, fame, and talent. The brickwork had been painted white and there was a fireplace with a chestnut mantle and a metallic hearth. Full-wall Tudor windows looking out onto the loud street below were minimally ornamented with beige drapes and gold tassels.

Edward and Kevin had introduced me to their guests. I'd read them all and so I'd been rightly petrified.

They politely greeted me but then turned their attention back to their host, who'd regaled with his encyclopedic knowledge of opera, classical music, and 18th century scandals.

"Francesca Cuzzoni was a star in the mid 1700s, a soprano who no man could hope to match. When she refused to sing an aria that Handel had written exclusively for her, he took her by the shoulders, shook her, and barked, 'I know you are a she-devil, but I am Beelzebub, the king of the devils, and I swear that if you don't sing that aria this very minute, I'll throw you out the window.'"

Joan—in my mind we were all already on a first name basis—touched her exposed clavicle and shook her head, squinting, enhancing her regal though somehow also mousy mien, breaking from her interminable notetaking. She was maybe the only one who recoiled at the barbarism of the story, as everyone else found it amusing. She soon returned to her automatism. Fanny cracked a joke about how that scare must have prompted the highest note the soprano hit in her illustrious career.

"How would such things fly these days, what with #MeToo?" asked

Suliman, his lilting English accent sounding like a snarky song. It made me think of Morrissey.

"I don't think we should talk about this," quipped Joan, with a twinge of defensiveness. "And please don't mention #MeToo in front of Violet Scott. She really detests being associated with it. She keeps saying, 'that's not me.'"

"Is Violet coming tonight?" asked Colin, ill at ease as he downed the remainder of his drink, which I think was a bourbon neat.

I continued to sit mutely. What highbrow insights or mordant analysis could I offer this group of cultivated people? I'd never been that sophisticated and struggled to keep up with their discussion on antiquity. I had never been a traditional thinker and easily reconciled the sacred and the profane cohabitating in the same artistic expression or even in the same person. I thought of my family and imagined how they would retreat from the conversation. In their black and white, cut and dry "neighborhood" milieu, things were either comedy or drama, dark or light, "classy" or degenerate, expensive or low rent. The moral, social, and intellectual ambiguity of these writers would have been beyond them. My family were not unintelligent, but they lacked intellectualism.

"Edward," began Suliman. "When were you last in Europe?"

"Last summer Kevin and I stayed in Stella Lucia Bonaventura's castle outside of Florence. She has this little guest villa for writers."

"Oh yes, I know Stella Lucia," said Suliman. "She once hosted me and Michael Cunningham during the same summer. My Italian is better than his, so our hostess favored me."

"Yes, that and you're a Pakistani Muslim," said Kevin. "She *favors* the exotic. I believe they call it 'virtue signaling' or maybe just good old-fashioned fetishism."

Edward scowled at Kevin, who'd shrugged and continued to bring bottles of sparkling water to the table. Apparently, he'd spend the morning shopping, the afternoon cooking, and the evening serving whenever Edward had one of his parties, but I'd later learn he'd do this to keep his husband vital, with something to look forward to and by which be engaged. The Chinese food paired with Kevin's salad and roasted potatoes that evening satiated. No one desired more upmarket fare.

It had been during the inaugural dinner when I learned that Kevin had been a writer but gave it up a few years earlier to nurse Ed and help him with his "plot walks." I'd asked him if he regretted the decision or resented Ed because of it and he said no in a way that made me believe him. You'd never know it to look at him, but Kevin, it seems, was always drunk during these soirees, which I'm sure helped mollify his social anxiety.

"Don't fuss, Ed," said Suliman. "Kevin is right. Why do you think she's always inviting Zadie Smith to stay with her?"

"She is one of those rich old women who never knew a desperate day in her life," began Kevin, "the kind of wealth that compels scenic slum tours through impoverished neighborhoods in Southern Italy, like maybe Naples or Calabria, to sightsee the homeless and the gutter rats and the families living ten to a room as if she were on Safari in Kenya!"

I'd known that Kevin had read the *New Yorker* essay about my parents (I had made very specific allusions to such slum tours in their Bronx neighborhoods when they were children) and made the reference as either a courtesy or an insult to me. I hadn't known him well enough at that point to read his intentions accurately. Either way, I felt instantly self-conscious and defensive of my own family of "gutter rats".

"Don't talk about her like that, Kevin," snapped Edward, red-faced.

"Oh, your favorite patron," said Kevin with faux contriteness, "Sorry!"

"Anyway," said Suliman, with piqued, smug eyebrows. "Even white people enjoying hip hop is now regarded as slum tourism."

Fanny had turned sourly to me with her signature long face and beady eyes hidden beneath too-large glass frames and mumbled in her equally trademark dour, raspy voice, "So, what's your story?"

For once, everyone's attention was on me and it felt unnerving but also satisfying, even if my private life had become the subject du jour.

"He is the one who just had a very popular little memoir published in *The New Yorker* about his family," said Kevin. "So, I called him up to come over."

"No book yet?" asked Colin.

"Not yet," said Kevin. "But the essay is all about how he sacrificed and slaved over his family who couldn't take care of themselves and took advantage of him, but he was always so timid and passive, and he let them."

Kevin's summation had hurt but it wasn't wrong.

"Julian," said Edward. "I read your piece and I want you to know, you were very courageous to write about your family the way you did. I almost lost a sister and a father for doing the same thing many years ago."

"Thank you, Edward," I said. "I'm afraid it's cost me already."

"His family are trying to convince him to not write the book," said Kevin, "And they even want you to have Remnick pull it from future prints, isn't that right, Julian?"

I had nodded and shrugged. Kevin ogled, his gaze cutting through the vase of daffodils, the decanter of wine, the matrix of glasses and plates and bowls of salad and fruit and lo mein and sesame chicken and egg drop soup, and though no one else would see it, his expression was on me, and it was one of determination, of a starved animal seeing a meal primed for consumption. Maybe I'd misread his stare. Perhaps I was only inflating my own ego. It was all I could offer these accomplished people: something to desire.

"I told Kevin when we started chatting on Facebook that they're all pretty upset with me," I said, "but I shouldn't be surprised. I have mixed feelings about the whole thing, to be honest."

"Well, you should be happy that your writing is getting any attention at all," said Colin.

"It's not a small thing," said Joan, not looking up from her doodle.

"Better a literary career than a family, anyway," said Fanny. "It requires less time and gives more rewards."

"Families are a millstone," said Suliman.

"No one needs them," said Kevin. "I made my own family here in New York. Biology is not your fault, and you don't owe it shit."

I faked a smile and forced myself to nod. I wasn't sure I agreed with their sentiments, but they were offering support and it would have been rude not to receive it as it was intended. I'd soon returned to my awkwardly quiet default and looked down at my plate, waiting for the conversation to move on.

I'd attended that first party with so many reservations, with such implacable guardedness and rigid prejudices, that I'd almost missed their warmth, their filial playfulness, their accessibility. Even though Ed and Kevin's generosity had been evident, it would take weeks for me to get over my own blinding, paralyzing insecurities, and exorcise myself of imposter syndrome.

CHAPTER 4

Amid the clatter of hurried waiters and chatty patrons, Caroline Herzer exuded the haughty stoicism of a medieval nun. The French café in the West Village was small and overcrowded and buzzed with all the frivolous self-importance of a Manhattan brunch. Caroline held a severe gaze that enhanced her unflappable bearing and everyone around her became trivial in contrast. Even as she sipped her black coffee and nibbled on her almond biscotti, she made the whole of Jane Street too quaint for her seriousness and its inhabitants too slight.

Her white hair had been cut into a bob. She wore soft colors to accent her pastel makeup, always applied with restraint. When she spoke, her face lit up as though she were issuing orders of national security and when she listened it was with the focused care of someone receiving life-or-death news. Though sixty-three, Caroline contained the vigor of a woman half her age. She was the kind of bulldog-in-cashmere advocate you'd want in your corner, and I counted myself lucky to call her my agent.

"You should have your friend send me a sample chapter and I'll see," she said in response to my pitch on Raul's behalf. He'd spoken for years about writing queer-slanted essays about everything from his Marxist grandfather to the border to underground sex in Mexico City to the mythology of Quetzalcoatl and the endless Mesoamerican lineage to how custom, history, and religion interacts with contemporary culture and modern personalities. He'd not written a word and likely would have killed me if he knew I was querying for him, especially when he was violently opposed to making a career of writing.

"I will let him know," I said.

"Now, getting back to *your* book." Caroline leaned back imperiously.

"It's not a book, yet."

"What are you doing about that?"

"They were hurt by the article, Caroline. I won't be able to get them to help me with a book."

"Oh, Julian, forget about asking for permission!" There was a smug laughter in her voice. "It's better to beg forgiveness." And then her voice became flat and jagged, as if she'd learned this advice only after too many tough lessons.

"Is it, though?"

Caroline had a way of looking through the people she addressed when they did or said something foolish. She believed they should have known better and her gaze implied disappointment but also patience. She knew the foolish speaker would eventually come to the realization that they've been foolish. The stare weighed and I could never bear it, so I looked down, into the rich taupe pool of my coffee mug that reflected the chandelier above our heads.

"The truth hurts, Julian, and the book will contain a lot more of it."

"Maybe I don't have to share so much."

Caroline shook her head. "We had an agreement."

Most memoirs are mawkish with too many twee metaphors and facile similes. Or they're too confrontational and suffer from a cringey cynicism. Sometimes they're so precious about their self-awareness they became meretricious. The few that work, at least for me, are the ones that braid journalistic autobiography with rigorous scholarship and theory and have a focused, central point of view or theme, not just a whole life. When I decided to take Raul's advice and sit down to write my own, I knew I had to write about myself in a revealing, frank way though also integrate enough sociocultural research and speculation to make my experiences and anguish somehow matter in a larger framework. My pain alone never would. Also, nothing ever happened to me. At least nothing worth writing about. Unlike my poor Uncle Angelo, who lost his wife, daughter, and son to myriad diseases and accidents all before they reached fifty. He had a real story to tell. He had real pain. Fiction was easier.

Originally, I thought about exploring my sexuality, about the plight of the bisexual, the "poor sad bisexual" that no one wants to play with, the in-between person, a Kinsey 4, in my case, the undependable type, the greedy one, the deceptive lover, the pink-purple-blue flag waver, the child of Woolf's Orlando, the orgy-hunter, the unfaithful, the myth. I could play victim to both sides. The heterosexuals were just as intolerant as the homosexuals. I belonged nowhere. Pity me. Read my book. Unfortunately, that level of navel-gazing and identity politicking didn't interest me. Also, I'm not bisexual. Another fiction.

I then considered writing a fictional account about my invented parents or my numbing childhood in Phoenicia in Upstate New York, but that would be an outright lie. My parents only took me to Phoenicia a few times during the summer and even after my mom settled in Montgomery I had only gone maybe once. I could have made up a tale about how I'd lost them to disease and disaster at an early age. I'd always hated stories about dead or dying parents. Parents are supposed to die. It's the natural order. Maybe not as young as mine in my fictive universe, but I hadn't been scarred by their deaths. I loved them. I missed them. My life would have probably been fuller with them in it, but I have little control over the hand I'd been dealt. Dave Eggars wrote about losing his parents and caring for his younger siblings but that was his hook: becoming an instant guardian, forgoing the freedom of his youth, assuming a daunting responsibility. As someone who always valued being footloose and fancy free, that scenario read like a real horror story to me. I wouldn't add to the glut of material in the world of enduring, sick, dependent parents. Gone guardians. Of moving on without unconditional love. Besides, that too would have been a lie.

I landed in the most obvious of places. A family saga about my very much alive parents and all the rest of them and their little tragedies and innumerable needs and demands.

"Why not meet with them?"

It took me a minute to process Caroline's request. Her outlandish request. After avoiding my angry, abusive family so successfully for the past few months since publication of the article the very last thing I wanted to do was purposely "meet with them." They would surely do everything they could to stop me from writing anything further about them. Any mention of a book would no doubt make them murderous.

"No, I can't right now. I guess you can say I am temporarily estranged."

"Well, instead of avoiding this unpleasantness, maybe lean into it. Meet with them separately. One on one. Schedule separate meetings with each of them. Hear them out."

"You think so?"

"Maybe your book could be about the effects of memoirs on private people. A mix of memoir and critical essay. The uninvited invasion on bystanders in a tell-all culture. Start with the article and how it's affected them and then dig deeper while writing about their reactions. Think Joan Didion or Maggie Nelson."

"Or Susan Sontag? Edmund White?"

"If you like."

"I'll think about it."

Caroline looked at me with pity. "Julian, I chose to represent you because I anticipated a book out of this association. I don't represent writers who limit their potential to magazine articles."

I looked away. She sighed.

"This is the age of 'My Truth,' right?" she said. "How you phenomenologically experience reality, and therefore, filter it, express it, believe it. That's what matters."

I'd agreed with her but was not sure how I felt about the reality she'd been describing.

"People want to buy the story you sell them, no matter how implausible.

Borges once said that in Israel the bookstores do not separate works by fiction or non-fiction, but rather group them together as "narrative." It's all literature. All storytelling."

Caroline knew better than I did and so I decided to give her what she wanted: a convincing, commanding story, despite the protests of my willfully illiterate family.

"What's happening with *The Touring Barbarism?*" I asked.

"The Darlington Brothers are interested in meeting with you when they return to New York next week," Caroline said. "They're still in LA."

The Darlington Brothers had just come off a three-season run of the multiple Emmy and Golden Globe winning dark comedy, *All of Susan* for Showtime. The show was about an accountant named Ivan Trenton who pursued women who reminded him of his dead wife, Susan. He would role play intimate encounters with them based on past experiences he'd had with Susan in hopes of reanimating her, at least psychologically, emotionally. The concept had been inspired by the Darlington Brothers' father, whose bereavement period for their mother had been long and problematic when they were kids, and their affinity for Hitchcock's *Vertigo*. Their show dealt with grief and solipsism and how loss could feed delusion and fantasy. Some feminist groups decried its treatment of the women Ivan used to regain Susan, but the artistry and depth with which they probed the relationships and the sensitive treatment of mortality and coping with death mitigated any controversies that arose around gender.

The logline read:

```
Ivan found Susan in other women. Their eyes,
their hands, their mannerisms, their scents,
their voices. If he interacted with enough of
them, he'd find a composite of his lost wife.
```

The studio rejected the description, finding it too narrow and odd, but the filmmakers stuck to their guns. They wanted even the official summary to have its own strange flavor. The show felt like a dense and complex novel, and I was eager to work with them. Writing for a cable series also promised gainful employment for at least a year with an increased likelihood of further opportunities. *The Touring Barbarism* was all true. Mary really was an anthropologist and Monroe really worked for Raytheon. Her intrusive methodologies did in fact accidentally create a small skirmish in a village in Northeastern India, which led to numerous hearings about her research grants and employment at Columbia University and inquiries into ethics violations headed up by The Hague and the American Anthropological Association. She nearly lost her career, though due to support from the department and some influential benefactors and colleagues, she was able to retain her job and the grant money. However, the Indian government banned her from further ethnographic research in the subcontinent.

"I think it's smart to pursue TV work this quickly," said Caroline. "I'm glad you were open to it. These days, the new model is if you write a good book, you probably won't get rich enough to quit your day job, but you could parlay that small success into more interesting employment in a more desirable field."

"I mean, look at Michael Chabon or AM Homes," I said.

"Right," said Caroline, bored but humoring me, "he's doing *Star Trek: Picard* and she's done *The L Word*, right?"

"And John Irving, and Margaret Atwood, and Tom Perrotta and Jonathan Ames."

"Yes, dear, the list goes on. It's no longer William Faulkner's paranoid time, where 'in Hollywood they stab you in the back while climbing a ladder'. I mean, even the University of Iowa's Writer's Workshop is condoning the porous relationship between literature and television. We're not very strange bedfellows anymore."

The Touring Barbarism's synopsis was even more evocative. The Darlington Brothers wrote it themselves to show me they got the themes. The casual indirectness of the catastrophes we'd delve. The studio said their long synopsis was too esoteric, but they used it anyway:

The Touring Barbarism SYNOPSIS: Mary and Monroe Clint are not your typical couple. Mary's self-esteem was a delicate thing that was sustained by long spells of solitude. She prided herself on her lack of need from others. She'd always rely on only herself to get what she wanted. Even if it sometimes meant starting wars. Monroe treated his three cats, Simone, Picasso, and Butters, and dog, Shiloh, as he would children or lovers, minus the sex. He would lay with them in bed under the covers and cuddle and caress and whisper endearments. But when out of the intimate safety of slumber and leisure he was all business and meted out trauma like snacks for the sake of hypervigilance. As a builder of bombs, Monroe knew a thing or two about danger. Pegasus had a creeping suspicion that his parents were not good people. Outwardly they did saintly things, like advocate for immigrants or the homeless or animals, but inside, where it counted, they broke bread with the devil. That Pegasus was a progressive and queer and effeminate was poetic retribution for Monroe's aggressive masculinity and his one and only desire to spawn a son as quintessentially macho.

If it weren't taken from my life, or at least the lives of people close to me, it could have been something I'd invented, a heavily symbolic meditation on my own morally ambiguous, emotionally volatile, dangerously eccentric family. Like Pegasus's formation as the antithesis of everything Monroe holds dear, my own homosexuality revealed itself as a devastation to my father, as I, his only child, would bear no seed. Though the book Caroline had pitched about the ethics of writing personal stories that involve others wouldn't happen right away, the cable series, ultimately picked up by MAX with me as one of the head writers, shoulder-to-shoulder with the Darlington Brothers, would. They'd offer me the job soon after meeting with me because they identified me as a fellow accommodator, a fellow ashamed child of shameless parents.

"I don't know what you told them, kiddo," Caroline would say to me over the phone a few weeks later, just after our meeting at the Players Club in Gramercy Park, "but they met our terms and want you as their head writer. There may be one or two others in the writing room to help with editing for practical purposes. TV shows sometimes film two episodes at a time. And let's face it, you're not really a name yet, are you?"

The Darlington Brothers were frustrated novelists and hired me because they valued my "literariness". They gave me surprisingly considerable poetic license. They said I should treat every episode as a stage play or even a prospective chapter. They said I should include notes directly to them about actors or staging or character background in between the dialogue and action sequences. It was an unorthodox approach, but I didn't mind. In fact, I'd preferred it. Teleplays were dry and technical, and literature is what I did. Living inside someone's head and sharing their experience with readers was the kind of intimacy that compelled me to write in the first place. The Darlington Brothers loved the bleak treatment of my family's story. I was frightened by how much they could relate to its characters.

On the topic of things frighteningly relatable, I called my mother after lunch with Caroline and told her I'd come for a visit soon.

My parents were so poor that rich people from Park Avenue would tour their neighborhoods like they were on safari in Kenya, spying the indigent as if they were wildlife in an exotic element. "Slumming," they called it. My grandfather Angelo would cite the 1936 film *My Man Godfrey* as an example of the tourists' audacity. In the film, socialites visited the slums of New York to find a homeless person in a scavenger hunt for a kind of show and tell during a party they'd been attending.

My mother's mother was a too-kind woman who opened her tiny Bronx tenement to the entire Arthur Avenue neighborhood. All the creeps, abusers, con artists, and leeches wormed their way into her heart and bedroom. She'd soon have eight children with five different men and not one of them a husband. My mother, now in her late sixties, witnessed untold cruelties during her childhood. Being poor might have taken away her softness but not her dignity. Annalisa Donizetti, no relation to the 19th century composer, became hard but not mean. She saw in her own mother, Philomena Theresa Maria Donizetti, a saintly woman who only loved too much, too hard, too many. That the world took advantage of her naivete was not her problem. It was theirs. Still, she would be damned to allow the same fate to befall her own family once she married my father, Adam Sorrento.

My father failed her in too many ways to innumerate here, but he'll get his due. He'd doomed her not just emotionally, but also financially. Growing up, it never failed to amaze me how someone who'd been so needy through much of her life could afford a whole house to herself and be so self-sustaining. As I became old enough to understand the machinations of my mother's fiscal survival, I figured out how she'd done it. Her scheme was immoral, but understandable. She had spent years conning parishioners out of their donations, skimming off the top with other church officials, doing creative things with records and taxes. She'd even convinced neighbors to give charity directly to her, never too proud to beg, her sad sob story eliciting untold quantities of pity and cash. Her act as town crier of the impure and hypocritical inspired the truly god-fearing to contribute to her "campaign".

With Adam and her three children, secure in suburban Bayside, Queens, Annalisa harnessed the same charitable spirit as her mother but did so with greater pragmatism. She joined the local parish, attended church weekly, volunteered, and head-started an outreach program to appeal to friends and neighbors. She sought out "the depraved" through friends who had a penchant for gossip and spearheaded campaigns to ban "incendiary" literature from our neighborhood libraries and grade schools. She organized demonstrations at strip clubs, movie theaters showing "torrid" films, and at the one sex shop that served the whole of the 43,800-resident community.

Mom's steely persona was necessitated by a childhood populated with monsters. Her mother's third baby daddy, Martin, had called Mom into the bedroom one night while her mother was playing gin Rummy down the street at her friend, Sara's. Loitering in the threshold, hiding behind the half-opened door, my mother saw he'd had his penis out, waiting for her. She was twelve. Another time when she was 17 and her own biological father Beppe tried to grab her breast at a cousin's communion, and she had to reprimand him in public. Another time when she was fourteen and her mother's friend Lucille had sex with Gregory, a police officer assigned to their precinct, in bed beside her as she pretended to sleep.

I'd always found her infantilization of me, though not James or Sophia, to border on the incestuous, but I understand now it was a means to compensate for the void left by her own mother, and all the awful men in her own childhood. My meekness with her was one ruled by empathy and served through affection.

When I was about twelve or thirteen, I would invite friends to my house after school to watch movies and play video games. There was John and Jeremy and Anthony and Chris and BJ and Matthew. We would kick off our sneakers, hit the kitchen for snacks, and then pile into my small bedroom to huddle around the television and binge 80s horror or sci fi like *An American Werewolf in London* or *The Shining* or *Gremlins* or *Back to the Future* or *The Fly* or we would play *Soul Caliber* and *The House of The Dead* on my Sega Dreamcast or *Metal Gear* and *Crash Bandicoot* on Sony PlayStation. My parents spoiled me, so I had both systems. We would glut ourselves on Oreos or Doritos or Sour Patch Kids. My parents always kept a stash of junk food in the house for when my friends would stop by. When I was alone, I was only allowed fruit and vegetables to nosh on.

My mother was fastidious about cleanliness and odors and would barge into my bedroom to demand we tell her which of us had missed the toilet bowl rim and peed on the floor and whose sneakers stank up the foyer. I had pleaded with my mother to not do this, but every time the boys would come over, she did, dismissing my pleas and overpowering me, shutting me up, shaming me and my friends. I never stood up to her. I only begged. I only pleaded. My pale nature, my passive position could never stop her from making a spectacle and embarrassing me and my friends. We were all her victims, all her targets. In time, I found that my meekness in these moments would eventually provide me a kind of protective barrier, a solace space in which I would move beyond shame and into a Zen-like acceptance of badly-behaved people, an acceptance of my own impotence. People will do what they please and make monsters of themselves in so doing and we must learn how to allow them that. We cannot control anyone. We can barely control ourselves.

CHAPTER 5

"You've got some imagination on you, mister," my mother said when I greeted her at the door. "I mean, really, my sister started a war in India now?!"

Annalisa Sorrento, of the once-destitute Donizetti crest, insisted we meet at her house, which for me required a two-hour train trip north from Penn Station. Mom was good at laying on guilt trips if more than two weeks passed without a visit. I'd taken to calling her once every other day to avoid the Sicilian melodrama.

"Well, yes, she did," I began, taking off my shoes, "while looking at primitive tribal groups, PTGs, in Bihar, outside the state's city, Patna. The Bhumij and the Kharia were the tribes."

"Oh, I don't know about all that. I mean, she was in India a few times, but I never heard about any wars."

"Well, she did. It's all in the article."

My mother shook her head, indicating nothing clear, and disappeared into the kitchen.

Mom had maintained the small, three-bedroom, two-bathroom townhouse in Goshen on her own. She'd given a 20% down payment, still only pennies in the early 1970s, from the money she'd saved from the charities and community, rented it out for thirty years to a family from Puerto Rico, and then kicked them out so she could move in when she and my father divorced. By then the mortgage had been paid off and her taxes were low. She'd saved money from all the years she worked and collected social security. She was shrewd that way. Growing up on the streets had taught her how to survive, conditioned the shame right out of her.

"Listen, I'm sorry I left so many messages," she began, stirring eggs and mushrooms and cheese and broccoli in an over-sized wood bowl at her granite counter. "And I'm sorry I cursed and called you a name. You know I am not usually like that."

My mother had taken elocution lessons when she finally came into money to rid herself of the neighborhood drawl, the fatal outer borough accent mocked and sneered at by the rest of the world, that media-saturated indicator of ignorance and classlessness, the universal marker of low education and nil culture. *The Godfather, The Sopranos, Goodfellas, The Jersey Shore*, all culprits in the distorted perception of our tribe. Nationally, few had been of that ilk, and the many I'd known, having grown up in their prime region, were not categorically unintelligent or immoral people. Many had so much common sense to almost register as a kind of genius. They possessed passions and knowledge and creative visions and abilities that impressed. Their manner and voices belied their intellects. It had taught my mother that the only thing that mattered were optics. How you spoke, dressed, stood, and walked, and maybe the references you made, determined to the greatest degree your place at the table.

It was the little details that gave her away. Like the granite countertop. Like her occasional slips when tired, revealing the accent when saying "caw-fee," or "flaw," meaning "floor". Like her framed photo of the New York City skyline. If she'd truly wished to pass herself off as a fellow WASP in her Anglo-Saxon enclave, she'd have to do a better job minding the trivia. Taste, whatever that meant anymore, and restraint in all manner of presentation would become a new charade, a higher stakes game.

"I'm used to you yelling at me and cursing," I said, adding, "calling me all the time."

"Well, I don't do that, though, Julian, you left me no choice this time."

"You think I didn't get our family, right?"

"I was moved by some of it."

I regretted not including in the article the Halloween costumes she used to make for me. The bumble bee, the alligator, the Dracula. It had taken me this long to realize how special it was that she'd done that. She could have just bought a costume at the store like all my friend's mothers did. It meant a lot more that she had spent all those hours shopping for supplies and cutting and sewing and coloring and sculpting and gluing and actually made something. Many somethings. Of course, this was out of necessity. We were too poor to afford expensive costumes. I would put all this in the book.

"But you won't turn it into a whole book, right Julian? Say you won't. You mentioned you'd might."

"I may. Probably, yes. I will."

She sighed as she began to rinse and slice a large head of Lacinato kale. She mixed extra virgin olive oil, sea salt, black pepper, parmigiana cheese, red pepper flakes, sliced garlic, and lemon juice into the chopped kale, which she'd slid into another wood bowl. I knew that my mother would take exception with my claim I'd grown up poor, because to her we were middle class. *She* had grown up poor. She couldn't deny that. Grandma Rosalie. What they'd all gone through.

"Maybe in the book you will capture my mother's goodness, her big heart."

Mom mixed the salad with her bare hands because she said that was the only way to truly get the olive oil and garlic to permeate the kale. My mother would never say it, but she meant my grandmother's giving nature. And the way they all used her. Beat her. Left her. The reputation. The way they talked about her. And the way she had treated Sophia because of it.

Mom sighed again and shook her head, maybe reacting to a memory, or maybe reading my mind and responding to my thoughts. There was a belief in witches in Southern Italy and especially in Sicily. They called them Donas de Fuera, the Ladies from the Outside, as Sicily at the time of this folklore in the 16th and 17th centuries was under Spanish rule. They claimed associations with fairies. Maybe mom was a witch.

"It hurts me to see your sister being as naive as my mother," she mumbled to herself.

Sophia, opening her house to the world. Sitting on the stoop talking to everyone who passes, again just like my grandmother. Hanging out with Arnold's friends. Kids half her age.

"It's trashy, Julian," she continued, as though continuing a conversation I'd had no part in, "come on."

Mom began to set the table. Even though it was just us and only lunch she put out the fancy china and silverware and cloth napkins, an Emily Post perfected table setting.

"Doug may cheat," she said, seemingly out of nowhere, minutes later, "but he provides."

Mom poured us both a glass of chianti in her crystal wine glasses as having any meal, aside from breakfast, without wine was unheard of.

"I never stole money from people. And what you wrote about your father."

I paused, masticated my next thought as we began eating. After swallowing my first bite, I cleared my throat and frowned at her.

"I didn't lie about anything."

"Maybe you just didn't remember things correctly," she said. "Just don't do the book."

She'd repeat herself whenever she doted or fretted. She was in full-fret mode.

"Look, ma, I am working on expanding the essay into a book because if I don't, I will lose my agent and it's important to me to fully understand the family and my childhood and, well, my whole life, really."

Though my mother at the time had been closing in on seventy, she kept the appearance and vigor of a much younger woman, much like Caroline, which is maybe why I'd been so quick to do whatever she commanded. My mother was stylish and focused on clean eating and staying active, which took the form, of course, of vigorous housecleaning, and I hoped I'd inherited those genes. To retain glamour and a sense of youth into senior years. When she pouted, as she had that afternoon, she looked girlish, sweet and innocent, and it was difficult to fight with her. Such guile served her well in life. It was another weapon in her street-smart arsenal.

"Listen, Dad actually came to my apartment and made a scene out front."

"Yes, well, I hear he's very mad at you," she said, almost rehearsed, or at least waiting for me to bring it up, "and so are Sophia and James and Doug and Arnold and Luz and—"

"I know, Mom, they've all left messages and texts and none of them were nice about it."

"Do you think they should have been, I mean, after what you wrote about them, Julian? I mean, really. But look, you did what was necessary to succeed and we're all happy to see you got up there."

Up there.

"There was a lot I didn't write about, things I still don't know or fully understand. Like that guy you were with, that Greek guy, the one who used to date Sophia."

My mother shook her head, sucked her teeth, a theatrical gesture, her moment in the spotlight.

"Don't you dare write about Dimitri Daviyas."

"It's not a secret, Mom. You dated him for three years after you left Dad."

"But no one needs to know that he was in a relationship with your sister when they were younger. It will make us look like Jerry Springer trash."

The fact that my mother dated my sister's ex-boyfriend was worthy of an entire episode of daytime talk.

"And don't write anymore about the other things, Julian."

"What other things?"

"You know the things! The sexual things. About my mother. When I was a kid, Julian."

I had planned on further investigating these claims from her adolescence and young adulthood, but I would handle it discreetly. I'd visit the now grown children of the offenders and ask them what it must feel like to have had fathers who did what they'd done to my mother.

"Mom, you should know—"

Before I could complete my plan, the doorbell rang. I was grateful for the interruption. My mother unhurriedly, even elegantly, stood, folded her cloth napkin, and sauntered across the dining room, into the living room, and then out of sight into the foyer, to answer. I couldn't see who had visited, but I heard their conversation. It was a man, an older man given his gravely, hoarse voice, likely around my mother's age, or older. They spoke cheerily about lawn maintenance.

"Annalisa, I've told you. I really don't mind doing it."

"Well, at least come in and meet my son. He's just taken the train up from the city for lunch."

I groaned and finished my wine before they reached the dining room.

I'd been right. The visitor was an old man, but surprisingly powerful in build. He looked like he could have been a wrestler or bodybuilder or construction worker in his earlier days. White-haired with white scruff and barrel chested, he also reminded me of Ernest Hemingway.

"Julian, this is Raymond, he lives across the street."

I stood and shook the aged giant's mighty paw, which was calloused and dry and stronger than mine.

"Pleased to meet you, Julian. Your mother talks about you all the time."

"Oh boy," I said.

"Only good things, and I look forward to reading your article."

"It's a good one, Raymond, even though Julian didn't mention my relationship with Dion from Dion and the Belmonts. We dated for a time, you know, when we were teenagers, way before he became a star."

That had been true. Dion and my mom did date well before she'd met Sophia and James's dad or mine. She'd throw it in everyone's faces whenever one of her two husbands did something to upset her, which had been daily: "I could have been married to a musical genius and had all the money in the world, but no, I settled for this bozo!"

This bozo could have been my dad or Sophia and James's.

I'd dedicate a chapter to the Dion fling in the book.

"Oh!" exclaimed Raymond, an earnest man, easily impressed. "I just ordered a copy on the Internet. I had to buy a six-month subscription, but it will be worth it, I'm sure. Your mother told me not to trouble myself, that she would lend me her copy once she was done reading it, but I wanted to support you by buying my own."

I looked away out of embarrassment of his kindness. "Thank you. Really."

"Raymond is a doll, Julian. He shovels my walkway when it snows and mows my lawn."

"Really? What a great guy."

"I cook him lunch, and sometimes dinner, every time he helps me with something."

"I would do these things, but I live pretty far," I said, realizing how awkward and defensive my excuse sounded.

"I have the time and I like being useful," said Raymond. "Plus, your mother is a fantastic cook!"

I excused myself and said I needed to use the restroom, walking past the half-bath connecting the dining room to the living room.

"Why not use this one?" asked my mother.

"Privacy," I said and darted up the stairs toward the master bath. I heard Raymond chuckle and my mother snicker. I'd wondered if they were seeing each other. Annalisa Donizetti Sorrento was not the single type, despite her penchant for autonomy and solitude. I suspected they were lovers, though she'd not tell me, especially not after what she perceived to be a slight against her reputation. I was surprised she'd mentioned my book at all. She'd probably told him well ahead of its release, not knowing how clear I'd been in my memory and how frank I'd been in my detailing. She was probably mortified at the prospect of him reading about her and my father and siblings. I bet she had never intended to share her copy of *The New Yorker* with him.

My mother never brought up the way she would humiliate me and my friends for their poor hygiene and malodorous feet. We had been boys and all boys smelled. As an adult looking back on her lot in life, I learned that all she had was presentiment. All she had was her fastidiousness. She could control her space. She could control the smell of her space. That was her value, her power, her contribution. Maybe I had been too rough on her in my essay in that regard, but I also knew I would write more about it in my book as there had been too many incidents to fit into the *New Yorker* article.

Along the way to the bathroom, I passed the guest room that I'd often shared with Raul. I had been too uncomfortable to have sex under my mother's roof, but Raul was just as forward and aggressive as he'd been in our apartment. There were also portraits of me as a boy, photos and paintings. I'd boasted a bouffant and clothes that had suddenly become fashionable again. Fanny packs. Corduroys. Denim jackets. Z Cavaricci pants. There was a painting of me and my father standing in front of a cherry blossom. Another of me and my mother before a fountain. Maybe it was Central Park. When she was younger my mother looked like Sophia Loren but as an older woman, she struck startling semblance to Ann Margaret. There were also photos and paintings of my sister and brother with their father and mine. At a certain point, they started to call my father "Dad." Along the walls were also portraits of Mary, Monroe, Pegasus, and other cousins, aunts, uncles, grandparents, siblings, and even some pets. Max, the first cat. Lady, the first dog. Godzilla, the first lizard. My mother's house was a monument to what our family had been.

CHAPTER 6

"It's not surprising to me that they want to focus on the weirdest aspect of your article," said Raul spread across his sofa in briefs, still semi-hard, intermittently berating me both for fun and for the sake of arousal. We'd established a strange routine. I'd come over to his too-spacious Brooklyn Heights co-op (he'd lived alone and didn't require so much space) and he'd lecture me on either a lacuna in my knowledge about world history or my moral code and then manhandle me to orgasm. He had certain sadistic tendencies that my masochism responded well to early on and our understanding of playful submission and domination allowed for the delicate dance of willing humiliation. This modus operandi dated back to college, but I suspect this new wave of abuses stemmed from being left out of the essay. Though I hadn't written about him in the article, I would likely include him in the book and already involved him in the series adaptation as a peace offering.

We'd only just begun to discuss the Darlington Brothers and my big MAX deal. It was a wild story and very new, something not yet seen. The other parts of my family's life, the poverty, the infidelities, the crimes, the puritanical fearmongering, all that had been told already in a million other books and movies and tv shows. My family wasn't so different in those respects, but Mary, Monroe, and Pegasus were true unicorns.

"I didn't even know half the shit you wrote about them," Raul continued. "I mean, I knew Mary did research in India and I knew Monroe worked for Raytheon, and I knew Pegasus was an eccentric who hung out with homeless kids, but I had no idea the extent of their stories."

"Yeah, they are very different from the rest of my family, I mean, despite, the questionable behaviors, they're the only truly educated ones, you know, which is why I think we see them so rarely."

My aunt, uncle, and cousin had distanced themselves when I was pretty young. My mom resented my aunt's education and career. I think she was threatened by it. My mom values education and class and how people come across in society, but she never had the guts to go out and better herself that way, aside from the elocution classes, of course. And my aunt, well, she was embarrassed by my mom. All the crazy religious stuff and the stealing from the donations. She thinks my mom is trash. And my dad with all his crimes is no better. I had kept in touch with Pegasus and because he hated his parents, he informed on them. He thinks they're total frauds. He calls them narcissists.

Raul stared at me for a while and then smirked. It was fiendish and adoring. His expressions always conveyed multiple messages.

"Come on, Julian," he said. "How much of all this is true?"

"It's all true, Raul."

"You're not stretching it a little?"

"It happened as I wrote it."

"Even the Vikings weren't honest, you know."

"Huh?"

Raul explained to me how the Vikings had been shitty record keepers. They never wrote anything down, so all the media we had received about the king of Sweden and Denmark, Ragnar Lodbrok, is really a jumble of myths and second-hand accounts. That figure was a composite of several people, actually.

"Well, that's not what I did," I said.

Raul always won his arguments not because they were better informed than most but because he was prescriptive and deflected and often gaslit and could make even his closest associates feel as though the relationship was only transactional when in that mode. On the subject of Vikings, *The Touring Barbarism*, was, I felt, a good title. The Darlington Brothers had come up with it.

"It has their hipster sensibility written all over it," said Raul.

The idea of taking a leave of absence from a reliable day job scared me, but my supervisor, Kathy, liked me and said I could return whenever I wanted. In her exact words, "I'm very happy for you, Julian, and this all sounds very exciting, but if you ever need to come back down to earth and have a real job again, we'll be here waiting." I'd saved enough money to sustain myself for a year, and MAX paid me twice my annual salary per episode, so an entire season would keep me afloat for over a decade if I budgeted wisely. With any luck, it would lead to more writing jobs, and I would never have to do social work again. Noble as it is, the job drained me, and though many of the individuals I served gave me guilt trips for leaving, I had to do what was best for me and my own mental health. Besides, in a city as big as New York with so many well-educated, ambitious, altruistic professionals, they would restaff my position with someone as competent, if not more so, in no time.

Raul had been staring at me again with his signature look of inscrutability. "Did rich people really tour the ghettos your parents grew up in?"

"They sure did."

Most people think slum tourism went out of style in the 19th century in America. It still thrives in places like India, Brazil, and South Africa, but few knew that it existed in New York into the 1970s. Poverty porn is alive and well and when I write the book, I will really expose it.

Raul raised an eyebrow and began playing with himself. "It's pretty amusing that your uncle shot all that testosterone and HGH and steroids into his balls to become a mega man only to end up siring a fruity, delicate son. Feels karmic."

"I think it's what started him on the crisis," I said, touching his stomach, so enviably smooth, working my way toward his underwear band. His happy trail was composed of short black curls that aligned symmetrically with the indentations of his obliques.

As I kissed Raul, I reached for his genitals, but he grabbed my hand, stopping me.

[46]

In my disappointment and shame, I recalled a company called Real Bronx Tours offering excursions through the Bronx to show visitors a real-life New York ghetto to sightsee 'gangland activity,' drug deals, murders, other crimes. It made a big stink and they stopped it eventually.

"You said you wanted to help me," I said, pulling away, irritated with his teases and evasions.

"Right," said Raul, moving back to the sofa. "My job is mind-numbing and immoral, so … I'm happy to help with anything creative and personal."

I had already started spreading the story out across ten episodes, but I needed help developing some of the ideas. Remembering the guidance issued directly by the Darlingtons, I kept the format as self-serving as possible: a weird, maybe unprofessional, hybrid of prose, essay, stage play, notebook, and teleplay.

```
INT. CLINT RESIDENCE — DAY
```

Though she might have been known in choice circles as the illustrious Dr. Donizetti-Clint, Mary's self-esteem was a delicate thing sustained by solitude. She prided herself on a lack of need from others. She'd always relied on herself to get what she wanted. Even if it sometimes meant starting wars. (Borrowing here from your synopsis a bit, Darlingtons)

Monroe was at work and Pegasus at school. Neither would be home for hours. Monroe's cats didn't like Mary, despite her best efforts and bribes. They especially took shelter when new people entered their hold. Lauren Gibbons, the reporter from *National Geographic* and disrupter of Mary's hermitage, smiles inscrutably at her host's offering of tea or coffee.

NOTE: The coffee had been made an hour earlier in anticipation of Lauren's arrival and after a protracted and humorous episode of Mary and Lauren going back and forth over whether to have tea or coffee, which the actors will ad lib, they decide on tea, though Mary has trouble getting the tin with the tea bags open, so they end up having the coffee anyway. Lauren takes it black and maybe in voice over we hear Mary stating that black coffee was for sociopaths.

They eventually get down to business.

"Okay," Raul interrupted, "how do you know what she was thinking and how do you know what was happening between her and that reporter?"

"Poetic license," I said, more annoyed than on guard. "All writers do it."

We continued together. I read from my notes on my laptop, adding minutiae to the meeting between my aunt and the reporter, and he helped me fill in holes and create drama. But first he forced me onto the floor, keeping the sofa for himself, and made me rub his feet as I recounted my narrative.

Mary studies Lauren's face and put her at around thirty, maybe younger. Half her age. Legacy media recruited young writers, especially the brands that catered to old readers. And National Geographic, with its own problematic legacy, had a lot of course correcting to do in the woke new world.

LAUREN

I was just going to say I won't
waste your time asking questions
that you've already answered.

MARY

Well, thank you for that.

Lauren tucks her short, flat hair behind her
ear and adjusted her glasses. She does this
whenever she wants to exude seriousness.

LAUREN

Columbia and The Hague wouldn't
talk to us, but they said you could
speak generally about your field
work in Patna and the effects as
you observed them.

MARY

Oh, yes, they consider those things
sensitive.

LAUREN

Right. Classified. What brought you
to India?

Here, Mary takes a minute to formulate a thorough
enough explanation that answers the question
but doesn't make her come across as a cynical,
meddling troublemaker. Before Lauren had

[49]

arrived, Mary spoke with her sister, Annalisa, a puritan who lived in Bayside and stole money from parishioners. (NOTE: THIS SCENE WILL BE WRITTEN AT SOME POINT AS A FLASHBACK). Annalisa, despite judging Mary harshly as teenagers, had assured her sister that she'd done nothing wrong. That is, nothing intentionally wrong. Intent mattered. It proved culpability and premeditation. Annalisa should know she was married to a con artist and gangster.

"Oh shit," said Raul. "Your dad is going to fuck you up!"
"He won't even know about it until it airs, if he even watches."
I continued with the paragraph-fragments-come-episode.

                    MARY
        I wanted to look at primitive
        tribal groups, PTGs, in Bihar,
        outside the state's city, Patna.
        The Bhumij and the Kharia.

                    LAUREN
        What exactly were you "looking at"?

                    MARY
        Social roles. How people present
        themselves in public within rural,
        impoverished communities.

                    LAUREN
        And you matched this against their

private lives, those things that
they withheld from other tribe
members?

                    MARY
Yes, I suppose I was measuring
authenticity. Social masks, in
other words.

Lauren's pause is loaded. Mary thinks her
expression signifies suspicion. The reporter
stares at her with an incredulity that makes her
smirk. Mary remembers Annalisa's words, "You
are a decent, well-intentioned person who was
just trying to do a little good in the world.
Everyone makes mistakes." NOTE: Perhaps this
is conveyed through voiceover or flashback.

                    LAUREN
        (looking at her notes)
Dr. Donizetti-Clint, I'm sorry,
but you originally stated that
you went to India to study
"how western media portrayals
of power influence tribes
otherwise unaccustomed to such
representation".

                    MARY
That's what the work became, yes.

                    LAUREN

So, that's not what you went
for? But you brought films and a
projector with a screen.

                     MARY

Yes, I did.

                    LAUREN

I'm sorry. I'm lost here.

                     MARY

I had always intended to show
them the movies and gauge
their receptivity to 'western
performance' and then determine
how those performances resonated
and influenced them, but I didn't
intend to do … what I ended up
doing.

                    LAUREN

Which was?

It is Mary's turn to exhibit an incredulous
expression.

                     MARY

Well, you know full well, don't
you? That's why you're here, isn't
it? Lauren looks down, suddenly off

                     [52]

guard.

                    MARY
I will tell you what I told
Columbia and The Hague, that if I
had known that they would take
these depictions of competition and
power as literally as they did, as
instructively as they had, I would
never have brought them, let alone
shown them.

                    LAUREN
The films included *Citizen Kane*,
Wall Street, *Dangerous Liaisons*,
The Godfather, and *The Great
Gatsby*. All English-language. Did
you subtitle them in Bengali or
Hindi?

                    MARY
No, I wanted the imagery and the
behavior to speak for themselves.

                    LAUREN
        (jotting notes in a notebook)
And they sure did, huh?

Mary pictures Annalisa sitting beside her,
holding her hand, assuring her that she was a
"decent, well-intentioned person doing good but

making mistakes like everyone else." Her sister, who championed the underdog, the wretched, the cast asides, like their mother, would not lavish praise of character so cavalierly. Mary was certain she'd earned it, that Annalisa had seen it, known it, and that if she navigated this interview correctly the world would too.

"Does your mom know she's in this?" asked Raul.
"She's barely in it," I said, continuing.

                    MARY
        I thought they would find the
        presentation of public identity
        and the battle for status and the
        desperate grab at reputation and
        glory and material gain absurd. I
        thought they would fail to identify
        with the characters and their
        actions. Find them barbaric.

                   LAUREN
        Would you paint a picture of what
        happened there? Columbia and The
        Hague classified your testimony.

                    MARY
        Well, I don't know if I would
        get in trouble then if I told
        you. There's still an active
        investigation, after all, and I

have a lot to lose here.

LAUREN

Your job?

MARY

My job, my entire career, in fact.
And maybe more.

LAUREN

You're not going to be charged with
a war crime.

MARY

Well, my sister doesn't think so
either, but what does she know? And
there are people at The Hague and
at the UN who believe differently.

Raul listened and smiled in a way that made me nervous. "In sinning, each man sins against all," he began, "and each man is at least partly guilty for another's sin. There is no isolated sin."

It had been a while since he'd quoted Dostoyevsky's *Demons* to me, something we'd done routinely in college.

"What?" I asked, the soles of his bare feet pressed against my chest.

At Columbia, Raul and I would also discuss Nietzsche. We'd lie in bed in the dorm, our legs splayed over each other, each of us reading one of his books, *The Genealogy of Morals* and *Beyond Good and Evil*, usually. We'd assume our usual positions of head to feet in our briefs, and we'd intermittently massage each other's ankles and calves and toes while quoting from our books and breaking into cold digressions.

Once, he'd gone too far, and I'd submitted for the first time, learning the bliss of pain.

"Some blood has to be spilled in the name of progress," Raul had said.

"Charlatan! You're supposed to be a communist." I'd bit his toe and he'd squirmed. "You sound like a fascist."

He had shoved his free foot into my throat until I apologized. I'd been unable to breath and wondered if he would have killed me if I hadn't.

"Even Stalin killed for utopia," he said, before beginning another dream about how he had destroyed *RFN*, this time with a data breach.

Adding irony to my mother's righteous crusade, Adam Sorrento, son of Angelo Sorrento of Bay Ridge, Brooklyn, was a contractor who made most of his money manufacturing counterfeit passports and drivers licenses. The Alto crime family of Staten Island subsidized his employment and used his construction company, Sorrento Remodeling, as a front. I realize this is a cliché full of awful stereotypes, but it's also the truth and sometimes there is a basis for such tropes. It was also believed his job required him to sometimes use violence to leverage transactions. Though I can produce no hard evidence, I recall seeing him return home late at night washing blood out of his shirt and socks on more than one occasion.

When I turned eighteen my father had me take out several lines of credit. Because his own credit was terrible and he owed the IRS several years of back taxes, he used these cards—and my name—to operate his "contracting company" for twenty years until it went bust and I was left holding all the debt, nearly $800 thousand in real estate acquisitions, supplies, and damages. The county judge froze my assets, including my bank account, and garnished my wages. Eventually, I had to file chapter 11. My dad had literally bankrupted me, despite years of my mother pleading with me not to help him, warning of his unintentional destructiveness.

My parents separated when I was twenty-two and, of course, had already moved out, though I'd wished they'd done so sooner. It was the one thing I requested every Christmas since I was seven. Their marriage was as horrific as George and Martha's in Edward Albee's *Who's Afraid of Virginia Woolf?* if Martha were puritanical and prone to moral condemnation and if George were mafia, much less cultured, and quicker to strike with fists and baseball bats than with clever barbs.

Intentional or not, the harm he caused me, to my financial situation, to my credit, did take its toll. Coupled with my mother leaving him, Dad stopped sleeping, stopped exercising—he'd been an avid runner, swimmer, and weightlifter—and stopped taking care of himself. He drank more, bathed less, and the emotional destitution began to show itself. His skin had become sallow, and he looked older. He began to move like an old man for once. He lost weight and took on a chronic, heavy sigh, "the Moorish sigh," he'd call it. Regret would give him cancer, I was sure. It would only be a matter of time.

If sight and smell were my mother's

domain, then surely sound was my father's. Whereas my mother policed the hygiene of our house, my father was critical of noise. If I or my friends would run up the stairs too quickly or close the door without turning the handle, causing the deadbolt to slam into the strike plate audibly, he would huff and puff and curse and growl and scream at us. My friends were afraid of my father, as was I. He had a tremendous temper and could turn vicious on a dime. Whereas one minute he'd be discussing butterflies and koi and Ancient Rome, the next he'd be red-faced and stomping and punching walls and making threats. As was the case with my mother, I never stood up to my father. I allowed him to run roughshod over my friends for very minor infractions. Over time they began to come over less often, not having the words as twelve-year-old boys to describe the uncomfortable atmosphere my parents had created. The passive-aggressive signals of invitation and welcome intermingled with scorn and shame.

The friends I kept in touch with as adults told me that when they looked back on those days, they said my house felt like a museum, where you could look but not touch, walk but walk softly, speak but in hushed voices, express but within limits. They said that the level of tension was palpable and made it hard to breathe. They said they felt sorry for me and understood that much of my childhood unhappiness, anger, and insecurity probably came from growing up in such a setting. I allowed my father to bully me, bully us. I could have told him to be nicer, to be patient, to speak to us with dignity and respect, as we were just kids being kids. Later I came to value how growing up within such a density of rancor and unpredictability served me. I could withstand silence as an adult. I could detach, even dissociate from conflict.

CHAPTER 7

My father, Adam Joseph Sorrento, met me at a diner in Sunnyside, not far from my Jackson Heights apartment, but far enough to keep him out of my neighborhood. The 7-train rattled overhead. The 46th Street gantry hosted a family of pigeons whose droppings came close to alighting on several passersby. The aromas of falafel, shawarma, and curry competed with the stink of car exhaust, sewage, and body odor. The Manhattan skyline was in sight on a clear day and the din of distant hip hop was always audible. Like Jackson Heights, Sunnyside was cultural spaghetti with heritages intertwined in a knot of backgrounds, languages, and ornamentations. Not a single nationhood lacked representation here.

"You really screwed the pooch on this one, kiddo," Dad said, exiting his silver minivan in the parking lot under the 7 in the middle of Queens Boulevard. Cars sped past us on either end as pigeons squawked and rats scurried for scraps. "What were you thinking writing this garbage? You have a good brain. You were supposed to be the boy with the golden pen. The scribe to make them all weep."

My father was self-taught and pompous because of it. I'd soon learn that most autodidacts were self-regarding and full of aggressive charisma. As commanded by his high tone ideas about his family and heritage, he even named me Julian after Julius Caesar.

"Can you not yell at me, please? I'm a thirty-five-year-old man."

"I don't give a fuck if you were ninety-five! I'd still yell at you because you fucked up and you're still my son and I still fucking love you!"

He put me in a headlock and messed up my hair before releasing me with enough brio to send me stumbling backward into his minivan door, which had been ajar, causing me to bang my elbow and twist my ankle. Red-faced with mussed hair, in pain, and slightly humiliated by the onlookers witnessing our strange Caucasian behavior, I finally convinced my father to continue the conversation at a hushed, or at least respectable, tone in Pete's Diner, not renovated since the early 80s and moderately crowded for a weekday afternoon.

"So, you just had to go in on the credit stuff, huh?" My dad slurped black coffee and nibbled on toasted rye. "You couldn't leave that out of it?"

"I wanted to tell the truth, but not all of it, yet. Have to leave something for the book, which—"

"There won't be a fucking book, son," he said without expression, but his face looked newly older. "And the 'truth'? Is that some kind of a joke, Julian? All that gangster shit? Are you trying to get me locked up? Or worse?"

"What's worse?"

"Did you ever consider how hard it was for me to ask you to do that for me? Do you think I'd have even asked if my back wasn't against the wall? And it almost killed me, you know! It made me fucking sick to my stomach! I could have gotten cancer worrying about it. Knowing I was hurting you this way. Your mother left me because of it."

I didn't have children, nor did I want them, but if I had, the last thing I'd ever do was put them on the line the way my father did me. It was reckless and selfish and upset the natural order of things. Parents were supposed to protect their offspring and sacrifice for their increase. My mother understood this and that's why she fought to stop me from helping him. That's why she left. And that's why I wrote the memoir and despite my father's protests, eventually the book. I could never say any of this to him. With his radical sensitivity to the truth, such admissions would have caused him to drop dead of a heart attack right then and there.

"I just thank God that you didn't mention anyone else's name," he said, harmlessly sticking the prongs of the fork into his hand.

"They'll be in the book, though."

He failed to find the humor in my joke, which was also half serious as I needed more content to fill chapters. Dad slammed the table hard enough for me to jump and several other diners to glance over at us.

"You promised," I said.

"I know you felt the need to get up there, but how do you just make shit up like that?"

Get up there.

"I didn't make anything up."

"It's like the 1919 World Series! Eight Chicago White Sox players threw the fucking game to the Cincinnati Reds! And for what? For a damn gambling bribe of one hundred thousand bucks! That's like maybe one and a half million dollars today when accounting for inflation."

"That's a weird comparison, but okay."

My father always reached into history, both recent and ancient, in a multitude of areas, be it military, political, philosophical, or even sports, to make points about faltering moral uprightness. It had been part of his character to illustrate lessons by citing the moments that shaped modern civilization. He also never missed an opportunity to prove to people, his own family included, just how learned he was.

"You lied."

"Stop saying that. I didn't lie."

"Then you're delusional or have a brain tumor or something. Have you gone for an MRI?"

"Jesus Christ."

My father, even a year later, still bore semblance to the decrepit old man I'd described in the article. Vain to a fault, he disarmed by not excoriating me for the unflattering portrait I'd painted of him in a magazine with a circulation of upwards of 1.2 million. If I was being fair, I'd acknowledge that maybe he had put on a little weight and his pigmentation had been somewhat restored to a flesh-like hue, but still, he looked much older than my mother and too old for someone his real age. Stress did leave its mark.

"Sophia and James are hurt," he said. "And pissed. They want to rip your head off. And don't let little Arnold get his hands on you. He said he will stomp you into the dirt."

"What a family."

"Well, Julian, come on, what did you think was going to happen? That we'd all be happy for you for making us look like chumps? For what? For you to make a name for yourself like a big shot? In the old neighborhood, you'd have already had your legs broken."

"What a dad."

My father then grabbed a bread knife and pointed it at me, his reddening fist hovering, trembling over the breadbasket and our coffees. It was a real threat. He would have gutted me right there in front of a dozen witnesses to correct my disrespect. He was old school savage, that way, despite all his self-ingested knowledge. He would cut me and then reference Shakespeare or Ancient Rome and make a point about honor and family crests and nobility and tough love and necessary reprimands.

"Are you serious?"

He lowered the cutlery and worked demonstratively—deep breathing and grimacing—at managing his infamous, unnerving temper.

"Just don't get smart with me," he said in a dramatic whisper, doing his best De Niro. "I'll slap you right here in front of everyone."

Though *The New Yorker* ran the piece over a year ago everyone was acting as if it had just been published. It was like time paused when I dropped out of their lives upon publication, and they'd kept all these thoughts and feelings contained until they saw me again and unleashed with fresh outrage. All the emails and texts and voicemail messages and late-night arrivals at my front door, and all the times I'd ignored them, or offered tepid replies, or placations had accumulated into a ball of animosity that they giddily spiked at my head upon finally seeing me again in person. It all messed with my sense of time.

"Write another article about how you lied. Tell them you wrote a work of fiction, not an autobiography. Tell them it was a nonsense story or something"

"It was a memoir. The basis for a book I am—"

"Tell them you'd like to make a public statement and come clean."

"My agent will drop me if I don't write something that can make her money. That's how this all works."

Despite sixty-odd years of carrying his fat-muscular frame around the sensory assault that was a lifetime in New York City, my dad still moved with the ferocity of a man in his twenties. No one in my orbit succumbed to their age. They fought like hell to stay alive and hold captive vigor and appearances. He shook his head maniacally and threw his hands up, mea culp-style, and let loose a hoarse, abrasive chortle.

"And that's another fucking thing," he began. "I hear you're turning the bullshit storyline of Aunt Mary and Uncle Monroe and your goofy cousin Pegasus into a show for HBO?"

Word had travelled fast. Everyone in my family was a gossip.

"Yeah, that's what the producers wanted. Just their story."

"Well, thank God you're leaving all the rest of us out of it, huh?"

"Look, Dad, I—"

"No, *you* look! You're not writing a book about us. If I have to get tough with your bitch agent and the faggot editors—sorry, son, I didn't mean that like that—at the frou frou *New Yorker*, I will stop that from happening. No more about us, you got that?"

I absorbed his ugly words and almost reminded him of his hoodlum upbringing but didn't want my life to be publicly threatened again. Still, his face had become serpentine.

"You're not hearing me!" He hissed like a cobra. "Write what you want, but don't put us in it."

The waitress, a frumpy and impatient woman of middle age with heavy make-up and chaotic hair, brought us our check, eager to get us out. We'd only had toast and coffee. Neither of us anticipated much of an appetite. Dad paid and I let him.

On the way to the car, I passed a homeless woman, maybe middle aged or maybe much older. It was hard to discern as her patina of filth and grief was dense. She'd been murmuring about "Jonathan" and "Claire" and "Shonda." Her rants were shot through with sobs, unintelligible gibberish, and guttural recriminations. All bile and agony. She was clearly arguing with demons, contending with contentious memories of those who had done her wrong. The woman had dried crust around her mouth and her eyes were heavy and big. Her hair was matted to her face. Her wrinkles were deep and intermingled with scars. She looked as though she'd been through a battle. A battle that left innumerable wounds. She reminded me of a service recipient with whom I'd grown close named Breanna. Breanna had been raped when she was fourteen by a boy in her Highbridge neighborhood. Thirty years later she had met her rapist's wife, Daniela, by chance at a party thrown by a friend. That evening she also learned that Daniela and her rapist had three children, all girls, and that he had died a few years earlier. A week later, Breanna's nervous breakdown stripped her of all functionality and before long she was living in the park a mile down the road, her job as a cashier at a department store gone vacant, her rent gone unpaid, her apartment gone haunted, her friends and family grown alienated.

My father snapped me back to the terrible present as he grabbed and hugged me. I heard him whimper into my shoulder as he held me close. I returned the embrace but not the emotion. He'd always tend toward the maudlin whenever drama was diffused as a relief or a victory. In his mind we'd both lost and won something. The essay had been written and that bell could not be un-rung, but I'd also protested his request to issue a public statement recanting my accusations, as he'd seen them.

For the book, I decided that I would lean more heavily into my father's relationship with the assortment of Staten Island toughs who littered my childhood. Their children and grandchildren could provide insights into the shady dealings my father had been involved in. Joe Black. Sal DiMaria. Frankie Caruso. Dad's chapters would be augmented with the machinations of degenerate New York underworld types and their merciless codas. It would for sure end my relationship with him, and very well lead to criminal charges, likely prison, and all the Italian Americans with their myriad complexes would come after me with a fury, but who cares? My father was a selfish, irresponsible man who ruined my name and hurt my mother and I only had left the capacity to care about very few things, like selling the damn book.

"You know, Julian, even after you told me you were, you know, the way you are, I never had a problem with it, I mean, none of us did, not even James or Dougie, and now look at little Vaughan in Arizona, all mincing and whatnot, but we accepted you, you know for who you were. And we even welcomed that Spanish guy you dated in college into our home. What was his name, Ricardo?"

Ricardo. Raul would have never let me live that one down.

I'd felt nauseated but didn't vomit. I pulled away. "So, I should be what? Grateful?"

"Yeah, you should be grateful. It wouldn't have been so easy for a lot of people who grew up like us. And then you go and write about us being poor degenerates and mobsters and thieves. You had a comfortable middle-class life, Julian. We weren't in the gutter. Why are you trying to hurt us?"

I stepped back. It took me a minute to catch my breath and twice as long to put my thoughts in order and make my next move.

Like my mother, my father never brought up the countless episodes with my friends, how he had terrified them when erupting like a volcano over nothing significant. I am sure if I asked, he would have said that his house was a sanctuary and silence helped him form and hear his own thoughts, develop his ideas, relish his passions, plan his future. I would have said, but, Dad, you had a child, and that child needed a childhood.

"Dad, I have to go. I'm sorry you didn't like the article."

"Yeah," he said, getting in his minivan, "A real pity to see talent wasted on the wrong idea."

He always had to be the last to say his piece. I let him think that he had, but the old man was sadly mistaken. The writer is the one who will always have the last word.

CHAPTER 8

As was often the case with Ed and Kevin's dinner parties, the guests were in constant rotation. I'd probably been to at least two dozen in the past year and of the original quartet, only Colin made an appearance on the evening attended by Violet Scott, a once popular actress who #MeTooed a studio executive and ended her own career in so doing, and Jackson Reilly, the heir to a pharmaceutical empire who dabbled in all forms of media including producing independent films, publishing graphic novels, and developing apps. Ed had not been a Renaissance man, but at least he could call his friends and acquaintances diverse and varied in their brilliance.

"It's all a construction," said Violet, groggy, yet alert. "Man makes everything and most of it isn't worth anything. The atomic bomb. Too many movies and television shows and books! Too many cars and guns and apps and drugs. I'm sorry, Jackson, but it's true. Too many apps and drugs. All constructions."

"So, what, we should stop, Violet?" asked Jackson, handsome but physically incongruent. His body was overly developed with synthetics, clearly, and accented under snug clothing, with a face of a prepubescent child. "Just laze around and bask in our complacency?"

"How about developing inner constructions?" said Violet, childlike in her naivete.

"Oh, jeez," said Kevin, well into his fifth cocktail, intolerant of spiritual assertions.

"Don't be cynical," said Violet to Kevin. She'd looked sincere, maybe even wounded.

Kevin stared into his drink and shrugged. Who could argue with Violet

Scott? After what she'd endured by The Creep, the name of whom was never mentioned in her company, and then by the system itself, the very industry that she'd helped bank hundreds of millions of dollars. Her skin was so white her veins presented themselves as if they'd been painted on. She could pass for a medical school mannequin. Every inch of her exposed itself as raw and fragile. People were delicate with her. Especially gay men who took her into their fold as something iconic. She'd regarded Ed and Kevin's home as a safe enough space to speak freely.

"You don't want to act anymore, Violet?" I asked stupidly. I'd known it was a stupid question because Ed, Kevin, Jackson, Colin, and Violet looked at me crookedly, noting the misstep.

"I can't even remember my own name on some days because that's what trauma does," she said, not looking at me, but instead at Colin, who blushed and wrinkled his brow. I thought I even saw him swallow hard as if in a lampoon or animated fable. A theatrical gulp.

"I'm sorry," I said and thought about *things that trauma did*. And the things we did to meet its damage, the ways in which the brain protects itself. Seeing my young cousin, Loretta, then only 44, wasting away in a hospital bed after her breast cancer reached her brain stung deeply, so deeply that I craved diversion. I became fixated on a handsome nurse and the association of the trauma of my cousin's sad state and the nurse's estimable beauty proved a mercy.

"It's what happens when you spend your life playing other people," added Violet. "Now, I always only want to ever be myself."

"That's commendable," said Colin, to which Violet again looked at him as if he'd just struck her.

"It's what happens when you fuck with powerful men," she said with discernable acid.

Colin excused himself to pee. Kevin looked at me with a softness I'd needed but hadn't known how to request.

After the awkward tension dissipated, Jackson turned to me with squinted eyes. "Tell me, Julian, do you have a producer for your little film, yet?"

"Oh, it's a series," I corrected with satisfaction, "and yes, MAX."

"Oh, *them*," he said, declaring his boredom.

"Yeah," I said, sheepishly, "and the Darlington Brothers are producing and directing."

"Oh, I know those boys," said Jackson. "Very good boys, indeed."

"Julian is writing all the teleplays," said Kevin, proudly, again gazing at me with tender curiosity.

"Busy beaver," said Jackson.

"As I understand it, the whole series will focus solely on your aunt and uncle?" said Ed.

"And cousin," I said, "Thankfully just them."

"Why, 'thankfully'?" asked Violet.

"My family is not happy with what I wrote."

"No one wants their dirty laundry aired," she said, looking at Colin as he returned to the table, looking unwell.

"What's all this about 'dirty laundry'?" he asked, almost knocking over his wine glass.

"We were just talking about the trouble Julian's *New Yorker* essay got him into with his family," said Ed.

"Oh, that thing," said Colin. "Well, memoirs are a deadly game."

"For the author?" asked Jackson.

"For the author's targets," said Colin.

I excused myself to pee. From the bathroom I could clearly hear the conversation continue without me.

"You know, Jackson, I must say, your physique is looking splendid, these days," said Ed.

"Thank you, Ed," said Jackson, I'm sure puffing out his chest and flexing his arms. "I do work hard at it."

"I would love to have your portrait painted by Christian Melendez," said

Ed. "Do you know him?"

"I don't but that sounds lovely," said Jackson.

"Yes, he is a friend of ours in Key West. He painted my beau Giancarlo, who has the most lithe, sinuous body you've ever seen. He is a vegan, don't you know, and he does this thing called intermittent fasting where he starves himself from seven at night to twelve the following afternoon. Makes him a total bitch, but he looks great. Wasp waisted and striated and plump in all the right places. Christian also painted our friend Alvin, who is an acrobat for Broadway who has also done some porn. He is a little muscleman. Shaped like a square with the biggest calves you've ever seen on a man."

"Were these portraits clothed?" asked Jackson.

"No, they were both au natural," said Ed.

"Well, getting naked for another man, Ed, I mean—"

"Oh, don't be a prude, Jackson," said Colin. "Christian is a professional and it's art, for Christ's sake!"

By the time I returned to the dining room I saw Violet staring hard at Colin. He flinched in his chair as if she'd thrown something at him.

"It's not that, Colin, but my family, of course," said Jackson.

"A very bad look to have the heir of a dynasty appearing in the buff for all to scrutinize," said Kevin, full of delight and mischief, glancing at me with a new familiarity and ease. "How would the board members react?"

"Well, so you get it."

Jackson was straight but Ed, Kevin, and Colin didn't care. They pursued him as if they'd had a shot all the same. Violet, that evening, was his bodyguard, keeping the predators at bay. She'd learned how to do such things the hard way. I'd wondered if she would eventually protect me from Kevin, but then I decided I'd give him unfettered access to me whenever he'd wanted it. Reciprocity. Quid pro quo. Passive personality.

As I was about to take another bite of the creme brûlée, the biggest cockroach I'd ever seen appeared on my plate. Ed and Kevin's house was as immaculate as possible given their employment of a cleaning lady who did diligent work weekly, but this being New York City on a warm day, the invasion was unstoppable. Without thinking I smacked the insect with my fork sending it across the table, where it bounced off Ed's chest and into his lap.

Ed leapt to his feet gasping and howling in horror. I imagined him having a heart attack and dying and me being forever stuck with the label of "icon killer."

"Ohmygod, Ed! I think it fell into your pocket!"

In a manic flurry, Ed pulled change and receipts and newspaper clippings from his pants pockets before realizing the attacker had fallen onto his chair and then the floor by his feet.

Colin and Jackson also jumped up and hissed in squeamish revilement as the vermin scurried under the table.

Kevin, unshaken by the ordeal, turned to Colin and Jackson and said with a lazy, or indifferent, glamour, "He's not a fan," and continued eating.

Violet too was cool. She stood up, took off her shoe, which had a chunky heel, and furtively closed in on the cockroach before bringing the shoe down, heel first, like a mallet.

The insect had been half crushed, its spared legs twitching with desperation and in agony. It was a hard kill. Violet struck the roach again and again and again, grunting and then crying and then screaming with each messy, measured, though forceful, blow. It looked as if she were reacting to something else and her frenzied, brutal murder of the little critter was a grisly sublimation.

Flatted intestines, mangled legs, cracked shells, mutilated wings, and a smeared hull strewn across Ed and Kevin's inlaid parquet wood floor and on Violet's probably expensive shoe. Violet was red faced. Wounded, to be sure, in her own way. The act was barbaric and required commitment and cruelty and vigor. She wiped away tears blackened by mascara and gritted her teeth. She languidly excused herself and hastily retreated to the bathroom to presumably wash her shoe and gather herself.

"Don't think your family's drugs can rehabilitate that poor little fucker, eh, Jackson?" said Colin.

Jackson looked at the brash Irish author and sniggered. Everyone sat and resumed their dessert, except for me who carried the contaminated remainder of the crème brûlée to the trash and then washed the plate in the kitchen sink. Soon, Violet was beside me.

"Are you okay?" I asked.

"No, but it doesn't matter."

"You should maybe go home and get some sleep," I said.

"Jackson is not safe here without me," she said.

"Jackson is a big boy, a *very* big boy, who can more than handle himself."

Kevin appeared with Jackson. I heard Ed and Colin laugh heartily from the living room.

"Ed and Colin are excluding us from their inside jokes and old, boring stories," said Kevin, elbowing me from the sink so he could start cleaning. The dishes were a precarious tower threatening collapse. "I don't give two shits what they go on about, but it's rude when we have guests like these two, who hardly ever stop by anymore, and it's no wonder with a host like Ed!"

Violet liked Kevin. I could tell because when he was around her shoulders settled and her smile looked genuine. It involved her eyes. When she faked her happiness her big giveaway was her eyes. Like most they didn't produce crow's feet. A real smile made you look older.

"We should be going anyway, Kevin," said Jackson, handing Violet her futuristic-looking cerulean jacket with eccentric zippers and exaggerated collars and outsized grommets.

"So soon?" Kevin pouted with suds coating his hands and forearms.

"I have a meeting in the morning," said Jackson. "App folks."

"And I am tired," added Violet.

"Of course," said Kevin, drying his hands, throwing his arms around Jackson and Violet with guileless warmth. "Thanks for coming, kids."

The goodbyes with Ed were equally congenial and reverential, though

Jackson and Violet became chilly when parting with Colin. The frosty tension between the three of them was obvious and I'd been curious to learn why. They shook hands and gave polite nods rather than hugs and air kisses.

After they left, Ed and Colin continued nibbling on cheese and discussing Mann and Rimbaud and Genet and whomever else long-dead writer struck their fancies. Kevin and I returned to the kitchen where he washed the dishes and I dried.

"We like you here," said Kevin, handing me a plate. "You're family now."

CHAPTER 9

I squeezed into my boxing helmet and slid my mouthguard over my teeth. Raul never went easy on me when sparring. It was a very public and acceptable iteration of our very private BDSM sessions. He'd pummel the hell out of me and get off on the domination as his clients or other members of the expensive club watched and cheered him on. I'd be equally turned on as he beat me silly. To be fair, it was also a rigorous workout, and I did pick up a skill or two. I'd been especially adept at blocking right hooks and anticipating upper cuts and absorbing direct blows.

That afternoon he had been particularly brutal, and my head rang from all the punches, none of which he pulled. He grunted and splashed spit and sweat onto me as he attacked. I shielded myself as best I could, cowering when he got too aggressive and even whimpering and groaning more than once. I'd desired him more during those moments when he wouldn't let up and hurt me. It had taken me a while to gain acceptance of my proclivities and to share them with someone, and no one ever gave me what I needed quite like Raul had, and with such minimal effort and no uncomfortable conversations about what we'd both desired. We read each other that way.

Something special about Raul that few knew about was his hyper-sensitivity surrounding nonhuman animals. Whenever we would watch a film or tv show that had a scene in which a nonhuman animal was hurt or killed he would become angry and storm off, even if we were in a theater. Sometimes he would even exclaim "This movie sucks!" before exiting the screening room.

As we showered in the gym's spa-like locker-room, I could hear Raul jerking off in the next stall. I worried that others might, too, and that he'd lose his job, but we were alone. He had been putting on a show for me, moaning and gasping demonstratively, to communicate how gratified he'd been by our workout. He'd told me that the part-time gig as a martial arts instructor helped mitigate all the sitting and suit-wearing required for his white-collar programming day job at *RFN*.

Raul was difficult to please, which is why I wanted him to help me with the adaptation. I knew his critical nature would improve it. He denigrated most new writers, filmmakers, and musicians. He'd made it a sport to list reasons why emerging artists—that is anyone who started producing work for public consumption after 2000—were derivative mercenaries, hacks who just sought fame. Any great work of art produced in the 21st century was either an anomaly or done so by wizened masters who'd begun their careers likely in the 60s or 70s and were hanging on. Any new media was a hollow tribute to the better expressions that had come earlier, and the producers of such new media were mere product makers. I asked him if this included me, and he'd said no, because he'd known me. I told him that invalidated his endorsement because what if he hadn't known me. I'd be written off before I'd even begun due to my birth date. His position was intellectually dishonest. I'd argued with him that many Generation X artists and leaders had a delayed start due to the Silent Generation and the Baby Boomers grabbing and holding onto power for dear life, denying us opportunities. It's sort of like being chained to the radiator in the basement for twenty years and then being chided for having kept a dirty house. We'd never even had the chance to clean!

We ate mock duck at the too-precious café next door. Raul and I brainstormed how we'd adapt Mary, Monroe, and Pegasus's exploits into the second episode of *The Touring Barbarism*. My chronicles were minimal and mainly probed their psyches like case studies.

"I think it's fascinating the way you spend so much time on his deformities and body obsessions," said Raul, wolfing tempeh and lentils. "Your Uncle Monroe, I mean."

"It's central to his personality so it has to be central to his episode," I said. When Uncle Monroe was thirty, he was in a bad motorcycle accident which left him with a permanent limp and facial disfigurements. He has a thick scar running from the right corner of his mouth, his nose bends to the right, and his right eye droops. Also, his jaw is uneven and juts out like a truck's grill. Apparently, it was the threat of death that occasioned the disaster. Monroe had passed a cemetery while riding one Sunday afternoon and felt a rush of defiance, a reminder that his life would someday end, the urgency to live with robust abandon, and so he sped and became reckless with life, but soon crashed.

"I think lean into his disfigurement and disability and how he overcompensates by building bombs for Raytheon and turning himself into a muscle freak and his weird cat obsession!" Raul practically drooled over these details as he espoused them.

```
INT. CLINT RESIDENCE — MORNING


Monroe   Clint   stares   at   his   unfortunate
reflection  in  the  bathroom  vanity  and  wishes
the  motorcycle  wreck  thirty  years  earlier  had
killed  him.  (NOTE: will have to insert flashback
of motorcycle accident).  The  pain  in  his  right
hip  radiates  from  his  sciatic  nerve  down  to  his
toes  and  leaves  his  limb  numb  and  useless.  He
limps  and  requires  a  cane  to  stay  upright  and
mobile.


He  hides  under  the  comforter  in  bed  long  after
Mary  wakes  and  begins  working.  When  she  was  in
the  field,  be  it  in  Chile,  Congo,  or  Cambodia,
he  would  while  away  the  entire  morning  under
```

covers with his cats, Picasso, Butters, Juice, and Sonia, gripping them to his chest and gut like a mother would her litter, extensions of his loins, furry babies that required affection and protection, assurance that they would be kept safe form the monstrous, too-fast, too indifferent world. Work could wait. As senior engineer and Northeast director of Phalanx assembly, he can do his high-level job remotely whenever he wanted, which was most days, and since his server was Raytheon issued, secured, and supervised, he could continue telecommuting at will.

Character NOTE for actor playing Monroe/ possibly depicted in a montage: He begins his rise the same way every afternoon with shots of testosterone into his ass and a protein shake that provides three times the daily recommendation for a man his size and age. Now sixty, he is determined to build his muscles as big and as hard as athletes half his age. He will have to become more than human if he hopes to protect his family and defeat the demons of his deductions and derangements.

He had converted his garage into a gym with benches, dumbbells, barbells, murphy racks, treadmills, cables, boxing bags, one heavy and one for speed, and yoga mats. Mirrors also abounded on all four walls and the ceiling as the garage doors had been replaced with drywall and a conventional door had been built into it. The room was cooled and ventilated as Monroe had an aversion to odors of any sort, except for his cats' urine, which he'd accepted as a natural occurrence. Humans were unnatural and so their odors offended. Monroe spends two hours a day in this room, a place of mental maintenance and spiritual stability.

"It kind of reads like J.G. Ballard, which means as a series I bet it will have the feel of a Cronenberg film," said Raul as he poked me with his bare foot, free of its flip flop, under the table.

"Or a Darlington Brothers film," I added.

Monroe downs his post-workout blueberry-banana-peanut butter-Greek yogurt shake and stands at his elevated desk while analyzing the most recent data sent by his staff that morning. He remains on his feet when he works to prevent atrophy. Despite all the weight he lifts, he knows his body will become soft if he spends the day sitting. His protein-enriched flatulence reeks of death which means he is healthy, eliminating the most noxious toxins from his tissue.

The cats lounge in the living room, basking in the slivers of sun that cut through the foyer, or else attacking their stuffed mice or plastic balls.

Suddenly, Monroe leaps back and shouts. The cats turn to him with bored eyes, but when he begins running full speed through the house screaming, "It's happening! It's finally happening!" the felines bow into an inverted U-shaped curve and hiss, their scruff raised, their defenses heightened.

Monroe rampages in his underwear through their basket of toys, knocking over their food bowl, stomping on their kitty litter, and shrieking at them as though they are feuding combatants and he a Nordic warrior. Pegasus and Mary are still on campus and the house is his temporary battle simulation.

I had a feeling that Raul approved of the structure, so far, with episode one focusing on Mary, episode two on Monroe, and episode three, presumably, about Pegasus, and then have them converge in episodes four through ten.

The Darlington Brothers and I never discussed it, but I began to find it odd and maybe telling that they only wanted to adapt the sections of my memoir that did not have me at all in it. The portions of the piece that were not at all about my meekness, no matter how mighty. The graphs about Mary, Monroe, and Pegasus were meant to support the graphs about me and my immediate family and perhaps thematically uphold the ideas of passivity crushed by aggression amid grace and inner, quiet strength.

Raul reached across the table and touched my hand, holding an almond croissant that I'd still not bitten into.

"So, Monroe works mostly from home on a protected server due to his agoraphobia?" he asked.

"Yes, but he also goes into the office a few times a week."

INT. RAYTHEON - MORNING

Despite his station, Monroe surrenders his cell phone to the locker outside the lab like everyone else. He deposits it into an encoded lockbox and enters through the double steel doors. Inside technicians work assiduously on the numerous constituent parts of the Phalanx CIWS, pronounced sea-wiz. The technology is designed to reduce collateral damage and only destroy intended targets, killing exclusively marked men and women. Mainly it is needed to defend against small boats, surface torpedoes, anti-ship missiles, fixed wing aircraft, and helicopters. With their barrel-shaped radome and automated nature some refer to the Phalanx CIWS as R2-D2.

Raul snatched my croissant and helped himself to half. "I thought all that stuff was classified."

"Everything is online," I said, grabbing the croissant back from him.

When we went back to my apartment an hour later, Raul tossed me to the floor and stripped me naked. We had violent sex, a continuation of our hard sparring. He left me sore and bruised and satisfied, eerily. It *was* eerie how much sex we had and yet he still seemed to need more and often pursued it with other men. How much could one want and get and still need? What were the limits of his libido? Was satiation even a possibility? I knew early on that I'd never be enough and if we ever got serious the relationship would have to remain open as he'd require a variety of cocks and holes and bodies and faces to gratify. I didn't judge, but I always felt bad that the corporeal in him was such a ravenous animal that could only stop when dead.

We lay on the floor, half nude, panting, sweating, regaining ourselves. I got up and got dressed and took notes about my second episode, which was still mostly in chapter form, and questioned my choice to include any of the insider stuff at Raytheon. Could I write it authentically and with true insight? Could I be that procedural? I didn't want to turn this show into *Law & Order* or *ER*. It wasn't necessarily about the machinations of the workplace, though Mary and Monroe's chosen professions mattered to their characters and to the story as they are the very things that compel Pegasus to act and spite them through his "lessons".

Monroe Clint's work life is downright Vonnegut. The office and lab, his colleagues, and their orders, feel surreal and absurd. Almost slapstick ready. There is even a sense of Kubrick within the sterile halls. As though a scene in *Dr. Strangelove.* The quiet menace of Raytheon is lost on the bomb builders as they were merely cogs in a massive machine and by following commands and meeting deadlines and hitting their numbers, their quotas, and studying formulas and percentages and functionality of parts and their relationship to the whole, the workers lost sight of the big picture of killing and maiming and razing entire cities and wiping out whole cultures. It is mundane daily. Tedious and trivial. It's how they can get up and arrive on time, achieve productivity, receive paychecks, support their families, embark on holidays, buy cars and houses and clothes, and generally feel accomplished.

Though Pegasus makes sporadic remarks about ethics and US sovereignty and hegemony and imperialism, Monroe dismisses his son's criticisms as products of youth, inexperience, and idealism fed by professors who extol the virtues of socialism because they hadn't earned enough to buy themselves an adequate life and so they took their economic frustrations and misgivings with capitalism out on their impressionable students. Groomers, he often calls them.

With Mary, it is different, as she's lived long enough to know better, but her impoverished youth in the Bronx with a mother who'd been a giver and had been taken for a fool by the entire neighborhood and sister, Annalisa, who both robbed and preached, even as she was pilfering, made her find sympathy for the marginalized and the maligned. Monroe appreciates that she'd seen in anthropology a way out of her family's disgraced legacy and a means to be proud even while doing charitable work. That she's being vilified and lampooned for inadvertently inciting an Indian civil war came to her and the entire family as a shock and it had grieved her.

INT. RAYTHEON - DAY

Dean Hornak, Monroe's chief technician, and Monroe test radar transmissions and microwave assemblies.

                    DEAN
          How's Peg?

Monroe climbs onto a stepstool and peers into
the oversized unit.

                    MONROE
          Ah, he's been taken under the wing
          of this cracked socialist professor
          of sociology.

                    DEAN
          Uh oh. Watch it there. You don't
          want a commie as a kid.

                    MONROE
          Yeah, you know, his heart is in
          the right place. He's studying
          homelessness this semester, but
          this guy, this teacher, Doctor
          Alessandro, is a real Marxist. I
          don't like it.

The men descend their stools, fold them up, and
carry them to the next metal giant.

                    DEAN
          What's Mary say about it?

                    MONROE
        Well, you know Mary, she's a
        bleeding heart.

As the men climb their little ladders and stick
their heads into the machines for inspection,
Dean hesitates, and —

                    DEAN
        Sweet Mary, how's she dealing with
        that India nonsense?

                    MONROE
        Well, the Hague came after her, but
        the college is behind her and she's
        keeping her funding, but they're
        investigating and not making our
        lives easy.

                    DEAN
        It was an accident, what the fuck
        do you expect when you're dealing
        with barbarians?

                    MONROE
            (leaning against his killer of
            weaker forces)
        Yup, let no good deed go
        unpunished.

Raul crawled over to me and rested his head in my lap as I typed the paragraph at my dining room table. I needed to first write the episode out in prose before I could adapt it into filmable action.

"Marriage is the death of every proud soul," he said, sadly. "Of all independence." Another quote from *Demons*. Had Raul imagined I wanted to marry him? Was he trying to preemptively dissuade me from reattaching to him? I'd mis-stepped a few years back and begun to cling, demanding more of him than occasional conversation and quick fucks. Had he been reading my mind? Was I that transparent?

I touched his head, ran my fingers through his thick shock of ink-black hair.

"Who wants to get married, Raul?"

He wrapped his arms around my legs and buried his face in my lap. "I have no idea who ever would," he said, muffled.

My brother James dated models (including a Playboy cover girl who was also an NYPD officer, which created a scandal the entire country heard about), aspiring actresses, and strippers, almost exclusively, and finally married one. Luz Osorio was from Bogota, Colombia. She was effortlessly charming and seduced our family when dating James, though became possessive and paranoid after marrying him, a decision that was occasioned by my brother's lack of caution. He'd gotten her pregnant when she was only twenty, the median age of conception for the women in my family, and soon after their Justice of the Peace ceremony, Vaughan was born. Luz would deny it if anyone asked, but she'd confided in me that she'd been raised by Marxist parents in a dogmatic commune, really a cult. When she and my brother first dated, we'd do everything together. Horseback riding weekly. Plays and museums and drinks and dinners, sharing dishes. Movie night was twice a week. She preferred love stories and I tended toward horror. We'd discuss art and books. Sometimes we went to cocktail parties before film premieres. She was smart and fun and cool, but when Vaughan was born, she'd changed. Maybe something hormonal kicked in or maybe she'd been playing us all along to snare my brother. He lacked backbone and

Excerpt of
My Mighty Meekness,
as published in
The New Yorker

was easily swayed, led away from us almost too readily, as if he'd waited his entire life for a beautiful woman to waltz in and steer him from our interdependent dysfunction. It was a shame that she fell out so badly with us as we'd bonded almost immediately. I'd finally had someone in my family with whom I could discuss books and film and art and culture. Luz and I were much closer in age than she and James. Luz also tricked my mother into believing that she regarded her as a second mom and my mom foolishly, cruelly took to Luz as a second daughter, one she favored over her own. Sophia added that slight to the already towering mountain of lifelong resentments for my mother.

When I told Luz that I wanted to be a writer, she'd encouraged me to leave college, steer clear of conventional full-time jobs, and to wait tables or bartend to free my mind and time for writing and networking. She said I should move to LA and try to get work on a TV show because that would help me get an agent. She'd known people in TV and film as she was a model for a short time and even acted briefly. She'd befriended the legendary studio executive Robert Evans, the titan who'd been responsible for *The Godfather* films, *Chinatown*, and *Rosemary's Baby*. He even called her apartment once when I was over. She'd been in the shower, and I answered. When he said who he was I thought it was a prank, but it hadn't been. He was interested in Luz for more than her limited acting ability. If she wanted to have a career as an actress, he'd make it happen, but at a cost. Clearly, her principles had been greater than the offer she'd not be able to refuse, and yet she refused and so became a nurse. Ten years later I would meet the son, a budding producer himself, of the Paramount executive vice president who'd actually had to fire Evans in the 1990s for his rampant drug addiction. By then I'd all but given up my passing dream of writing and had earned an MSW, got licensed, and became a social worker. When she and my brother had begun dating, Luz, had rear-ended a fire truck at sixty miles per hour, killing a firefighter riding on the back. She had been drunk. She survived the accident though required reconstructive surgeries to repair the scars the windshield caused when it exploded into her face. My brother used his connections as a police officer to have her sentence reduced from ten consecutive years in prison to imprisonment on weekends for five years, ten years of community service, a 30-day stay in rehab, and an annually documented lifetime in AA. They also paid out over a million dollars to the firefighter's family in a civil suit, something that cost both her and my brother years of savings, their condominium, and several more years of garnished wages. While it hurt them both financially, it destroyed a large piece of Luz.

After finding one of a litany of phone numbers of a woman in my brother's pants pocket, Luz subjected me to a tirade about what a creep he was, what a weakling, what an insecure momma's boy, and how he wasn't even the most handsome man she had ever dated and how he was selfish in bed and how he had been abusive and cruel and immature and lazy and dumb and ignorant about world affairs and uncultured and uncouth and an embarrassment to bring to her society parties at art galleries and upscale restaurants. I allowed her to vent even though she'd been saying the nastiest things about my brother, who I still had looked up to as a kind of role model, but I never stopped her, I never challenged her, I never defended him, and I regretted it for years. He may have been some of those things, maybe even all those things, but he was also my brother, my heroic brother, with all his warts and flaws and shortcomings and immoralities, and I should have said something.

After that first tome of invectives, Luz felt emboldened to badmouth him interminably to me. It taught me the value of keeping my mouth shut and permitting free rein to people during their diatribes, to be there for others as a sounding board, to provide them ample rope with which to hang themselves, to collect and accumulate self-damning dirt on the mindless talkers.

CHAPTER 10

Luz had texted me on a Tuesday morning and asked if we could FaceTime later in the day. 5PM EDT/ 2PM PST. I'd agreed but facing her turned my stomach. I knew the interaction would be uncomfortable. I hadn't seen her in about five years, though James had emailed me photos of her, himself, and Vaughan on various vacations. The Grand Canyon. Zion National Park. Las Vegas. San Diego. They took myriad road trips and from Phoenix any number of fun destinations were a mere several-hour car ride away. Sometimes they drove to Mexico. San Carlos, usually. Now pushing forty, she was still as beautiful and youthful as she'd been when I met her almost twenty years ago. She smiled warmly as we greeted each other on Facetime.

"Julian," she began with teeth whiter than before and skin clearly Botoxed. She was too young for Botox. "You're looking well."

"Thanks, Luz, you are too."

Her cosmetic face seemed almost waxen the closer I looked. The new oddness of her features was not evident in the photos because she was inanimate, but when speaking, making expressions, an unnaturalness to her beauty revealed itself. If this was Luz at thirty-five, pray tell, what would she look like at sixty-five?

"Maybe we should just get right down to it, if that's okay?"

"Sure," I said, trying not to fixate on her plastic skin, permanently puckered lips, and immovable brow.

"You know how hard it was for me to come here, right? I mean, to New York, when I was only eighteen to study nursing, leaving my life and family in Bogota, learning English on my own, making my own way, making my own life."

"I do know that, Luz."

"And yet in your article you describe me as a gold digger."

I stammered, hemmed and hawed, reverted back to the boy she'd known all those years ago, every measure of success slipping from my face, compromising my rehearsed demeanor.

"Luz, I didn't—"

"You wrote I trapped your brother. You wrote I became pregnant with Vaughan to trap him. You wrote I manipulated you and your mother and father."

"Well, maybe you did."

Luz emitted a faux gasp. A scoff? She smirked and looked off camera at something, someone. When she looked back at me, she was cool with calculation in otherwise vacant eyes.

"Have you ever wondered if maybe you are in such need of acceptance and attention that you have to make things up, twist things into lies, and cause trouble just to get people to notice you? Has that ever occurred to you?"

I slouched. "No, not really."

Luz clasped her hands together, resting her elbows on the table. She looked as though she were about to start praying when she buried her chin in her knuckles. It was as if this had all weighed too much, and she suddenly needed added support from God or her own limbs.

"And you wrote about the accident, Julian. How could you do that to us? Do you know how much that hurt your brother? And my son?"

I presented all the facts as they occurred in my memoir but what I had left out was how Luz had begun an anarchistic underground of radical socialists. They wrote, published, and disseminated zines about the evils of capitalism and the best way to upend a political system. She had a network of hundreds across the country. Many had been living in the Southwest which is probably why she'd urged my brother to move to Arizona. He was so clueless about everything I wouldn't be surprised if he had no idea. Raul knew about Luz and her samizdat through the associations with his grandfather. Being the heir of a revolutionary made one privy to the illicit goings-on of insurgents. She looked down on Raul because he was Mexican. She claimed South American superiority as a Colombian. I would have Raul help me with the research as there was no way this wouldn't be making it into my book.

"It was a big part of our lives, Luz, but I am sorry if it hurt you all."

"Not *our* lives, Julian. *My* life. Your article was exploitative. A selfish grab for attention."

She was angry and her waxen face petrified with the urge to convey an emotion that it could not. Her tawny skin blushed, becoming almost burgundy, and beads of sweat formed across her brow where faint lines from the fifteen-year-old scars could still be detected, though faintly. Her lips, so full now with collagen, furled, and her blindingly white teeth were flashed like a predator that needed to kill even though it was not hungry.

"I'm sorry you feel that way, but you changed so much. We were friends. Do you remember all the fun we had in the beginning? The horseback riding, the plays, the museums."

"You were different then, too. The Julian Sorrento I knew all those years ago would never have done something like this to me, to his brother, to his nephew."

I could play the asshole. She was leaving me little choice in the matter and God knows the shit I'd be writing about her secret club of incendiaries would probably lead to criminal charges. I imagined her and my father going to trial and getting locked up. A gift to myself. Vengeance was ugly and maybe the punishments would exceed their crimes, but the fact of the matter is that they did break the law in their own ways, and they were menaces to good American decency, and what is more, they fucked with me and weren't sorry. Maybe if they had been supportive of my *New Yorker* essay, I might have let it go, but they hadn't been. They'd been downright awful. Also, this little article gave me the first taste of what life could be like, free of the shackles of social work, of servitude, of a menial salary, of needy people, of an abusive system, of heartbreak and frustration, and now I had an agent, and she was a shark who wanted blood from me too, and I would give it, in the form of a book and a cable series, and I would have a new career, a new chance before it was too late, before I grew anymore ashamed of myself and disappointed with life.

"He didn't have much to write about back then," I said with dispassion. "It took 'all those years' to accumulate all these stories."

"And the horrible fantasy about my family? What made you come up with such a creative backstory?"

"You. You must have forgotten, but you told me these things. When we would drink and you'd get hammered, you really let it all fly."

Oh, Luz. You must have also forgotten then what you spilled when soused about the group you'd founded and all the treacherous, treasonous literature you and your cohorts produced and handed out.

Luz's dark eyes, once like a doe's but now more like pockets of coal, renewed with nebulous intentions, gazed through the camera, across 2,500 miles, into the screen, penetrating time and space, unsettling me in my Jackson Heights apartment, stories above the earth. Her looks could be felt like a cosmic slap.

"My parents were socialists, that's the only truth."

"You said specifically 'communists'. You told me they used to translate Trotsky and Marx into Spanish for schools in the countryside outside of Bogota. You said they were part of a commune, a sort of cult, even, that met every Sunday to discuss environmentalism and the collective and the 'evils of capitalism' and individuality."

"If I ever said those things I don't remember and none of it is true."

"So, you either blacked out when you drank, or *you* lied?"

"It's monstrous of you to bring up what happens to me when I drink, knowing what I did."

"You're right, it is, but you're accusing me of lying, Luz. I have to defend myself here."

When Vaughan was born and Luz turned against my family, my mother snapped and told my brother to get a lawyer to make sure she didn't run off to Colombia with their newborn son. Luz never forgave my mother for that admonishment. She also began a campaign to smear us should it all ever come to litigation. She had my computer hacked by a friend who worked for CNN as a programmer. He'd combed through my search history and downloads for anything at all criminal. I knew that because I'm gay, Luz, despite her progressive patina, hoped she'd find images or videos of underage boys, something that would not just get me barred from ever seeing Vaughan but also prosecuted and publicly shamed. It was an evil maneuver, but somehow, I forgave her. This vile detail was not included in *My Mighty Meekness*, but it would be in the book.

And yet, I admired Luz. To have done what she did, setting off for a new country alone while so young, she had to be self-interested and strong. Anyone, including her admiring brother-in-law, had been expendable if they proved themselves obstacles. I guess I'd been deemed an obstacle by association. I had even once driven her to my brother's police station in the South Bronx to confront him after discovering he'd cheated on her with a South African cocktail waitress from Brooklyn Heights. She'd taken Vaughan, then only six months old, with her into the station in a stroller and made a scene in front of the other officers, my brother's sergeant and lieutenant and captain, and all the secretaries and perps. Apparently, she'd somehow found out that the cocktail waitress was in the precinct visiting him during his lunch break. As I waited in my jeep Cherokee in front, I saw the cocktail waitress run out first, crying and panicked, followed by Luz, visibly incensed, rolling Vaughan at full speed. My brother, both pissed and panicked, ran out after her, followed by two officers, friends of James's, who'd been trying to contain the situation. The whole scene was comical, but also nerve-wracking. Afterward, my brother stormed up to me and asked, "What the fuck were you thinking?" I didn't mention this episode during our meeting, but it will be in my book.

"You should tell that magazine you made a lot of this up," she said.

"But I didn't."

Luz sighed. This certainly weighed and there was no hiding it. "Just … don't write anymore, okay?"

I tried not to smile, and so instead I frowned.

"I am expanding the essay into a book. There will be more. A lot more."

Luz's lips curled as if she were about to curse or threaten me, but then her face become once again expressionless.

"I guess there's not much more to say, then, Julian. This is a disappointment. I am disappointed in you."

I stared at her slack jawed. "I am disappointed in everyone."

Luz chuckled, her face appearing for once organic, young again, like the Luz I had known. Soft and endearing, the face of a person who'd been incapable of cruelty and teachery. I'd only known that face during the first few years of her relationship with my brother and the early years of our friendship.

They didn't publish *The Bell Jar* in the United States until 1971, not until Sylvia Plath's mother died, to spare her the shame of her daughter's confessions. It was published in England seven years earlier. Confessions. A confessional. I supposed that's what I had written, but my essay, and eventually my book, was unlike Plath's novel. *My Mighty Meekness* was not intended to be a fiction. It was published as a memoir, fully non-fiction. This was not the early 1970s and my book was not meant to hurt anyone.

Luz, now suddenly unconditionally in love with my brother years later, not once brought up the foul things she had said about him, all the denouncements of his character and abilities, the trampling over his intellect and soul. I had been a meticulous chronicler of her assertions, and her loose lips gifted me generous fodder for the book that would surely catalogue her long list of pejoratives. Secretly, I'd hoped it would break them up once published.

"Send my love to James and Vaughan," I said, sounding flip, though not meaning to.

Luz's face changed again. Morose suddenly. There was expression, human emotion. Sadness, primarily. Maybe concern.

"God, there's not much left in there, huh?" she said, looking closely at me through her computer's camera, seeking proof of conscience, glimmers of humanity, perhaps finding a reflection as chilly as her own.

Without realizing it, I nodded in agreement. I must have looked dumb or maybe sociopathic, a nefarious con man admitting his misdeeds to one of his victims. I am sure that is how she would have read it, dismissing the possibility of having taken me off guard, as a mere human flustered in a moment of incrimination. The most understandable thing. She'd not buy that.

I caught myself, already too late, knowing the admission would travel the filial circuit, even though my family had been fragmented beyond mending, and ended the call. I couldn't be sure, but I'd sworn I could hear the breathy growls of a man—or men—in the background.

CHAPTER 11

Raul led the way as I scrambled to keep up on Lake Minnewaska's lush, steep strip of New York State's Bear Mountain. In the center the crystalline lake sparkled as the midday sun hit it. Nearby West Point Academy trained future mechanical engineers, economists, and soldiers. I watched Raul effortlessly bound up the mountain, traversing felled trees, unwieldy roots, interlocked vines, and thick, grubby brush. He was good at spotting poison ivy and oak and nimble when bushwhacking with one hand while cutting through spiderwebs with the other. His bare legs stretched and contracted, showing off the muscles, striations, and vascularity I'd come to idealize.

"I feel like one of those insecure white fools that Melville or Conrad or Hemingway wrote about," he said, breathlessly. "You know, those jackasses who exploit the world, heading off on needlessly dangerous missions, and all for the sake of ego edification!"

Other hikers took different routes, safer routes. For Raul if it wasn't dangerous or at least arduous it wasn't worth doing. And I followed along dutifully.

"But if it were not for these communions with nature," he said, grunting through the last few feet of the ascent, "I'd likely take a flamethrower to my office."

Raul would make these pronouncements about mass murder more frequently lately and with a cavalier, throwaway ease that really spooked me. He said nothing else until we reached the summit.

I'd packed my book and laptop along with peanut butter and jelly sandwiches, a few apples, several bags of chips, and bottles of water so we could work while eating. The picnic area was a wide plateau that overlooked the lake and the dense forest that surrounded it. We were alone amid half a dozen vacant picnic tables.

Raul leaned forward. "Start reading."

EXT/ INT. NYC MONTAGE/ VARIOUS LOCATIONS — DAY

When he isn't in class or having lunch during breaks with Dr. Alessandro, Pegasus Clint loiters in Hamilton Heights with Joe, a hustler who never charges him. He also never fucks him. Like many young professionals, Joe had previously rented a room in a four-bedroom pre-war apartment along Riverside Drive. The kind with rent stabilization, ten-foot ceilings, and one hundred-year-old crown molding. His ability to pay his way was spotty and soon the other roommates voted to evict. He'd been living in the park since then, some two months ago. Fortunately for Joe the weather has been up until then moderate. Pegasus brings him lunch on Tuesdays and Thursdays from a local bodega. Ham sandwich on Tuesdays and tuna on Thursdays.

                    JOE
          (eating the tuna, it being a
          Thursday)
          How long have you been doing this
          for me, man?

                    PEGASUS
          A few weeks, I guess.

                        JOE

What are you getting from being so
nice to me? It's not like I let you
screw me or anything.

                      PEGASUS

I'm not being nice to you for sex,
Joe.

                        JOE

Well, what then?

                      PEGASUS

I like your company.

                        JOE

And you get to be the cool kid in
class talking about how you hang
out with a homeless whore, right?

                      PEGASUS

I don't do that.

                        JOE

It's the kind of thing a liberal
brat from Columbia would do.

                      PEGASUS

I'm not a liberal brat.

In truth, Pegasus befriended Joe and spent a

few days a week for several hours at a time
with him because Dr. Alessandro had assigned
a "social problems" project and Pegasus chose
homelessness. His report requires he gets to
know a young homeless person, write a thorough
behavioral analysis of them, and integrate
academic research into the study, while also
positing a realistic solution to the problem,
something that could be submitted to the City
Council.

"Does Mary know Dr. Alessandro?" asked Raul. "Anthropology and
sociology are related fields and Columbia is a small pond."

"They know of each other, yeah, met at a few events on campus, heard of
each other through common students, but they didn't socialize or anything."

"Did he know Pegasus was her son?"

"Oh yeah, and he got a kick out of having him do this assignment,
knowing it would push her and Monroe to their breaking points."

"Nice," Raul said, smiling callously.

Raul thought we were all hypocrites and frauds. Me, my family. He'd felt
entitled to his moral superiority as only he had descended from a folk hero.
He'd always relished media and literature that punished people in power,
people who were cruel to animals, people who hewed to civilized stricture.
He liked to see the privileged squirm.

INT. CLINT HOUSEHOLD — EVENING

The evening of that day, as Mary prepares
dinner, broccoli rabe with garlic and salmon,
Pegasus enters with Joe, the young man who, to
Mary, smells distinctly of urine and turpentine.

Caucasian, maybe Italian or Turkish based on his
features, she thinks, always the anthropologist
at work. She notices patches of actual dirt on
his clothes and his blackened fingernails. His
shaggy black hair looks heavy with grease, and
Mary is certain his left eye is infected.

Her judgements are quick and sharp, and she
loathes them, but still they come in VOICE OVER.
Joe's whole presence is potent and leaves her
dizzy with an alarming annoyance. She's hardly
ever been puritanical, but a certain degree
of filth and odor offends even her well-worn
sensibilities. She never makes a comment about
his looks or smells, not even when he takes
off his windswept sneakers and reveals stained
socks and releases yet another wave of rank
odor.

                    PEGASUS
        This is Joe. He's a friend … from
        school.

                    MARY
            (stammering, assaying her guest)
        J-J-Joe?

                    JOE
            (softly)
        Joe Hartley.

                    [104]

MARY's V.O.

"Hartley." So, then he'd been
neither Italian nor Turkish, but
English in origin. Northern England
to be precise. Perhaps Kent or
Devon or Hampshire. Old English:
"Heorot" or "Hart" means "Leah"
wood: Wood Clearing. I wonder what
wood Joe would be clearing.

MARY

Are you two working on your
sociology project tonight? Pegasus,
you didn't tell me.

PEGASUS

Yeah, … but I figured he would come
earlier and have dinner with us.

Joe smiles loopily and with eyelids half-mast,
but Mary does not smell alcohol or marijuana.
Something odorless, then. Xanax maybe?

MARY

Of course. Why don't you boys get
cleaned up and I'll set the table.

And then they were off to Pegasus's bedroom, where
Mary fears Joe would spread his contamination.
Despite her field work, filth depresses Mary.
It has a measurable effect on her. When she

moved into their current house, which had been old, maybe built in the 1930s, and owned by an elderly couple, maybe in their 80s, the grime and mold and dust were so thick she swore the house hadn't been cleaned in at least a decade. At a certain point, dirtiness becomes a moral issue. Mary judges those previous owners as bad people. Anyone who allowed their possessions and space to fall into such squalor deserves harsh thoughts. Even poverty is no excuse for filthiness. Even the tribes she'd studied in developing nations managed their own brand of cleanliness.

As she set the table, Mary thinks of all the things Joe might be bringing into her home. Cockroaches. Bed bugs. Fleas. Scabies. Syphilis. (NOTE: voice over, maybe)

Dinner feels overlong and is marked by awkward pauses and clumsy gestures.

                    JOE
          My dad was a bit of a drifter. He
          went where the work was and dragged
          me and mom with him.

                    MARY
              (picking at her fish)
          What line of work?

                    [106]

                    JOE

He was a repairman, lots of odd
jobs.

                   MARY

I see, and where were you born?

                    JOE

In a small town outside of Chicago,
but mostly raised in Michigan,
until we hit the road when I was
ten.

                   MARY

So, where are your parents now?

So many questions, thinks Pegasus. An
inquisition, really.

                    JOE

They split up. I think my mom is in
Tallahassee with her sister and my
dad, last I checked, was maybe in
Portland.

                   MARY

Oregon?

                    JOE

Maine.

Mary begins working on her second glass of chianti.

                    MARY
          And now, you're here alone
          studying?

That's when Joe glances at Pegasus for a cue, and Mary realizes that something is amiss.

                    PEGASUS
          Nah, Joe is not formally enrolled
          at Columbia.

                    MARY
               (trying not to sound persecutory
               but failing miserably)
          Oh, so, just auditing classes,
          then?

                    PEGASUS
          He's participating in the sociology
          project, but he's not a student. At
          all.

Mary stares, waiting.

                    PEGASUS
          He's actually—

                         JOE
          (plainly)
     I'm a sex worker, ma'am.

Mary swallows her last sip of wine and smiles,
making every effort to maintain the enlightened
front, the progressive effect of being
unaffected. Mary believes she'd failed at this,
too.

                        MARY
          Peg, a word?

Joe raises his eyebrows and continues to shovel
copious servings of roasted vegetables onto his
dish. He is ravenous and Mary is beginning to
think he might also be homeless.

INT. PEGASUS'S BEDROOM — EVENING

A few minutes later. Mary stares at Pegasus,
awaiting an explanation.

                        MARY
          (gently, with feigned patience)
          Honey. I'm not sure what's
          happening here.

                      PEGASUS
     Dr. Alessandro said I had to do
     something good for someone in need.

For the community. For a grade.
So, Joe is the person I found. We
met outside of the Hungarian cafe
on Amsterdam. He was looking for a
job, and he thought he could find a
john for the night.

                    MARY
        (in a wheeze)
    A john.

                    PEGASUS
    Yeah, when he can't get a john to
    spend the night with, he has to
    stay in a hostel or on the street.

                    MARY
    You barely know him, Peg. Can we
    trust that he won't rob from us
    or kill us in our sleep? Do you
    realize how dangerous and reckless
    this is?

                    PEGASUS
    Isn't that a little hypocritical,
    considering what you do for a—

                    MARY
    Don't start that, again, Pegasus.

    NOTE: Pegasus had made it a habit of lecturing

Mary on cultural appropriation and the crimes of anthropology. God knows, since Dr. Wong's campaign against her and her work in India began, Pegasus had seen his mother as a something close to a villain.

> PEGASUS
>
> Look, it'll only be for a few
> nights, and it'll strictly be for
> the project.

Mary weighs the request against all the bad things Dr. Wong had written about her and all the accusations Pegasus has leveled against her and to her surprise relents. With provision.

> MARY
>
> He can't have anyone here, Pegasus.
> No johns.

INT. DINING ROOM — EVENING

A few minutes later. Joe has already finished all the food and wine.

> PEGASUS
>
> My mom said you could stay the
> week, Joe. But no johns.

> JOE
>
> How am I supposed to make money?

                    MARY
          (trying hard to sound congenial)
     Well, you'll be staying with us,
     and your room and board will be
     covered, so you won't have to worry
     about money for this week.

                    JOE
     Okay, fine, fair enough. I have a
     big appetite, though, so you know,
     prepare yourself.

Mary looks at the empty plate and smiles.

                    MARY
     Why not take a shower and get
     settled?

She probably looked desperate and possibly even
frightened when she made the request because
Joe studies her face and body language, rigid
and billowy at the same time; she could feel
these things when done to her, and Joe is not a
tactful observer, but he thankfully submits, and
borrows sweatpants and underwear and a t-shirt
from Pegasus and showers before bed.

NOTE about character: Mary could have refused
Joe. It was her house and even Pegasus was a
guest in it. She'd yielded because the young

                    [112]

man seemed grateful and desperate and it would
only be a night or two, she'd decided. Or so she
thought. Mary would learn later that she could
not decide such things. She also could not have
foreseen that there would be more to come. She'd
thrown Joe's clothes in the wash and added too
much detergent. She would not take any chances
with this one.

"God, I love how judgmental she is," said Raul. "I barely know her, but it
seems like you really captured her, that entitled, elitist, full of crap liberalism
that so many professors suffer from."

"Yeah, I guess that's her, then."

"Now, finally, the fucking story is underway! I love to watch the mighty
squirm. Man, I would love to watch the jackoffs at my job squirm."

On the way back down the mountain, deep in the diagonal woods,
surrounded by skittish deer, curious black bear, patient tics, and busy spiders,
Raul took me against a maple, dropped my pants and underwear, and did me
without a condom, but with ample ardor, and he muffled my cries of pain
and ecstasy.

It was then and there, bent into a tree, balls to the wind, bare-assed, and
subjugated, that I realized Raul hadn't intended to help me with the series
at all. He only wanted to feel like he was taking part in its formation. It was
pretext for sex. It was pretext for unlimited judgement. It was pretext for
sublimation for the murderous rage he had for his job. It was pretext for ...
for ...

We are mutts, which is why my brother James's surname is Bartha. It's Hungarian. Before my father, my mother was briefly married to another man, a police officer from Westchester named David, with whom she had my siblings, my half-siblings, though we never referred to each other as such. James was a dozen years my senior. He, too, became a cop and then a sergeant and eventually a lieutenant when he retired five years ago at forty-two. He'd since moved his son and wife to Phoenix, Arizona, a state conservative enough to feed his reactionary worldview.

When we were younger, James possessed a handsome face and a muscular physique (some say he looked like John Gavin from *Psycho*, others like George Clooney in his prime). He would purposely have sex with women in front of me, knowing it turned me on. He would also walk around in tight briefs to show off his endowments. Knowing my predilections, he was aware of the power he had over me. Even though James teased me with something forbidden, and he'd accepted my queerness and even seemed to enjoy hitting me in the groin on a regular schedule, which led me to believe that maybe he'd acquired the same gene with which I'd been gifted. I'd once caught him pleasuring himself to a Muscle

& Fitness cover featuring a then-younger Arnold Schwarzenegger. I must have been thirteen and he twenty-five. He twisted my arm hard enough to break it and made me swear to never tell. And I never did. Well, until this essay.

My brother used to insinuate himself into my group of friends mainly because they all revered him and his adult body. He had big, impressive muscles that he would show off like a peacock, shirtless, in his underwear, showcasing what us prepubescent boys could only ever dream of possessing. He was our star alpha and we his fanbase of omegas. So much of my homosexuality was formed during these years when my young friends would romanticize his manhood and idolize his power. James in his weird way got a kick out of the exaltation. It flattered him. He would routinely and with systematic care commend each one of my friends for their talents or appearance or intelligence. Chris was handsome enough to be a model. Jeremy was athletic enough to play high school basketball. BJ was talented enough to become a professional guitar player. John was smart enough to get into Harvard. Anthony had a great sense of style. Matt was a dynamic illustrator and should draw comics for a living. I was never praised by

James. He instead would use me as a basis for comparison to my superior friends. He would say it was a pity I was not as smart as so and so or as handsome as so and so or as athletic as so and so.

James even used to pit us against each other in wrestling matches that he would orchestrate and referee, and I would always lose to each one of my friends. I would go limp and let them pin me. James was sure to ridicule me for not putting up a fight, for lacking balls and fire. At the time I didn't understand why I would become a ragdoll and let my friends beat me, but now I am impressed with my selflessness, my violent opposition to competition and ranking and shows of strength. I didn't need to win to feel good about myself. I could get out of the way and let others who needed proof of their worth take the trophy and acclaim.

CHAPTER 12

James texted me to say he'd flown in from Phoenix for a friend's wedding in Northport, Long Island. He asked to meet to discuss my article. Apparently, Luz had told him I was expanding it into a book, and he too was not at all pleased. When we met a day later, I imagined him greeting me with punches and kicks—a rage-fueled beatdown for which I should be grateful. Instead, he disarmed me with weird warmth, fraternal grabs for my nipples, headlocks, and hair mussing. He'd been this familiar when we were younger, but not for decades since.

"You look skinny," were the first words out of his mouth when we met on Main Street in Downtown Flushing for dim sum. My choice, as I'd known he loathed Queens and especially Flushing, finding the pollution and traffic and odors and throngs of Chinese and Korean residents and shoppers off-putting. Perhaps it had been passive aggressive of me to make such a selection.

"Quit working out, huh?"

"Thanks," I said, my voice toneless, "You look good, too."

"Ah!" he scoffed with faux-affection and forced jocularity as he smacked me across the head. His assaults were more annoying than painful.

We walked up the block to the original Joe's Shanghai, forced into the street more than once by deliveries of fish and produce obscuring the sidewalk in front of restaurants and grocers. The crates oozed suspicious liquids and emitted questionable stenches.

"This fucking place," he began, only five minutes into our reunion after several years. "Used to be all White when I was growing up. Maybe a handful of Orientals. Now I feel like I'm in China!"

I'd forgotten how brazen he'd been in his bigoted decrees. He was a post-modern Archie Bunker. The crotchety, racist observations were acceptable in his mind, despite the years of progress and political correctness and cancel culture. To him, it was still customary to make criticisms out loud. He'd felt he had license because at least he wasn't conquering and enslaving. The perception was deranged, but as a former New York City police officer he felt he'd earned the opinions, which made it even more nauseating.

"Who's getting married?" I asked as we waited for our table. Aside from a few tourists likely migrated from the Mid-west or TriBeCa and probably curio hunting after watching an old Food Network segment with Anthony Bourdain or Guy Fieri about the authentic and affordable cuisine offered in the neighborhood, James and I were the only Caucasians.

"Dennis O'Connor, remember him?"

I had remembered Dennis O'Connor, a firefighter who once dangled me by my ankles over a lobster tank in a Whitestone fish shop when I was six. He was also the first person to teach me about sex when he drunkenly demonstrated one evening during a party how important it was that a vagina contract at the right ankle on a penis for optimal orgasm. He showed me how it should be done by forming a vagina with one hand and a penis with the other. I was nine at the time. When my parents found out about the lesson years later, they barred him from our house. James hated me for telling.

"Sure, I remember him."

We sat and I ordered appetizers, which James sneered at and poked with his fork (of course he asked for a fork) before devouring. He made squeamish faces every time I selected items from the roaming cart. Siu mai. Har gau. Cheong fan. Char siu bao. Sesame prawn roast. It was odd that someone who'd been raised in a place like Queens was still so ignorant of other cultures. I always thought it was tragic that after almost forty years, up until the time of his "escape" to the Southwest, he was never curious about the races and heritages that surrounded him or took advantage of exploring the varied nationhood only a stone's throw away. He simply had no interest in their histories or customs or art or food or language or communities.

"So, anyway, why the fuck did you write all that shit in your article? Was getting yourself up there that important to you?"

Up there.

"Because it was a memoir and it all really happened."

"That's stupid to make a big deal of it! I mean, I did hit you a lot because you were a little asshole who deserved it and it was funny seeing you cry and writhe around on the floor in pain, but there was nothing more to it than that!"

James looked around nervously, worrying no doubt that the other diners would hear us, assuming they all concealed their understanding of English to spy on us. Even his paranoia was racist.

He should have only known what I had planned for the chapters about him in my book. My theory is that 'straight' guys who get joy out of beating up other guys, especially with frequent low blows, of which James was so fond, are probably gay. It's the only socially acceptable time a straight man can touch another straight man's genitals. I mean, professional wrestlers and action stars and MMA fighters, paragons of heteronormative masculinity, get away with it on a regular basis. I had already begun to outline the pages about how he would get an erection every time he assaulted me. Indeed, as I recall, he often groped me and seemed to get a thrill out of it. He'd started when I was still a boy, only thirteen. He would have been in his mid-twenties. To think that he could have sexualized his wrestling matches with me. My account will detail all the occasions he exposed himself to me from under a towel, all the times he wore sweatpants without underwear, the instances when he slapped me with his penis and rested his testicles on my head as I watched TV from bed because he found it funny, of course. Borderline molestation of a minor disguised as innocent straight guy tomfoolery. I could only hope these passages wouldn't give my mother a stroke.

James's face became dumb as he thought about the insinuations made by the article. Something might have even registered but then he shook his head while squinting as if he'd been bothered by a gnat.

I shrugged. "I spoke with Luz."

"I know. She told me."

"She was pretty pissed."

"You did her wrong. She's a good person and you wrote fucked up shit about her."

"It was necessary to my life story."

"You sound like a douchebag right now."

"If it happened and I remember it then it's fair game. I am not out to hurt anyone, James."

James pondered this as he fought with his cheong fan, slippery as a slug.

"You didn't have to write about the car accident. It's the worst thing that's ever happened to her and she didn't need to relive it and you didn't have to tell the world about it."

Truthfully, I'd regretted including that incident. In the future I would cherry-pick more carefully my damning episodes, that is, after I finished the book. That would by necessity be rife with damning episodes.

"I know, you're right."

After we ate, I suggested we walk around a bit and James agreed only if we strayed from Downtown and headed into the more quasi-suburban part of Flushing where there were no stores but instead lawns and houses and fewer people and quieter cars and milder odors.

"What's with your haircut?" he asked after an extended pause filled with ghoulish stares at a group of young black men playing basketball in a high school playground and then at a pair of old Indian men who were walking too slowly for him in front of us.

"What do you mean?"

"It's too short on the sides and looks silly."

"My crown is thinning," I said, wincing, "and this makes it less obvious."

"Well, it looks silly."

"You already said that."

For as long as I could remember, James was an expert at noticing and pointing out flaws in my appearance or intelligence or behavior. He seemed to relish inventorying my inadequacies and making sure I knew what they were. He wanted me not just humble but insecure. From childhood when he would make it a point to praise my friends for their strength or athletic prowess or musical abilities to my adolescence when he derided my virginity as something shameful. Commenting on my male friends' physiques and faces and fashions also seemed queer. I once worked out with James and several friends in the police athletic league gym and my sneaker laces came loose while sparring and he said loud enough for everyone to hear that I was so weak with such girly fingers I couldn't manage to tie my laces tightly enough. On another occasion when lifting weights with him I exhaled while he was spotting me, and he announced to everyone in ear shot that my breath stank. Countless times whenever I'd do something clumsy or make an error in logic, he'd be swift to proclaim I had no common sense even though I was allegedly "book smart". Oddly, the one thing he never mocked was my homosexuality. In that area he was surprisingly supportive, even enthusiastic.

"You still dating that Mexican?" he asked out of nowhere.

"Raul? We still hang out, yeah. Also, he's American."

"Ah, hooking up, right?" He seemed far too excited.

"Yeah, I guess we still are."

"So, which one of you is the man and which one is the woman?"

I cringed and rolled my eyes at him. "We're both men, James."

James wrinkled his brow and scrunched his nose while balling his fist and half-punching the air to suggest sex. "I mean, which one fucks?"

"Raul is the top."

Again, he lit up. "So, he fucks you?"

"Are we really having this conversation?"

James shrugged as if his line inquiry intimated nothing deeper. "I'm fascinated by the whole thing."

"Maybe you should try being with a man, then."

"Men are disgusting. They fart and have hair all over their bodies and their balls smell."

"Not the men I've been with."

James made a face to communicate revolt. I smiled at myself as I recalled him once admitting to me when he was drunk that he used to occasionally receive oral sex from men when he was in his twenties, "back when he would get drunk and go clubbing." He hadn't thought of himself as gay. "It was just a blowjob," he claimed, and *he* never touched *them*. "A mouth was a mouth," he'd argued. He'd gone on to tell me that I'd be surprised by how many Italian guys who call themselves "straight" in Whitestone "suck dick".

We entered a surprisingly verdant park surrounded by a dozen plots of community vegetable gardens and towering, old trees amid tall, unmanicured grass and gargantuan roots and vines. It was uncultivated and savage, like something you'd see in Louisiana or Florida. In the center was a playground with water fountains and benches and monkey bars and swings. A group of elderly Chinese people were practicing Tai Chi on the one manicured swath of grass in the whole park and by the concrete benches and chess tables another smaller group played mahjong. We sat on the swings.

"So," James continued, "do you guys do anything weird and kinky? I hear gay dudes are freaks in bed."

It had been perversely satisfying that James solicited so much intimate detail about my sex life. I hesitated before answering and he looked at me in such a way as to suggest that my reaction could either mend our tenuous relationship or end it; such was the danger of irreparably bruising his flimsy ego. Fortunately, I'd trained myself well to never show my hand after so many years of hiding in the closet and navigating tricky political waters at work and in my newfound literary milieu.

"He's a little bit of a sadist, you know," I said with a smirk.

"He beats you up?" he asked in an almost ecstatic gasp.

"I'd rather not go into detail."

James looked disappointed or maybe I'd misread his expression. Perhaps he'd been repressing a craving. "Ah, come on."

"Maybe I'll put it in a book someday."

James flashed me a jaundiced eye. The mere mention of my writing a book was enough to unsettle.

The probes into my sex life surprised me. I'd suspected for years that he wanted to cross the line, maybe not with me, but as his half-brother I was familiar and safe and could serve as a guide into an otherwise forbidding world of penetration and submission and managing phalluses that weren't one's own. Now on his way to fifty, for how long had he deprived himself these tendencies or urgings? What could such containment do to a man? In James's case, certainly nothing good. It was possible I'd seen him take home a few men. There could have been rumors. The kind of gossip that spreads around a neighborhood like Whitestone. Maybe he'd experimented with his roommate Terrance. They'd lived together for four years before James met Luz. Terrance always commented on James's body and supposedly enormous prick. He'd frequently grabbed him with a harmless familiarity to which James cottoned. Who knows? Maybe there would be a chapter or two on my brother's fluid sexuality. His son, my nephew, sweet, sad Vaughan, the inheritor of his predilection.

"Man, look at how skinny you are," he said, squeezing my arm.

"You said that already, pick a new insult."

"You were getting fit there for a while in your twenties, maybe you thought you could take me."

I was too tired for this. "I never imagined fighting you, James."

James was off the swing and on his feet in front of me. He clawed at my head and chest and caught both my hair and collar in his attack. Effortlessly, he yanked me from the swing and into his chest where he held me in a bearhug. I struggled to break free, but he was too strong.

"Say you're not going to write the book!" he growled. "Say it!"

We clumsily staggered across the playground, brushing past the mahjong players who cursed at us in Mandarin and onto the manicured lawn, close to the Tai Chi practitioners. We'd broken their focus and they stared at us as we fell over each other and began to wrestle.

"You fucking maniac!" I screamed at him as I struggled to break free from his grip.

His foot ended up in my gut and I wheezed for air. Soon he was back on top of me, wrapping his meaty arms around me, squeezing my chest and belly, burrowing his face in my neck. It felt almost erotic, and I swear I'd detected tumescence on his part. We slipped on mud or dog shit and landed hard atop each other, and I tasted dirt. Our shirts were stained green and brown as we slid across wet grass and pockets of soggy soil. My head started to ring from the impact of the fall.

"What is wrong with you?" I pleaded but he just grinned and leapt into me again, this time prompting us to tumble down an embankment.

We ended up in a marsh. Water bugs, beetles, and frogs scurried clear of our rampage.

I tried to shove him off me, but my hand slipped, and I smacked him full-force square in the face leaving a red welt across his forehead and right cheek. This got him angrier. He bared his teeth like a rat and grabbed me by the throat. I was on my feet again and clung to his wrist, terrified that he'd snapped and was really going to kill me this time. The murderous closeted New York cop that I'd known so well during my childhood had reemerged.

"There's not going to be a book, right, Julian? Right?!"

He backed me into an oak tree and growled as he drove his knee into my groin. His signature strike. I crumbled to the ground as he unhanded me. I held myself, fought the urge to cry or vomit. The Chinese witnesses gasped in warbled unison. I was on my knees in the swamp, and he stared down at me. Curiously, I was wondering in that moment if he ever felt bad about hurting me so often. Maybe the allegations wouldn't be so veiled after all. Maybe the molestation would be less borderline and more apparent. Maybe there would be no disguise for his "innocent straight guy tomfoolery".

During this most recent rendezvous, James had failed to bring up the way he'd reduced me in front of my group of childhood friends. Up until this sudden beatdown, I had wondered if he still thought I was inferior to them. More still, had he ever, or had he only made those pronouncements to hurt me. I also wondered if he'd made the unfavorable comparisons to toughen me up, to thicken my skin, to push me to improve. He knew what we hadn't yet known. The world was as hard as a tortoise shell and as unforgiving as a feasting shark. We were all animals, and, in this kingdom, we needed to pick a role: predator or prey.

"Put that in your fucking book," he said and left. He'd regret the things I'd put in my book.

CHAPTER 13

Kevin's "office," an inconspicuous gay speakeasy two blocks east from his and Edward's apartment named The Starfish, a cheeky wink at the queer allure of anal sex, no doubt, was small and cramped, oblong-shaped and illuminated in red, blue, and green, like an exploded Christmas tree. Suspended TV screens played experimental—and sometimes pornographic—films curated by Ralph, a fifty-year old writer who had tended bar there since its inception 25 years earlier. Sometimes he'd play excerpts from Maya Deren and Kenneth Anger shorts.

Devon, a bald and brawny art director who spent most of the year in Los Angeles but kept a pied-à-terre in nearby Hell's Kitchen, had been on his fifth Manhattan by the time we arrived.

"I'm being canceled!"

"What did you do?!" asked Kevin.

"What didn't she do?" hissed Mark, Devon's long-time friend and sometime lover who worked as an administrator for the NY Board of Education. With a white and black goat-tee, Mark had a wizened refinement about him.

"I was with my cousin on Long Island, and we were playing with his Boston terrier, and the dog makes this indescribable shrieking sound when looking out the back door because it wants to kill squirrels and when you hold her when this is happening, she goes ballistic and it's funny, but the animal is not being hurt! She's just frustrated and desperate to, you know, maim something! But my cousin's dimwitted sister-in-law recorded it on her phone and put it on Tik Tok and in like a week it got like five million views and thousands of comments, calling me an animal abuser! Can you imagine?

I'm at my cousin's house playing with his stupid dog, never imagining that in that moment, in that very private moment, I would be thrust into worldwide notoriety!"

"When I used to write, I would use social media, mind you, for like years, to promote my writing and I never got more than 80 likes and maybe a handful of sales, but you do something dumb and suddenly you go viral," said Kevin.

"A dangerous new world, Kevin," said Ralph, who'd been eavesdropping while mixing cocktails.

The immediate, tangible effect of social media was nothing to complain about as a writer. If someone were to use it smartly, which is to say, "stupidly," like Devon's cousin's in-law, the amount of attention one could curry would be worth more than an entire Random House public relations department. And a whole hell of a lot cheaper and quicker, too. The celebrity was instant, and nothing had to be spent, save for a few minutes to record and upload. Of course, this type of fame was fleeting and quickly replaced by the next new dumb shiny object.

"Ralphie, meet Julian. He's a social worker from Queens and now a writer with a book deal and TV show on the way! He found me and Ed on Facebook."

"Oh, another one?" said "Ralphie," drying the bar.

"A *different* one, wiseass," corrected Kevin.

Devon and Mark continued their conversation about cancel culture and canines at the bar with Ralph proffering periodic comments as Kevin and I found a private table in the back.

"I wrote my entire short story collection back here," he said.

"It wasn't distracting?"

"Not at all. So much of my work is—*was*—auto fiction so it was good to have the people I was writing about in front of me, you know, when doing so. Sort of like a portrait artist who needs the model to hold a pose for a few hours while he paints."

"Uh huh," I eyeballed the young twinks across from us making out. One's neck was hickey riddled and the other's pants were open. "To be so young and shameless."

"You're not so old, Julian."

I glanced back at the brazen lovers. "Too old to do that in public, I assure you."

"I wish I had someone to do that with, regardless of where."

"You have Edward."

"Not really. I mean, I have him as a soulmate, yeah, sure, but there is nothing like that there," said Kevin as he gestured toward the amorous boys. "We have an arrangement and Ed is very popular with the young guys, but I haven't had as much luck."

"So, what was it like in Memphis, growing up there, gay?"

"How'd you know it was Memphis?"

"Your Wikipedia article."

"Right. I always forget I have one of those. Memphis was tragic, you know. It's a fine place for a straight, white, male musician looking to sing country music, but that's about it, and for a homo like me, back then as a kid, it was downright scary."

"I bet. Queens wasn't so great, either."

"I'm sure. Guidos and smog and ugly architecture."

"Hah! Yeah."

"You get used to people being a certain way. You learn how to accept their limitations and you find a way to even accept the way they keep letting you down."

I nodded and thought about my youth with all the limitations and disappointments and how they would be magnified into something dreadful and deadly.

"Aside from the racists and homophobes, and yes there are in fact as many bigots as you'd think down there, you also have to contend with the religious zealots and the closeted husbands with families who fuck you in private and threaten your life at the very mention of ever exposing them."

"Wow, it's cinematic."

"Maybe even literary?"

I looked again at the young lovers. "Sure, that too."

Kevin looked, too. "I've fucked all types, Julian."

"I'm sure."

"And been fucked by all types, too."

I touched Kevin's knee with discretion. "I'm sorry, Kevin."

"No one can really hurt me anymore, and yet, I still get hurt, so go figure."

Kevin watched the young men. Was he waiting for them to see him, call him over? Join them? He'd wanted to be invited to take part, to be a part. I'd not yet known Kevin well enough to make these sweeping assumptions about him, but there was something telling about the way he watched, the way he looked at people, at me, with an expectancy, a request to be brought in and held close. I'd been tired and knew Raul would be pestering me soon for sex, so felt I should go, but I'd be lying if I said I didn't want to hold Kevin, not as a lover, but as a brother, as a friend.

CHAPTER 14

Raul and I had an early dinner in a Tibetan-Nepalese restaurant in Jackson Heights's historic district. He chose Gyagoh, a Tibetan dish in the Han style comprised of meatballs, bamboo shoots, vermicelli, and mushrooms and often enjoyed by senior monks during crucial rituals, and I ate Dal Bhat, the quintessential meal of Nepal made of rice and vegetable curry. We'd both felt bloated afterward and decided to walk along Roosevelt Avenue to talk about *The Touring Barbarism*, though the overhead rattle of the 7 train was not conducive to any substantive conversation.

We turned down a side street, a quiet tree-lined block where the streetlamps cast heavy shadows that reminded me of a Howard Hawks film, or some 1940s noir. On either side of us were stately houses built in the 1920s, some of which belonged to jazz legends. Matching the melodramatic mood, Raul moved like a predator, furtive and observant, ready to kill and devour. He administered dominance tests to all young men who came our way. He'd glance up, catch the man's eye, and nod with a clenched jaw, as if to invite combat or sex. I found the challenges unnecessary, though for him it was ingrained, a ritual practiced for years. In New York at night every passerby, man or boy, posed a potential threat, or an unpromised dalliance.

"So," began Raul, "How did it go last night with Kevin?"

I'd stopped talking with Raul about my weekly jaunts to Kevin and Ed's because he always ridiculed me for spending time with them, suggesting I'd either been using them or they were turning me into an elitist. Neither was the case. I just enjoyed their company and felt good about myself being in their fold. I only mentioned going to The Starfish with Kevin because it seemed less rarified than their "celebrity soirees" or our "intellectual circle jerks". It was common. That most common thing: two friends at a bar.

"Oh, it was fine, he and I went—"

"By the way," said Raul, cutting me off without hesitation, as we passed The Chateau, an ornate building from the early 1920s, "Montgomery Clift used to live there."

"Oh yeah?"

It was an example of French renaissance revival. Built in 1922. I'd Googled it later that evening. I'd always needed to know at least as much as Raul about trivia. I'd also learned that Charlie Chaplin also lived in the area for some time.

INT. CLINT RESIDENCE — DAY

Two weeks on and very much at home, Joe, it dawns on Mary and Monroe, has no intention of leaving. Also, Joe has not been one for regular bathing. His feet stink. When he reclines on the sofa, much of most days, he buries his reeking feet under the throw pillows, making them too smell. It becomes abundantly clear that his aim when urinating is poor as he often misses the toilet and leaves yellow orange drops on the toilet rim and even small puddles on the floor around the bowl. Joe eats junk food and farts frequently. He acts like this is acceptable behavior. His appetite is voracious, and he regularly finishes trail mix or cereal or milk or eggs with little regard for anyone else in the house. When Joe watches television, much of most days, he does so at such a volume that no one else is able to concentrate on their work or relaxation. Joe is clumsy and careless and breaks things on an almost daily schedule. Vases. Plates. Glasses. Chairs. Antiques. All the rare collectibles that Mary had brought back from her travels to Asia or Africa or South America. Joe picks his nose. Joe picks his scabs. Joe's attitude is generally poor. Even Monroe's many cats hiss at him, claw at his feet, and pee on his dirty laundry. His presence is a plague and the only one not bothered by it is Pegasus. His intrusive guest's behavior beguiles. Pegasus studies his emaciated, filthy body and imagines doing foul things to it.

"Wait!" said Raul, stopping me mid-stride with a forearm to the chest. "Is *that* true? Your cousin did this dude?"

"Eventually. Their courtship was slow. Don't spoil it."

We continued down 82nd Street, past Indian spice shops, Colombian bakeries, and Peruvian restaurants, and ascended the decaying stairs for the elevated subway to Manhattan, though that's not where we ended up. On the too-crowded 7 train, Raul and I, pressed against the rattling doors by throngs of riders who'd themselves struggled for air and space, gazed out the windows at the neighborhoods below us. We were silent because I never felt comfortable talking about sex or other intimacies when surrounded by strangers with questionable politics. It might have been New York City, but people were people and in a city with 9 million of them, probability had it that much of them were likely closeted bigots. As we approached the former ruins of the Fun Factory graffiti palace and PS1, overlooking the vista that would inspire Universal Studios' now bygone King Kong attraction, Raul and I glanced at the Silver Cup studio marquee, a leftover from the early 80s, and descended the rusted staircase into Long Island City.

"So, your aunt and uncle just accepted Joe's bullshit?" asked Raul as we made our way into a maze of factories and warehouses, many of which had become condos and art galleries.

"That's how I envisioned it in my book, and I guess that's how the Darlington Brothers want it for their show."

My aunt and uncle suffered in silence for fear of looking bourgeoise if they complained or kicked him out. Monroe already had a complex because all of Mary's colleagues and students gave him shit for working at Raytheon. And Mary, well, she was still trying to live down the disaster she created in India.

INT. CLINT RESIDENCE — LIVING ROOM — DAY

Mary cleans around Pegasus and Joe as they lounge on the sofa and binge Netflix.

                MARY
      Maybe you boys would like to go out
      today? It's beautiful. Sunny and
      dry.

                JOE
      (scratching his crotch)
    Nah.

Mary turns away and imagines an infestation of pubic lice infiltrating her upholstery.

NOTE: Perhaps an absurdist fantasy sequence?

I stopped at the pier overlooking the East River. People jogged, biked, walked dogs. Lovers necked. Children chased each other. I looked across the river at the Manhattan skyline and remembered all the Sundays my parents would take me to dinner and to a Broadway show. I suddenly felt lonely but didn't know why. The loneliness stirred panic and I soon found myself on the verge of crying. Had I wronged them by writing the article? Would the book be a final straw? Was I sabotaging the one good, reliable thing in my life? And for what? To feel as though I'd achieved something tangible? Could it be worth it? I quickly brought myself back to *The Touring Barbarism*. Creative work always anchored me when I spiraled.

INT. CLINT RESIDENCE — PEGASUS'S BEDOOM — EVENING

Pegasus finds Joe's chalk white body oddly beautiful. His deep blue veins and spare blond hair delicately coating his arms and legs, none on his stomach or chest, and all his crevices and bulges conspire to arouse in Pegasus insatiable hunger. He wants to bite into Joe's supple calves, his surprisingly brown nipples, his bulbous ass. Joe doesn't exercise but he, like Pegasus, is young and active and has a fast metabolism and good genes, and his physique is naturally athletic. With the thick, unruly chestnut bouffant, he is a David.

Pegasus masturbates to Joe while he sleeps. He knows this is creepy and dangerous, but he doesn't care. He watches Joe, who snores softly on the floor beside his bed, and imagines lovemaking. NOTE: Maybe another fantasy sequence of Joe and Pegasus having sex while Pegasus masturbates.

"Pegasus is kind of a pervert, huh?" asked Raul, leaning over the promenade's railing, cringing at the rank odor rising from the river.

"I don't know if he's perverted." I turned away from the skyline, away from the reeking river, away from Raul. "He was falling in love."

"I'm not judging, Julian."

Without realizing it, I began walking away. Raul followed.

INT. DOWNTOWN PRINCETON — DAY

Giving Mary a much-needed reprieve, Pegasus convinces Joe to go out. They take the bus into nearby downtown Princeton. As they exit the bus, Joe laughs at Pegasus as he discusses Princeton's rivalry with Columbia, its jockeying for top status in U.S. News & World Report's annual college and university rankings. Joe thinks his concerns are laughable in their pretenses.

> JOE
>
> Do you really think people care about that shit?

> PEGASUS
>
> Of course, they do.

> JOE
>
> It doesn't matter. Not when people are starving to death and genocide is still a thing.

Joe is right and Pegasus feels small. Joe soon

restores Pegasus to full size by holding his
hand as they walk across the 18th century campus,
stopping off at a local café for lattes and
scones, and into an alley where they kiss.

"Well, that came sooner than I'd expected," said Raul as we entered
Socrates Sculpture Park.

"Yeah, sooner than Pegasus expected, too," I said, studying the public
art on exhibit around me and not knowing how we arrived here. I'd been
either too consumed by relaying plot points or too enamored of Raul to pay
attention to where we'd been wandering.

"So, are they still fucking?" Raul drifted from the concrete walkway
onto a cropped lawn with industrial art installations forewarning climate
catastrophes. He interacted with the art by walking through it, steel
structures ambiguously rendered into either skyscrapers or trees, twisting
into the earth upside down.

"I don't talk to Pegasus much anymore, so I don't really know."

"I guess you can make up their ending, being the writer and all."

He was right, on some level. The Darlington Brothers wanted an
unhappy ending, so, I'll have to give them that.

INT. BUS — EVENING

On the bus back home, Pegasus rests his head on
Joe's shoulder.

                    JOE
          Are you going to hurt me?

                  PEGASUS
          Can I hurt you?

                            JOE
              (dead serious)
        Not even if you tried.

Pegasus nods, knowing Joe's wisdom is more
impressive than he estimates, and maybe deeper
than the academics in his department, Dr.
Alessandro excluded. The boys cuddle on the
remainder of the nighttime bus ride through
Astoria and talk about dumpster diving, sex
work, and shelters. Pegasus hates himself for a
moment when he fetishizes the despair, finding
romantic allusions to Pasolini, Burroughs, and
Genet, but then accepts his references as the
musings of a scholarly mind hard at work on
altruistic solutions.

"I am coming up with a plan to fuck over the warlords I work for," said
Raul as we left the sculpture park and got lost in the shadows of nuclear
power plants, construction sites, and crumbling facades.

My blood ran cold as there was something sincere, sinister, and close to
specific in this admission, unlike all the other times when he'd say ambiguous,
outrageous, provocative things to shock me. I nodded and feigned interest.

"Did you hear me?" he said.

"Yeah, sure. So, okay."

He smirked at my fatuous irreverence. "I don't mean to make you an
accomplice, but I will need to tell someone and you're the only one I trust,
though lord knows why, given the way you're betraying your family."

I sneered. "Fuck you—"

Raul tugged at my shirt, stopping me before a firehouse. Before I could
defend myself any further, he had me against the brick and mortar and

shoved his tongue down my throat. We kissed hard enough to break skin. I bled from my top lip as his canine had caught me. I winced and he licked it clean. We pressed against each other but when a pair of firefighters emerged to smoke, we separated and continued walking. I was done discussing *The Touring Barbarism*. At least for the evening.

Now in her mid-forties, my sister Sophia Bartha-Byrne was a troublemaker as a teenager and gave the assistant principal of her junior high school a heart attack by making him chase her after she cut class for the 20th time her senior year. She dropped out of high school, earned her GED, and married a plumber named Doug, who himself had been a truant, in and out of jail throughout his adolescence, and had the stitches and malformed nose to prove it.

Ever the rebel, Sophia got caught up in drugs and prostitution before she met Doug and wasn't shy about broadcasting her popularity among the lustful young men of Northern Queens and Western Long Island to me, James, and our parents. My mother's first husband, David, the Hungarian cop, was an adulterer who slept around so much on my mom he gave her herpes and chlamydia. Sophia must have been conditioned to men being unfaithful because when Doug began routinely sleeping around on her, she didn't seem to mind, as long as he gave her a weekly allowance rather than an STD.

Intent on inflicting maximum harm to the family name, Sophia did everything she could to distress my parents. Her biological father couldn't be bothered with her attention-seeking antics and was hardly in the picture. He used his clout as a police sergeant on several occasions to bail Sophia out of jail after countless fights at school and in the neighborhood, as Sophia ran with a surly, bellicose group of girls identified as some officials as a gang.

In high school I was bullied by a kid named Davis. He would spray fine droplets of spit into the back of my head when behind me. He would shove me against the locker whenever he passed me. He would gesture in an effeminate way as if to mock my gentle, or fey, manner. He would blow me kisses during class. He would tell everyone I was staring at his ass. He would trip me. He would pants me. He would slap me across the back of the neck, leaving red welts. My passivity was a kind of resistance. I could take the indignities of his insults with a quiet grit and never report him to the teachers or my parents. I could continue with my life while he sought to cut me down and tarnish my reputation. It didn't matter because I had grown a leathery flesh that was impermeable.

Once, I did make the mistake of venting to my sister about Davis and she without hesitation showed up at my school one afternoon during dismissal, insisted that I point out Davis, and when I did, she proceeded to snatch his ear with one hand

and his throat with the other, spin him into a nearby car, and then send him face first into the pavement. As his lanky, awkward fifteen-year-old body was tossed around like a gazelle in the jaw of a lioness, a massive crowd of students congregated to watch the thrilling episode. As Davis lay on the ground, dazed and bruised, my sister kicked him once in the face, causing it to blow up like a balloon, leaving my bully temporarily deformed, and she told him who she was, Julian Sorrento's sister, and if his behavior should persist, she would be back to finish what she had started, though she'd said it with much less eloquence. Though I was moved by my sister coming to my rescue I also had to live with two more years of everyone making fun of me for needing my sister to come to my rescue. I credited the months of abuse I'd received from Davis for making the years of mockery from everyone else tolerable. It started to become a test of my ever-expanding threshold. I could shut down and remain untouched by their words and notes and banners and gossip. I could be a teenage martyr. The martyrdom would continue well into adulthood.

CHAPTER 15

Sophia had wanted me to take the LIRR to her house on Long Island to discuss the article, and the threat of a book. The last thing I'd do would be to trap myself in her house with Doug and Arnold, too far from a train or bus and too long a wait for an Uber or Lyft. I asked her to instead come to The Starlight Diner on Horace Haring, just off the Long Island Expressway in South Flushing, not far from where we'd grown up. The Starlight Diner was old. It was opened in 1933 by the current owner's grandparents, who'd emigrated from Athens. It was greasy spoon but clean and well maintained. Not unlike Pete's Diner in Sunnyside. Families in Queens were not unlike families in New Jersey in that we made diner visits a routine part of our lives. We especially hewed to the old ones that remained within one immigrant family, usually Greek or Italian, sometimes Jewish.

The Starlight was convenient enough, she'd said, and provided I paid, she'd weather the traffic. We met for lunch on a Friday. The diners were regulars. I'd recognized some of them from my youth as it had been years since I'd been back. To my adolescent brain they all always looked old, so the fact that they'd aged twenty years didn't make much of a difference. The thought startled. Had I look indistinguishable from a seventy-five-year-old to a teenager?

Sophia wore baggy sweatpants and a faded t-shirt evidently from "Virginia Beach." I tried not to judge her, but she'd always chosen comfort over style. Perhaps comfort was her style. Sophia had not always been overweight, and she was once conscious of her looks. I feared that the drama of being in our family, or maybe just of being in the world, eventually caught up to her. She suddenly wore psychosis, or perhaps just fatigue, on her sleeve.

She bore the inevitability of everyone too sensitive for modern life. Less a cautionary tale than a preview of the ineluctable, Sophia's haggard, slovenly appearance was a reminder of where we'd all be heading. It was resolutely American.

"Thanks for getting dressed up," I said.

"Funny, asshole. You're a funny asshole."

My mother had always been ashamed of Sophia's penchant for profanity. She swore like a truckdriver, my mother always said.

"Could you not curse too loud? There are old people here with heart conditions."

"Who gives a shit! We have more important things to talk about than my language, dickhead. Don't start sounding like mommy, criticizing me the first chance you get. Fuck, fuck, fuck. How's that?"

She was a snake charmer, my sister. I could hear my mother's pointed insults whenever I spent time with Sophia. *She dresses like a slob. She should lose weight. She should have gone for elocution lessons like me. I wish she would have stayed in school. She is so uneducated. She is so uncouth!* I appreciated that my mother, having gone through the worst of life early on, knew how unforgiving the world was and only wanted her daughter to be as well-equipped as possible to face it. The disadvantages were many, and as far as my mother was concerned, in Sophia's case, self-imposed. She had nothing systemic against her.

"Speaking of mom, what did she say about your article?"

"She said I have a great imagination."

Sophia snorted in laughter. "That's just another way of saying you're a liar."

The waitress appeared beside us. A tired looking woman either in her forties or seventies whom I'd recognized as always being in either her forties or her seventies, even when I was sixteen. Her nametag read: ROSE. She still smelled of wet cigarettes and burned coffee.

"What'll it be, hon?" she asked Sophia.

"He's buying, so I'll take a cheeseburger with fries, a Pepsi, a side of waffles, and a slice of carrot cake."

Rose looked at me, expressionlessly.

"I'll just have a coffee and some toast. Whole wheat, please."

Rose grunted and walked off. I turned to Sophia who was smirking at me.

"I didn't lie about anything," I said.

"You could never do wrong in mom's eyes. You could fucking kill someone and she would find excuses for you."

"She is hard on you. Yes, I know, but she just worries that you're too generous and you let too many people take advantage of you like grandma."

"I would be fucking honored to be like our grandmother! That woman was a goddamn saint. You know what I always say, better to be so good you get abused than be a bitch like mom that no one can stand to be around."

She was right about that, and I didn't want to argue about my mother's favoritism. That's not why we were here.

"Mom may be a bitch and full of shit, but she is not a thief, Julian. She didn't con anyone out of their money. Where the hell did you get that?"

I began playing with the salt and pepper shakers, rearranging them, clinking them together. Anything to avoid looking at Sophia's wounded, weary eyes. The whole tableau became depressing. The décor of The Starlight had not changed since the mid-80s. The faux wood paneling. The browns and yellows. The frayed, stained carpeting. The ersatz stain glass chandeliers. I remembered going every Tuesday afternoon with my dad after school. With Sophia and her black-and-blue personality in the context, it all pressed against me.

"There were things I was privy to that you and James were not. You were both out of the house by the time they ... I was alone with her and dad, okay. For years. Alone. I saw what they did."

"And James!" Sophia began noodling with her keys, outsized with many ornaments like lip gloss, pepper spray, souvenirs from Miami, the Bahamas, and Puerto Rico. "What you wrote about him. Disgusting, Julian. But hey, you're up there now, so..."

Up there!

"I already dealt with him, too."

"Did he kick your ass? He should have. Dougie wants to. So does Arnie. No one is happy with you. No one is okay with what you did."

I put the salt and pepper shakers back in their upright positions.

"I never sold it for sex, Julian." Sophia stopped fussing with her ten-pound keys and looked at me plainly with no affect, her face a ruined canvas, marked by years of wear and cheap makeup and tears, a face with no decoration, no concealment, a face of a person who'd absorbed every blow. "And my drug problems were not yours to write about."

I swallowed hard and cleared my throat. "I should have told you. I'm sorry."

"My kid is not a gangster. My husband was never a pimp."

"Sophia, you don't know—"

"About them?" She leaned forward and hissed. I thought she might slap me across the table. "I know everything! You made us look like trash, Julian."

I now began manipulating the packets of sugar and Splenda. Tearing them open, spilling them out, folding the corners into dime store origami. I made little mountains out of the piles of sugar. I didn't know how to respond to Sophia. She watched me for a moment and then grew bored and began to check her phone for texts or calls. I wouldn't have been surprised if she'd begun playing Roulette or some other game.

"Just so you know ... I didn't mean to hurt anyone."

She scoffed. "That's what everyone says who hurts people."

Rose arrived with our food and Sophia ate as I sipped my coffee, nibbled on my bland toast. We didn't talk much anymore as she'd consumed herself with the robust meal and myriad games on her phone, most of which emanated obnoxious sounds that attracted challenging glances, audible scoffs, and several complaints from our fellow diners. Rose eventually asked Sophia to lower the volume. She did so but only after mumbling, "Uptight assholes." I'd have been embarrassed by her display, but I'd grown accustomed to it and even expected it whenever we were in public together. Before I could say anything, I noticed a turquoise feather jutting from Sophia's shirt, just under her right breast. I don't know why it had taken me so long to catch it.

"Are you molting?" I asked, pointing to the feather.

She looked down at the feather, groaned, and plucked it from her shirt before tossing in onto the table.

"Fucking Doug. He's starting a zoo in our house."

"An aviary?"

"Whatever. He's into birds now."

I could have pressed for details about Doug's aviary but feared that small talk about something other than the memoir and my portrayal of the family would make me too nostalgic for better times, i.e., the countless times I swallowed shit and smiled. Sophia began on her dessert, and I fell silent again, enduring her boorish medley of masticating sounds.

"So, that's it?" she said, a few minutes later, finishing her slice of cake, wiping her mouth, belching softly into her napkin. "Nothing else to say?"

"What should I say, Sophia?"

"Why you wrote that garbage. I mean, I know why. You wanted to get famous. I know that much."

"I didn't want to 'get famous.' I didn't want to hurt anyone. I wrote things as I remembered them and as they've bothered me all these years. I had to finally get it out. I deserved to get it out. After the shit you all put me through. This is the minimum of what I deserve!"

"So, this was like therapy or something, then?"

"Maybe, yeah!"

"Therapy that *we* all have to pay for?"

We were at an impasse. I asked Rose for the bill and paid, leaving her a sizable tip, an apology for Sophia's behavior, really. My sister shook her head and continued playing her games. Though in her mid-forties, she still acted like a recalcitrant teenager. It was as if she'd been stunted at sixteen, a perpetual adolescent, forever defying the dictates of polite society. Civilization advanced, but Sophia remained proudly obstinate.

"Why don't you just fuck back off to Tucson or India or wherever else you were happier?" she finally said. Her go-to Parthian shot.

"I think about it every goddamn day, believe me."

It was true. I'd spent two years in Tucson barely scrapping by on an adjunct's salary, teaching psychology and gender courses at Pima Community College, and three months with a friend and his family in India, mostly Pune and Kolkata. I'd tried to find a job to stay and wept when I left. I'd never known even a second of loneliness in India, something that I could not say about life in the United States, especially in New York. Neither place afforded me enough to live for the long-term, but with my new writing life allowing remote work, the thought of escape was again on the table and Sophia knew and her query was a reasonable one.

"So, just go! Disappear! We'd all be happier, too"

As we left the diner, I couldn't stand the awkward tension between us, so I changed subjects clumsily.

"How's your dad?"

"Fuck you care."

"I care, of course, I do!"

In front of the diner was a bus stop with a line of people, mostly elderly or very young, students heading to Queens College, a few stops away. The traffic on the Long Island Expressway roared over our conversation, and we often had to shout to hear each other, which ended the possibility of a private chat. I tried to lead her away from the onlookers at the bus stop and closer to the parking lot, hoping she'd get in her car and drive away.

"His dementia is getting worse and that witch he's married to is always complaining and keeping him locked up in that little apartment in the slums to control him!"

"She's probably just worried about him hurting himself. And I can't imagine it's easy to take of someone like him?"

"The fuck does that mean? 'Like him'?"

"With his condition, I mean. It sounds difficult, you know."

"Like your father was such a fucking peach!"

"I never said he was. He's more like a rotten apple!"

She didn't find this funny, and she recoiled from her own comment, "I didn't mean that. Your father was always so good to me. Adam treated me like his real daughter."

In fact, before I came along a decade later, my father spoiled Sophia and James. Let them get away with murder. My mother still blamed him for having "ruined" them, turning them into "greedy, selfish ingrates."

"I know, and he feels the same about you. Like you're his real daughter. But both my dad and yours treated our mother like crap."

Sophia looked at me with disoriented eyes. As if she'd just witnessed some unspeakable trauma. That look that survivors of assault have, a faraway unfocused gaze.

"You're such a liar, man. Why do you lie?"

"I am not a liar. I did not lie."

"Oh, and Aunt Mary and Uncle Monroe? Are you fucking kidding me? A TV show about their shit? Are you stupid?"

"What's the problem with that now?"

And with that, Sophia allowed whatever composure and civility she'd mustered for the past hour to fall away, and she began to beat me in front of the retirees and students waiting for the bus. She punched and slapped me, and I turned away and shielded my head as her blows landed on my back, shoulders, and the hands protecting my skull. I could hear the elderly people gasp and the students hype the beating. Some laughed.

"You're a fucking liar! Why are you such a fucking liar?! Go ahead and write your stupid fucking book of lies! Why don't you just go run to mommy like a little bitch?! Why don't you just fuck off back to India and Arizona?! Why don't you just fucking die?!"

[148]

After a minute she'd thankfully tired herself out, panting and wheezing. She stared at me and as I shielded my face from further blows, I saw she was crying.

"Why the fuck did you put that shit with Dimitri in there? The whole world can now have a good laugh about mom fucking my boyfriend! That was just fucking cruel!"

She held herself and started slowly back to her car where she blasted the radio—contemporary pop—and sped off demonstratively. I looked at the people waiting for the bus. One of the students said through mocking laughter, "Yo, she fucked your shit up!"

I also laughed at myself as I began the two-mile trek toward the subway station downtown. The tops of my hands, my crown, and my right shoulder blade ached, and I'd imagined were either bruising or swelling. Sophia packed quite a punch. She could have brought up the time she'd stuck up for me when she'd beaten up and scared shitless my high school bully, but she hadn't. I could have also told her that her good intentions yielded a greater wave of bullying by thousands instead of only one. My meekness in the face of class-wide hounding continues to gird me from the opinions of others. Once you stop caring so much about judgments you achieve a sort of freedom to live without the kind of self-consciousness that could be quite inhibiting.

I knew how to fill the chapters about Sophia. I would go to the notorious, storied Farrington Street and question the other sex workers and maybe even the johns. I'd dive deeply into my sister's exploits while also writing an analysis of sex work in modern America. How for some it is a pleasurable choice that has dignity and provides a living, and for others how it is an act of desperation and degradation, the product of a merciless capitalist society. In Sophia's case it was neither. She did it to hurt our parents, James, and me. She did it to impress Doug. She did it to ruin Arnold, filling her unstable boy with shame and rage. I could also dig into her gang affiliation as a teenager. The brutal, mean things she did to other girls and boys as part of initiation and to prove her mettle. The police record a mile long. The diet pills in her thirties and how skinny and crazy she became. The flirtatious afternoons in the backyard with Arnold's athletic friends, just boys barely 18 at the time. The portrait would be monstrous. I'd do such damage. She'd been too impatient with me. Too much of a bully. Like James. Like my Dad. Spite is not petty. It is not grotesque. It is a profound reaction to injustice, and it is beautiful.

CHAPTER 16

I'd developed a—maybe perverse—interest in seeing how everyone's midlife crises manifested and how they navigated them. Raul surrendered to his promiscuity, his need for frequent anonymous sex, increasingly aggressive and degrading, I to my article and its success, despite or *because of* the grief it's caused my family, Sophia to binge eating, eschewing self-consciousness *and* self-esteem, James to hostile policing, Monroe to excessive bodybuilding. I thought about all this as Raul and I ascended the wide spiral of the Guggenheim, surveying Cecilia Vicuna's exhibition. Museums always opened the door to existential musings like aging, insecurity, loneliness, and where we find purpose in those horrifying nuisances.

"You know," began Raul, gesturing at Vicuna's work, "she once painted my grandfather."

"No kidding? That's incredible. Do you guys still have it?"

"My parents do. They'll leave it to MoMA when they die."

Raul smelled like soap, cologne, deodorant, and dried blood. Fresh from a shower after hours of combat, clearly. He'd just come from a morning of teaching hipsters and yuppies mixed martial arts in Bushwick. His black backpack had been slung around him. I wondered who'd seen him naked at the dojo as he showered, and afterward, when he dried himself and dressed. Had there been roaming queer eyes? Had male students loitered to catch a glimpse of Sensei Sandoval as he disrobed?

Mostly I was worried that the topic would turn to his plans for *RFN*. That night in Socrates Sculpture Park had spooked me. Would he try again to make me complicit in a scheme to commit some sort of grand crime, be it white collar or violent?

I cleared my throat. "Was this while he was living in Santiago?"

"No, they were here in Manhattan together for a time."

Vicuna's work, a monsoon of threads and knots, reminded me of the otherworldly nightmares of Louise Bourgeois, Eva Hess, and Lee Bontecou. There was something corporeal yet formless about their art, tangible but ethereal. These women seemed to be embracing the unalterable alterations of civilization. We build bombs and contaminate nature and encroach and spread our technological germs and we pay for the expansion, the entitlement. The apocalypse in the worlds of the artists is a cosmic necessity. Possibly even a pleasure. *About to Happen* was the name of the Chilean renaissance woman's show. She also painted and made experimental art films. The whole of the great and awful 20th century had been contained in their conceptual dramas.

I stepped around, under, and through Vicuna's raw wool, her heavy fibers, dangling, draping, slithering across the floor, inspecting the dyed crimson, looking up at the ropes suspended around me. Raul toured the space with me, as amused by my fascination with the art as by the constructions themselves. Vicuna was telling us that colonization was all around us.

Did Raul suggest the Vicuna show for context? To help me shape the episode with my mom and aunt? The great women of art and memoir, of political revolt and television? Of their fucked-up girlhoods

NOTE about characters' backgrounds: Annalisa and Mary had been the closest friends and most vindictive rivals as kids. Mary had committed herself unapologetically to school. She knew at a young age that she'd be an anthropologist. For some children, they'd proclaim a vague notion of their futures and careers. They'd like to be a doctor or a lawyer or an actor. Mary's ambitions were specific and narrow. She wanted to be a cultural anthropologist who conducted most of her field work in India. Her love affair with the country began in junior high school when she read *Passage to India* by E.M. Forster. And when the time came to enroll in a specialized high school (Bronx Science) to get into the best college program (Dartmouth) she did so without hesitation, even at the cost of her parents and sister. She left them for New Hampshire without the guilt that might have prevented someone hindered by obligations to stay behind and play nursemaid and doormat, like Annalisa, for example. <u>NOTE: Perhaps all these scenes with them during their childhoods could be rendered with flashbacks throughout each episode in a parallel timeline.</u>

"What are those welts on your neck?" asked Raul, interrupting the saga of Annalisa and Mary.

"Oh, I met with Sophia the other day."

"Damn. Not even your brother left any lasting impressions."

"James knows how to hit me so no one can ever tell."

<u>NOTES on characters' histories:</u> The Donizetti Sisters were a study in contrasts. The daughters of the saintly, martyr-like, Philomena Theresa Maria Donizetti of the Bronx, the girls viewed their mothers through vastly different lenses. For Annalisa, Philomena was a sucker, a foolish giver who gave until it hurt and not just herself, but the entire family. It hurt their

reputation, their comforts, and their financial situation. For Mary, Philomena represented the best in humanity, someone who gave selflessly and maintained an open-door policy for a neighborhood wrought with domestic abuse, poverty, and food scarcity. Mary sought to emulate her mother's altruistic nature as an adult when she decided on cultural anthropology.

As kids, Annalisa spent much of her time caring for their blind grandmother and dysfunctional parents, while Mary focused her energies of excelling in all her classes and remaining on her path toward becoming an academic. It never dawned on Annalisa that Mary had been critical—indeed even ashamed—of her the same way she'd been critical and undoubtedly ashamed of her own daughter Sophia, who reminded her too much of their mother, Philomena.

I was surprised that Raul didn't question my decision to bring Sophia into the story. He usually relished the opportunity to interrupt and challenge my creative decisions, finding mistakes in my judgment and room for improvement through his own suggestions. Anything at all to minimize my abilities and effort and regard his own. I'd eyeballed him to see if he made a face, but he hadn't. Maybe he wasn't paying attention. Maybe he was waiting for the right moment to list all the ways in which I'd erred in this story's telling.

NOTE on characters' backgrounds: Mary feels that Annalisa settled in her life, in her marriage, and lacked not just sophistication, culture, and education, but also compassion and wisdom, as indicated by her shame of their mother and Annalisa's daughter. Mary saw their mother on parity with Mother Teresa, someone Mary had studied and planned to emulate as a cultural anthropologist in India. Of course, Pegasus tortured his mother for the idolatry by challenging all of this as a form of imperialism. Mother Teresa had been criticized by the head of the Hindu nationalist group Rashtriya Swayamzevak Sangh (RSS) for having had ulterior motives of converting the poor in Calcutta to Christianity, as well as allegations of misusing funds, poor medical treatments, and religious evangelism in the institutes she founded. He also frequently referenced Christopher Hitchens's documentary *Hell's Angel*, which goes into her relationships with Charles Keating and Jean-Claude Duvalier, Haitian dictator, and the conditions of her institutes, which were apparently deplorable and akin to Nazi concentration camps like Bergen-Belsen, and finally, what Hitchens called, participating in "the cult of death and suffering."

"I am so relieved you have Pegasus challenging her worship of that cunt," said Raul.

"That may be a bit much, calling Mother Teresa a cunt."

We caught affronted glances from nearby visitors. Catholic, most likely.

"You just said it yourself."

"I didn't call her a cunt."

"What you described was cunt-like behavior."

We entered a gallery of the museum's wide upward spiral where giant, heavy cloths hung in beige, pink, purple, and red. It looked like a giant octopus in suspension, though without a discernable body, tentacles dangling, running partially across the floor. The material was unspun wool meant to intimate quipus, cords knotted to record information, something created by the Inca, banned by the Spanish in 1583, or so stated the description posted to the wall beside it. The tendrils sometimes looked like nets and occasionally held found objects. One looked like a heart.

Vicuna's voice competed with our own as video footage of ancient textiles was projected onto the wool. She mumbled inscrutable words, perhaps messages, and sometimes she shouted in an unknown language, at least, unknown to me. I thought she was yelling at us.

INT. CLINT RESIDENCE — DAY

Mary, Pegasus, and Joe sit in the living room discussing Mother Theresa.

                MARY
       (quoting from an article)
   In AsiaNews, which is a Vatican-
   affiliates news agency, Peg, the
   Reverend Bernardo Cervellera said,
   "She didn't have a plan to conquer
   the world. Her idea was to be
   obedient to God."

              PEGASUS
   To *her* God!

JOE

She exploited all those poor,
uneducated people.

MARY

Okay, I'm not about to argue the
merits of Mother Teresa ... I mean,
what have either of you ever done?

PEGASUS

Well, I brought Joe home to live
with us. 'For real' charitable. Not
like Mother Teresa, who—

MARY
(touching her temple)
Okay, enough, Peg. Just be quiet.

MORE FLASHBACKS: Annalisa and Mary share moments
of closeness: they go to the local movie theater
as teenagers on Saturdays to see the latest
Faye Dunaway or Goldie Hawn or Diana Ross or
John Travolta. They get lunch at a nearby diner
and discuss the plot and the performances,
daydreaming about Marlon Brando and Al Pacino
and Warren Beatty. They share milkshakes or
waffles with ice cream or French fries. They do
things young women, especially sisters, do, if
the subjects of school, career, and mother are
never broached.

BACKGROUND NOTE: At Dartmouth, Mary met Monroe Clint and Annalisa instantly disliked him. A "too white" sort of man from New Jersey—blue eyed, blond haired, creamy skin, unlike she and her family, the dark Italians—who'd take her sister away and confirm her intelligence, enable the life of ease and comfort in what would decades later become a trendy part of Queens and cement her standing in society, if she wanted it. But Mary never wanted it, which made it even tougher, and if anything, Clint's career as a builder of weapons of mass destruction problematized Mary's life and career as a progressive scholar. He was civil and polite, even as he became weird in his advanced years with the collection of cats and the bodybuilding supplements. It had been a creepy midlife meltdown, one that mixed outdated notions of gender essentialism.

INT. CLINT RESIDENCE — DAY

1990s. Annalisa and Mary tend to a two-year old Pegasus.

                    ANNALISA
          I don't think he likes our family
          very much, Mary.

                    MARY
          He doesn't like people much. It's
          not personal.

The timeline would be tricky to show in a series without too many jumps back and forth in periods. I thought about the film version of Michael Cunningham's *The Hours*. That had worked well enough. There would be flashbacks in the episode, but most of the story unfolds when Pegasus was in his early twenties, which would make it modern day. Mary and Monroe were my mother's age. They're currently in their sixties. Maybe a little older. I don't really know how old anyone in my family is. They all lie.

MORE NOTES ABOUT THE CHARACTERS' BACK STORIES:
The Indian scandal brought out the best and worst in Annalisa. She was there to support her sister when Columbia and The Hague came down on her, but secretly she was glad Mary suffered, relieved to see her fall, thrilled at the prospect of her career ending unceremoniously, being internationally vilified. There was poignancy in the incident and its connection to Mother Teresa's own work not far from Kolkata in Bihar, just 320 miles north. The entire state of Bengal had been plagued by well-intentioned white women.

Though Monroe Clint was Dartmouth-educated and a rather brilliant scientist, his ethic and personality were decidedly blue collar. He was also a fierce ally to Mary and when the incident rocked her career and turned her into a nearly household name in the worst possible way, he stood by her, even when her own family, Annalisa included, were quick to judge and ridicule.

INT. CLINT RESIDENCE — DINNING ROOM — EVENING

Annalisa and Mary eat dinner.

                    ANNALISA
          Well, you should have stayed in
          America, Mary. You go looking for
          trouble when you travel to those
          places.

                    MARY
          What do you mean by 'those places,'
          Annalisa?

                    ANNALISA
          Those places … where the people …
          will eat you alive.

PERHAPS THROUGH MARY'S VOICE OVER: Annalisa's
bigotries were expressions of her unformed
brain, Mary always thought. Had her sister
taken her studies seriously when younger and
not sacrificed at the altar of her mother's
desperation and her grandmother's dependence
and their father's philandering, she'd have
been a whole person who didn't look down on
other people or speak reductively and hatefully
about entire countries and indeed continents.
Classic ignorance, but maybe not of the willful
variety.

"You know," began Raul, cutting me off as he was wont to do, "I just read in *Scientific American* that from a neuroscience perspective, the memories we keep dredging up are the least reliable."

I didn't reply, trying to conceal my perturbance. I'd read the article, too. The major points had been covered by *The New York Times*. Something about how when we keep bringing an event to the surface, re-telling it, we must write over and re-encode it and we end up revising it each time, essentially fabricating it, eventually, turning it into a narrative, which is what it is, right? A story? So … maybe it's not true at all? And the truest memories are like dinosaur bones that need to be re-assembled to see what they looked like. This is just an elaborate way of saying memories are subjective. Something we all already know.

"I love these paintings," said Raul, flippant in his diversion. "They remind me of the portrait she did of my grandfather."

In one of the museum's many alcoves, Vicuna's paintings were mounted in symmetrical alignment. Raul was already closely inspecting one. An ivory-white human-leopard-giant clutching trees, one turquoise and one pink. Teats and eyes filled her coat, respectively sagging and peering from her belly. She smirked menacingly, pleased with her unusual appearance and threatening manifestation. The title card read "Leoparda de Ojitos," "Eyed Leopard." Vicuna painted it in 1976 and it was weird and shocking, which was acceptable in fine art, even encouraged, but in a story, a novel, or a TV show, weird and shocking had to be meaningful and earned.

"Ferocious," I said.

"*Fucking* ferocious," Raul added.

NOTE: Annalisa did a poor job of hiding her disgust with Monroe's disfigurement. Something that Mary chalked up to her shallowness and limited life experiences. Mary also gave grief to Annalisa for her treatment of her daughter.

She always extended great admiration for her niece who took so much after her mother. Annalisa took umbrage with this kindness.

INT. GREEK RESTAURANT — EVENING

Annalisa and Mary eat lunch in a busy Greek restaurant.

                    ANNALISA
          I don't like you undermining me to
          my daughter.

                    MARY
          Maybe if you were kinder to her
          yourself, Annalisa, then --

                    ANNALISA
              (poking at her grilled calamari)
          Mary, she is becoming our mother!

                    MARY
          And how beautiful is it that she
          is? We should celebrate that. Mom
          was a saint. Like Mother Teresa.

                    ANNALISA
              (trembling)
          I don't understand you, Mary.

                          MARY
            (touching her sister's hand)
        You don't understand what about me,
        Annalisa?

Annalisa tries to tell her but can't find the
words. She stares at her blackened squid and
shrugs.

NOTE: Mary also had grievances with Annalisa's
younger son, Julian, who she believed swayed
Pegasus's political leanings. She valued him as
a member of a marginalized group, like her own
son, and in that respect, she appreciated him.

"Wow." Raul had moved on to a new wing in the museum, a fun house
of Vicuna's curious neuroses. Wires, ropes, flags hung from the ceiling and
piled in unruly, squirming masses across the waxed concrete. "How very
indulgent of you to write yourself into the show."

"I *am* in the book, you know, *my* memoir. It's about me mostly, Raul. It's
reasonable."

"Solipsistic. Narcissistic. But, sure, reasonable, too."

NOTE: Mary and Annalisa's older son, James, had
fallen out of touch after he moved to Arizona,
as neither he nor she made any effort to stay
in touch.

Annalisa also has a chronic habit of criticizing
Mary's taste in decor and clothing, finding
her aesthetic dowdy, even "matronly," but as

a woman of the mind and spirit, Mary deflects
these insults and levels her own.

INT. CLINT RESIDENCE — DAY

Mary and Annalisa argue in the kitchen.

                    MARY
        Maybe if you used your brain more,
        you'd see things more deeply and
        realize how materialistic you
        are. You dress well and decorate
        well, but that's all. Life on the
        surface. Nothing deeper.

Annalisa begins to cry.

On the winding descent toward the exit, another painting caught my eye.
For all her abstractions, arresting surrealness, and gruesome commentary,
Vicuna produced one piece that ended up staying with me, a portrait of a
woman who could have been a young girl or an old lady sitting cross-legged
and holding either beans or embers or bugs as if an offering.

"Don't worry" Raul whispered in my ear, with another non-sequitur, this
one demented. "I'm not planning on shooting up the dipshits at *RFN* or
anything like that."

I looked again at the painting because what else was there to do? The
ageless female held in her beseeching expression the wisdom of youth and
fear of obsolescence.

Excerpt of
My Mighty Meekness,
as published in
The New Yorker

In his day, Angelo was a gambler, some might say degenerate, as he'd lost two cars, a house, and his and my grandmother Rosalie's retirement savings in his weekly poker, blackjack, and gin games. He was also a belligerent drunk. Rosalie was old-fashioned strong, made of rubber and steel, but even she had been able to withstand only so much before throwing herself down the stairs, abandoning Angelo and his unstable, brutal world. I had been only four at the time, so I'm unable to recall her.

My father had told me stories about how Grandpa would come home drunk from losing a card game, stinking like beer and cigar smoke. My grandmother would sometimes have friends over and he would yell at them to get out of his house, accusing them of brainwashing my grandmother against him, eating all his food, and gossiping about him. He would take their teacups or mugs of coffee and ceramic plates that held either pastries or fruit and smash them into the sink with theatrical grandeur.

My grandfather was a skilled craftsman. He could whittle wood. He could lay brick. He could construct frames. He could cut marble and granite. He could manipulate steel. He could build anything with his bare hands. I, on the other hand, had trouble with hammering nails and assembling Ikea furniture. We sometimes had backyard parties and would invite the extended family and friends and neighbors. One year when I was in high school the theme during a late summer party was farm life. So, my father rented chickens and pigs from a local farm and my grandfather and brother spent the week constructing enclosures in our yard. I tried to help but had difficulty with almost every facet of the labor. My brother, as was customary, laughed and hurled insults about my lack of common sense and physical ineptitude, but what stung during that would-be bonding exercise was the way my grandfather had sided with him and laughed at me with my brother. Grandpa had joked about how at least my parents had one son, even if they'd been stuck with two girls.

I lived with the complex I'd developed that day for at least a decade until I learned that I did not have to be good at everything, or even anything, and I could value the abilities of others even if I could not find those same attributes within myself.

CHAPTER 17

The trek from Jackson Heights to Bay Ridge on the 7 to the D to the R took nearly two hours but it had been almost a year since I'd seen my grandfather and five years shy of ninety, he wasn't getting any younger. Angelo Sorrento lived in a walk-in studio—really the finished basement of a two-family home—on Marine Avenue, a block from the Atlantic Ocean. Superstorm Sandy had nearly drowned him a decade ago, but he was stubborn and refused to leave. The owner of the building and upstairs resident, Bruno Giuseppe Belladonna, was an old family friend of my father who checked in on grandpa daily and reported back to Dad, who himself dropped in weekly, though never on a set schedule, which unnerved me as the last thing I'd be able to bear was my grandfather *and* father at the same time discussing my mischaracterizations of them in the essay and my plans for the book.

Grandpa still dressed like an old-world gentleman. I'd seen photos and movies of Italian immigrants in the 1940s and 1950s and they all wore the same fedoras, neckties, and three-piece suits, like Grandpa in his beige tweeds. He moved with a sprightly force that time hadn't diminished. He offered me a half-smile, half-grimace, and patted my arm.

"I read your letter," I said.

He nodded and then grabbed my wrist. "Well, good, it was written to be read, after all."

I followed dutifully as he led me inside.

His apartment was tidy and looked decorated a hundred years ago but not touched since. Taupe cloth doilies, curios packed with antiques like limited edition collector plates, tin coffee pots, ceramic decanters, porcelain figurines, a vintage singer sewing machine, Victorian-era utensils, mugs from the 1940s, all relics from his time as a young man in the New York seventy years ago. Immaculate, but unmolested, Grandpa Angelo's little home was a portal to another world, and it oddly comforted. It made me remember my father's cologne and my mother's perfume.

"You look like you could eat," he said.

I wondered how he had the energy for such an effort to keep everything so clean. I was almost a little over a third of my grandfather's age and I felt a hair's breadth away from giving in, bucking all maintenance. Was I too young or too old to contemplate such a colossal resignation? Not just quit cleaning, but also quit laundry, quit working, quit writing, quit socializing, quit cooking, quit exercising. Embrace the delayed decline and welcome it head-on — accept poverty, accept obscurity, accept loneliness, accept filth, accept odors, accept going broke on ordering in, accept the growth of my nascent midlife paunch.

"You look like you could use a good long sleep," he said.

Not only was everything sterile, but also brown. Brown fabrics. Brown wood. Brown tablecloth. Brown carpeting. Brown base molding. Brown was the color of my youth. I can no longer see shit and not think of my childhood.

"You must understand how much it hurt to read your article, Julian."

I sat at grandpa's little wood dining table as he served me an espresso and a plate of S cookies.

"I didn't mean to hurt anyone."

"I didn't kill your grandmother." Grandpa sat and sipped his espresso.

"Maybe not intentionally," I started but then stopped when I saw the way he'd been looking at me, as if I'd just stuck him with one of his antique forks. "I didn't mean that the way it sounded."

"You could be careless and clumsy, Julian. So carless and clumsy."

"I just want to write. I just wanted to capture who we were. Who we *are*, I mean. And what has changed. The good, the bad, the ugly. Unfiltered."

"You seemed to focus on the bad, though. And even that wasn't enough. You had to distort even that. Dial it all the way up. And now … a book, I hear? Is that really necessary?"

"We don't see things as they are, we see things as we are."

I'd quoted Anais Nin, not thinking grandpa would know the reference, but I'd underestimated how well read he'd been.

"When dealing with people as narcissistic as Henry and June Miller, it would take a perceptive woman to see that."

"You know Anais Nin's work?"

"I know the quote. I'm not a moron, Julian, though I'm sure that's how you'd like to see me."

My grandfather had had an affair with the wife of his bocce ball mate for several years when my grandmother was still alive. The wife's name was Theresa, and she was a librarian who read voraciously. Angelo began reading to impress her. My father told me that his mother, my Grandma Rosalie, began to get suspicious when he started bringing home books by Henry Miller, Micky Spillane, and Ernest Hemingway.

I picked at my S cookie. "Grandpa…"

"What can you do to make this all right with the family? What can be done? No use feeling bad and pouting now."

Nothing could be done because I'd done nothing wrong. I'd often tended to overstate or theatrically emphasize or maybe sometimes even exaggerate when recounting incidents and my family would be quick and all too happy to call me out on my hyperbole, labeling me a "drama queen" or "a Spielberg" due to my penchant for fantasy and making life more cinematic than it really was, but I hadn't done that with *My Mighty Meekness*. In fact, I was deliberate in stating things simply without heightened drama or embellishment. I would be even more journalistic in my book.

"I wonder how many more lies you will fill your book with."

I looked over his shoulder at the antediluvian credenza atop of which were a collection of gild-framed photos ranging from this past year to grandpa's boyhood in both Naples and the Bronx in the early 1930s. There were also photos of Rosalie, the grandmother I hardly knew, looking pretty but dowdy, balancing elegance with ordinariness. The photos of my father as a boy and as a man, in military regalia and in construction gear, in a suit and in a tank top made me saddest. The photos of James and Sophia as kids and with me during my high school and college graduations did, too. Grandpa had displayed a generous number of photos of my mom and of me, like dad, from childhood to adulthood and all the awkward years in between. I felt like I had murdered a family. Not my own but someone else's.

"How did she fall down the stairs?"

Grandpa's response chilled me. He sniggered and then brought his plate and espresso cup to the sink to handwash them. He used copious amounts of soap and the water steamed, reddening his hands, already arthritic with veins as thick as fingers and wrists like bags of rocks. I watched him scorch himself and not react to the injury, though it didn't seem like he was demonstrating an endurance test. Rather, it was a matter-of-fact resilience.

"Rosalie spoiled me, Julian, but you wouldn't know that because you weren't old enough to have seen us together. She cooked the best meals, healthy and filling and flavorful. She cleaned like a professional. We could eat off the floor if we wanted to. She sewed even better than I could, and I was the tailor! She taught me something every day. I am half the person I was before she fell down those stairs. The fall killed half of me, you understand. I have had to go on living as a half-person for forty years."

His diatribe was by design an indictment of my abusive thinking. If I pressed the theory that Rosalie's death had been planned or even spontaneously carried out with malice, I'd be guilty at this point of elder abuse. I could accept that I was that kind of grandson, that kind of writer. I would further investigate this death, this possible crime. Men of his age did such things in their youth. They were of a time that excused brutality toward women. William S. Burroughs. Norman Mailer. Roman Polanski. Men could do vile things, murderous things, and get away with them. Could Grandpa be such a man? Perhaps my memoir would answer the question, and the question needed to be asked even if the search for the truth would conflagrate the whole family. My book—for there would certainly be a book and it would be full of unkind accusations as I was not in the business of writing hagiographies—would be a cudgel with which I'd bludgeon him and my family and the cherished memory of my long-dead grandmother.

"Rosalie wouldn't have approved of what you've done."

I gripped the tiny ceramic handle of the espresso cup and almost broke it clean off. "What I've done?"

My father routinely reminded me that his father hadn't been there for him when he was starting out, just after high school. My dad wanted to go to college, but Grandpa thought it was a waste of time and money, so he encouraged Dad to get a job in construction to make a living as young as possible so he could build and save and start a family and provide for them. He became a brick layer and my grandfather celebrated that. Grandpa never saw the value in education. He was young and ignorant, only in his forties then. It wasn't until my father was already grown and working and had to support me and James and Sophia that Grandpa had begun to understand the importance of knowledge. Dad wanted to be an architect, but when he would ask my grandfather for money for books he'd say, "What do you need those for?" What a damn ignorant fool Grandpa was. I don't think Dad ever forgave him for that.

My father would tell me every time I spoke with him how grateful I should be that I at least had a father who always encouraged my dreams and pursuits no matter how impractical. I fell easily under the influence of his emotional blackmail, which is why I never hesitated lending him money or signing my name for him on credit card applications or loans or mortgages.

"I also never really drank, at least not as much as you portrayed in your article, and I only gambled occasionally with close friends, but never to the extent that I lost my shirt, also as you'd written I had. Ginn rummy was my game, and sometimes blackjack or poker, but those were harmless pastimes, and the stakes were never higher than maybe $20 dollars, which in those days was maybe the equivalent of $100 today. Certainly not enough to make someone go poor!"

Grandpa was stupid like a fox. Clever in the way people born during The Silent Generation were. Keeping their cards close to their chest, managing the strings of the entire world like a giant marionette. They were, after all, the progenitors of the Baby Boomers, my mother and father, those who clung to power with an indestructible death grip.

An ugly thought occurred to me. Had my family, like too many families, taken advantage of my gratitude for their acceptance of me? Did they think it was okay to take me for granted because they believed I was desperate for support and should be appreciative that they offered it? Was I even in a family or was it a coven and grandpa the altar of their circle, or maybe we were a confederacy, and Angelo the head of our union? Either way, I was no longer at home here, not with my grandfather and not with any of them, not after these encounters where I was left to feel as if I'd transgressed a sacred moral.

"I think I need to go, grandpa," I said, leaving my espresso cup half full and my S cookies half eaten.

He nodded with a grin that could have been construed as sinister or merely condescending.

"Do what you want," he said, beginning to clean my mess before I had a chance to do so myself. "Your kind always does."

Neither grandpa nor I recalled the backyard farm animal enclosure disgrace from my youth. He'd been too old to answer for it at this point, anyway. He was of a generation that demanded capable manual laborers of all men, even if it was not their vocation, so to him I'd always be a half man in failing to gain this virtue. And to him it was a virtue. He'd probably been more ashamed of me for not meeting this masculine expectancy than my queerness. I could live with his disappointment. It was not my problem as much as it was his. And that level of meekness which I counted as mighty would protect me from the devaluations of others well into my own old age.

A troubling new thought occurred to me after leaving Grandpa's apartment. Standing on the southernmost tip of Brooklyn and staring into the murky, polluted waters of the Atlantic below, I thought about the seconds before Grandma's fall. Had she been scared or angry, or both. Had she cried or prayed. Had she put up a fight? I thought about the minutes before the fall. Had she been attempting to escape or confront? Had she been ascending or descending? What had brought her to the top of the stairs? I thought about the hours and days and weeks and years before the fall. Had she regretted her decisions? Had she resented Grandpa? Had she thought about getting out of her life? Did such thoughts occur to women of her generation? Had she envisioned a better life for herself? My book would be a tribute to her pain and surrender. I would avenge her murder.

I turned around to face the subway, but I didn't move an inch.

CHAPTER 18

Marcel Laurent spun a strange story about the uneasy relationship between his family and country. Kevin had spent all day at the gym and then ordered Thai food for dinner. The young Parisian prodigy regaled us—that is me, Kevin, Ed, and Fanny, as everyone else were either on tours or holiday or writing—with the details of his new work-in-progress called *My Parents Shot Themselves with Destitute Bullets*. The work, like his previous two books, *The Completion of Marcel* and *Those Who Canceled My Father*, would likely further his reputation as France's folk hero, an exemplar of the industrious poor, the virtues of farmer grit, and unexpected places (re: poor and uneducated) we find sparkling intellectuals. Everything in France was class warfare and Marcel had the biggest gun.

"My father was an ignorant farmer, and my mother was not much smarter," said Marcel, "and so, naturally, they voted against their own interests by casting their ballots for Le Pen, much the same as your American hillbillies and rednecks did for Trump. These people don't know any better and they are easily fooled and so they elect the person who promises a restoration of old times when the country was white and straight and dropping atomic bombs on other sovereign nations. The so-called 'great days.'"

"I don't understand your title," I said, to which Kevin snorted and Ed gave me a cross look.

Fanny, reliably neutral, just shrugged and muttered, "What's there to understand?"

Marcel, though only twenty-seven, looked to be in his mid-forties, ghostly pale and thin, with premature wrinkles and sallow complexion. A cherubic beauty in adolescence who embraced the marks of old age too soon, marks left by cigarettes, cocktails, and precociousness.

"My parents," began Marcel, extra slow and deliberate, his rheumy eyes encased within dark bags, speaking to me as if I were a moron and maybe I was, "ignorant and destitute, by voting for Le Pen, that is, voting, again, against their own interests, ended up shooting only themselves, as 'in the foot,' as you say, or 'cutting off their noses to spite their faces.'"

"I get it now," I said.

"Of course, you get it, Julian," said Kevin, putting a warm hand on my leg. "You're currently living it."

"Well." I sat up and smiled through gritted teeth. "My circumstances are different from Marcel's."

"Only as far as countries go," said Ed. "You're both poor boys from proletariat families who have made yourselves into erudite writers and have written books about those families and now those families hate you both. Quite similar."

I had never thought of my family as "proletariat" or myself as "erudite," for that matter, but Edward was the grand master of observation and concise assessment, so I couldn't argue his usage of terms.

"Julian," began Marcel, "How did you wrong your family? By telling the truth?"

"I guess there is such a thing as too much truth," I said, finishing my glass of cabernet, which Kevin refilled immediately and with urgency.

"Nonsense," said Marcel. "There could never be too much truth. We should all say the truth again and again, over and over, until we ache from knowing it."

"That's much too ascetic a way to live," said Fanny. "We're not monks. We don't need to be so spartan about it. There should be some mystery, some romance, some tall tale telling, even."

"'Tall tale telling,' Fanny?" quipped Kevin with a chuckle.

"Yeah, tall tale telling, what's wrong with that, Kevin? Let the fabulists entertain us. Why not?"

Kevin giggled into his bourbon and burped.

"Well," began Edward, "I think, like a good memoir or novel, life should be a mix of fact and fiction, and let the lines blur, I say."

"By keeping it unclear, though," said Marcel stretching his lanky body and yawning, "that is where the troubles start!"

Kevin planned the dinner early so that Ed and Fanny could make the 8:00 PM showing of *Marietta and Elena*, a Castilian lesbian melodrama set in 1930s Seville with Franco's genocide in the background, at the theater around the corner. Though we'd been invited to join them, Kevin insisted that Marcel and I go with him to The Starfish. We all walked Ed and Fanny to the theater before heading to the bar. New York could be impatient with slow-moving elders, despite their intellectual prowess and professional victories.

In under an hour, we were all drunk in the backroom of the bar. From curated buckets of galvanized steel plumed bouquets of kitschy fake flowers encased under oversized glass cloches. Kevin joked about how the owner was trying to spruce up the place and appeal to a higher pedigree of customer, those who'd spend premiums on multiple bottles of prohibitive French wine and top shelf liquor. He laughed at these efforts.

"We're all here to get shitfaced fast and fuck hard," said Kevin, slurring and blushing. "And then come back tomorrow night and do it again. I mean, 'know your clientele,' am I right?"

Marcel and I were not as incoherent as Kevin, though in our boozy fog we laughed and agreed. Soon we were joined by an excitable young man, maybe twenty or younger, named Milo Riddle from Tampa, Florida, he'd said. The intrusive boy had bloodshot eyes, a red nose, and spoke with a nervy cadence. I was sure he'd been doing lines of coke before appearing.

"You're Marcel Laurent! And you're Kevin Tracy, of course! Married to the illustrious Edward Gray!"

"You've identified us!" Kevin faux-gasped, touching my stomach. "Kill him!"

"It would be my honor!" shouted Milo in a howl that was endearing in its awkwardness.

"Milo," said Kevin, in a slow, rumbling drawl intimating irritation. "We've met. Many times already. You do this every Thursday night. Do you just keep forgetting or is it shtick?"

Milo, who'd apparently known Kevin well, disregarded the insult and continued his blue streak, rambling about his rich and probably queer uncle Ken back in Tallahassee, who'd spoiled him on first editions of old books. Milo had whipped out his smart phone and began sharing photos of his library back in Tampa.

"Here are Ed's first editions, a whole shelf, you know, back home in swampland."

Milo showed Kevin a montage of Ed's books, their shopworn spines standing in formation like weary but preserved soldiers, something I'd find out later he'd done every Thursday night.

"They're all here," said Milo, breathless, sweaty. "*A Young Man's Private Tale*, *The Gorgeous Attic is Lonely*, and *The Goodbye Sonata*. And the memoir, *My Incarnations*. All here!"

Kevin yawned and nodded, both scowling and smirking at the same time.

"I even have some of your cohorts' first runs. I mean Fanny's, Suliman's, Colin's, Fen's. The whole coterie! And now even yours, Marcel's!"

Milo was as knowledgeable about contemporary writers as he was grateful to suddenly be in their company.

"Why don't you sit, Milo," said Marcel, calm, if not curt.

Milo sat but gesticulated with greater ardor when he spoke. He swung his arms carelessly when acting out scenarios involving the family he'd abandoned in the swamps, "left to the palmettos," as he'd put it. On several occasions he'd inadvertently hit the barback as he attempted to clear our table, snarling, and muttering under his breath each time. "Watch it, twat!"

"But what I really want to share with you all is the plot of my new novel," Milo continued, hopped up on our attention and oblivious to the annoyance of the stranger he'd struck, "and who knows, maybe I could get some blurbs out of you all sometime! No pressure of anything!"

Milo began his pitch about his novel called *Group Shows*, a satire about the art world. He acknowledged that we've had so many of those in the past few years. Low hanging fruit. But this one promised to be absurdist and extreme, like maybe Jonathan Swift. It's about this thing he called "gunshot chic." Wealthy socialites pay to have themselves shot as a status symbol. It's like an underground cottage industry. Those who die, and of course, some of them accidentally do, are exhibited in a museum like a piece of art. "The beauty of carnage," he called it.

"Why would anyone want to be shot?" asked Marcel, creepy in his sedate tone.

"Christopher Lee Burden did it in 1971! It has like a street glamor to it. To be a victim and survive. To be part of the violent zeitgeist and live to talk about it or not, to be killed, and have your murdered body be on display for visitors to gawk at, like a piece of art, something made by the current cultural moment, the contemporary cruelty. The indifference and the rage and …"

Milo's eyes glazed over, and he stared at the disco ball in the distance and trailed off. We all waited for him to return, but Kevin grew bored and sighed loudly enough to break Milo of his spell. When he began talking again, he did so with increased volatility and swung his hands feverishly as he returned to the subject of his family.

"My family is so fucked up! Did I mention?"

"They all are, kiddo," said Kevin. "We're gay. Even the good ones are fucked up when you're gay."

"Mine, especially," said Milo, as he raised his hands and beat the air, apparently emulating his father. "My dad used to slap the shit out of my mom, and my grandmother, my dad's mom, who lived with us, said to mom, get this, 'there are two sides to every story, Pam,' and Pam is my mom, right? My grandma was old as shit, like ninety, and she used to read this manual about how to be a proper housewife and make your husband happy, like,

[178]

how to please your man, type shit, okay? There were actual manuals for that nonsense back in the 50s and stuff. And because my mom didn't cook or clean or do laundry, I mean she wasn't lazy or anything, but she was an artist and she used to paint really well, my grandma thought it was okay for my dad to get pissed and break plates and punch walls and slap her when she got out of line, because, you know, she 'failed him as a wife'. She didn't keep a home for him. I just couldn't take that shit anymore and so I left. And that was it."

As Milo ended his sentence, on the word "it," he'd swung his arms again, wilder than the other times, and smacked the glass cloche with the back of his clumsy hand, sending it to the floor, smashing into a thousand sharp pieces. Marcel closed his eyes and sighed with a precious fatigue. Kevin laughed with a new nastiness. I leapt to my feet to grab a rag from the bar and paper towels from the bathroom. When I returned, Milo was crying, on his knees, trying to gather the shards with his shaking hands, as Kevin and Marcel watched with derision. I knelt beside him and helped clean up the mess before the barback could see and have us ejected.

"It's okay," I said. "Accidents happen."

"Well, this is boring," said Kevin, who left us for the bar.

As we swept up and discarded the shards of the cloche, Milo continued to prattle on about his family and Floridian politics and book bans and trans youth and gun control, but then he stopped and began to stare again, his eyes glazing over and fixing on nothing. Maybe the disco ball. Maybe a prospective trick amid the swaying, gyrating bodies of inebriated patrons. Maybe he'd been astral projecting to another plane, an improved dimension, one without abusive families who condoned abuse, one in which he'd been elevated to a celebrated author and not just a pining sycophant.

"Okay," he said softly. "Okay. Okay."

"'Okay,' what? What's okay?"

"Uncle Ken," began Milo, cool but angry, "is my mother's younger brother, very effeminate, and I mean, more than even me, but never seen with a man, or even woman, but his feminine manner was enough for my dad to berate him and, like, just totally bar him from of our house. He bought me all those rare, old books, all those first editions, to antagonize my demented dad and to maybe fuel my emancipation."

"Oh, well, it's good you had someone there who supported—"

Before I could finish my sentence Milo turned away from me, lumbered through the crowd, and tumbled into the bathroom, pushing his way past the great density of horny, drunk, amused men embroiled in one another's rapt dramas. I returned to Marcel who lazily scrolled his iPhone.

"I love that Kevin invited us here and then ditched us for trade," he said.

I checked my palms for grains of glass, noticing remnants of the bell jar jutting from the bouquet of ersatz flowers in the galvanized steel vase.

"Tell me, Julian," said Marcel, crossing his leg, rubbing the tip of his sneaker, a beaten-up converse, against my shin. "I read your little article and wonder how much of your family's destitution is true."

I grinned and sat back, moving my leg away from his foot. "It's all true, Marcel. And there will be much more once I finish the book."

"I mean," he began, "we were so poor my mother began to see flies and roaches and rodents everywhere she went, even if they weren't really there, suddenly a Monarch was a fly, a beetle a roach, a squirrel a rat, all haunting signifiers of failure and indigence. Squalor attached itself to her as this fetid specter."

Had Marcel really been doubting my account? Was he competing with me? I see your hardship and I raise you a privation. Deprivation Olympics. The expression he held suggested envy, I told myself. It was a scowl, or a cringe. Was it meant to intimate mistrust or competition? Either way, it gave me a chill. Marcel had decided to take that moment to show me his fangs. We'd only just met a few hours earlier, but we'd known of each other's work for months and we'd heard too much about each other through Ed and Kevin for as long. He giggled and continued scrolling on his phone. I wanted to remind him that he'd achieved literary stardom in his early twenties and I only now well into my thirties. When I was his age, I was still forced to work deadening jobs in at-risk schools, mental health clinics, tutoring agencies. It was the kind of sentiment that when said aloud made one look like an out-of-touch ingrate, so I kept quiet.

A rumble broke the tension between us when one of the patrons screamed for a medic prompting a chorus of gasps and cries and trundling to and from the bathroom. Marcel stuck out his tongue and rolled his eyes. King Cunt.

"What now?" asked Marcel. "What is this shithole? Why did Kevin bring us here?"

Without looking at Marcel, I jumped up and hurried toward the bathroom, making eye contact with Kevin, who'd been kissing a burly, bearded man I'd later learn was a police officer from Staten Island named Tony who'd been separated from his wife and estranged from his two sons. Kevin looked irritated, not by Tony, but by the commotion that was apparently ruining his evening, his new attempt to make me jealous, no doubt.

I pulled, shoved, pushed, and pleaded my way toward the threshold whereupon my suspicions were confirmed. Milo's body looked thinner and smaller dead than alive as if he'd shrank as soon as he'd passed. His exuberance and pain and anger and ambition and reverence must have inflated him in life, mimicking a look of largeness, an illusion of dimension. His sweaty, pasty face had become suddenly serene, and the sallow hue was newly flesh colored, even sanguine. His deflated hull slumped atop the toilet with his tangled legs pressed against the stall door, revealing his demise as though an exhibition, not dissimilar to the characters in his story.

A drag queen performed CPR for ten minutes to no avail while we watched as if it were theater.

"What a pity," said someone from behind, but when I turned what I saw was a mass of faces, blushing or ashen, drunkenly confused or soberly indifferent, and all peering into the bathroom at the appalling spectacle.

"Inevitable, though, what with his life," said another.

"Families," mumbled Kevin, appearing behind me, his arms slung across my chest, his head on my shoulder. "Fucking families."

CHAPTER 19

It was Raul's idea to meet at the Bronx Zoo. He was strategic that way. By ensuring our get-togethers to discuss *The Touring Barbarism* were in public places we'd avoid ever being alone. I think he could detect that I'd begun to develop feelings again and wanted to prevent re-attachment. If I could give sex without emotional clinging, we'd have met for every story session at either his place or mine, but I wasn't able to do that and without having to ever say it, thankfully, he understood and made provisions.

We stood before the lion enclosure and watched as an enormous male licked his burgundy chops. The color of old, dried blood from a last kill, if it were in the wild. In containment, it was the marker of a recent feeding. It being a workday in autumn, Raul and I were among only a few visitors. Mercifully, a handful of children abounded.

"I have a fantasy of breaking in and setting them all free in New York, but not here, not in the Bronx," began Raul, making eye contact with the giant feline, "I'd bring them to SoHo or TriBeCa or the Upper East Side. Maybe Park Slope or Long Island City. Set them all loose in one of those awful neighborhoods. Just. Let. Them. Feast."

I nodded and shrugged, intent on showing him how unimpressed I was by his gruesome desire.

"Nibble on the yuppies and hipsters and frat boys and old money, right?"

The lion looked at us and chuffed. Raul snickered and walked away. I followed. I always followed because he always led.

"So, where are we in the series?" he asked.

INT. CLINT RESIDENCE — DAY

Pegasus sprawls across the sofa as Phyllis
roams the living room inspecting the keepsakes
from other countries, Jonah thumbs through
books about astronomy from Monroe's study, Paul
watches a Knicks game on the TV, and Joe naps
in the loveseat. Mary and Monroe, just returned
from a play by Tom Stoppard and dinner at their
favorite Ethiopian restaurant in Hell's Kitchen,
stand in the doorway, their lips atwitch and
their cores in convulsion. The calm set by art
and cuisine upturned by novel stenches and
sights infiltrating home.

                    MARY
          (aquiver)
     Pegasus?

                    PEGASUS
          (without reverence)
     Mom. This is Phyllis, Jonah,
     and Paul. Friends of Joe's from
     Riverside Park. They'll be staying
     with us for a while.

                    MARY
          (in an honest, unadulterated
          wheeze)
     But where? Where, Peg? Where will

they stay?

                    PEGASUS
We have the guest room that Joe is
in. We can blow up the inflatable
mattress and we also have the sofa
here. There's really plenty of
room.

                    JONAH
I'd be happy to sleep on the
kitchen floor. I don't need
anything fancy. As long as there
are no bugs or rats and it's not
too cold or hot.

                    PHYLLIS
And I don't need too much to eat.
My stomach has shrunk over the
years and I'm not at all picky.

                    PAUL
We just want to say how generous it
is of you, ma'am. It's really nice
of you to take us in like this.

                    MARY
    (again with immediate honesty in
    her wheeze)
Take you in? We've taken you in?

                              PEGASUS
          Well. I suppose I have and so by
          extension so have you.

          Monroe's cats poke at the strangers' feet,
          circle them with suspicion, tentatively nudging
          them.

Raul groaned and I knew what was on his mind because he had
mentioned it a few times already. He doubted my veracity, my accuracy
of recollection, the reliability of my memory. I also thought about letting
Pegasus see the script once written, but I wouldn't give him the opportunity
to request revisions. It would be a hollow gesture. Raul could groan all he
liked. As long as he didn't start scheming *RFN's* downfall again, I'd be fine.

We were in front of the tapirs, and I thought about *2001: A Spacey
Odyssey.* The scene during which the Australopithecus beats the creature to
death and Kubrick transitions from the tossing of its femur into a spaceship
floating in space. Unless I have conflated the scenes in the film. My memory
rejiggers events, puts them out of sequence, and occasionally combines
details from other moments.

It made me think everyone could have been right about my distortions,
but then I put the possibility out of my head and continued the episode
summary. The tapir grew surly anyway. It upturned its snorkel nose at us and
showed us its horse-mouth.

          INT. CLINT RESIDENCE — LIVING ROOM — EVENING

          Hours later. Paul, Phyllis, and Jonah loiter
          about. Jonah plays with the cats. Pegasus and Joe
          hang out. Mary and Monroe scrutinize everyone.

PAUL
(scratching the head of
the black one with his index
fingernail)
Nice cats.

MARY
Not mine. Monroe's.

JOE
Or maybe they're nobody's? Maybe
they are their own people.

Monroe groans and Mary rolls her eyes. Inside,
convulsions ripple through their nervous systems.
Being corrected for misspoken immoralities
rankle them.

MARY
Maybe ownership is what some people
need. Even animals.

JOE
Spoken like a true anthropologist.

Mary's face folds inward, a kind of crinkle, as
if it has been struck.

JONAH
(hoisting the astronomy book in
the air)

```
          The moon is actually an
          astrological body or a satellite.
          It can't really be classified as a
          true moon, anymore. This book is
          woefully outdated.
```

"They sound somewhat similar," said Raul. "Just positing different points."

"That's the idea. It's a formalistic choice."

```
     Monroe nods with a reactionary sneer.
```

```
                    PHYLLIS
               (fingering a terra cotta bowl
                from Ecuador)
          All these foreign artifacts. It
          must feel so empowering to own
          parts of other cultures. Like
          you're collecting the world.
```

```
     Mary finds Phyllis's delivery earnest, but she's
     been conditioned to accept such statements as
     facetious and doesn't know how to respond.
```

"This is also more like a play than a traditional screenplay," said Raul.

"The Darlington Brothers are experimenters, okay? They don't want tradition."

```
                    PAUL
          Personal ecologies are what matter
```

most now. The interaction between environment and self and how our microorganisms mingle. We brought the whole city into your little home, so you'll never get sick again, what with all our personal tolerances to germs.

NOTE ON MARY'S MINDSET: It was a nightmare, then, Mary thinks. One from which she will not waken without mass murder or fleeing her spiteful, insidious child and her inept, guilty husband. She, too, has been guilty, though. It would be a public penance. She will capitalize on this punishment. She will show the critical world who she was, and of what she's been capable. Mercies for the most targeted.

"You're letting her off too easy," said Raul, now staring at Savanah elephants. "She's too self-aware."

"Yeah, but look at what she's doing with that awareness, the most cynical, disingenuous thing."

The elephants seemed perturbed by our presence, maybe they could pick up on our tension or on Raul's impatience, or my defensiveness. Their eyes were wide and maniacal. They threw their heads back in an arc and doused themselves with dirt. Suddenly their tusks were high, their jumbo ears fanned, and their tails stiffened. By the time they began to approach the fence of the enclosure, we'd gotten the message: it was our signal to leave them be, and so we did.

MONTAGE: The homeless people leave their stink

on the area rug and sofa and towels and curtains. They leave their filth in the sinks and tubs and counters and wood floors. They leave their remarks impugning how Mary and Monroe live in the air and in the hallways and in the attic and in the cellar. They leave traces of multiplying mites and righteous reprimands. They disease the house. Pegasus will furnish no remedy, no inoculation. He will allow the vector for the contamination. He will revere the contagion.

MONTAGE CONTINUED: Mary and Monroe feel themselves judged, albeit silently, by the squatters. Jonah, Phyllis, and Paul pass them in the night and make comments on some of their pricier possessions, questioning the value and its necessity. They discuss the bounty of food in the fridge and cupboards and wonder aloud how much of it often went bad. They whisper to each other about the abuses of utilities and how much it must cost every month to keep the house cool or warm or lit or secure or gas accessible and shake their heads at the excess of options on the many televisions. All the apps. All the tv shows. So many movies.

INT. CLINT RESIDENCE (STUDY) — EVENING

A week into the squatter's (permanent) stay, Joe approaches Mary and Monroe.

                    JOE

Don't mind them. They've been on
the streets for a while. They've
forgotten what creature comforts
are. How important they are to
people like you.

                    MARY
        (sitting up on the desk chair
        that newly smelled to her like
        sweaty feet or dirty ass)
People like us?

                  MONROE

People like us, who let people like
you into our home for indefinite
stays?

Joe smiles. He gets the rise for which he'd
worked for months.

                    JOE
        (flatly)
People who like their comforts.

Pegasus appears beside Joe.

                    MARY

How much longer will they need to
stay?

PEGASUS
Until they find homes and jobs, I
suppose.

MARY
(dire and cold)
Why not help facilitate that,
perhaps? Maybe as part of your
goodwill project?

Pegasus fights a smile. He relishes his mother's
cruelty because it means she cares.

Becoming cold, becoming cruel, not caring about anything, was my
Aunt Mary's way of rising above the hot, kind, caring passions of my family.
It was a way to turn American. To shake the Italian off her.

"Those suckers at *RFN* are not going to know what hit them," said Raul
out of nowhere, another of his infamous admissions. And to his comment
I nodded as I always had, never challenging, never questioning, but always
terrified of the next words out of his mouth, his actual plan and God help
me, the inevitable execution of it.

As we headed for the exit, the zebras, giraffes, monkeys, pangolins,
aardvarks, gorillas, shoebills, toucans, reptiles, and serpents seemed to join
the elephants, lemurs, lions, and tapirs in their displeasure with our visit.
Maybe it was just feeding time or the witching hour, but their chorus felt
like a dismissal.

Excerpt of
My Mighty Meekness,
as published in
The New Yorker

Doug was a plumber in the US-Local 1 union, but like my father, his respectable blue collar day job was only a cover for his real profession, a more reliably lucrative racket. In Doug's case, the covert swindle was prostitution. Sophia had first inspired him and then guided him, knowing the intricacies of the trade and competition intimately. Doug was a natural pimp. His sex workers (he called them "his girls") respected him, and his johns (he called them "his boys") feared him. It helped that they'd known of his volatile reputation through the intimate New York wise guy grapevine.

Doug and Sophia took me to the South Street Seaport one Sunday during an early aughts summer. I must have been about 18 and Arnold was only seven. My sister had gotten into a verbal altercation with the server at a Mexican restaurant in the food court. They'd exchanged accusations over the order. I don't remember the minutiae of the debate, but it escalated when the server called my sister a bitch, and she'd responded by tossing a fajita at him. Doug and Arnold were holding a table for us so were not there to witness the incident. I had stood by, idle as can be, and did or said nothing as was my passive way, but Doug, when he'd heard about what occurred five minutes later after Sophia told him, became an unstoppable menace. He first denigrated my loyalty and manhood, claiming I should have defended Sophia. He then screamed at the server and his half dozen fellow workers, insinuating decapitation and dismemberment. The manager and security were called, and we were escorted off the premises.

On the drive home, Sophia supported and even fueled Doug's mean rant centered on how my meekness was pathetic and dangerous, claiming I was much too frightened and weak to be a true man or worthy of a place in our tough, noble family. In the moment I could not see how my defense of Sophia, who had been so abrasive with the server, could have helped the situation. I imagined it would have only inflamed it, but assuming any deferential posture or standing down during combat to someone like Doug meant giving in and therefore cowardice.

CHAPTER 20

Doug reminded me that Queens had produced many infamous straight white men. Donald Trump had been from Jamaica Estates. Harvey Weinstein hailed from Flushing. Bernie Madoff grew up in Far Rockaway. Ron Jeremy was a Bayside resident. Lucky Luciano is buried in St. John's Cemetery in Middle Village. Then there were the untold number of anonymous bigots who'd abused animals, their wives, girlfriends, and children. The neighborhood toughs. Doug grew up in Forest Hills and claimed to have been friends with Joey and Dee Dee Ramone. He'd regale me with his criminal adolescent exploits every time I saw him.

"Did I ever tell you about that time Joey, Dee Dee, and me broke into the abandoned tenement across the street from this yuppie apartment complex and watched people fuck? We used to climb out on the fire escape and cheer the guys on and most of them saw and heard us through the windows and smiled as we watched, like they was trying to impress us by how hard and how long they could fuck. We were kids. It wasn't gay or anything."

Doug picked me up at my apartment an hour earlier and had been driving around aimlessly since, from Jackson Heights to Corona to Elmhurst to Sunnyside to Astoria and back again, prattling on about the misadventures of his recalcitrant youth.

"God, these hoods were real shitholes when I was kid," he began. "I'd used to fuck with the Colombian and Dominican girls around here. Your brother, too. Hell, he eventually even married one, right? And we'd get into beefs with their brothers and cousins and me and the guys would come down here and crack a few skulls every once in a while, you know, just to remind these wetbacks who was boss."

I wish I had the guts to reprimand his racist language, but I was far too frightened of him, and I hated myself because of it. "Where are we going, Doug?"

"Just cruising, kid."

Doug was pushing fifty so I, at thirty-five was still a "kid," I suppose.

"Your dad and sister tell me you're writing a TV show about your holier-than-thou aunt and uncle and wack-o cousin."

He only partially paid attention to the road. He mostly looked at me when he spoke and, on several occasions, he came close to clipping pedestrians, many of whom threatened with clenched fists and profanities in other tongues.

"Yeah, that's really happening."

"You got yourself all the way up there, didn't you?"

All the way up there!

I wanted to groan out loud but didn't have the energy to deal with Doug's reaction to such a gesture. He was dementedly sensitive. If someone were to hurt his feelings, he'd both cry and pummel the offender toothless. He was that kind of roughneck. The type that both wept and killed. We once saw a maudlin movie about Irish immigrants when I was in my twenties in Kew Gardens and he sobbed audibly through the whole thing, turned to me when it was over with red, puffy eyes, and said, "You and me, we're through," meaning that I only brought him to movies that revealed his vulnerabilities. When he saw I had dry eyes he said, "I thought gay guys were weak but now I see you're fucking strong." On the way home from the theater a man stepped in front of his car at a stoplight as it turned green and Doug beeped at him, prompting the guy to flip him off. Doug sprang from his car and beat the man's face against his bumper, leaving him a bloody mess. He was that kind of roughneck.

"So, I'm a pimp who ran whores on Farrington, huh?"

Farrington was a street along the Whitestone Expressway, behind a Blockbuster Video, and across the highway from *The New York Times* printing plant. During my adolescent years Farrington was rife with tales of sexually transmitted infections, stabbings, rapes, castrations, and even partial cannibalism run rampant. Many of the sex workers were trans women and many of the johns knew, which is why they frequented the spot, but for those who were ignorant to the culture, violence often ensued, and the sex workers often came out on top.

"Those fugly he-she bitches with AIDS and shit? That's how I made my living to support your sister and your nephew, you little twat? Go ahead and tell me to my face that's how I supported them!"

His transphobia was grotesque, but my tongue was tied as I was sure he was going to punch me, and I braced myself for the blow. Doug hit hard. I once accidentally kneed him in the balls when we were wrestling when I was just a teenager and he punched me so hard in the small of my back it still hurts almost twenty years later. I gripped the door handle, and I prepared to bolt from his Range Rover, which was fastidious in its spotlessness, but I stopped myself from running. I waited for the punch that never came, and I was disappointed. Maybe a big part of me wanted something more severe than my sister or brother had doled out, something more tangible than my father's threats, something more direct than my mother's passive aggression, something more intimate than Luz's two-thousand-mile glare.

"So, Sophia said you're into birds now."

Doug's entire personality changed, and he was suddenly boyish, eager to discuss his latest passion with me.

"Yo, Julian, I have an African Grey Congo named Tippi, like from the old movie with the birds, and two macaws, a green wing named Hitch, after the filmmaker of that movie about the birds, and a blue and yellow named Marion, named after the character from that movie about the birds directed by Hitch. Sophia busts my balls over them, but I can tell she loves them. I mean, yeah, they're messy and needy and loud, but so is she! I'm also building a pigeon coop in my yard. Arnie and me built it ourselves out of lumber and wire mesh. I have the quails in the basement for the eggs. They're dirty and they sit in their own shit. Their nails get infected and break off after a while because of, you know … they sit in their own shit all day. We watched that old horror movie about the birds by that guy Hitch, and I'm not shitting you, but the fucking male macaw laughed every time the stupid humans were attacked! It's a regular aviary over at our place now. You should come by and see them."

The thought was outlandish. It would be akin to a free bird willingly stepping into a cage.

Doug then went into how he might even buy a bird store not far from where they live. The owner apparently wants to move to Florida to breed birds exclusively and Doug would take over. The current owner claims to have established vendors and clients down there, so maybe it's not a bad idea. Doug said he'd keep his day job and hire a manager, and then joked about offering me the job. Doug's version of a midlife crisis was cute in its way, but I'd sooner leap off the George Washington Bridge before becoming a part of it.

"I have a job," I said.

"Yeah, as an assassin of family members! I hear you're writing a whole fucking book about us now?"

This time I did groan, and he heard me. He smacked me across the side of my head with the back of his hand, catching my ear. I heard ringing. I somehow felt calmer.

"Don't be disrespectful," he said, his fat, rosy cheeks a hot purple.

"Look, I didn't *assassinate* anyone. None of you are public figures so none of you have characters to assassinate."

"Dipshit. Check this out, we are on social media. We have friends, neighbors. We live our lives. It don't matter if we're not famous, like your faggot friends in the city."

Aside from Doug's casual homophobia and general bigotry, he also suffered from a major misperception of the people I hang out with. Could Doug wrap his head around the fact that they're working class, too. They pay rents and mortgages and feed themselves and their families. They just made choices to cure cancer rather than build houses. They made choices to write novels and make films rather than sell smart phones or do people's taxes or fix bad plumbing. They made choices to make art and get paid for it rather than working on cars or laying floors or picking up trash. Doug was not alone in his rigid dichotomies. Everyone in my family was saddled with them. Either you were intellectual, and the world opened to you, or you were streetwise, hustling to get by. There was no room in their worlds for one person inhabiting both realms.

"You put on these airs, and you so badly want to be accepted by these 'important people' who shit and fart and piss and put on their pants one leg at a time like every other poor sucker and they get old and they die and there is nothing special about them and they're no better than nobody else and you just suck their dicks like they're God or something."

As he spoke, Doug tightened his grip around the wheel and accelerated, nearly hitting a middle-aged Latin couple as they staggered out of his path.

"I don't worship anyone, Doug." I looked back at the shaken couple. They held each other and threw their hands in the air as they hurled expletives at us, understandably.

Doug's cell vibrated, and he looked at it, which terrified me as he was still speeding. He could have easily killed someone. In fact, I am certain that he had. In my book I decided I would detail his many violent crimes, all the nightclub assaults with broken beer bottles, the basketball scrape wherein he brutalized his opponents with crowbars, the locker room beat downs with dumbbells. Everyone in my family was prone to savagery, but Doug was the worst, the most homicidal.

"Motherfucker!" Doug punched his dashboard, and his rosy cheeks again became a menacing purple.

"You're coming with me. I gotta go to Astoria to see a guy."

Fuck. I knew what this meant. His rage at the text coupled with his language only meant one thing. We were going to "see a guy" about his involvement with Doug's gambling and racketeering businesses, which meant I was about to be made a witness to something I'd only ever heard about during my adolescence but somehow managed to dodge being directly implicated in my whole life.

He continued to berate my ethics and integrity for the duration of the ten-minute drive from Elmhurst to Astoria in a diatribe that was downright Mamet.

"You should realize by now that all people are full of shit and they're selfish and they're mean and they lie and they'd fuck over their own grandmothers if it meant getting a leg up on the other guy and they'd leave you rotting in the street and steal the gold from your teeth and the cash out of your wallet and your fucking wedding band to hawk it for a little mullah and I've seen best friends fuck each other's girls and kids crack each other over the head with wooden blocks for the last piece of candy. That's what people are. They're fucking mongrels. I don't care if you talk fancy and have ten degrees and all the money in the world and all the rewards you can stuff up your ass and all the fans who want to lick your asshole. You're as much a rat as the loser at the bar drinking away his kid's college fund or the degenerate gambler selling his wife's jewelry to pay off his debt or the pathetic bastard who has to scrub toilets for a living."

I let him rave at me because I'd hoped that by blowing off some steam he'd come at "the guy" we were about to visit with a little less fury.

We arrived at a two-family attached house, all yellow brick with over-sized, gaudy Greco-Roman statuary, on a quiet, tree-lined street near Astoria Park.

"I can wait here," I said.

"Nah, you should see this."

Doug pulled from the backseat a small, metallic, rusted birdcage.

"What's that for?" I asked.

"Birds," he answered.

I felt lightheaded at the prospect of what might happen inside. Not to me, but to the host of our visit.

The man who answered the door was young, maybe in his early twenties. He was tall and thin with disproportionately muscular arms. He was the kind of guy you'd see at the gym who only did curls and skull crushers and ignored the rest of his body. A young, straight man proclivity. He also wore a tight black "Megadeath" t-shirt and denim shorts. His hair was thick, long, and black. He had Greek features.

"Fuck, Dougie," said the young man, glancing at the birdcage in Doug's hand.

"Iannos," said Doug. "You alone?"

Iannos nodded yes. Even from the threshold I could tell that the apartment smelled like weed and saw that the sink was full of several empty beer bottles.

"Oh good," said Doug, swinging the metallic birdcage made for finches or sparrows into the Greek's face.

Ioannos made a strange sound, halfway between a gasp and gurgle, as he staggered back and off his feet. Doug walked inside. I stood still.

"Close the door, Julian."

I followed him in and obliged because shock does that to you. It compels you to follow orders, even if they're outrageous.

Ioannos turned to us from the floor like a child caught by a teacher red-handed.

"What did I say you'd have to do if you were late with payment?"

"Come on, man," Ioannos managed through a mouth full of blood and maybe a few teeth. "I said you'd have it this weekend. It's just a few days, Doug."

"Late is late. A few days or a few years, there's no difference. C'mon, you know."

"I thought you were joking about that."

"I never joke about money, malaka. Little faggot. No offense, Julian."

I instinctively nodded, caring nothing at all about political correctness or manners as I was too focused on not wetting myself.

Ioannos tried to stand but Doug clocked him again with the birdcage, this time against the side of his head, sending him into the stove, where he whimpered and curled into a ball. Doug handed me the birdcage and pulled off Ioannos's socks, then pants, then shirt, and finally his underwear. The young Greek man had a good body, but it had been tellingly reduced by drugs.

Doug left. I followed close behind, gripping the dented birdcage and making sure not to look at the bloody, sobbing, naked man, now *our* victim.

I kept quiet until we got to the car where I continued to hug Doug's weapon like a life preserver. "Doug, what the fuck?"

Doug drove slowly as though what'd he just done wasn't a crime, as if we'd had all the time in the world, out for a Sunday morning joyride. He turned to me with a face that I'd not seen since I was a kid, a time when he and my sister had been fighting in the middle of the night over his alcoholism and womanizing. I asked what was wrong, emerging from my nephew's bedroom, where I'd been sleeping on the floor, and he looked at me with that same face, purple with broken veins and bunched squirrel cheeks and yellow teeth and red eyes and a sideways, bulbous nose and he said, "This doesn't concern you."

Up until the grisly encounter with Ioannis, I had been waiting for Doug to resurrect the awful memory of the South Street Seaport ordeal, but he did not. Perhaps he had forgotten or maybe he was tired to talking about it. I hate conflict, still to this day, and go out of my way to avoid it. I suppose you could call me a pacifist. An eye for an eye leaves the whole world blind, and all other idioms to that effect apply. And this event would surely be featured in my book, another in a long string of arrogant horrors exacted by Doug in all his entitled rage, so straight and so white.

We drove for a few minutes before he answered me.

"Thought you'd enjoy that, as a writer and all. Something to put in your book!"

CHAPTER 21

Raul surprised me by showing up at my door unannounced. Something archaic in this age of cell phones. At first, I thought it might be my father again dropping by to harass me. Raul carried a canvas shopping bag heavy with produce and meat and wore his clingiest attire, a form-fitting beige t-shirt and snug gray jeans. Brown and mustard sneakers. A silver necklace tight around his thick neck. He aroused long-dormant sensations.

"Did you hear that Saudi Arabia is creating an indoor city only 660 feet wide and 110 miles long called The Line? The future of all cities, they say. I just read about it on the way over."

Raul pushed me against the wall of the foyer and kissed my neck and then my mouth, his restless tongue poking my uvula. He pulled away, smirking, and walked inside.

"In the future no one will live outside," I said, closing the door.

"We'll directly inhale each other's carbon dioxide, killing ourselves, but sparing the planet our pollution."

"I like it," I said, still tasting his tongue.

"I knew you would."

Raul put up a pot of coffee. He always inhabited my space as if it were his own. He had a gift for making himself at home wherever he was no matter how alien or improper. In fact, he'd made himself so comfortable that he immediately removed his shoes, socks, and pants. His wore Batman briefs.

"Did we have something planned today that I missed?" I felt foolish asking but his appearance had really thrown me.

"I'm going to cook us dinner. Shakshuka! Remember I'd make it for dinner all the time?"

I had only just started adapting the next chapter about Pegasus's professor, Dr. Brian Alessandro, and wasn't completely ready to start discussing it, but Shakshuka was the best thing Raul had ever made for me, and I wasn't about to look his gift horse in the mouth.

Raul paused, holding a pound of lamb. He waited for the coffee to finish brewing and began pulling the groceries from the bag. Raul in his underwear and bare feet was stork-like, big feet with thin ankles connecting to legs that swelled in all the right places. When he turned back to smile at me, I was reminded of a Disney character, a prince, maybe.

My aunt, uncle, and cousin are only peripheral characters in my article and inevitable book, but the Darlington Brothers asked me to focus on them pretty much exclusively for the series. Why? Maybe because their story is the most gothic in its awful ghoulishness. It has all the unbelievably terrible bullshit that attends being alive. Poverty. Exploitation. War. Malice. Indifference. Even if it lacks disease and obsolescence, it represents those horrors in the failure of family and society and humanity itself. It's to pull the grief out of hidden places for a collective catharsis. It's a public service.

The ingredients that Raul pulled from the canvas grocery bag seemed interminable. Bell peppers, fresh cilantro, red onions, tofu, garlic, tomatoes, ground cinnamon, ground cloves, ground turmeric, ground cumin, paprika, eggs, and, of course, lamb. Raul stir fried without scientific precision. When I asked him how long we should let the produce and herbs cook before tossing in the tofu, eggs, and meat, he said, "A while." For him, cooking, like sex and fighting, was intuitive

INT. CLINT HOUSEHOLD — DAY

Dr. Alessandro is an average height, somewhat handsome from certain angles, and awkward, clearly struggling with the discomfort of his own skin. He dresses plainly so as not to call attention to himself.

                    MARY
     How long have you been living in
     the shelter, Brian?

                DR. ALESSANDRO
          (with a soft voice)
     The entire semester, ma'am.

                   MONROE
          (behind Mary fixing himself a
          marguerita)
     Even with a doctorate from Yale?

                DR. ALESSANDRO
     Even with a doctorate from Yale,
     sir.

                   MONROE
     Columbia must pay well, though?
     Mary does okay.

                DR. ALESSANDRO
     Not for adjuncts. Mary is tenured.

Mary and Monroe exchange suspicious glances.

                   PEGASUS
          (sitting beside Dr. Alessandro)
     It will only be for a few weeks,

```
              mom.  Until Dr. Alessandro can
              contract a few more adjunct
              appointments.


                     DR. ALESSANDRO
              I may just bite the bullet and take
              a staff position at a charter in
              Brooklyn.


                     PEGASUS
              You're too brilliant to leave the
              university, Dr. A.


         Joe, Phyllis, Jonah, and Paul sit together,
         squeeze onto a love seat, recently showered with
         fresh clothing, smiling with folded hands like
         Stepford children. Interesting, Mary has thought
         on many recent occasions, how quickly they all
         adapted.  NOTE: Maybe convey via voiceover?
```

Raul cooked the lamb, the hot oil bouncing off his chest and face. I'd begun picking at the pile of excess tomatoes and onions. I thought about telling him about the incident the other day with Doug but decide against it. Why give him more fodder. He already hated my family enough.

He once told me my family was sick. Sick beyond the typical Caucasian middle-class dysfunction that bores us in movies. It was next level, he'd told me. He implored me not to feel bad about the memoir, as they deserved my ridicule. They pull their shit with impunity, he'd said. He was right. My family weren't evil, not inherently, but their behavior was largely reprehensible, and they'd implicated me in too much of it for too long. The article was a receipt, then, and the book would allow no refunds.

                    MONROE
          (sitting beside Mary, sipping
          his cocktail)
     So, Dr. Alessandro.

                DR. ALESSANDRO
     Please call me Brian.

                    MONROE
     So, Brian, did you assign this
     goodwill project to our son, to
     your class, that is, because of
     your current situation?

                DR. ALESSANDRO
     Your son is a generous spirit, sir.

Pegasus holds Joe's hand. It is a new frontier
for the boys and an unexplored realm for Mary and
Monroe. Dr. Alessandro smiles at the gesture. Mary
thinks the whole interaction feels ritualistic
and the mood of the scene reads like a cult with
Dr. Alessandro as their perverted, charismatic
leader. <u>NOTE:</u> <u>All this should be communicated</u>
<u>either through the expressions by the actress</u>
<u>who will play Mary or with voice over.</u>

The story had begun to feel like the saga of a cult, and I did take liberties
with the telling. It was not my memoir, so it didn't have to be entirely true,
but to what end, I wondered. It would be changing the focus. We're telling
a story about a well-intentioned young man who punishes his parents for

their bad behavior and unethical jobs. Making Dr. Alessandro a cult leader diverts from that. Maybe it enhances it. It shows that there is organization and intention, that Pegasus's censure is part of a larger underworld system that is working to catch the frauds and destroyers. Raul hadn't said anything about the detour, which meant he probably approved.

We began eating. The shakshuka was spicy and heavy, but flavorful. It bloated me because I ate too much too fast. Raul was more careful, disciplined. He practiced portion control and calorie restriction. As a fighter and a self-adoring aesthete, he'd left himself no other choice.

Raul kept touching my bare foot with his own. The cool, rough, soft flesh of feet on feet aroused. I felt a decade younger each time he made contact. He snarled boyishly every time he bit into the lamb as if he were promising a caveman romp after the meal. Either way, it was all terribly electrifying—his bare legs, the Batman underwear, the delectable meal, the discussion.

With *My Mighty Meekness* and now *The Touring Barbarism* I began to think I was being hoisted by my own petard, or undone by my own doing, or blown to bits by my own bomb. I'd never find an idiom adequate to match Shakespeare's, but the feeling of unintentional self-harm had never been greater. Raul washed the dishes even though he'd cooked, and I felt obligated to thank him in many untoward ways.

MONTAGE: Dr. Alessandro delivers his excoriations sweetly, and almost undetectably. On the two days a week when he was not on campus, he'd helps Mary with research, offers himself as a sounding board, weeds in the garden with her, sometimes mows the lawn, sometimes rakes the leaves, sometimes cooks dinners, and often offers to clean or do the laundry, but he also let little observations and suggestions slip as if unintentionally.

INT. LIVING ROOM — MORNING

Dr. Alessandro and Mary sort through documents in the living room.

> DR. ALESSANDRO
> (holding up her latest article about a nearly extinct tribe in Brazil's Amazon)
> Mary, the way you word these last few paragraphs … well, they feel a lot like virtue-signaling.

> MARY
> I don't do that. I know what that is, but I don't do it.

> DR. ALESSANDRO
> It's something I've come across in a lot of your past work, and I know Columbia has a tendency to encourage that sort of thing, but these young kids, these generation Z students, they'll nail you on it, believe you me.

EXT. VEGETABLE GARDEN -- DAY

Dr. Alessandro and Mary weed in the garden.

                    DR. ALESSANDRO
          (examining the weeds he'd just
          plucked)
     I can smell the pesticide here. You
     know, it's carcinogenic, of course.
     You should consider your family's
     health and try a natural remedy.

                         MARY
          (gloved and knee deep in a mound
          of wet soil)
     The gardener told me it was safe.

                    DR. ALESSANDRO
     For example, citronella grass
     repels mosquitos and petunias keep
     away aphids and beetles and squash
     bugs. There are also marigolds,
     which scare off nematodes.

INT. KITCHEN -- EVENING

Dr. Alessandro and Mary cook.

                    DR. ALESSANDRO
     You should consider switching to
     extra virgin olive oil instead of
     vegetable oil and paprika, cumin,
     and turmeric instead of salt. It's
     all much healthier. Monroe is not a
     kid anymore. And neither are you,

right?

                    MARY
          (ardently deboning a chicken)
     I am careful with their diets!

                 DR. ALESSANDRO
     Is that poultry even organic,
     though?

Mary looks at the fowl and purses her lips as
she continues to work on its carcass.

Raul offered ideas as we wiped the grease, herbs, and sauce off the stove,
floor, and counter. He was a carless chef and shakshuka was a messy dish. He
suggested Dr. Alessandro's course of interrogation from here on out.

NOTE: Dr. Alessandro wears his psychologist's
cap whenever it serves him, which when with
Mary or Monroe is always.

INT. DINING ROOM — DAY

Dr. Alessandro and Monroe work quietly at the
table.

                 DR. ALESSANDRO
     You know, Monroe, the bombs Saudi
     Arabia and United Arab Emirates
     have dropped in Yemen were made in
     Tucson by Raytheon?

                    [211]

                    MONROE
I do know that, but you should
realize two things. One, Yemen is
in the middle of a civil war and
two, we are only contracted to
make and ship the item. Like gun
manufacturers, we don't use the
guns on victims. We entrust states
to do the right thing when selling
them to customers.

                 DR. ALESSANDRO
With all due respect, that is a
specious defense, sir. If a maniac
buys a gun you made and uses it to
kill three dozen children, you find
yourself in no way complicit with
that mass murder? I mean, you are
providing the means of major harm.

Monroe's unnatural muscles tense as do the furs
of the cats that surrounded him.

                    MONROE
As cold as it sounds, no.

                 DR. ALESSANDRO
It doesn't trouble you,
though, to commit your life to
the proliferation of so much

                    [212]

destruction?

Monroe's veins, full of synthetic enablers
and capillary expanders, rise far above the
muscles, threatening a snap or a burst. His jaw
clenches and the cats hiss before scattering.
Dr. Alessandro finds himself stirred by the
prospect of a physical confrontation with the
aging behemoth.

                    MONROE
        I am a forward-thinking person,
        Doctor Brian, and I have no room
        in my life for moral ambiguities
        when there are real forces in the
        world that would oppress people in
        real ways or bring down corporate
        buildings full of innocent citizens
        just trying to provide for their
        families. My line of thinking is
        cool in its logic and humane in the
        big picture salvation our business
        and our labors provide.

As Raul recounted the scene that had been living in his head, he crouched
before me and scrubbed a stain of grease on the decrepit tiles between us. I
caught a whiff of his endogenous fragrance and something automatic inside
me became unclean.

Raul caught me staring at the pulsations of his neck, every heartbeat a
stringlike twitch up to his jaw. I gasped, smiled, and shrugged, returning to
the story.

                    DR. ALESSANDRO
You've traveled to Tucson twice
in the past month alone since
I've been here. Do you personally
oversee the manufacturing of these
things, Monroe?

                    MONROE
Of course, I do, as a point of
pride. Quality assurance is central
to my role in this company.

                    DR. ALESSANDRO
What are your thoughts about
Raytheon's production of the Joint
Standoff Weapon, which they say
is used as a delivery vehicle for
cluster bombs and kills thousands
of civilians every year around the
world.

                    MONROE
My thoughts are this, *Doctor*.
Raytheon employs one hundred and
seventy-four thousand people! And
they all support families. Feed
families. Raise children. And
defend this country against those
intent on hurting us for our way of
life.

Dr. Alessandro frowned, though it looked like he might cry or scream.

> DR. ALESSANDRO
> And all in the name of freedom and profiteering, right?

Monroe catches himself, exhales gruffly, and wipes his nose. He grabs a cat, the tuxedo one, and pets her forcefully, kissing her head to the point of annoyance. He exits the living room, leaving Brian alone, freeing the tuxedo, and when he gets to the —

INT. BASEMENT — DAY

— punches the hell out the heavy bag, grunting and snorting and cursing throughout the throttling. Dr. Alessandro hears him and smiles at the rise he'd achieved.

Pegasus, Joe, Jonah, Phyllis, and Paul spy on the interaction and its fallout from the KITCHEN. They provide a secret audience that snicker and gently cheer Dr. Alessandro's exercise in antagonism. Everyone enjoys seeing Monroe seethe, repress, and sublimate his umbrage. Dr. Alessandro turns to his admirers and smiles in a way that suggests there is more to come.

I rinsed the sponge after wiping the suds off the sink, and Raul brushed against my butt when he moved toward the cupboard to put away the cleaned glasses.

INT. MARY'S STUDY - DUSK

Dr. Alessandro thumbs through the titles of Mary's book collection, a full-walled bookcase that expanded the entire width of her small study and then folded into an L.

                    DR. ALESSANDRO
          I could never fetishize poverty
          like you, Mary.

Mary stops jotting whatever notes she's been making at her desk and turns to Brian.

                         MARY
          Do you think I fetishize poverty?

                    DR. ALESSANDRO
          By exoticizing tribes with no money
          and only limited access to … you
          don't think you do?

                         MARY
          I study cultures in developing
          countries to better understand and
          help preserve them.

Dr. Alessandro begins surveying a new wall of

books perpendicular to the other.

                    DR. ALESSANDRO
          Against deforestation, right?

Mary returns to her notes at the desk.

                    MARY
          And demagogues.

                    DR. ALESSANDRO
          Like Brazil and their new fascist?

Mary, not turning back to her persistent visitor,
mumbles to herself.

                    DR. ALESSANDRO
          Of all the books you have here not
          one explores the very pervasive
          post-structural critiques of
          colonialism.

                    MARY
          I don't like post-colonial theory.
          Foucault was a con artist who
          ripped off Erving Goffman. Derrida,
          Butler, Guattari. They were all
          opportunists and careerists seeking
          to carve out departments in
          nonsense for themselves. Complete
          frauds.

DR. ALESSANDRO
Some say anthropology is the new
colonialism.

MARY
That's absurd. As an academic,
Brian, you should know better than
to proliferate such garbage.

DR. ALESSANDRO
Well, you do move into other
people's lands and impose yourself
on them, altering—as we know
as was the case in India—their
practices and behavior and in so
doing violating their customs and
privacy.

MARY
How ignorant do you have to—

DR. ALESSANDRO
Watching the behavior of the thing
changes the behavior of the thing.

Mary tosses a textbook, heavy and hard, across
the room, missing Brian by inches, but shattering
a small clay ashtray that Mary had brought back
from Turkey ten years earlier. Brian shakes his
head, playing up his disappointment as though
it were kabuki theater. Mary covers her mouth,

surprised at her own outburst.

The people in the threshold, her son and Joe, Paul, Phyllis, and Jonah, watch in a menagerie of startled and unapproving faces. A wall of recriminating expressions.

DR. ALESSANDRO
We see it now, Mary, the propensity for cruelty and lack of mindfulness.

The wall of startled expressions opens to Dr. Alessandro as he leaves the anthropologist to her books and broken clay, to her meanness and lack of self-criticism, to her world free of examination and penalty.

"So, now that we're finally alone, I should tell you about my plans for RFN," began Raul, prompting panic, of course. Without thinking, I touched his arm, to silence him, to seduce him, and it seemed to work as he instinctively pushed his pelvis into me. I grabbed his shirt and pulled him in. His breath was hot with a flavorful musk. My fear of learning his criminal plot had been temporarily abated. He shoved me into the refrigerator and began nibbling on my ear. I licked his neck. The brine was pungent.

We made love on the kitchen floor. Afterward, I held him.

"I'm going to leak kompromat on RFN's biggest personalities," he said, plainly, and I said nothing, hoping he'd stopped talking. "Their CEO, their Senior VP, and three of their top journalists."

Raul mumbled about "inappropriate touching" and an "open marriage" and "racial and homophobic comments" and how he had enough proof of these accusations to bury them all under a mountain of dirt: emails that should have been deleted, accidental voice mail recordings, hot mics that captured guests off air. But less accidentally, he had spent the last two years secretly recording conversations and taking photos of his own. The evidence would be hard to counter, he'd assured. I was relieved to know that his agenda had not included a bomb or a semiautomatic and that the killing would be of reputations and careers instead of bodies. Still, this would certainly be the end of *his* career if anyone were to find out he was the whistleblower, if you could call what he had planned to do whistleblowing. I worried that they would sue him or even have him hurt. People in power with great resources were masters of spite and retaliation.

We eventually fell asleep and woke up in the middle of the night still on the kitchen floor. A car alarm had pierced through the apartment. I staggered to my bed and told Raul to follow me. He said he needed to use the bathroom and called me "Leonard."

I fell back to sleep before he came out, and by the time I woke up again in the morning to a different car alarm he was gone.

Vaughan apparently also reaped the gay gene, though hadn't denied it like James. Effeminate, he was bullied in his expectedly tiny-minded Mesa high school. He'd attempted suicide twice and once even cut himself deeply enough to require staples and a mandated 30-day stay in a psychiatric hospital.

During one Christmas dinner I was talking with my family about Ancient Egypt, a subject I knew well as I had written an essay about it for my World History class that was excerpted in the college paper. I'd also spent a month in the country between my junior and senior years in college. Vaughan, though only in grade school at the time, corrected me on a fact about Ramses II, something he'd learned a week earlier in his social studies class, and proceeded to inventory at least three things I'd gotten wrong, about Hatshepsut, the Valley of the Kings, and Cleopatra. As his knowledge was fresher, more recent, I guess he'd been better positioned in that moment to talk with authority on the topic, but my family, so lacking in nuance or contextualization, immediately leapt. They turned the whole of my intellectual pursuits, accomplishments, and identity into a stack of frauds, lies, and general con artistry. They'd claimed young Vaughan had been the one to expose me as a phony and that he would bear the designation of "the truly smart one" in our otherwise willfully ignorant, peasant family.

I came close to crying with frustration and outrage. Their evaluations and insults were an injustice to my efforts and victories. I steeled myself in the bathroom shortly after, muffling my cries of rage and self-loathing into a towel and then washed my face and sat emotionless and silent for the rest of dinner, feigning pleasantries to avoid further abuses. I knew then that holding on to any source of pride would be foolish. I'd always fallen back on my family's perception of me as being intelligent. That was the one thing I could be proud of and hide behind, if not anything else like athleticism or labor or leadership. I'd been stripped of even that.

CHAPTER 22

Vaughan gave no warning that he would FaceTime me. He called on a Friday afternoon when I'd been transcribing notes for the cable series. First, he texted.

Vaughan: Uncle Julian, what are you doing?

Me: Hey, Vaughan. Just writing.

Vaughan: Not a book about us, I hope. LOL!

My nephew bothered with me so infrequently, I felt bad cutting the written conversation short, but I'd needed to work on the show. I also worried he'd soon sour the dialogue with the scorn and ridicule of which his parents had both been experts. Surely, nastiness and bitterness had been genetic, if not learned.

His face flashed across my screen as my phone vibrated. It was uncharacteristic of him to call, so I urgently answered. He wore no shirt and, now twenty-one, his body looked leaner than I'd remembered it. Hairless and well defined. I tried to shut out any hint of sexualization, though it would be a cruel irony if I'd preyed on him the way my brother had preyed on me at his age, and even younger. He also had two tattoos on his chest of sharks, above each nipple, circling the areolas.

"Uncle Julian!"

"Is everything okay, Vaughan?"

"I just wanted to chat because it's been a while and after your *New Yorker* article and how much it upset my parents, I thought I should call, and we should talk."

"Right, we should."

"You basically outed me, you know."

I was a villain, after all. I did hurt people. Vaughan was amongst the most innocent, the most vulnerable. He was me in my younger years. Had I hoped to hurt my younger self or the person I'd eventually become? Did I mean to hurt James and Luz by striking down their son?

"I know, and I'm sorry I did that."

"Don't say sorry. You're not really sorry. And I'm not really upset. You helped me."

"I helped you?"

"I'm writing a memoir, too, now."

"You are?"

"Yeah, about me and this older man I'm calling Gerald."

I settled in my chair and submitted to what I knew would become a long conversation.

"Who is Gerald, Vaughan?"

"He's this history professor at Arizona State. He lives in Phoenix. He's very conservative. Like Doug Doucey-Jeff Flake-level-conservative. He even contributes to their campaigns and is close with the head of the RNC here, Kelli Ward. He has a wife and two sons. Total closet case. But he and I meet once a week in some shitty motel room near campus and ... he gets off ... on cleaning my feet."

My stomach turned as Vaughan went into detail about his sex life with this apparently sixty-two-year-old teacher and friend of the neocons of the Sonoran Desert.

"Listen, Vaughan, I don't need to—"

"Yes, you do need to listen ... because ... it's the least you can do."

I nodded and waited for further gory description.

"He likes my feet dirty, so before I meet him, I walk through the yard barefoot, and I stick my feet in the muddy puddles after the monsoons and I keep them in my socks and sneakers, so they start to reek, and he spends the whole time cleaning them with a warm washcloth and soap and when they are clean, he worships them and kisses them. My left pinkie toe has become infected because of this but he likes to treat it with Neosporin and rubbing alcohol."

This all felt vaguely like the plot of any number of Hervé Guibert autofictions, as he mentioned he'd been reading gay French literature from the 80s, and I wondered if my well-read, provocateur nephew wasn't making his lurid saga up whole cloth to shock and impress me, his older, literary uncle from sophisticated, jaded New York. Or maybe it was a penalty. Could he be so clever at such a young age to torment me with the threat of corruption? That is, the possibility that my essay had so badly molested his image that he unconsciously began acting out as I'd portrayed him. He was smart, by Arizona standards, but could he have been that smart to punish me in such a highbrow way?

"Obviously, my parents don't know about my fetish or Gerald, so please keep it to yourself. Actually, I can't believe I just told you all of that knowing how untrustworthy you are."

Ah, this was a test then, of my loyalty, of my journalistic integrity. Of course, there would be no way I wouldn't write about this admission in my book. Vaughan was not the target, but his parents surely were, as was this Gerald character and his corrupt cohorts, their politics a deadly game that I would win with names and dates and locations and eyewitness testimonials. It would surely secure me an appearance on MSNBC and CNN. Joe and Mika would love to hear all the slimy goings on in the GOP. It was their raison d'etre—the discussion about how evil politicians could be.

"Yeah, of course, Vaughan, I won't tell, anyone, but please be careful."

"I'm not afraid of Gerald, I mean sure, he's big and strong for an old guy, but if he ever tried to fuck with me, I'd rip his balls off and send them to his sons in a FedEx box."

He certainly had my brother's killer instincts.

"I'd better go, Vaughan. I'm up against a deadline. Good luck with your book."

Vaughan shrugged and put on a t-shirt. "I'll probably write it as an essay first. Like you, right? First as an essay and now as a book. Mom told me."

Vaughan looked off into the distance, maybe at his door or window as a new light shone on his face.

"Would you mind taking a look when I'm done and let me know how it is?"

"Of course."

The camera became jerky as Vaughan pulled it from wherever his phone had been docked. He stood up with it and the perspective shifted, briefly revealing a stack of books, the titles of which I could not discern, a pair of boxing gloves, no doubt given to him by my brother, and a poster of Zac Efron, showcasing his Olympian physique in *Baywatch*, behind him.

"Cool." He nodded with a gentle smirk and disconnected.

Before they moved to Long Island when Vaughan was eleven, I'd visit them several times a month, usually on Saturdays, and Vaughan and I would spend hours drawing animals and superheroes on the kitchen table. I would tell him all the time to focus on developing an original style because style is what would set him apart from other artists. Luz would cook us dinner, and we'd all watch a movie, a Marvel spectacle or 80s comedy. Sometimes I'd sleep over and head back home on Sunday mornings. Vaughan would sometimes stare at my face as I drew. I wasn't sure if he was happy to have an adult take an interest in his creative endeavors or if he'd been infatuated with me. I understood the allure for boys of adult males, their full bloom on display, a promise of what to anticipate. I first knew I was gay when I'd begun staring the same way at James.

Vaughan had always been a timid kid, despite having had parents like James and Luz, prime movers, alpha dogs, aggressive capitalists. I'd read about how shameless adults raised ashamed children, and this could have explained him. James could be apoplectic in his rage and unreasonably short in his patience. Luz was domineering and controlling. She'd pester and bark orders for fear that something might go misunderstood or ignored. She'd insulted, or at the very least, annoyed, many people, including both of my parents, with the constant reminders of things that needed to get done for birthday parties or supervision of their pets when they went away, as if we'd all been too dull to understand the expectations during the first go round.

I exercised in my living room in hopes of forcing the awful imagery of Vaughan with Gerald out of my head. I had trouble reconciling the memory of Vaughan as that precocious, curious eleven-year-old drawing portraits of Doctor Doom and Superman and giraffes and elephants with the imagery of him now having his feet worshipped by an old, closeted puritan. I dreaded the essay he'd be sending. How vividly would he chronicle their encounters and how much further would the interactions go, if not in reality, then in his mind?

I would salvage the unfortunate reading by culling from it what I needed for my book. Hopefully, Vaughan would provide places and names of other people associated with Gerald. I would duly thank Vaughan for helping me with the research of the book in the acknowledgment section, if not in the footnotes.

Sometimes Vaughan would drop disarming admissions on me, like that time when we'd watch WWE wrestling matches when he was around ten and he said it made his penis hard. It terrified me that I'd had anything to do with that kind of physiological response and I'd never so much as tousle his hair after that. When he was sixteen, he called me to tell me he had discovered William S. Burroughs and had read *Queer, Naked Lunch, Cities of the Red Night, Wild Boys,* and *Exterminator,* and fantasized about caging all straight men, starving them, and hosting orgies atop their conquered cadavers. I'd been less concerned about his desire to partake in a same-sex orgy than I was about his dreams of oppression and murder. I had told him that he had a vivid imagination, and he should next read Jean Genet, which he'd done posthaste and found further fuel for his lascivious, homicidal fire.

He especially admired Genet's description of the protagonist skull fucking his dead landlord in *Our Lady of The Flowers*. I wondered at what point I should have notified his parents or the authorities. I'd play through active shooting scenarios wherein he killed all the bullies in his high school. Lord knows how easily he'd be able to get a hold of a semi-automatic in Arizona. Panic attacks struck me routinely until he graduated. I prayed he'd make it through without incident.

Tall with aquiline features, lustrous black hair, big, dark brown eyes, and deep tan skin, Vaughan, with an Italian-Hungarian father and Colombian mother, was "ethnically ambiguous," as is the buzz term, and cut a striking figure, one that I am sure appealed to both boys and girls, men and women. Phoenix was a rapidly growing city and its gay culture, as I understood it, was expanding with equal velocity. I worried about Vaughan getting bruised, taken advantage of, falling in with drugs and unsafe sex, and I started to picture overdoses and disease and brutal beatings. I'd reminded myself that I was not responsible for the behavior of my family members and had no influence over their decisions.

A big part of me was still wrestling with the inadequacies implanted and fed by my family ever since the Christmas dinner when Vaughan schooled me on Ancient Egypt. He was good enough not to mention it and I certainly had no plans to examine it any further. Vaughan could take the crown of academic excellence. I had no use to feel good about myself anymore. That was another thing my meekness gave me: a complete humility, a total renunciation of ego.

He'd changed greatly since the last time I'd seen him. He began to remind me of one of the four homeless youths—Sean, Rosa, Peter, and Derrick— I had chaperoned on a field trip to Italy. We'd hoped to expand their horizons, show them what the world had to offer. Incentivize them to keep the jobs we'd found for them and provide for themselves the wonders of travel and experience. Of course, as we chaperons slept, they snuck out of their hotel rooms, made their way to the bar on the ground floor, and drank themselves drunk, as Italy's drinking age is 18 and minimally enforced. The next day, on our visit to the Vatican City, they were all terribly hung over, and naturally, Derrick puked on the floor of the Sistine Chapel, triggering Sean, Peter, and Rosa to follow suit, and prompting the Swiss Guard to expel us from the sacred structure. I could picture Vaughan doing such things when in Europe, when under the care of a concerned adult.

Later that evening as I'd tried to shake off the conversation with my nephew by watching a Jean-Luc Godard marathon on the Criterion Channel, my phone began vibrating. I checked it and saw that Vaughan had sent a series of texts. The first two made me smile: a photo of a drawing he had done when he was a kid of Spiderman, the next was a drawing I had done at around the same time of an elephant and giraffe embracing, and the text that followed read: I have gone from this ... to this ... What followed left me nauseated: a drawing of a foot, presumably his, filthy and infected, pock-marked, and fungal. An oversized, cartoonish tongue licked the sole. Though the subject was off-putting, his artistry was impressive. His final text:

    What do you think of my style now?

CHAPTER 23

Raul led me through the Metropolitan Museum of Art, which even on a Tuesday in the fall was bustling with mostly retirees, tourists, and high school sophomores on class trips. It was becoming a habit, strolling around museums while discussing episode summaries of *The Touring Barbarism*. Raul claimed the mausoleum-like acrid air and lack of natural light helped him focus, even though he seemed to be eluding me through the stately, maze-like building.

Had he been playing a game? Had I offended him? When we dated, he would harbor resentments that manifested in bizarre and apathetic behavior. He'd sometimes become avoidant and hostile. When we went out during these periods, he'd walk several feet ahead of me, ignore me, and sneer at me when I talked to mutual friends during dinner parties. Maybe he regretted telling me about his plot to destroy *RFN* and felt vulnerable with me now knowing his scheme. I hadn't brought it up and decided I would play dumb if he did, pretending that I had been sleeping while he spoke about it on my kitchen floor the other night.

"Is everything okay?" I asked after double-timing it to catch up to him.

"Why wouldn't it be?"

Marveling ostentatiously at Hendrick Sorgh's *A Kitchen* in an exhibition of Dutch masterpieces was a handsome man in cerulean blue tights, a blousy cream top, and a maroon scarf whom both Raul and I had recognized.

"Leonard," Raul said. "You gorgeous frog!"

Leonard Denis was a French ballet dancer for New York City Ballet that Raul "dated" after we broke up. We'd only met once.

"Raul," said Leonard, turning with only a feint hint of an accent as he'd been in New York since his middle teenage years and was now almost forty. I imagined he still danced based on the pronounced musculature of his legs, swelling and indenting like a billowing jellyfish at every movement. "Quelle surprise!"

Raul, more alive than he'd been all morning with me, thrust his body into Leonard's and the two men embraced warmly, nearly erotically as their midsections met, occasioning a slight gyration of the hips, followed by two air cheek kisses.

"You remember Julian," said Raul, gesturing to me as if I were a chore.

"Yes, Julian, how are you these days?"

"Good," I said glancing at his marvelous legs, but quickly averting my eyes for fear of giving him a compliment. "I am developing my *New Yorker* article into a book and writing a cable series." I couldn't help but showoff.

"I have been hearing all about it. Look at you!"

I smiled politely before turning away to study the 15th century painting of two female servants preparing produce and fish.

"The Darlington Brothers are directing the show," said Raul.

Leonard bugged his eyes unconvincingly and exclaimed in an equally put-on tone, "How wonderful!"

I was not convinced that Leonard thought the adaptation was "wonderful," as I knew his type, the ones who frowned on television as low culture and only regarded opera, ballet, fine art, and some literature as highbrow enough to be worthy of his attention and, very rarely, praise.

Leonard smiled at Raul, and I could have sworn Raul rolled his eyes, though it was quick and subtle, and I could not be sure. Had I been the butt of their inside joke? The possibility put me in a murderous mood. I cleared my throat in a way that was not at all judicious and Leonard blushed, knowing that he'd been put on the spot to end this encounter.

"Well, I will let you get on with your afternoon," said Leonard. "Raul, please come by and see me when you can. We're performing *The Goldberg Variations* for another month."

"Robbins does Bach! I'll make it my business to come."

"You always do!" said the vulgar Frenchman, eliciting laughter from my equally vulgar ex. The two men embraced and parted obscenely with playful ass grabs and giggles and lingering gazes.

"Be seeing you, Julian," Leonard said to me flippantly before walking self-importantly out of the wing.

"That guy is such a cunt," I said, hating myself for revealing my jealousy.

"Catty bitch," said Raul smiling with a superiority that made me want to punch him.

We moved around the room of Dutch masters, discussing *The Touring Barbarism* while finding mitigating diversion and inspiration in maids, provincial life, parties, and still life renditions of fruits and flowers by Vermeer, Metsu, Haverman, and Hals. Raul periodically glanced back, maybe hoping to find Leonard loitering nearby.

INT. CLINT RESIDENCE — DAY

Mary and Monroe sit stone-faced on the sofa ensconced in Monroe's many cats as they listen to their son explain how Joe and Dr. Alessandro are a "thruple". The term is new to them, but they understand the meaning. Paul, Phyllis, and Jonah listen raptly from across the room on dining room chairs as though they are a co-op committee hearing requests and complaints from hopeful, disenfranchised tenants.

MARY

This is unethical, Dr. Alessandro.
I will report you to the ombudsman
and human resources and the dean on

Monday morning.

```
          DR. ALESSANDRO
If I lose my job I will never get
out of here, Dr. Donizetti-Clint.


          PEGASUS
It's true, Mom. He'll be stuck with
us forever. Besides, if you report
him, we'll run off to Berlin or
Granada and you'll never see me.
```

Mary and Monroe look at each other, hoping the other would have a solution or at least something sagacious to say about the situation. Mary exudes frustration as Dr. Alessandro and her son's assertions shut down all assumptions. While it is morally squeamish territory it is not illegal as Pegasus was an adult and the relationship is seemingly consensual.

Raul touched my hand as we entered the Fabergé egg exhibition inhabited by elderly women and delicate men pompously scrutinizing the displays. "Were they really a threesome?"

"Does it matter?"

"No," said Raul, touching my back. "Not really."

I saw Leonard on the other end of the wing standing before the famed *Lilies-of-the-Valley Basket*, a late nineteenth century oddity that looked like an HR Geiger design for some science fiction horror, despite its pearls, diamonds, and cabriole legs. He alternatively studied it adoringly and assayed my discussion with Raul. I couldn't read his eyes from so far away, but he saw us, and he kept looking.

<u>MONTAGE:</u> As he had with Joe, Pegasus initiates the romance with Dr. Alessandro. Their sex is gentle, careful, and quiet enough for nightly coital congressional summits under Mary and Monroe's roof to not call attention to themselves. Phyllis, Paul, and Jonah spy on them and sometimes ridicule the "acts against God" they are committing. Their concerns are ignorable and even laughable and on more than one occasion Pegasus reminds them that they are still guests in his house, and he'll put them back out on the streets if they question the propriety of his behavior again. <u>NOTE: The actors may ad lib these exchanges.</u>

<u>NOTE: The following scene may require an intimacy coordinator and the actors should perform to their comfort levels</u>: Dr. Alessandro assumes his favorite position—on his back. Pegasus straddles his face as Joe hoists his long legs up in the air, allowing his oversized feet to rest on his shoulders as he plows away into him. Dr. Alessandro tells the young men that he relishes being the pig on their roast, the kabob on their spit. Dr. Alessandro is taller and more substantially built than the thin boys and so their topping of him takes effort and stamina that only men of their age could muster. Dr. Alessandro surrenders to the domination and

encourages verbal abuse.

"This is getting me hard," said Raul as he awkwardly slouched, trying to hide his tumescence while entering the Greco-Roman section of the museum bright with sunlight through an atrium, the statues of the semi-nude and naked sentries doing little to help his condition. "Are you sure The Darlington Brothers will shoot this?"

"One is gay and the other is gay-friendly," I said. "Plus, they consider themselves Avant-Garde progressives and MAX loves graphic gay sex. Just think of *Oz* or *Six Feet Under* or *Game of Thrones.*"

"*The White Lotus*, too."

"Yup. Ass eating, right?"

Raul stared at the statue of a youthful Hercules. With his haughty, assured posture, the figure showcased for spectators its sinew, mass, and genitalia. Raul was too easy to turn on and impossible to turn off. He'd demand a release from me for getting him worked up. And then we both saw Leonard leering at us from the other side of the exhibition, skulking lecherously by a Roman statue of a young man. Raul turned back to me and again his hand brushed my hip.

INT. PEGASUS'S BEDDROOM — NIGHT

Sitting naked in Pegasus's bedroom on the floor in a circle, Dr. Alessandro, Joe, and Pegasus take turns revealing desires that they'd claimed to have told no one else. Though Joe thought up the idea, Dr. Alessandro facilitates, and Pegasus shares first.

PEGASUS
(staring at Joe as both young

men begin playing with
themselves)
I always thought it would be hot
to have a bodybuilder tied to my
bed for me to torture and abuse
and berate. Just someone big
and powerful and helpless and
humiliated.

DR. ALESSANDRO
(massaging Pegasus's feet)
Very exciting to dominate and
humiliate a bigger man?

JOE
I would love to be taken apart by
a group of construction workers. I
used to watch these burley, dirty
guys bust up the street or put-up
buildings along Riverside from my
little bed inside the park and I
would secretly beat off to them,
and I was under all these blankets
or cardboard, or in the bushes, so
they couldn't see what I was doing.

PEGASUS
What about you, Dr. A?

DR. ALESSANDRO
This is it. What I am doing with

you two. This is *my* fantasy.

                    JOE
Young, barely legal.

               DR. ALESSANDRO
And completely in charge of me.

"Did you get the foot fetish stuff from your nephew?" asked Raul, as we found ourselves in the Japanese wing, staring at a row of cypress sculptures of male and female deities from the 10th century.

"I regret that I ever told you about that," I said, kicking myself for divulging the details of my interaction with Vaughan a few days earlier. Thankfully, I'd stopped short of showing him the drawing my nephew had sent me. "And I don't have a foot fetish!"

"It does get kind of perverse, no?" said Raul, finding Leonard watching us from across the Michael C. Rockefeller African Art wing.

"It gets perverse," I said, turning to Leonard.

We'd parked ourselves in front of a 16th century ivory mask from Nigeria, the queen mother, Iyoba. It looked as though she were frowning at us, which felt appropriate given the nature of what we'd been discussing.

Leonard slunk around a 19th century male power figure, a Congolese carving with an expression both forlorn and stoic. Typical, I thought, that he'd spend his time seducing a male in power.

Raul touched my ass for Leonard to see, which made the Frenchman smirk.

MONTAGE: Dr. Alessandro treats Joe and Pegasus
to one film per week, usually in Manhattan
or Brooklyn, and almost always something
international or art house. He sits between them,

and the men keep their hands tucked between one another's legs, frequently tickling one another. They sustain erections for the entirety of the films, no matter the subject matter. Even epics about war or bigoted persecution, intimate dramas centering on disease or old age—nothing mutes the cries of their orgy.

They nibble on each other's earlobes and suck necks, pinch nipples, bite lips. They don't care who sees or who they offend. They are a traveling bacchanal, and they celebrate their lust for each other in ways so unabated and unapologetic it provokes comments and groans from many onlookers. More than once, they are discharged from restaurants, department stores, and movie theaters.

During an after-dinner stroll through Washington Square Park, Dr. Alessandro holds his young lovers' hands.

DR. ALESSANDRO
I wish I could merge with you both.

PEGASUS
We consume you and you consume us.

INT. BOOK STORE — DAY

Dr. Alessandro, Pegasus, and Joe are caught

with their hands down each other's pants in the erotica section and are not only barred for life but held for the police. The gross indecency charges come with hefty fines and a court appearance. No one says anything to Mary or Monroe. <u>NOTE: These scenes will be filmed/cut in a montage.</u>

<u>NOTE for the actors: Character motivation:</u> Eventually Pegasus and Joe will compete for their elder's favor and during sex will see who can make him moan loudest. Joe, free of bourgeoise decorum, approaches the task with a savage abandon and often emerges the victor, but it is with Pegasus, frail and wan, that Dr. Alessandro feels safest and most loved, and finds himself able to make love most often.

"This is the most interesting aspect of their relationship," said Raul, watching Leonard watch us in the Egyptian art wing. "The competition for Dr. Alessandro's preference."

We were beside the red quartzite face of Senwosret III, over three thousand years old and only missing a nose and ears. He, too, looked to be scowling at us and our dirty tales of Pegasus and company. Leonard milled about a male god statue made of granodiorite, unsurprisingly. The ancient statue held a was-scepter before him with a suspended hand due to his missing arm. The implement that denoted dominion looked a lot like a long, thin phallus. I bet Leonard thought it was and that's what had first attracted him to the piece.

We exited the Egyptian wing and noticed the banner for *Goya's Mental Crisis: The Art of His Black Period*, a discussion about the artist's mental illness and the works produced during the 1820s in the Grace Rainey Rogers Auditorium.

"Wanna see this?" asked Raul, to which I nodded in the affirmative.

Before long we were in the Grace Rainey Rogers Auditorium and Leonard followed us in, sitting audaciously beside Raul, who was stuck in the middle. The curator, an old woman fashionably dressed, began talking about Goya, his fear of old age, his descent into madness, his visual reactions to the Peninsular War, and his 14 Black Paintings. We were seated in the back row of the dimly lit, moderately crowded theater.

"Goya's deafness was a mystery," began the curator as she projected on the screen behind her Goya's *The Drowning Dog*, an upsetting and minimalist painting in which the small head of maybe a Labrador looks skyward, peering from a brown mass, possibly mud, for salvation. "It is said, that is what drove his anxiety about madness and fear of old age."

I whispered further plot details into Raul's ear as I slid my hand over his right thigh. I'd noticed that Leonard had his hand on Raúl's left knee. A challenge, I thought.

INT. CLINT RESIDENCE — EVENING

At the dinner table, Dr. Alessandro, Pegasus, and Joe are discreet in their play. They slip their hands or bare feet into one another's laps unbeknownst to Mary or Monroe or to Phyllis, Paul, and Jonah. They text each other pornographic snapshots they'd taken earlier. They go into detail about what they will do to each other later in the night. Mary and Monroe are not stupid, so they assume the three men were engaging in covert communications about eventual coitus.

DR. ALESSANDRO

Your son is a stellar student. He
regularly leads class discussions.
and his reports dig deeper than
those of any other student. He is
incisive and bold in his analyses.

MONROE

Seems the apple has not fallen too
far from the tree.

DR. ALESSANDRO

Another scientist ready to bud.

A NOTE for the actor playing Joe: Joe, without
family or money or prospects, imagines college and
graduate school and all the career advancements
they could engender and discards them as distant
fantasies. He'd resigned himself to his lot and
would go on hustling and attaching himself to
people with warm beds and full refrigerators
for as long as he could until he'd either got
lucky or cashed out.

JOE

I am a scientist of the gutter.

Mary and Monroe turn to him with unreadable
expressions. Dr. Alessandro thinks they look
for once sympathetic, but Pegasus knows better.
Their faces are meant to convey apathy born of

blame. They are libertarians in progressive's
clothing and attribute success and failure to
the engines within people.

                    PHYLLIS
          The gutter has plenty of lab work
          that needs doing.

Raul smirked and kissed me. "You find room to care about Joe," he said. "That's sweet."

Leonard slid his hand up Raul's left leg, but I stopped it short of his crotch. He looked at me and frowned, as though I'd disappointed him, breached some unsigned, though implicit, contract. I touched Raul until he engorged.

"His mental and physical collapses seemed to have occurred shortly after the French declared war on Spain," the curator continued, projecting now Goya's *Two Old Ones Eating Soup*, shriveled, ghoulish men hunched over bowls of presumably soup, one grinning dementedly and the other potentially a corpse. "And it should be noted that most of these works during this time were painted on the walls of his home."

Raul turned to Leonard and kissed him. Not to be outdone, I opened Raul's pants and began to masturbate him. Leonard gasped. Raul looked at me as if I were mad but didn't stop me. The combination of Leonard's jealousy and Raul's plan to flatten *RFN* thrilled me. Leonard watched my hand pump up and down as Raul fought the urge to whimper. I threw a sweatshirt I had been lugging around over Raul's lap and tried to concentrate the motion to my wrist to avoid unwanted attention and subsequent interruption.

"Other post-mortem possibilities include paranoid dementia, caused by brain trauma," said the curator, while projecting Goya's *Deaf Man*, a Santa Claus gripping a cane endures a demon howling into his ear, "which culminated in these black paintings for which he is still so known and the demons of which he painted that have provided a kind of personal Rorschach for centuries of admirers."

Raul grabbed my jerking hand and exhaled sharply before wincing and shuddering. We'd both broken a sweat and Raul, the restraint winding him, fought for breath. I kissed his cheek and smiled at Leonard, who grimaced grandly.

CHAPTER 24

The Starfish hosted a memorial on the one-week anniversary of Milo's overdose. Though Kevin had been in the middle of preparing a pizza party he took a break to pay his respects. Photos of Milo had been posted on the wall behind the bar and the suspended TVs played footage of him dancing and singing. Flowers were strewn across the bar and on the stage in the back where drag queens usually performed on Tuesdays and Saturdays. An older man who looked new and out of place cried in the corner over scotch. I thought it might have been the uncle he spoke about, the queer idol who'd once saved him. I'd forgotten his name.

Kevin took my arm. "Come on, babe, we have a dinner party to host and a bit of life to celebrate."

As Kevin pulled me through the swinging front door, I glanced back at the crying scotch drinker and thought he looked like an older, haggard version of Milo, a boy in middle age and too soon decrepit.

***

Ed and Kevin's pizza party unfolded like a fever dream. The strangest parts felt the most real and the most real felt strangest. We all ate too little and drank too much and spoke too fast, careless with our expressions and resentments, and feelings were hurt, and antiques were smashed, and we were all left a little older and bruised if not maybe thrilled and breathless.

In addition to Joan and Colin, the regulars, the guests included Giancarlo Salamone, Ed's lover, a cultivated cancer researcher from Sicily who was probably the wealthiest person in the room by a mile, Fen Chen, a Princeton professor who'd inherited Ed's department chair and also wrote fiction, winning every major literary prize in so doing, Alvin Becker, a Broadway tumbler who played Tumblebrutus in *CATS* and a gazelle in *The Lion King* when he was not filming amateur pornography, and Linus Fielding, a middle-aged actor who became a respected audiobook narrator when the roles began to dwindle. Linus required a cane and wore a cast on his ankle as he'd broken it recently during a hiking incident in Montreal. Everyone threw back sidecars and highballs and cosmopolitans and the memoirists spoke about their victims.

"I used to tell the friends who hadn't made it into one of my books that they should be thankful!" said Joan, still reeling from an unfortunate social media fusillade as she tapped the pen against her pad as if she were gearing up for a marathon stretch of doodles. "It's like discovering some awful gossip wherein you're the subject."

"Yes, Joan, and the fiction stings more than the memoir, which is surprising to me," said Colin. "You'd think that a work of fiction, never mind if it's a roman a clef, would obfuscate the truth of the identity, but I guess I understand now."

"Well, with a memoir," began Edward, "you have to depict things as they really happened, but with autofiction, as they call it now, you know, you can take the likeness of a person and twist it into a made-up narrative, and in the process make pointed observations and have them do things that are less than reputable. I have lost many friends over novels, but never because of a memoir."

"Well, I am about to lose more than just a few friends," sighed Joan, picking at her plate of olives and almonds, her pen ready in her free hand like a sword.

"Oh, Joan," said Linus, "Don't let those cyber-vermin get you down."

"Maybe I should stop tweeting, after all," she said.

"I have been telling you for years to stay off social media," said Kevin.

"Oh, leave her be, Kevin," barked Ed.

"No, he's right. It's too precarious. Treachery lurks behind every post. My agent and publicist and manager all encouraged me to engage with the community and I did, but I don't know, perhaps I am too old and out of touch."

"Nonsense," said Colin.

Joan had posted something about an agent friend who couldn't get her straight white male clients published, regardless of how good their books were, due to identity politics, and the internet went crazy. Thousands of comments appeared on her Twitter feed calling her a "racist," a "dinosaur," a "has-been," a "delusional idiot," and worse. She'd since removed the post, which invited another wave of accusations and pejoratives. Some people even posted charts showcasing the disproportionate number of straight white men being published and the stark comparisons to the dearth of "marginalized" writers.

Earlier in the evening Joan had explained to me that she'd "only meant well." Watching her at the dining room table, writing with ardor, digging the tip of the pen through the pages of her pad, I felt sorry for her and others of her generation. They'd been stuck with antiquated positions that were not always hateful, but the fashion of the day had changed, and they'd suddenly become enemies of goodwill. Joan told me that she had only meant that if these straight white male writers were self-reflexive and dissecting with a jaundiced eye their own privilege and toxicity then maybe we would be better off as a culture. She was not wrong.

"Don't worry too much about it, Joan," said Fen. "It will pass. These things always do. You're far too important a writer to be cancelled, anyway."

"Far too gifted," groused Colin, drunker than everyone else, who'd begun a tirade about talent, and who has it and who doesn't. He exclaimed that plenty of people can write and that plenty of people are technicians. They can dance and sing and act and draw but do they have more than just craft. I mean, can they see anything deeply at all? Is there an original vision at play? An original voice? This is a matter of soul, that kind of artistry. Many writers.

Few artists. Many technicians. Few do it soulfully. He was not wrong.

"I find that white people don't hate minorities," began Fen, "but rather so many of them don't go out of their way to include them."

All the white people in attendance nodded sagaciously, fearful of negating Fen's observation as the only nonwhite person at the party that evening. Giancarlo and Alvin hadn't contributed a word to the discussion since it began and quietly sipped their drinks and occasionally held hands and rubbed one another's leg. I, too, had been too quiet, having drank too much to not sound foolish if I'd opened my mouth, though I'd also realized that no one had been coherent enough to have remembered.

"I just get tired of the left cannibalizing their own," said Alvin, finally, to which Giancarlo squeezed his hand. "What? It's true. The house is on fire but let's keep complaining about the termites in the basement!"

"Well, if you leave termites to their own devices the house will eventually collapse," said Kevin, winking at me from across the room.

"But if it's on fire it will burn down first!"

"Oh," said Kevin, giggling, blowing me a kiss, "Let's just drink more. Climate change will do us all in before long, anyway!"

"So, Alvin," said Linus. "Ed tells me you're something of a tumbler?"

"The best in all of New York," added Giancarlo with a pang of jealous bite.

"Let's see something!" said Ed, deflecting Giancarlo's snark.

Alvin had been so inebriated he didn't put up his usual faux protest but instead instantly leapt to his feet, kicked off his Pumas, stepped away from the dining table and dipped forward into a mid-air flip. He landed elegantly though with force just short of the coffee table in the living room before flipping again backwards and nearly alighting on Colin, who gasped and chuckled. Alvin then did a handstand and walked a good seven feet down the hall toward the bathroom. Everyone applauded and whistled.

I noticed that while Alvin regaled the crowd with his boozy athleticism, Giancarlo began to fidget and shift in his seat. He looked agitated. In fact, all evening he'd appeared annoyed, and he, like everyone else, drank a lot more than usual. It was as if some fog had consumed us, some miasma had infected us, some mood had permeated us, and we were in the throes of a new ecstasy, even if some of us fell under the sway of different energies.

Alvin came back flipping violently down the hall as we all proffered "ooohhhs" and "aaahhhs," though his muscular body picked up momentum and inertia was not a friend. He hadn't been able to stop in time to avoid smashing into an end table on which a small statue of a naked man with a gigantic phallus fell and broke. His prick had cracked clean off. Alvin landed hard on his ass and when he discovered what he'd done he cried, holding the statue and his enormous phallus up for us to see.

"I've broken off his dick!" he wept, to which everyone laughed heartily, even Giancarlo.

Later, Kevin and I talked alone in the living room.

"You know, my family should be grateful that I didn't write about my psychotic Uncle Sal, who nearly killed several people in various fits of rage!"

Through the corner of my eye, I saw Giancarlo look up from his phone. Kevin leaned in. "Good lord that is sexy."

I went into detail for Kevin. One of his victims was a Puerto Rican man who had stolen from his son, back in the 70s, another an Italian racketeer who insulted his wife, also in the 70s, and then with another he'd gotten into a parking dispute in the 90s. I was a teenager then and remember this one, well. Uncle Sal does have a big heart, though, and for like forty years cared for a pigeon coop on the roof of his tenement on Arthur Avenue and used to always buy sandwiches for the homeless people in the park by Fordham.

"You should write a whole book about this guy," said Kevin, touching my knee. "Lovely, terrifying Uncle Sal."

I could hear Giancarlo snicker. I knew what "real" Italians thought about Italian Americans. That our ancestors were peasant farmers, desperate crooks, and murderous thugs, riff raff rejects from the motherland. The lowest of the culture, expelled from the ancient country. The diaspora did the slender boot a favor by eradicating us like a case of athlete's foot.

"Or how about my very tragic Uncle Carmine ... neither his wife nor son nor two daughters ever even made it to 50!"

"Jesus fuck," said Kevin, nursing his highball to his chest as though it were a crucifix and then kissing my neck as if to assure me I was still sexy despite my dreadful filial sagas.

I told Kevin about Uncle Carmine's biblical losses beginning with his wife, my Aunt Patricia, who'd died at 44 of lung cancer in 1996, and then his older daughter, my cousin Malena, at 48 of breast cancer in 2015, and his younger daughter, my favorite, sweet cousin Loretta, also of breast cancer at age 44 only last year. His horrible, lost son Andrew, had died of diabetes at 48, in prison in 2013 while serving a life sentence after killing his wife Carla in front of his son, Andrew, Jr.

"Your family has known so much grief and loss, Julian, and I am so sorry, kid." I'd never known Kevin to speak as earnestly, and it disarmed me. Even Giancarlo now looked at me with big, empathetic eyes.

I could have told him about my mother's three abortions. I'd have had two younger brothers and another older sister. And they would have been full-blooded and closer to my age. I'd spare my mother that.

"So many fucking things I could have included in that fucking book. Like how my father used to casually walk around the house during parties, lift empty glasses and mugs, and smash them into pieces against the sink, if people didn't clean up after themselves right away!"

"Ha!" Kevin picked at the assortment of cured cheeses and salted nuts on the coffee table. "He sounds like me! Or at least the me I wish I could be!"

Radiohead's *No Surprises* began playing on the radio as an argument about American opera grew louder in the dining room. Giancarlo approached the radio, turned it up, and began to sing along, alternating between falsetto and soprano. His vibrato shook the room when he hit his crescendos and made Colin's rheumy eyes well. Alvin, Ed, Kevin, and I listened with reverence.

"And no alarms and no surprises! No alarms and no surprises! No alarms and no surprises! Silent. Silent."

Alvin looked worried about his important Sicilian scientist. He stood and hesitated. The song ended and Giancarlo turned off the radio.

"Cancer cells acquire genetic mutations over time, which makes their cells behave unpredictably." Giancarlo spoke matter-of-factly. "These mutations eventually become resistant to treatment, making it ineffective. Cancer will always outsmart us, and we will never beat it."

"Well, fuck," said Colin, and poured himself another drink.

"Oh, well, how awful," sighed Ed. "I am glad my time is almost up then."

"It's a miracle anyone lives as long as you, my dear," said Kevin, his hands on me again.

Alvin pouted and with slouched shoulders and heavy hands walked to his lover, the renowned cancer researcher, the European aristocrat, the implacable, the unimpressible, the invincible Dr. Giancarlo Mario Antonio Salamone. Their hold lingered before the fireplace and then the acrobatic pornographer led the way to the front door, into the crisp city night, and back home to their palatial haven. Kevin held me in a cuddle, throwing his right leg over mine, resting his head on my shoulder. I reciprocated the affection because he'd deserved that much, and I owed him. Everyone had owed him.

Excerpt of
My Mighty Meekness,
as published in
The New Yorker

Arnold Byrne was as tough a boy as you'd expect spawned by people like Sophia Bartha and Doug Byrne. Indeed, still very much a "boy" in his early twenties. I can't recall ever seeing him without a black eye or swollen face or sideways nose or in a cast or a splint or with a limp. His favorite thing in the world was a bloody fight. Doug encouraged him to learn boxing, which he did and in which he excelled, earning numerous regional titles, but the training only fueled his lust for violence, and he soon joined a local Flushing gang. When one of his friends, a fellow gang member named Dennis, was stabbed to death in Fresh Meadows during a fight with a rival Dominican gang from St. Albans, Doug and Sophia finally intervened and forced him to get work as a carpenter's apprentice to keep him off the streets.

The one time I did stick up for Sophia was when Arnold was about twenty and he'd been berating her for interfering in an argument between he and his girlfriend at the time named Maria. I told him not to talk to his mother with so much disrespect and he told me to shut up and mind my own business. I guess I had lost my temper and got in his face and began screaming at him. He stared at me in disbelief and then took me by the neck and tossed me across the living room. Sophia and Maria tried to get between us, but he shoved them out of the way and onto the floor. He slapped me repeatedly because he claimed I'd been too much of a weakling to handle his punches. That he would break me with one blow. I could not fight back. Not because he was stronger than me or angrier or a better fighter, but because he was my nephew and fighting was not one of the amendments in my constitution.

If I had any sense of pride or ego left, it would have mortified me that my young nephew had manhandled me and beaten me up in front of his girlfriend and my sister, but I hadn't and so it didn't. Of course, Doug and James, and even Grandpa and Dad, made fun of me for getting my ass whupped by "Little Arnie," who had not been so little at the time of the thrashing. I could accept a younger, bigger, more powerful man besting me in a physical quarrel, but my own blood, my own nephew, made it a great indignity for me, if not my family.

CHAPTER 25

Arnold drove in from Long Island and asked me to meet him at a dive bar on Steinway Street in Astoria. I obliged though played through every potential scenario for violence and how I would handle it. He was as prone to tempestuous outbursts as his father but unlike Doug, Arnold lacked the mitigating torpor and wisdom of old age, however minimal both might have been in my brother-in-law. I knew Arnold had friends in Astoria and expected some would be there.

Loitering in front of Barry's Pub, I realized that I was not necessarily trying to make amends with my family but rather giving them room to express their misgivings over my essay. I knew my meetings with them wouldn't change anything in my writing as *My Mighty Meekness* had already been published and people were reading it and soon there would be a whole book. These farcical interactions could at least potentially provide a palliative for the sting of the punches I'd thrown.

I'd been watching the odd confluence of patrons entering and exiting the bar—businessmen, construction workers, young men poorly dressed, barely any women at all, and almost all white—when Arnold showed up. He'd grown bigger since I'd last seen him. I wondered if he'd been taking steroids. I wondered if he'd been consulting Uncle Monroe.

Arnold was handsome, even pretty. His long nose with a prominent bridge that ran into an upward pointed tip. His eyes lime green with thick, long lashes. His lips large and femininely shaped. An enviable jawline and pronounced cheekbones. A forehead as protuberant as a caveman's. He was bald. His pale eyes were bloodshot and searching and he smelled of weed.

He growled in a rumble, "Uncle Jules," as he swept me up in his massive,

Cro-Magnon arms.

I returned the embrace and kissed him on the neck.

"How are you doing, Arnie?"

He was no longer that lanky, goofy, 90-pound boy I used to dangle from the ankles when we play fought. Now he was a twenty-four-year-old man who could just as easily dangle me.

"You really fucked over the family," he said, grumbling as he opened the door into Barry's.

I nodded and followed him in, knowing this would be one of the toughest interactions. Arnold had shown tremendous promise as a kid, excelling in all subjects, and exhibiting a great interest in art and law at an early age. What changed him is anyone's guess but there are more than a few possibilities. His mother's several breast cancer battles, something Sophia with her unflappable toughness braved with tenacity and grit, numerous theatrical fights between his mother and father, and bullies who preyed on his soft nature. In the span of the seven years between 11 and 18, Arnold grew into an intimidating, impatient, fearless brute who hurt antagonists quickly and without much warning and remained stuck in that mold. He stopped tolerating even sideways glances. Because the world was hard, he became hard. Because people abused weak things, he became abusive. I almost couldn't fault him for transforming into a barbarian. Life requires barbarians.

Barry's Pub was old New York filthy with visible grime and plumes of dust floating in the light that cut through the stain glass windows and blood stains that marred the walls and floor and tabletops and that distinct pungent cocktail of stale beer, damp cigarettes, and poor hygiene. It was the middle of the day so the men on the stools were alone, as were the ones passed out at the tables. It was a lonely afternoon, and I suspect the drinks mollified their temporal tortures.

We sat in the darkest, bleakest, most degraded corner of the unkempt tavern and Arnold ordered us Coronas. The stench of the place nauseated me, so I sipped mine to stop from puking. The bartender was an overweight man about my age whom Arnold told me was Barry's younger brother, Donnie. They were from an Irish family of teamsters and raised in Kew Gardens, not far from Doug.

"Barry and Donnie know my dad so whenever I come to the city, I like to visit them," said Arnold.

"Your parents are pissed at me."

"Can you fucking blame them, Uncle Jules?"

"I keep saying the same thing to everyone—I didn't write this to hurt anyone."

Arnie cringed incredulously as if I'd said something outlandish. "But you hurt *everyone*."

"Arnie …"

"What the fuck did you do it for?"

I stared at the Corona label, my mind drifting. "It's hard to explain…"

"Try me."

"I needed to get things off my chest," I said, making no effort to obfuscate my frustration with this interminable litany of inquisitions. How many more family members would require explanations?

"You couldn't find the balls to say this shit to our faces?" Arnold grabbed the feeble, wooden table on either side and rattled it, his indignation, righteous always only to him, nearly boiling over, moving apace from 0 to 100 within seconds, as was his character. "That's how a man blows off steam. He confronts the people he has beef with."

Donnie looked over at us with raised eyebrows, so did some of the patrons, barely coherent though they were.

"Arnie," said Donnie with a stern purr, to which Arnold nodded and put his hand up.

"He gets really mad when people act up in here," said Arnold.

"Then keep your temper," I said, annoyed that my nephew would even entertain becoming aggressive with me.

Arnold chewed the inside of his cheek and winced, balling meaty white fists, exhaling, and sitting back in his chair. He was of the school of the outer borough neighborhoods in which all exponents felt it necessary to demonstrate the full range of their emotional experience. I found it performative and exhausting, a show of noxious prowess.

"You should know I didn't even write everything that was on my mind."

"That's why you're writing a whole fucking book about us now?"

He was right about that. That was why I was writing a "whole fucking book" about them, to detail the many things the people in the family did that I had left out of the article, shit that would have gotten them arrested. Shit that *will* get them arrested.

Arnold's eyes became dark and heavy, the stress of this encounter aging him prematurely. He studied my face as if he were looking for signs of intelligence.

I turned away, unable to deal with the incredulity any longer, of everyone doubting my veracity, of being called a liar and an opportunist and an exploiter, never in so many words.

"Of course, my father did crooked shit! Who hasn't? But he never ran whores, and your father was no fuckin' gangster."

Donnie and the patrons were looking at us. We'd both gotten loud again without realizing it. A new face appeared in the crowd, someone I recognized from Arnold's childhood, one of his friends. He looked different with long hair and shaggy beard.

"Vinny!" said Arnold. "Fucking Vinny Locarno!"

Vinny Locarno. His nose, eyes, and gait gave him away. He wore a black leather jacket over black sweatpants and white sneakers. He too smelled like pot, though mixed with the kind of musky cologne guys who frequent nightclubs wear. He'd apparently bathed in it. His left eye was blackened and the area surrounding it swollen. The bottom half of his left lip was also engorged and split. Arnold and his friends were almost always disfigured from recent fights.

"What's up, son?" said Vinny, shaking hands with Arnold before grabbing him in a studied, careful hug.

"This is my Uncle Julian," said Arnold, sitting again.

I shook the shopworn hand, calloused and clammy. Vinny sat at the table beside us, closer to me.

"Here, this is for your old man," said Vinny, passing a wad of cash across the table to Vinny, who took it and tucked it into his pocket. "From the other night."

"I heard he beat your ass," said Arnold.

"He doesn't fuck around when it comes to poker."

Arnold chuckled. "No, he does not."

Donnie brought Vinny a Corona and he chugged it. There was an extended stretch of silence that discomfited and then Vinny began to size me up in a way that was not at all tactful. I looked at my phone to diffuse the awkward tension.

"This is the guy, right?" he asked Arnold. "The one who wrote that article?"

Arnold nodded. I swallowed hard. With his long shaggy hair and emaciated body, Vinny looked to me like a low-rent Christ.

"You've got some atoning to do, brother," Vinny said to me.

"So, I keep hearing." I guess I was glad to know that Arnold spoke about me and the essay even if it was in likely nothing but negative terms.

"We were just talking about it," said Arnold.

"Sophia, Arnie's mom, is good people and what you wrote … you wrote some fucked up shit about her, man," said Vinny. "And Arnie says you're writing a book now about everyone? Dude, just fucking stop already."

"Sophia, *Arnie's mom*, is also my sister, and I think that entitles me to write whatever I like about her," I said, knowing it was untrue that I had the right to write whatever I pleased about her. There was still a line and maybe I'd crossed it, but it was not the place of Greasy Jesus to scold me for it.

Arnold's eyes became sharp and darted back and forth between me and

Vinny, watching, waiting, measuring.

"Don't make it right, chief," said Vinny. "If it was me, and you wrote that shit about my mother, I don't care if you're her brother or my uncle, I'd whoop your ass."

"Yeah, well, thank Christ we're not related, or the article I'd have written would have been a lot nastier," I said, shocked with how easily the words tumbled from my tongue.

Arnold's eyes bulged and his mouth made a puckered hole. "Ohhhhh, shit," he whispered.

Vinny stared at me with half a smirk, looking dumb and amused at the same time.

"And if you were my uncle, I'd lie about knowing you," said Vinny, before adding, "fucking faggot."

Without thinking I shoved Vinny off the chair. It was a smooth, quick action, and it happened without any forethought. It was simply an impulse, like swatting a fly alighting on your hand or swinging at a ball torpedoing toward your face. Vinny fell hard, knocking over the table next to him and creating a commotion loud enough for the other patrons to look again at us, grousing and cursing for disturbing their drunken solitudes. Of course, Donnie rushed over.

"That's it, Arnie, you gotta get out! I don't care what your pop is going to say, I can't have you guys coming in here and making trouble."

Arnold apologized and we left. Vinny, embarrassed and incensed, left first, brushing himself off as he kicked the pub's front door open and disappeared into the bright white daylight.

"I'm sorry, too," I said to Donnie, standing Vinny's toppled chair and the table beside it upright. "I've never done that before."

As I exited, I caught a glimpse of Arnold handing cash to Donnie and apologizing again. In a flash, Arnold's storyline became clear and it would involve the bigoted junky, the derelict Jesus, Vinny Locarno. Arnold had sold drugs in the past and it would not take too much to craft a convincing plot about his enterprise with Locarno. I would lead authorities to Vinny through Arnold by way of the book.

As though the thug could hear my thoughts and the plan they coalesced around, Vinny grabbed me by the shirt and slammed me into the brick face of the pub. He flashed yellow teeth. Just as quickly, Arnold's massive paw was around Vinny's throat, and he ripped my attacker away, tossing him into a parked sedan.

"Touch my uncle again and I break your fingers," said Arnold. "Call him a 'faggot' again and I break your jaw."

Vinny looked at Arnold with disbelief and then at me with a vileness that gave me the fantods. I remained braced against the bar's storefront in case he charged again, ready to fight back with a maniacal flurry of kicks and punches, though knew I wouldn't need to, now that my hulking, fearsome nephew had come to my rescue. It was both emasculating and affirming at the same time.

"Fuck this, man," said Vinny, straightening himself out and walking down Steinway.

"You alright?" Arnold asked me.

"Yeah, I'm fine."

Arnold had changed enough in the few years since that unfortunate episode where he tossed me across the living room and thankfully grown into too much of a gentleman to ever mention it. I felt saddest that Arnold had become a man with such rage and hatred and such a lack of stillness that fisticuffs were to him a normal and acceptable means of resolving a problem. Again, I reminded myself that passivity, meekness, passivism was truly the only sustainable form of protest and resistance.

"Look, Uncle Jules, you showed me you had real steel in your balls to write what you did and then to keep meeting with us and taking our shit for it … and again, today, just now, letting Vinny have it for mouthing off to you, that was real tough and you're a man, so don't let anyone tell you you ain't. You got yourself up there all on your own and that's somethin.'"

Up there ...

I wasn't sure where this was going but I knew Arnold's sentiments were pure and true, his knack for guile limited to flirting with women at clubs when drunk.

"Just don't write the book, Uncle Julian." Arnold's eyes were vulnerable and the desperation on his face made my blood run cold because I knew what I would be writing about him and the rest of the family. I would not be able to stop myself at this point. In the book Arnold would be treated as badly as everyone else but at least he would be granted a business mind, a warlord of a subterranean empire, a dealer on parity with the Sacklers. And Vinny would hopefully fall hardest.

I promised nothing but I hugged him anyway. He held me for a moment, uncaring about the optics of two grown men embracing for too long. He'd offered me a ride home, but I insisted on walking. Something new developed in our relationship. A kind of street wisdom based on dominance testing, maybe. I knew I was not of his world, and he knew any effort on my part to show that I could be, would be earnest at most, if not fully convincing. I'd not hear from him again for a few weeks when the war with my family would reach a new escalation.

CHAPTER 26

Raul and I sat on the steps leading to Low Library at Columbia University. We'd met on campus over two decades earlier in Dr. Conrad Stephens's course on French literature and disease. Alma Mater spread her arms magisterially behind us. Students mingled. Some studied, some courted. It had been nearly a week since Raul and I last saw each other, that afternoon in the museum with Leonard. Raul was less guarded than usual, even flirtatious. The incident at The Met changed things and that change was palpable. It was not like me to initiate, and I was never the aggressor. I was prone to shame and panic over socially awkward situations, which he knew, so the fact that I did *that* to him in a public space was probably not just surprising, but maybe also thrilling.

It made me sad to think that soon he would be on the lam for hitting *RFN* with a massive data breach, or worse, in prison. Either way, we'd not be able to sit together again.

"Do you remember what writer we met over?" I asked, touching Raul's knee.

"Do you remember *when!*" Raul sat up, as he had been reclining, and put his hand on my back and started making little circles.

"It was, like, fifteen years ago this past September, and we were in Dr. Stephens's class..."

"About French writers and the way they romanticize illness, right?" Raul wrapped his arm around me and rested his head on my shoulder. I tingled everywhere.

"It was Hervé Guibert," I said, squeezing his leg, pulling it closer to mine. We were now in full embrace, an unambiguous cuddle.

"I called you 'perverse' for digging his work so much," said Raul, chuckling into my chest, biting my shirt.

"When I thought it was brilliant that Guibert described AIDS as a modern invention, a kind of gift."

"Do you remember his book about the homeless guys who tried to out disgust each other?" asked Raul, sliding his hand up my leg toward my crotch. "They would, like, escalate their challenges to repulse."

"*Les Lubies d'Arthur*," I said in perfect French. I could only speak French when citing film or book titles.

I thought about the book by Guibert that I thought Vaughan was copying about the kid with the pustules who looked like Buster Keaton, a skateboarder who killed himself because he had AIDS. *Crazy For Vincent*. I groaned imagining him with that old, closeted neocon in Phoenix.

Raul secretly completed the ascent toward my groin and grabbing my package, squeezing it twice as if he were fluffing a pillow or examining a breast. I laughed and pushed him carefully onto the ground, leaned over him, and kissed him softly on the mouth. He pulled me in and kissed me back. Columbia and its inhabitants were so liberal that even if any of them took exception with our PDA none would say a thing about it. They'd not even give us a second glance. Besides, as alumni, we felt we had the right to do as we pleased on the grounds, as we had as students all those years ago.

"So," I began, still hovering over him, our mouths inches apart, "Leonard."

"Oh, God." Raul pushed me away and sat up. "Jealous much?"

I slid away from him by perhaps as much as a foot. "Well, you have to admit, the whole thing was strange."

What I'd done to him in The Metropolitan Museum of Art was perverted, yes, very, but it was *my* choice.

Raul looked angry, maybe even disgusted. Had I ruined what could have been an otherwise nice afternoon? Something resembling old times. I turned away and watched young coeds toss a frisbee to each other. I watched the students seduce each other. I watched their naïve, inexperienced faces still unaccustomed to disappointment and loss. I envied them and pitied them at the same time, even as some caught me watching.

A few minutes later we were strolling through the campus, regaining the days of our precocious scholarship, laughing at our younger selves for claiming to know what we thought we knew, and finding parallels to the story Pegasus and Joe and Dr. Alessandro in *The Touring Barbarism*.

We passed St. Paul's Chapel, the scene of our first gamble. He'd gone down on me in one of the confessionals. I worried the priest would hear us, leaving us unabsolved of our sins. Raul grabbed my hand, which startled me in the best possible way. Our chasms would be perpetually emptied and refilled.

INT. CLINT RESIDENCE — MASTER BEDROOM — EVENING

Mary and Monroe sit on their bed, cross legged, and stare into each other's eyes, while holding hands. They seem to be meditating, humming with relaxed jaws and straight spines. The visions within them and between them merge and then dissipate and what remains is clarity and direction. They speak in a trancelike state with a stuffy boxiness.

                    MARY
     We were wrong.

                    MONROE
     We often are, Mary.

                    MARY
     You were wrong to build those

bombs.

                    MONROE
And you were wrong to interfere in
tribal practices.

                    MARY
Pegasus was right to chastise us.

                    MONROE
He was right to bring all those
people into our home.

                    MARY
He tried to teach us, but we have
been resisting his lessons.

                    MONROE
Maybe it's about time we showed him
what we've learned.

We passed Low Library and Raul smiled. He leaned into me and kissed
my neck, and I remembered the time we'd had sex in the janitor's closet
on the second floor. He'd gagged me with his sweatshirt to keep me from
moaning for fear we'd get caught. He'd hurt me upon penetration because he
hadn't lubricated properly but we were only kids at the time so who could
blame him for not knowing. I held the memory of the rush, the defiant pride
in transgression, screwing in sovereign, dignified places and almost getting
caught by sovereign, dignified people, and then we moved on.

INT. LIVING ROOM — DAY

Mary and Monroe stand in the living room before their son, his lover, and their teacher, and apologize. Joe and Pegasus are on either side of Dr. Alessandro, holding hands like proper cultists

                    DR. ALESSANDRO
        Why are you sorry, Dr. Donizetti-
        Clint? *Mr.* Clint?

                    MONROE
        I'm a doctor, too, *Brian*.

                    DR. ALESSANDRO
        Of course, you are.

                    MARY
            (genuinely contrite)
        Pegasus, and Joe, and Doctor
        Alessandro. We have been frauds,
        you see.

                    JOE
        We saw. We still see!

                    MONROE
        And we would like to make things
        right.

MARY

After many hours sitting with *it*,
sitting with ourselves, cutting
through the clutter of this
material world and all our hang
ups, we were able to figure out the
ways in which we have deviated from
our path.

DR. ALESSANDRO

I hope you meditated on the
parts you played in India and at
Raytheon.

MONROE

Those were the very foundations of
our wrongs. They took up the bulk
of our psychic commitments.

MARY

We thought we were doing good, and
we never wanted to hurt anyone, but
these were the jobs we chose, and
the contributions we made.

PEGASUS

You will also have to apologize to
Phyllis, Paul, and Jonah for making
them feel uncomfortable here.

MONROE
We intend to, son.

As we discussed the script, we strolled past Harkness Theater on the south end of campus, just beside Butler Library, not far from the journalism building where they award the Pulitzers. Raul grabbed me by the collar and kissed me insatiably, like biting into an apple, and when he pulled away it was slowly, and a fine line of saliva dangled between us like a gossamer spiderweb. When we were sophomores Raul and I made love in the backstage of the theater, behind the sandbags and crates of props. And all while the actors rehearsed. He was inside me and the actors playing Konstantin and Irina and Pyotr reciting Chekhov's dialogue were only a few yards from us on the other side of the curtain. A weird turn-on. After finishing, we remained there for an hour until the actors left.

We headed off campus and ended up on Broadway walking north, passing the main entrance, and ended up at Teachers College, a series of dark red brick buildings in rectangular formation that ran to Amsterdam. We paused at the corner in front of Horace Mann to reflect further on our libidinous youth.

INT. KITCHEN — EVENING

Mary and Monroe find Paul, Phyllis, and Jonah in the kitchen playing gin rummy and drinking their best scotch.

MONROE
We are sorry if we made you
ever feel at all unwelcome or
uncomfortable here.

MARY

We are happy to have you, in fact.

PHYLLIS

Your son is an angel.

PAUL

He is surely at least a saint.

JONAH

At the very least a martyr.

Mary and Monroe think for a moment that this is
their home, they pay the mortgage and the taxes
and the utilities, and it is they who suffer,
so if there are any angels, saints, or martyrs
it would surely be them.

MARY

In any event, please stay as long
as you like.

MONROE

And make yourselves at home.

Phyllis, Jonah, and Paul laugh. A drunken,
hard laugh that suggests something callous and
satiric. They are laughing at their apologizers.
Mary and Monroe know it, too, and they accept
the ridicule, maybe even welcome it.

PHYLLIS
And what's yours is ours, right?

PAUL
And su casa es mi casa, eh?

JONAH
Guests are God, no?

Mary and Monroe turn away from the squatters whom they now anoint guests and shuffle back into their bedroom, the only untouched part of their house. They will continue to meditate, seeking further revelations and transcendences. They will gird themselves from their sins and the punishments and the company that consumed their sanctuary. Mary and Monroe know little salvation, but they will keep looking.

Inside Horace Mann, we fondled each other under the desk while listening to Dr. Weintraub prattle on about Thorndike and Bandura. I held him from behind, sniffing his collar as he rubbed my arms that held him. I recalled a rugby player named Philip watching us, getting turned on.

We walked, hand in hand, back onto campus. We were not ready to let this enchanted day close. We needed to keep it open through the grit of our desire and the fuel of our erotic memories and the story we'd keep telling.

INT. CLINT RESIDENCE — DINING ROOM — EVENING

The next day. Phyllis, Paul, and Jonah join Pegasus, Joe, and Dr. Alessandro in the dining

room during dinner, which Mary and Monroe prepare
as a sort of contrition banquet. There is ham,
brisket, honeyed brussels sprouts, and apple
pie. They had spent the day shopping, cooking,
and baking. It is a supper that would affirm
their grace and hospitality.

Phyllis, Paul, and Jonah, drink fast and full
just as quickly, belch, fart, and chortle
through dessert. Dr. Alessandro, Pegasus, and
Joe observe patiently, almost obediently. Mary
and Monroe oblige the boorish display.

                    PHYLLLIS
            (red-faced with a stained blouse
            she'd taken from Mary's closet)
        You want our blessing, do you?

                    PAUL
            (mashed potatoes and pie crust
            caught in his beard)
        They do.

                    JONAH
            (wine drippling down his stubbly
            chin)
        They want us to absolve them.

                    MONROE
            (unsure, awkwardly playing with
            his utensils)

We were hoping things could be
pleasant here from now on.

                    MARY
          (folding and refolding her cloth
          napkin in her lap)
     We want a harmonic home. We want to
     be family now.

Dr. Alessandro, Joe, and Pegasus whisper amongst
themselves as Phyllis, Jonah, and Paul laugh
themselves to tears and a coughing fit. Mary
and Monroe look at each other and then at their
son and his coterie and then at the squatters/
guests. They think to themselves, why are they
laughing? We are being sincere! (<u>NOTE: This</u>
<u>will be communicated by the expressions of the</u>
<u>actors playing Mary and Monroe. Or maybe through</u>
<u>voice over.</u>)

We loitered before Schermerhorn Hall, and I studied the patina roofed
building of wending corridors where Thomas Hunt Morgan won the
1933 Nobel Prize in Physiology or Medicine for uncovering the genetic
characteristic of the fruit fly and where Raul Sandovar had frequently defiled
me. We had christened many rooms there, too.

"Raul," I began, trying to put into words a request for him to forgo the
plot to undo *RFN*, but I knew it would sound ludicrous to say such things
out loud, I also knew I'd be wasting my breath. He was going to do whatever
it was that was in his mind to do.

"What?" he asked.

"Never mind."

CHAPTER 27

The day had finally come for an in-person meeting with elusive Caroline and the mythic Darlington Brothers at a French bistro on the Upper West Side. Though the restaurant was Michelin-starred and therefore prohibitively priced, the last time I'd dined there with Caroline a gigantic cockroach ran across my foot in the bathroom. Charming and expensive. The day at Columbia only half a week ago lingered fondly and I missed Raul in a way that was alien and familiar. I wished he'd been here holding my hand, reminding me of our lascivious college days, filling in the silent gaps, defending me as only he could. But he was not here. I was alone at this roast.

Caroline and Ernest and Logan Darlington had already polished off a bottle of Beaujolais and most of the appetizers—crackers with caviar, mini beef tourtieres, and shrimp tartlets—when I arrived.

Ernest was shorter than Logan but better built. A squat athlete maybe. Logan had the prettier face but was rail thin. They both had thick black mops of hair and spoke with a strange mix of cockney and Boston accents. I'd read in a *Variety* profile that they were born in the English countryside and raised in Massachusetts, though traveled to London for summers and winters throughout their youth, so the hybrid voices made sense.

"I'm relieved we can finally do this," said Caroline, purposefully holding a cracker with caviar as if it were fine china.

"I know, I don't know why I never thought to arrange a luncheon," I said, sounding like an idiot for using the word 'luncheon.'

"'Luncheon,'" murmured Ernest to Logan, to which both men giggled like misfits.

"It's nice to see you again, Ethan, Logan," I said, shaking their hands and sitting across from them.

The brothers had eyes that intimated telepathy. They glanced at each other but stared at others, as though they'd sent and received signals from each other in preparation for mind alteration of targets or combatants. I was sure that everyone in their world were either targets or combatants, except for each other. They were each other's savior and ally.

"How is our little baby developing, Julian?" asked Logan, clearly drunker than Ethan. "Are you incubating him responsibly?"

"Yeah, oh yes, it's—*he's*—almost done," I said. "Well, the first draft of the season, anyway. I have one episode left."

"I was reading your *New Yorker* piece again over the weekend and Logan and I think maybe it's not a bad idea to incorporate some of your other zany family members into the series," said Ernest.

This was the request I'd most feared and most welcomed.

"Oh, okay, like who?"

"Maybe your tragic mother or your crazy brother-in-law or your queer nephew in Arizona," said Logan. "Such fun characters."

A waiter brought a bottle of cabernet to the table and poured a drop for Caroline to taste. She sniffed, drank, swished, and nodded. The waiter filled our glasses.

"You know, gentleman," began Caroline, reclining in her chair as if it were a chez and this were a lounge in a 1940s noir to which she'd bought the rights. "The contract was explicit about which characters would be portrayed in the series. We'd have to get the lawyers back into the conversation before anything is decided creatively."

"Of course, Caroline," said Ernest, looking bizarrely like a Peter Lorre caricature with colossal eyes and outsized bags, dark and heavy, that communicated terminal boredom. "This is just a casual chat about where we might like to go, maybe even down the line, should MAX decide to do season two with us."

I could feel Logan staring at me and when I turned to him, he wore his sad face, beseeching, pitying, and fretful. He was likely always fretful.

"Are *you* okay with that, though, Julian?" asked Logan.

"Why wouldn't I be?" I'd been too assured, knowing the further damage this would do to my family and to our ever-tenuous relationship. I grabbed my glass of cabernet and started to drink.

Everyone laughed, though there was no joy, only a kind of cynical, defeated mischief found in end times gallows humor. Caroline shrugged with an air of superior apathy, a narcotized smirk, and eyes nearly soldered shut with too much mascara. She reminded me in that moment of Patsy Stone as played by Joanna Lumley in *Absolutely Fabulous*.

"But keep in mind," began Caroline, unexpectedly the most sober in attendance, "These are not really characters in a fictional story, right? They are Julian's relatives. His family."

This was a new Caroline. For months she had been encouraging me to "burn down my family" and write freely about myself and the people I knew and sometimes loved. She'd championed memoir as the new fiction, as important to 21st century storytelling as the novel was to the 20th. She urged me to treat my words as assassination attempts on those who'd mistreated me. Her concern about the propriety of the cable series astounded me.

I finished my glass of wine and poured another.

"I think there is a difference between literature and visual media," I said.

"A double standard," said Caroline.

"No, a *difference*."

"And what *is* the difference, Julian?" asked Logan.

"Well, for starters," I began, "no one reads anymore, so no one will ever know if you write something hurtful about them in a book."

"It's true," said Caroline. "If you want to bury a secret, publish it."

I spoke with intention and treaded carefully, prattling on about how depictions of real-life people in visual media automatically feels sensationalist, even gratuitous, because you're showing non-scripted behavior and consequences, and so it's always too graphic and in bad taste, even when it's not meant to be. Ernest and Logan gawked at me with stony faces. Caroline refilled her glass. Another bottle of Beaujolais arrived.

"So … we're in the business of exploitation, then," said Ernest, picking at the diamond stud in his right ear. "Did you realize that, Logan?"

"And here I thought we were fellow storytellers," said Logan, taking off and putting back on the gold ring on his right index finger.

"Anyway, said Ernest. "Your take is almost impossible. Even reality shows are scripted. And documentaries are constructed through the literal and figurative lens of a director."

I grew hot under the bright exposure of my ignorance. I knew nothing about film and TV. I was a fraud and they found me out. I panicked.

"Look, I did not call what you do exploitation," I said. "Lord knows, I'd sell out my mother if it meant a big TV or movie deal, I mean—"

Caroline, though visibly unnerved by the unrest amongst the brothers, saved the day by talking about how I'd been made in the mold of John Steinbeck in that I wrote sobering prose about the underclass. Caroline was the consummate host and any chink in the cordial armor was enough to fluster her to the point of discernable panic. She told them how much I loved the movies and Hollywood and all the glamor and pageantry. She'd recreated me before my very eyes. I had no idea who the person was she'd been talking about.

I also wasn't entirely sure how I had started this row, and as I moved in on my third glass of cabernet, I took a deep breath and inverted my eyebrows, playing stupid as I had when called on by a teacher during a class in which I'd been unprepared.

"Well, there are so many things to consider and it's all so ambiguous and who is to say what is moral or immoral, right?" I hemmed and hawed and sniggered and drank. "I mean, 'exploitation' is a big word, no? It's imperative to weigh intention against effect in these matters."

"What a load," said Ernest.

"A load of shit!" added Logan.

"A load of jizz!" said Ernest, not to be outdone by his brother.

Both men shared sardonic laughter. Caroline made a face, broadcasting her revulsion.

"Look," began Ernest, "If the actors involved consent to the scenes and no one is coerced into doing something they're uncomfortable with and if the people, or the families of the people, if the people are dead, being portrayed are okay with the depiction, and if the communities being represented are okay with it, then I suppose it's all perfectly fine, right?"

"Well," I began, emboldened by the drinks, "my family has not been okay with any part of the article and the book I am writing, and they're relieved to know they won't be portrayed in the series, though I have yet to hear from my aunt and uncle and cousin, but I can't imagine they'll accept how they're going to be shown in *The Touring Barbarism.*"

"Shall we cancel the whole production, then, Julian?" said Logan, his eyes sharp like those of a killer. A killer of careers.

"Just scrap a year of pre-production and all the writing you've done?" added Ethan, his mouth revealing fangs.

I finished my glass of wine and started another.

"I've heard enough!" Caroline was again on her feet, her cloth napkin crumpled and, in the air, her wine glass nearly toppled, her chair making a shrill screeching sound against the inlaid wood floor, and tripping over Logan's big, inconsiderate feet, too far to the side as he'd sat wide-legged, manspreading, occasioning the precocious filmmaker to reel and fumble with the literary agent's chaotic hands as they clawed the air for purchase. He caught her and she was temporarily stabilized.

"If you want to kill this project, Julian, that is fine, but I will be keeping my commission and I will move on without you," she said, adjusting her beige Hermes cashmere scarf and gripping her pink Chanel. "I am not in the habit of wasting time or fucking with my own reputation."

Logan looked like he'd seen a ghost and even Ernest approximated something approaching terror. The Darlington Brothers had homicide written all over them. The room itself took on a frost that was thick with disease, a crisis on parity with a nuclear meltdown and all the radiation poisoning it would beget.

I spoiled everything. Years and years of sacrifice and effort and networking and praying and scheming and ass kissing and costly improvements, and I'd undone it all in a single evening. I'd started a fire, spread a cancer, and it was up to only me to put out the flame, snuff out the metastasis.

"Caroline," I said firmly though with unambiguous despondency. "Come on! It was a joke. Just a joke! Of course, we are going to make *The Touring Barbarism*! Of course, I will write the rest of my lunatic family into the second and, God-willing, third season!"

Caroline paused at the entrance and turned back to the table. She looked for a moment like a schoolgirl who'd been scolded by her parents only to have them do an about-face and seek amends by proffering a bowl of candy or a day at the amusement park. She relented and sat with less slapstick than when she stood. I'm not sure any of them had ever seen her so humbled and I can only attribute the effectiveness of my plea to the cracking of my voice and the despair in my tone.

Ernest refilled her glass of wine, and she drank. "Well," she said. "Now that that's settled."

I may have still been on leave from my senses, but I reached across the table and took the Darlington Brothers by their hands, heavy, hairy, sweaty, and looked into their eyes, doing my best DeNiro, and in a quiet, focused purr freighted with dire seriousness, said:

"We are going to make great media together, the kind of content that breaks ratings and wins awards and is written about in *The Nation* and *The Atlantic* and *The New Yorker*, and, like, all Monday morning water cooler moments you could hope for! I mean, the type of show that cracks everyone's top ten lists, the type of show all critics, when they look back on decades from now, will count as the best in television of the 21st century, and we will ride my family's idiosyncrasies and crimes and bad behavior all the way to the bank. I have earned this success and for trusting me, you will, too."

The Darlingtons cringed and pulled their hands away. Caroline chuckled and drank some more. She searched my face for anything recognizable. I excused myself and went to the bathroom.

On the toilet, leaning my head against the door, I could hear them down the hall laughing and joking, and then when I directed my listening to the subjects of their discussions, I could eventually make out, or maybe just imagine, the things they'd been saying.

"Well, there is a cash cow if ever there was one. The kid is really just an okay writer but dear God what a fucked-up family." "A fucking goldmine! I am grateful those barbarians gave birth to someone smart enough to know the lucrative value of such dysfunction." "They're degenerates, and MAX loves degenerate behavior. It's art in their hands." "I don't know what I was saying before about them being 'real people'. They're total characters perfect for a lampoon!"

The room spun as I searched for the cockroach, but he wasn't to be found. There was only a giant Raid trap and a spot of black mold.

CHAPTER 28

I'd spent the week after that dinner with Caroline and the Darlington Brothers replaying what they'd maybe said about my family, and about me. I rationalized well. At the end of the day the book, and future books, the cable series, and subsequent seasons would all serve me, my career, and my legacy. For fear of sounding like Ayn Rand, social work was a coward's game. I was a writer and I wanted success and I wouldn't lie to myself anymore about wanting it. There was no shame in it. But I did not intend to ruin my family and I was not sure how much any of my projects really would ruin them. It's not like any of them were public figures or running for office or holding high-profile corporate jobs where their questionable characters could be seen as liabilities. We also never had good relationships. I was continually the uncle on the periphery, the brother to be endured, the son to be used and treated as a prop for infantilization. What had I owed them?

On my way home from the supermarket, shlepping four canvas shopping bags that began to chaff my palms after several blocks, I found Pegasus, Aunt Mary, and Uncle Monroe sitting on the front stoop of my building. It was a surreal image, shockingly out of context. Though they lived close—Astoria was a mere three miles away—their world was so foreign to me and the rest of my family that they might as well have been living in Australia. We'd also not seen each other in many years.

"Julian," said Aunt Mary, flatly though with a glimmer of a smile.

"What're you doing here?" I asked, not intending to sound accusatorial or defensive, but failing at both.

"We need to talk to you, Julian," said Mary, stepping closer, "About your article and this cable series we hear you're writing about us."

Pegasus and Monroe could barely contain their hatred for me. Their faces fixed masks of scorn and blame.

"I haven't seen you for a while," I began, putting on a congenial show while trying to make it to my front door.

"Look, Julian, you owe us reparations!" snapped Monroe, poking me in the chest.

Mary grabbed his hand and became ghostly white. "Monroe, you said you wouldn't!"

Monroe gathered himself and stepped back. Pegasus looked as if he'd gotten off on the assault. I was sickened by the prospect of what else would transpire during this ensnarement.

"Monroe was damaged, Julian, by your essay, and so was I," said Mary.

"And so was I, for fuck's sake!" screamed Pegasus in a warbled screech, which prompted his father to comfort him and at least two passersby to stop and gawk.

"How would you ever know the extent of my job details, Julian?" Monroe was again in my face, and he trembled with an ashen pallor. "Hmm? I certainly never told you because they are classified, and I would never have jeopardized my livelihood that way!"

I stepped back and into the door, banging my elbow.

"You understand what you've done, don't you? Raytheon terminated me. And I'm under investigation for leaking classified information, which could be interpreted by certain juries and judges as treason! Which means, I could go to prison, you little fuck!"

Monroe shoved me again, and again I banged into the door. This was not right. Mary, Monroe, and Pegasus were the progressive, passive subset of my volatile, violent family. They weren't supposed to get physical with me. We were supposed to engage in battle of wits, citing academics and history and relying on sound science, not brute force.

"Tell him about you, Mom!" Pegasus yelled like a mad child.

"Pegasus," whispered Mary to her son as if he'd been a wild dog off his leash, before returning to me with an aged face, a face weathered by some fierce and unforgiving frenzy. "Columbia's been investigating me, Julian. And I was close to being brought back, but the article, your article … and now the MAX show that they're talking about … they had to distance themselves from me, Julian. And so…"

"And so now both of my parents are out of jobs, you asshole!" hollered Pegasus clawing at me, sending me again into the door, prompting several new pedestrians to stop and stare at the crazy people making a scene. He went on about how Dr. Alessandro and Joe left him. He blamed my "literary crucifixion."

"Okay, I understand, I'm sorry," I started, to which Pegasus scoffed and lunged for my throat, though was intercepted by his parents.

"What can I do?" I asked.

"Do not let this damned television show happen, at the very least, have some sense of decency and cancel your contract," pleaded Monroe, "Maybe we can salvage some parts of our lives."

"We appreciate that this is a big break for you," began Mary, struggling to remain steady, her eyes pink, her voice tremulous, "I know you decided on psychology, after all, but I do recall the wonderful short stories you'd shared with me and your mother when you were in high school, and I knew you'd one day succeed, and it would be inevitable and great, but not this, not with this, not like this."

I could have lied. To get them off my front stoop, I should have told them what they wanted to hear. If I was smart that's what I would have done. But clearly, I was not smart.

"I can't do that, Aunt Mary, I'm sorry."

Again, Pegasus lunged at me as he squawked like a poked macaw. Again, his parents restrained him. I fumbled with my keys and then I saw them. Phyllis, Jonah, and Paul, their clothes clean and form-fitting, looking every bit the part of conventional citizens. They tentatively approached.

"We asked them to meet us here," said Mary.

"You know, you *writer*," said Phyllis, her voice sounding like it had been passed through a cheese grater, and not at all as I had expected, "you had no business writing about our private lives! Grifter!"

"And to do so with such irresponsible abandon," added Jonah, sluggish and barely coherent. "You misrepresented the lot of us! Swine!"

Paul groaned like he was passing a kidney stone and then centered himself and mustered the will to let me have it, too. "Maybe we didn't want the whole world finding out our business! Maybe we didn't want to become world-known *hoboes!*"

Jonah, Phyllis, and Paul looked beaten down by circumstance. I had known they'd been well cared for by Mary and Monroe, but still they looked as though they had been through an awful ordeal. Their collective dishevelment reminded me of one of the worst stories from my time as a social worker. The deranged director of a group home who'd taken some of our service recipients in for extended stays of rehabilitation and career counseling, brought four of them home where she orchestrated a kind of fight club in her basement, inciting them to engage each other as violently as possible. Maury, one of the frail older men in the group, had died during the serial, organized altercations, and the director had hidden his body in a storage space for six months before the odor of his decomposition alerted the manager and eventually the police.

I now knew that this carousel would never stop rotating and I could never get off. They wanted me to undo something that had already been well done. I noticed several of the bystanders witnessing this gross exhibition of private wrongs publicly punished—something I recognize I'd done in my very essay and would more thoroughly do in the book, oh the irony—were neighbors and all they wanted was to get back home.

"Look, there's really nothing I can do about any of it now," I said, pointing to the small crowd gathering behind my accusers, "and we are blocking the entrance and these people would like to get in!"

"Oh, no, it's okay, Julian," said Carlos Estrada, a neighbor from down the hall, "There's no rush."

Mr. Estrada had clearly been enjoying the lashing, an otherwise suitable diversion on a slow Thursday afternoon. As had the others in the audience. They waited and listened, expecting the perverse production to yield further tension and titillation.

"Okay, here," I said, studying Phyllis, Paul, and Jonah, and their desiccated, oversized mouths, starved and ready to further punish, "Please take these."

I held out the bags of groceries, waiting for the squatters to snatch them, which they did while exaggerating their protuberant bottom lips, kinked eyes, and yawning wrinkles. They crudely, demonstratively inspected the contents in the canvas bags—apples, oranges, broccoli, kale, asparagus stalks, chicken thighs, peanut butter, blueberry jam, gluten free bread, eggs, oat milk, toilet paper, paper towels—and shrugged, disappointed, perhaps hoping for alcohol or steak, chocolate or candy, and shuffled away, leaving me with my wretched distant family, soon to be again estranged.

"I'm ready to go," said Monroe. "I need to feed the cats."

Mary nodded and touched his shoulder, turning and leaving before him, signaling for him to follow. Pegasus lingered and I expected him to assault me again, but he didn't, and he soon followed his parents to the subway down the block. Looking at the general indignation that Monroe wore and the heavy burden of shame that Pegasus carried, I again felt grateful for being my own father's sole son, sole child, and how I would sire no progeny, end the surname with me, with my work, my books.

CHAPTER 29

Against my better judgment, I invited Raul to Ed and Kevin's Indian-cuisine dinner party in honor of Suliman. A few days earlier news broke that a would-be assassin named Kareem Bigloo attacked him. I'd not seen Suliman in months. He'd managed to dodge his fatwa for twenty years until his luck ran out while giving a reading on stage in Newark. Bigloo was a 26-year-old Muslim man—a T-Mobile store manager in Fort Lee whose family emigrated from Iran when he was a kid—who hoped to cash in on the three-million-dollar bounty offered by ISIS resulting in the esteemed, notorious Pakistani American writer's death. He managed to stab Suliman seven times before horrified audience members ripped him away. Two punctures had been especially devastating, costing Suliman a right ear and a great loss of blood from his neck. He would survive the attack, but recovery would be long and slow. The attending physicians confirmed he would remain in the hospital hooked up to various tubes and machines that kept him alive for many more months.

"It's really horrific," said Ed, as he ate chicken vindaloo. "He made it decades without incident and then this, the moment he drops his guard."

"It goes to show, you're never safe," said Colin, cutting a vegetable samosa up into bite-sized pieces. "And people never forget."

Earlier, Kevin had told me he thought the party would be in bad taste, but Ed needed something to look forward to, something to take his mind off work, his ailing friend, and his own decrepitude.

Fanny poked at a bowl of chicken tikka masala with her fork before nibbling. "His book sales have never been better."

"I read in *The Times* this morning that several of his titles are seeing a one hundred and fifty percent increase," said Joan, eyeballing the Indian spread without touching any of it save for a piece of dry naan while recurrently jotting ideas in her little notebook.

"Has anyone spoken to him yet?" asked Fen, sipping lassi.

"I've been communicating to him through his agent," said Colin. "He is responsive and talking."

On the way over I read that the attacker's mother has disowned him. It was the very least she could do. There was also a movement online to have Suliman short listed for the Nobel in literature. He had been speaking his mind freely at great risk to his life and family and reputation for over forty years. He deserved the plaudits. He earned the best adjectives—brave, courageous, heroic. What happened to him was unspeakable. It rattled me. A writer could be killed for what he writes.

"It takes serious balls to do what he's done," said Raul, commanding everyone's temporary attention with his phrasing. They'd been unaccustomed to masculinist assertions.

"So, Raul," said Edward, smiling and nodding pleasantly at Raul, a gesture of provisional approval, "Julian told me your grandfather was Guadalupe Sandoval."

"Yes, sir," said Raul, with a deferential smirk.

"I met him once in the mid 70s at a reading in Tucson," said Edward. "He was a lovely man, a gentleman, and a hell of a writer."

"Thank you. We're all very proud of what he's accomplished."

"I met him at a conference in Detroit in the early 80s," said Joan. "A very elegant and elemental spirit."

Raul smiled at Joan's description, maybe finding the word choice condescending like when some disingenuous white people say that well-spoken black people are "articulate." I'm sure that one of the reasons he never pursued writing was because holding the Sandoval surname proved daunting, too much to live up to. At least I, a writer from nothing, had nothing to live up to.

And then the atoms in the room shifted. Raul, spookily still, mastered their universe, rearranging the molecules. He was a magician of mood. He mocked everyone with haughty posturing, inside jokes, discreet giggles. Groans and eyerolls. I knew where he'd come from. No one else there, despite knowing the work of his lauded grandfather, had a clue what he'd endured. His return to Tucson after being away for so long, seeking an origin story, restoration of family, and reclamation of identity, proved a disappointment. The origins were a forgotten litany of stories that had been for so long only orally retold. No record survived. The family showed their true faces, a mob of degenerate users, broken down and always taking. The identity shriveled in the arid plains, sizzling under the Sonoran sun like shed snakeskin.

Raul spoke affectedly to, I believe, spoof the very scene in which he found himself. I am unsure that anyone noticed or cared as they knew their scene was beyond spoofery.

"I have to say," began Raul to Joan, still in lampoon mode. "I thought the backlash on Twitter and with the critics of your novel *Redhead* was unfair and unwarranted and *not* bona fide criticism of your craft."

"Well, thank you for saying that, but it sure did leave marks, all the same," said Joan.

"I warned her," began Edward. "I said, do you remember Joan, if you write a dark fictionalized version of Lucille Ball's life people will criticize you. You cannot get away with sullying the memory of beloved American icons. The idolators will not stand for it."

I knew that Joan hadn't intended to desecrate Ball's memory but instead sought to criticize the industry that mistreated her. It must have shocked her that everyone misread her intentions, but America was still the old wild west, after all. They all want to kill the old sheriff in town to make way for the new arrival. Joan's hand had been automatically doodling until the sketches took shape as letters and eventually whole concepts, but she broke away from it to smile warmly at me, maybe knowing my thoughts. I offered a look of friendly stoicism meant to indicate she would never be alone in a cultural scrap.

Kevin chewed on a mouthful of basmati and smiled up at me with insatiable eyes, unbothered by Raul's presence.

During dessert and Riesling, Raul and I chatted alone in the living room. Near the fireplace I recounted the events of the final episode of *The Touring Barbarism*, no doubt colored by my run-in with Mary, Monroe, and Pegasus. Though while the confrontation unfolded, I had felt nervous and guilty. I found myself, only minutes afterward, angry and offended that they'd demanded reparations, expecting my bloodletting.

"So, how are we ending the season, Julian?" asked Raul, scrutinizing a pair of small clay busts of Ed and Kevin on the mantle. "My time in New York is nigh."

I thought about Raul's plan and stepped mindlessly into the hearth, feeling the burn on my calves and almost knocking over a set of pokers.

INT. CLINT RESIDENCE — EVENING

Dr. Alessandro, Pegasus, and Joe decide that there needs to be an outward show of penance. Phyllis, Paul, and Jonah agree.

MONTAGE: Mary and Monroe cook them three meals a day, clean up after them, do their laundry, generally, submit too willingly to servitude.

INT. KITCHEN — DAY

Monroe mops the floor. Mary cooks a pot of stew. The cats lounge.

MONROE
I don't know why they're making us

do this. We've apologized several
times.

                    MARY
It's clearly not enough, Monroe.

Monroe checks his veins for a suitable pump
as his fitness routines have been limited to
housekeeping.

                    MONROE
Apologies are not in words, but in
actions.

                    MARY
These are acts of contrition, then.

The cats lick themselves and study the humans
as they toil.

Raul watched the famous writers pick at the assortment of sweets and
sipped their wine. I could tell he was already undressing them and would
soon share with me their faults, their hypocrisies, their corruptions, their
pretenses.

Raul turned away from the crowd and stepped closer to me, closer to
the fire. Raul's musk was freed by the heat of the fireplace. It warmed me as
much as the embers.

"What are you boys up to?" asked Kevin, appearing beside Raul.

"Julian's project," said Raul, sitting on the camel leather sofa from the 70s,
shopworn though still sturdy and plush. "You know the Darlington Brothers
are adapting some of his memoir into a cable series for MAX."

"I read about that," said Kevin. "How exciting. Maybe we can do a plot walk. I always help Ed with his."

Kevin slid his arm across the small of my back and I let him, if for no other reason than to make Raul jealous. The memory of Leonard was still fresh. Raul noticed and quickly looked away, pretended to be interested in the bowl of salted nuts.

"Okay, but let's sit," I said.

Kevin sat to my right, Raul to my left. Raul pressed his right leg against mine, maybe to remind me of my place or to anchor me for support. Kevin's hand was on my leg, and he leaned close enough for me to smell whiskey on his breath.

"This is about your aunt and uncle and cousin?" asked Kevin.

"The last episode of the first season," I said.

"What's the problem? Where are you stuck?"

I watched Ed as he directed the attention of his guests our way, which made me nervous as the last thing I wanted was for them to join Kevin's plot walk of my show. They were trained assassins, and their critiques would sideline me indefinitely.

I explained to Kevin how I had wanted to have my aunt and uncle sort of martyr themselves at the altar of their son's righteousness. Kevin, his socked foot touching mine, said he liked the sound of that, but I told him that Raul worried it robbed them of agency. Kevin asked me to share the plot.

MONTAGE: Phyllis, Paul, and Jonah begin creating work for Mary and Monroe by spilling food, defecating on the floor, peeing in the cupboards, and trekking mud through the house from the yard on rainy days. Mary and Monroe grin and bear it, though, and they work assiduously to keep the house spotless, sacred in its pristine order.

INT. KITCHEN - EVENING

                    PHYLLIS
          You like to degrade yourselves this
          way.

                    JONAH
          Cleaning up our shit.

                    PAUL
          Finally, someone to lick our boots.

Pegasus observes obediently, unobtrusively. Dr.
Alessandro, ever the Svengali, shadows his every
move and prevents him from ever intervening
or objecting to the rough treatment of his
parents. Joe, too, restrains Pegasus in his
weaker moments.

                    DR. ALESSANDRO
          Let them have this.

                    PEGASUS
          Phyllis, Paul, and Jonah?

                    DR. ALESSANDRO
          Your parents.

"Do we really need more stories about masochism?" asked Ed, suddenly
sitting across from me on a rickety old chair, a true antique. "Mainstream
audiences find that kind of behavior repugnant, even though it's all I write

[290]

about."

"Is this your cable series, Julian?" asked Fanny, sitting on a recliner beside Ed. "*The Daily Beast* had a piece on it."

"Yes," said Kevin, approximating the mien of a covetous teenage girl, "I am doing a plot walk with him."

"Is your story about martyrs?" asked Joan, sitting with Fen and Colin on a perpendicular sofa, a hunter green import from Milan.

"It's about atonement, I think," I said, turning to Raul.

Raul touched me. It must have made for a sensual tableau, being sandwiched between Raul and Kevin, their hands on my knees, their thighs pressed up against mine, me blushing in the middle, reaching for both, seeking them, allowing them to steer me. I thought about atonement and punishment.

"So, did your aunt and uncle really become servants to their son and these people?" asked Fen, having clearly overheard enough of the story, or maybe she'd read my article, after all.

I groaned and continued telling the story.

As their dominant presence grows, Dr. Alessandro, Pegasus, and Joe care less about discretion and propriety and began to have sex with their bedroom door open. They do this to goad Phyllis, Jonah, and Paul, and to disgust and scandalize Mary and Monroe. It would be Mary and Monroe, in the end, who would be cleaning up after them, washing stains from their sheets.

MONROE
Why are you punishing us like this, Pegasus?

                         MARY
        Leave him. He's testing us.

                        MONROE
        Testing what? Our limits?

    Mary thought about this and didn't even smile
    at Monroe's failed joke. Our integrity, she
    thought. NOTE: To be conveyed in voice over.

"This is a cruel story," said Fen.

It was cruel and I had every right to make it cruel. I could humiliate Pegasus and his parents and ruin the likelihood of a second season in one fell swoop.

"Good storytelling," began Joan, "is compassionate, no matter how much you first make your characters suffer and lose, you must have compassion."

"It's true," added Ed. "I became a better writer when I stopped trying to impress people with my wordplay and how shocking I could be. I became better when I began treating my characters with kindness."

I couldn't believe what I was hearing. This all felt upside down. These old cynics, sophisticates of the rarified order of letters, were encouraging me, the nobody, the wannabe, the outsider, to be more compassionate, to be gentler, and to my own family, no less. How many of them had exploited strangers and friends and family for fame and profit or because they couldn't differentiate fact from fiction and only sought to tell a good story?

"I have been telling him," Raul said, "you have to go easier on these characters. You can't make them suffer or lower themselves just for the sake of narrative surprise."

I looked to my left at the man who'd been both opponent and ally and wanted to assault and embrace him.

"Yes, it seems like you are trying to degrade these characters to make a point about how extreme you could be, which is a small talent and one that will be forgotten," said Colin.

"Try to balance your savagery with wit and find some humanity," said Fanny, "The best writers have done this. You don't have to be mawkish but be humane."

I turned to Kevin. "Be humane, babe," he said, drunk but focused with pink eyes. "Just be humane."

A few minutes later, Raul and I walked to the subway station where he'd board his train south into Brooklyn and I'd board mine east to Queens. I replayed the advice of the authors, uncharacteristic of their lot, and weighed it against my own scorn for my family. The better choice would win out in the end, but I was still unsure of the direction.

"Joan seems coy," said Raul, checking out a well-built boy passing us on 6th Avenue. "Like she is pretending to be this teetotaler but is really a judgmental bitch."

"Probably," I said, watching the boy disappear into traffic.

"And what's with that weird thing she's always doing? Doodling during dinner and when we're talking?"

"I think it's a condition or something, it helps her think," I said, feeling myself become defensive of these strangers, these successful authors who didn't need my defense. "She's always writing, I read somewhere."

I saw a sex shop and almost pulled Raul into it just to shut him up, just to distract him, compel him to engage something else other than his own tired opinions and half-assed assessments of people. His cynicism was a rotten piece of meat, and I was gagging on the maggots.

"And then there's Fanny. She's all shtick all the time. Like she's following a script written in 1975."

I rolled my eyes at him and chuckled. He was now going out of his way to berate as much as possible. He'd have been better off physically assaulting them then and there, but instead he dragged their characters through the streets, smashed them into storefronts, pissed and shat all over their very good names.

"Well, I think she's funny, and so do millions of other people."

"And don't get me started on Kevin." Raul checked his phone after a notification buzzed loudly enough to cut through the city's ambient noise. Could it be Leonard requesting a rendezvous? "He wants to fuck you, you know."

"I don't know ..."

"This people are even worse than the phonies I work with," said Raul. "At least they're all honest enough to admit they do it for the money. Finance people may be full of shit, but at least they're honest about their greed and shallowness."

The need to tackle him into traffic, kick his mouth toothless, and stuff him into a manhole had never been greater. If I could no longer fuck him, I could fight him. If I could no longer love him, I could hate him. If I could no longer hold him, I could kill him. He would always get the best of me and now he was spoiling whatever world I had made for myself just before his grand, self-aggrandizing exit.

"Man, you're tough tonight," I said, subduing my ambivalent lovechild of desire and rage.

"And Ed, Little Lord Fauntleroy in the body of a bloated 80-year-old pervert."

"You're being unkind," I said, turning to him with a cringe.

"They're every bit as bad as—"

I stopped dead in my tracks and shook, people muttered obscenities under their breath as they were forced to walk around me. I hissed at them to fuck off, but only so loud that they couldn't hear. I didn't really seek an altercation.

"You're being unkind!"

Raul stared at me, his kaleidoscopic array of expressions shifting from surprised to annoyed to excited. He looked at my mouth for a moment before kissing me with wet hostility. My bottom lip nearly bled when pressed against his canines. He pulled away and smiled.

"You obviously like art, Julian," he said. "I mean, we spend most of our time together at museums or galleries."

I watched the train arrive behind him. "Yeah, Raul, I like art, so what?"

"You know of Egon Schiele, right?"

"Of course."

"So, in around 1910, he painted a series of what most people until recently thought were self-portraits."

We briefly made eye contact again. "And?"

"Turns out, they may have instead been his gay friends, perhaps even lovers."

I watched the train pull away. "Interesting, but why bring him up?"

Raul squinted. "Something about hiding in plain sight maybe."

"I don't follow."

He looked at me as if I were a fool. "Don't you?"

I surveyed his face, searching for evidence of seriousness, not just about the example he shared, but about his agenda and how soon he would implement it.

"Raul," I finally said. "Don't do it. Whatever your plan is, please don't."

He smiled at me with a novel sweetness. "It's already done, Julian."

In the cramped, rumbling, malodorous subway ride home I thought not about Raul's cryptic, theatrical answer to my plea, but to his question, and found kinship not with him, not anymore, but with the other writers. They too knew how to dole out harm artfully.

CHAPTER 30

I had not spoken with Raul since Kevin and Ed's party over a week ago. He'd ignored my texts and left my calls unanswered, which was not disconcerting as he sometimes behaved this way in the past. It wasn't until I received a text from an unrecognizable number, which I later realized was from a burner phone, that I became alarmed. The text contained a link to a *New York Times* article breaking the story about Aaron Bliss, *RFN*'s CEO, Dennis Mulvaney, *RFN*'s senior vice president, and Jackie Meadows and Richard Acini, *RFN*'s highest profile journalists, and all their racist rants, abuses of power, and sexual indiscretions as caught on voice recordings, that which Raul had amassed over several years. He'd done it, though no one would know but me as *The Times* credited the whistleblower as anonymous. Soon Reuters and the Associated Press syndicated it. MSNBC, CNN, and FOX repeated the lurid details during their hourly carousel of repetitive programs, each of the pundits putting their own spin on the accounts. Even ABC's Nightline, CBS's Evening News, and NBC's Nightly News mixed it heavily into the cycle.

Aaron Bliss's personal narrative read like a character arc on *Succession*. He became *RFN*'s CEO after marrying Claire Remington, the daughter of the founder, Jonas Remington, a few years before Jonas's colon cancer killed him. He outmaneuvered Jonas's two sons, Christopher and George, by wooing the board of directors in clearly effective ways. That was twenty-five years ago when Aaron was a younger man of forty-seven. Now seventy-two, Aaron and Claire's childless marriage had grown stale, even putrid, and he predictably, inevitably found himself romantically entangled with executive assistants, aspiring journalists, and financial analysts, provided they were young, pretty, and ambitious. Raul had overheard him joke to Dennis Mulvaney about many of these episodes in the bathroom, while Raul was hidden on the toilet.

Dennis Mulvaney and Aaron Bliss had been friends since the mid-1970s. They had met at Dartmouth during Alpha Chi Alpha's initiation week. Identifying each other as outraged white men while donning red baseball caps on campus, Dennis and Aaron hit it off immediately and stayed close into their adulthood. Aaron, no stranger to cronyism, hired Dennis as a vice president of the world news division at RFN as soon as he was made CEO. It had been Dennis's second job. He'd left a position as a senior analyst at Bear Stearns for it. Dennis's proud bigoted pronouncements, while at home in Alpha Chi Alpha's cold green brick house with the volleyball court and pig spit in the backyard, found little acceptance in big media, his thinly veiled racist anecdotes instantly chided. Aaron had told him to keep the problematic language between them and be mindful of eavesdroppers. To be clear, Aaron supported his longtime friend's racism. He just didn't want to be put in a position where he would have to defend or fire him for it. Raul, ever present, judicious, and quick with his iPhone, was able to spy on at least three incidents wherein Dennis let fly his violent words.

Jackie Meadows was a finance and journalism double major at Northwestern. With her uncommonly good looks, she bartended and modeled her way through college. She had no problem getting hired at RFN after Aaron received her audition tape. She had worn a form-fitting white blouse and short black skirt. Soon after appearing as their star anchor, she initiated a five-year affair with Aaron. Claire had known but didn't care. She'd had plenty of lovers of her own. Her marriage to Aaron was transactional. She made him a king and he ran her father's business, and therefore legacy, respectably.

Richard Asini became RFN's chief financial news reporter and anchor after a strong run at CNBC. Tall, olive-skinned, athletic, and charming, Richard cut as striking a figure as Jackie, with whom he began an unwise affair. It was perilous territory for both superstars as they'd be instantly terminated if Aaron found out. They treaded lightly, avoiding each other whenever possible. Raul had only known about their relationship because Richard bragged to his young, impressionable male assistant about his conquests when drunk at office parties. Raul only attended them for the sake of his covert operation.

At the MET all those weeks ago, Raul said there would be five targets. I imagine he had insufficient dirt on the fifth and decided to spare him or her. I was afraid for Raul, though also mightily impressed and even moved. He'd done what he said he would do, endangering himself in the process. He'd always loathed these people. Not just the powerbrokers at *RFN*, but all the children and beneficiaries of the colonizers across the country and Western world. He'd often cite his Tohono heritage, the agonies of his ancestors, the generational trauma that attached to his DNA like an oncogene, to his skin like fleas, to his psyche like a nightmare. Hundreds of years' worth of dehumanization, specious reasoning, relegation to reservations, rape, pillaging, slaughter. He'd carried in his gut the inherent resentment for whites his whole life. I never had the nerve to ask him if that mistrust and loathing carried over to me. I liked to think of myself as an exception, but he knew my family, their limited positions, their sinful prejudices. I sometimes thought that the book would prove to him that I was not them, that I could punish them for their crimes, blood be damned. I once made the mistake of claiming that I was not in the lineage of any colonists as an Italian American, that my ancestors were farmers and peasants in Italy during the English, French, Spanish, Dutch, Swedish, and Russian pilgrimages. By the time we arrived in the late 19th century as poor immigrants we were treated like rats ourselves. Even Theodore Roosevelt called us "dirty beggars" and "violent criminals," and condoned Louisiana's lynching of Italian prisoners in 1891, calling it "a rather good thing". My defense did not go over well. He reminded me that despite that unfortunate moment—and it was only a moment—in history, Italians had been fully stitched into the American fabric and were now viewed as white as their English, French, and Dutch counterparts.

I started to text "They deserved it" to the burner but then stopped myself. It was clearly Raul, and he clearly wanted no trace back to his cell, even if he was likely going to toss it, if he hadn't already.

An hour later I was at Raul's apartment. I buzzed the intercom, but there was no answer. I called and texted his original number, but, of course, he didn't respond. I tried to peek into his third-floor window, but the lights were off. I waited twenty minutes until someone finally came out. I grabbed the door before it closed and slipped inside. I knocked on his door gently at first and then after a few minutes began banging. It was ludicrous of me to be impatient. He probably wasn't even home. He'd likely already quit his job, moved out, and was somewhere in the world. Anywhere in the world. Nowhere in the world.

I'm not sure that what Raul had done was a crime. However, it was certainly grounds for termination and likely a lawsuit for libel, providing they could prove Raul had made up the allegations and doctored the recordings. I suppose if Aaron Bliss had influential friends in high enough places, like, say, the offices of the district attorney or the governor, he could convince them to charge Raul with illegal wiretapping, which was a hefty charge. A felony in New York, I believe. More than any of this, though, I am sure that Raul, like myself, was most worried that Bliss or Mulvaney would have him crippled, disfigured, or killed—"disappeared"—for his trespasses. Most provocateurs do not emerge unscathed when they poke such bears.

I guess my pounding had alerted the neighbors because someone called the super, an older man maybe in his early seventies, though regal with shaggy silver hair and a thick Croatian accent.

"Raul left," he said abruptly before I could say anything.

"He left?"

"He moved out on Tuesday morning," said the super.

"Did he say where he was going? Did he leave an address for forwarding mail?"

The super sighed with a wince, as though the question crossed a line. "He told me nothing."

I returned home where I toiled away on the book, alone now. Intermittently I watched MSNBC or PBS or scanned *The New York Times* or *The Atlantic* to follow the fallout from Raul's data leak. The board of directors had called for Bliss's immediate suspension and Mulvaney's termination. In a bold reaction that did not help his cause, Bliss termed Meadows and Asini. His lawyers claimed "cause," as in their willful affair and coverups caused damage to *RFN*'s reputation and therefore its stock, which tumbled throughout the course of the week, anyway.

CHAPTER 31

Raul's disappearance set in motion a great expansion. The expansion of my *New Yorker* article into a book. Also, the expansion of my capacity to write frankly, even coldly, about people I'd known my whole life. His pain and anger gave me the permission to go after the truth, despite the damage. Truth became a question itself. I'd still not decided on a satisfying definition. Even objective truths could be obscured by perception, twisted into something else by memory. I'd wondered if the meetings with my family were not instances of ethnographic research as much as they were justifications for procrastination. To the dismay of the purists in my life, I wrote most of my book in the Notes app of my iPhone. I primarily did this because the book came together for me while revisiting the places where Raul and I had been. The memories seemed to fuel my agency.

Before embarking on the tour of our many splendored scenes, I began in my apartment and wrote about my mother. What had been in *The New Yorker* only a few pages turned into an overlong chapter in my book. Over the course of the six months that it took me to write a draft of my memoir that was suitable enough for submission to Caroline, I uncovered the now grown children of my maternal grandfather. The adults who knew little to nothing about my mother, their half sibling. The offspring of Grandpa's mistresses, the woman with whom he'd cheated on his wife, my mother's doormat mother, were awful people. My parent's parents were awful people, and I sought comments.

Jill lived in White Plains and had two children. She lived in a big house and her husband was a commercial airline pilot. She was a receptionist for a Park Avenue plastic surgeon. She met with me after I hunted her down through my mother's Ancestry results at a café on Madison and 71st. I'd bought Mom a genetic test and subscription to do such research. Jill spoke to me but refused to go on record. I included transcriptions of our interview anyway, much of which centered on how her mother had saved my mother's father by taking her away from my grandmother, Philomena Theresa Maria Donizetti, as her giving nature was "taking from" him. Philomena Theresa Maria invited in the world and in so doing pushed her husband out. Jill's brother Charlie was a divorce attorney in Queens and was himself divorced. His son lived with his ex-wife in Brooklyn. He was polite and eloquent, and he did go on record reiterating Jill's version of events when we met at the Brooklyn Museum of Art. Their father, my mother's father, had died years earlier from pneumonia at 82.

Raul had stripped me naked in the middle of the living room and manhandled me gently. I imagined him here again and sitting beside me.

I mentioned to Jill and Charlie that I would be writing about their father's sexually inappropriate relationship with his daughter, my mother, and they were horrified. They threatened to file a lawsuit if I went ahead with the story, but I assured them I indeed would and couldn't be cowed. I told them I welcomed a trial so that everyone could hear firsthand the litany of times he touched my mother inappropriately, made lewd comments to her, and treated her as a spectator to his affairs with other women. He'd also beat her mother in front of her, and on several occasions exposed himself to her. Of course, my mother would likely disown me if I included these accounts and many of them were inflamed based on her very vague allusions, but nothing would stop me from speaking the truth at this point, whatever that was.

Though she would not see it that way, my mother was the reason I was doing this. My aim was to vindicate her. To provide a psychological basis for her criminal behavior as an adult, the pilfering from church funds, the bilking of donations from members of her community and congregation, and her moral trespasses into puritanical campaigns. She had witnessed a horrible man do horrible things to her and her mother. Who wouldn't grow up sexually repressed, who wouldn't have an affair with her daughter's ex, who wouldn't use nonprofit money from a tax-exempt organization to fund "ethic" cleansing crusades?

I'd spent a week at home writing and rewriting the chapter on my mother and took my workshop to Raul's boxing gym to develop the chapter on my father. I'd visit it a few days a week for about a week and a half, maybe two, to recall the thrashing Raul had given me in the ring, before spectators. I'd always appreciated his domination. It had a calming effect.

There is something about getting hit that centers a person. Even with the mouthguard and the headgear, the blows brought clarity and toughened the will. Maybe I would not have written about these things if not for Raul, if not for his punches. A bloody lip, a swollen nose, a black eye. The injuries are harmless and temporary, but they remind us that we are made of tougher material.

The chapter on my father will make him violent, I thought while sparring with a guy named Floyd, who'd been friends with Raul. He had a long reach and a hard right hook. Each time he connected with my face, his knuckles shook lose any remaining uncertainties about my father's temper and lethal insecurities. He would come after me for writing about his illicit nocturnal activities with his sociopathic cohorts.

Between sparring sessions, I cooled down on a bench facing the ring, and jotted paragraphs about Dad into my iPhone, while alternating between watching other men and women spar. The ambiance of grunts and cheers and boxing mitts hitting heavy bags or heavy bodies helped me focus, gave me the bravery to complete the chapter.

For the chapter about Luz, it felt necessary to be in the country. I'd spent a long day in Lake Minnewaska writing about her while retracing the steps Raul and I had taken along "our" trailhead. Bear Mountain was dense with gnats and mosquitos and spiderwebs and ticks. I blew them out of my nose and picked them from my ears as I stopped periodically to jot down paragraphs about my sister-in-law's subterranean anarchism.

I passed the tree that Raul had pushed me against. He'd thrust himself carefully inside me and held me tightly as he gyrated his hips as if he were wrestling a bear, as if he'd been writhing through a wormhole, as if an orgasm would save him from something.

Luz had preyed on college students because they were idealistic, ignorant to matters of how the world worked outside of academic theory, and full of emotion. They'd all only recently learned about Che, Mao, and Marx, and even Raul's legendary grandfather, Guadalupe Sandoval, and their idealizations of revolutionary figures made them prime targets. Luz's zine would be put together for no money. It was on a volunteer basis that members researched profiles of historic figures, wrote political and philosophical analyses, organized meetings at their local café or bookstore, accumulated email addresses, and disseminated the fruits of their labor during protests of politicians, business leaders, and corporations.

Other times, Raul and I would walk through the slanted woods along the mountain with a horticultural app and try to identify types of plants and trees. We searched for toads and turtles. We inspected insects. We diagnosed bacterial spread, fungal proliferation. Whether it was sex or nature appreciation, we'd restored ourselves in each other's company, becoming young again, if only for the time being.

James was a raging capitalist and believed ardently in law and order, and penalty. Perhaps he knew about Luz's extracurricular work and turned a blind eye to it, or maybe he really did not know what she'd been doing. He was always oblivious to the obvious.

I tripped over a rock while jotting down a sentence about how Luz had drawn from her childhood in the cult with her parents in Colombia and ended up in a gooseberry bush, scratched and bruised and blemished with mud and grass. It felt karmic. Instantly karmic. Luz, the witch, knowing what I'd been writing about her, put the hidden rock in my path to bring me down. I brushed twigs and dirt from my phone and continued writing.

One of the reasons I am drawn to writing and particularly memoir writing is its promise of crystalizing moments. All the idioms about life being fleeting and too short are true, and by trying to take snapshots of interactions or events or tender exchanges with people you care about, you preserve them, and the memories are kept. It does not counter time or defeat death, but it does mitigate the anxiety of aging and dying. As I walked through Socrates Sculpture Park, I remember the way I felt spending the long day with Raul and having his full attention as I spoke about Aunt Mary, Uncle Monroe, and Cousin Pegasus, and their squatters. I remember the way he glanced at me, the sensation of the back of his hand brushing against mine, the minty aroma of his breath, the springlike fragrance of his body, and that kiss before the fire station.

Competing with these recollections were the various bits of the chapter about James, and my own long day with him that ended in public assault. Pushing through were the early childhood episodes when he would jokingly poke me in the crotch, grab my testicles, and make erotic threats. He'd often go into detail about how he'd fucked women, describing his technique, and how it important it was he worked out his "favorite muscle". He once demanded I pull down my pants when I was seventeen to show him "what I got". Much like my mother and her father, James overstepped with me when I was still only a boy. James's prancing around in his underwear whenever I would stay at his apartment, showing off his ample endowments, was an underhanded temptation. He wasn't just showboating, he was goading, he was seducing, he was exposing. My young mind fixated on the envy and desire he evoked and missed the seductive qualities of what he'd been doing.

Raul had told me all he needed by saying little to nothing. His sidelong stares, his chuckling at jokes he'd replayed in his head, never sharing with me, and that day surrounded by the sculptures of the industrial art installations portending environmental collapse, he'd said the most, even though we'd only been talking about the series. It was in the way he listened even as he contextualized my little familial story with the art that encased us in certain ecological finality. The metallic constructions that had mimicked the natural world's nervous breakdown had made him especially sagacious in his stares and active listening and I felt seen, amidst the supreme milieu of all things ending.

Even the bragging that James had done about his conquests and the sex he'd had in front of voyeurs were acts of performance and for the benefit of his male watchers and admirers, not the least of which was me. He wanted us to become aroused by his aptitude, by his body, by his pleasure. He wanted other men to be envious of him, to desire him, to feel damaged by him. He wanted me to remain envious and full of need. He felt entitled to touch me and abuse me, stopping short of the final incrimination, the incontrovertible action. Still, he touched, still he damaged.

After my three-day stay in Long Island City and Socrates Sculpture Park to get the chapter about James done and out of my life, I moved on to a series of visits at the Guggenheim, where the new exhibit was Francis Bacon, and began work on the chapter about Sophia. The last time I had been to the museum Cecilia Vicuna's corpus had been on display and Raul had been with me. Somehow, writing about my sister in a cultural institution as exulted as the Guggenheim felt incongruous, but given Bacon's violent, terrifying art, also correct. Sophia was not terrifying, but she was ferocious. Everyone in my family was.

Bacon's grotesqueries set against the memory of Vicuna's dignities with Raul's company while thinking about Sophia's sex work left me a little unsteady. I sat on a bench and wrote my way through it. Doug had put her to work soon into their relationship. He saw in her all the necessary ingredients for a successful prostitute: a good work ethic, malleability of a moral compass, resilience, toughness, beauty, and a willingness to accommodate.

Unlike our mother, Sophia never saw herself as better than anyone else. In fact, she was most at home with "low lives", the "dregs," the desperate and the derelict. Perhaps because of our mother, Sophia sought these types to befriend and even with whom fall in love. Doug, precisely. The other sex workers on Farrington might not have been as presentable as Sophia, but my sister never noticed, or if she did, she didn't say anything, and she'd counted herself among them. Their testimonies, which I'd collected after four or five all-night trips to the strip as a sort of anthropological study, confirmed my assumptions about Sophia's approach to the work and to the scene.

When we were last at the museum, Raul spoke about his grandfather and the portrait that Vicuna painted of him. I thought about my book and how each chapter was a series of portraits of my family members. I'd been painting Sophia's portrait with words rather than oils or acrylics. And like Bacon's treatment of his twisted monstrosities, I too strove to capture pain, grief, and all the beauty and ugliness of humiliation and sacrifice and fear. I wondered how much of these passages would inspire disgust and honor, and if they'd be viewed as violations or flatteries. With Sophia, one could never know.

I eventually made my way to the Bronx Zoo, where I bought multiple daily passes to loiter for several days and write about my grandfather. When Raul and I visited the zoo, the animals seemed to read our moods. They reacted to our nervous energies and made it clear we were not welcome, upsetting their peace, as it were. Alone with my thoughts about Angelo and my recall of Raul, the caged creatures took on a deeper personhood and I felt guilty about participating in their exploitation.

I imagined my grandmother Rosalie, his long-suffering wife, as a kind of caged animal, her freedom and pride stripped from her, put on display for others—neighbors, Angelo's friends—to gawk at, to ridicule. She'd been of her time, subservient to her husband who'd blown their savings, forfeited their house, and jeopardized their safety.

Raul and I shared things with each other that we'd never told anyone else. My fondness for submission. His fondness for inflicting pain. My desire to ruin my family. His desire to end white people. We trusted each other that way and it was when we were not talking, not discussing *The Touring Barbarism*, that we connected most deeply. Talking ruined these moments. I wondered if I'd ever find anyone else who could make me feel that way, and I hoped he also had such concerns.

Angelo slept around on grandma. He'd toss the dinners across the room if they were not cooked properly. He'd throw clothing out that sat in the hamper for more than a few days. He'd piss on the floor if she hadn't cleaned within the week. He was primitive that way. A bully. He'd killed her. There was no doubt in my mind. In my book I built a case for the murder. There was no statute of limitations in New York for murder and I prayed that my accusations would reopen the very cold case.

While back home for a respite—a long one-week stretch sequestering myself from the world—I gently began my chapter about Doug. The memory, really a fantasy, that intruded most on my hermitage was the one of Raul, always Raul, cooking me Shakshuka before we made love and fell asleep on the kitchen floor. He'd called me "Leonard" later that night, ending the fantasy.

Doug ran my sister and his other sex workers on Farrington with an iron fist. People in the neighborhood referred to him as "The Collector" because if he didn't collect profit, he collected anatomy. Sophia claimed to know nothing about this and everyone else in my family also played dumb. A would-be John once beat up a trans prostitute after discovering her secret, so Doug broke his wrist and collected his index finger and pinkie with garden shears. A John once raped my sister's friend, a skinny Ukrainian girl, without paying her, so Doug collected his left testicle. In addition to the shears, Doug also carried gauze, peroxide, and Ziplock bags. He was considerate in his care after dismemberment.

Raul once mortified me in front of friends by joking that he'd kick my ass in the backyard of a former colleague's Long Island house. We were off to Fire Island that weekend and stayed with Selina and Smith in their Bayport bungalow. As a black belt, Raul's fists and feet were technically lethal weapons, and he, in fact, very easily could dispatch me without breaking a sweat, but still, for him to publicly announce it in mixed company upset me.

I'd shut down and pouted through the weekend, slipping into an inconsolable despondency, something that would happen when I'd been made to feel in any way inferior, something that was usually by my own doing. I'd begun to recognize that these spells harkened back to the mistreatment by Doug, my father, grandpa, and James during my boyhood. Shame and insecurity were permanent fixtures and the men in my family had installed them like unremovable floor joists fixed for fear of bringing down the house.

As I'd curled into the fetal position with Raul that night on the cold kitchen floor and fell asleep with his warm breath on my neck, his long leg slung over mine, and his arm trapping me under heavy bone and muscle, I thought about Doug and the first time I'd ever masturbated. It had been beside him on his bedroom floor. Whenever I slept at Doug and Sophia's, I'd make a bed on the floor beside their bed. They were in their early twenties when they got their own place, and I was maybe eleven or twelve at the time. I'd gotten hard listening to him snore and surreptitiously pleasured myself. I wondered if he'd ever knew. Doug would also give the police a cut of his earnings for them to overlook the serial maiming and the prostitution. As far as they saw it, he was performing a public service, debilitating thieves, cheaters, and rapists, while providing a much-needed outlet for the potential mass shooters seeking validation.

In The Metropolitan Museum of Art, I found the exhibits— the Dutch, the Fabergé eggs, the Greco-Romans, the Japanese, the Ancient Egyptian, and the sub-Saharan African—Raul and I had walked past and the theater in which I'd given him the hand job. I remembered Leonard and the face he'd made when I'd bested him at the crass combat. I'd only told Raul about Vaughan's affair with the older Republican donor—his history professor, Gerald Watson, of Arizona State University—earlier in the day and he'd kept bringing it up despite my efforts to redirect our conversation to *The Touring Barbarism.*

Vaughan, like Leonard, was the kind of delicate homosexual that wore knowledge and references like suits of armor, hoping to deflect criticism or handedly absorb the blows of dismissal and apathy. I could already tell that my nephew would grow up too soon and be like Raul's French twat. By permanently scandalizing him in my book, Vaughan would have to assume a greater character, a tougher skin, something real and concrete to which anchor himself. I was doing him a favor by exposing his secret. If I was being honest with myself, I cared more about bruising the old guard, ruining this Professor Watson, harming the reputation of ASU, and sowing doubt in the southwestern neocons than I did about saving Vaughan from anything. He was a smart kid and didn't need his uncle to save him. Besides, if he didn't want the sordid details of their affair, and the support from Dr. Watson's friends in high government places, he shouldn't have told me about them. He knew I was writing a book.

I finished *My Mighty Meekness* weeks later at Columbia. The regaining of time had become meta. I recalled the last occasion Raul and I had been on campus while recalling my years in college with him. Memories of memories while remembering. My mind felt knotted, and everything ran into each other. Suddenly the past had flattened, and I could not discern what had happened a week ago from a decade ago. The events of my adolescence intermingled with the events from the other day.

It was fitting, but not really, that I'd write the last words of the memoir sitting on the steps of Low Library about Arnold dealing drugs, Alma Mater exultant behind me. The young man would always be a boy in an overgrown body he'd never learn to wear with overgrown emotions which he'd ever learn to manage. He'd become his father and would break everyone.

Raul had seen me the way I'd needed to be seen before meeting my family. He'd thought I might have come from money because of the way I spoke and the things I'd known about rarified circles. He thought my family might be elitist prudes, maybe in keeping with the WASPs of New England, because of my steady, sturdy manner. When he realized I was of dirt and trash but still presented as I had, he'd somehow seen me even clearer, and I loved him for it.

In the chapter about Arnold, I wrote that he'd started his business by selling dime bags of high-grade marijuana but would soon grow his enterprise into a franchised clandestine pharmacy. Fentanyl, Special K, molly, LSD, psylocibin, and cocaine. There would be nothing he'd not be able to get for his clientele. From Long Island, he'd bring his company into the Bronx, Staten Island, Queens, Brooklyn, Manhattan, and eventually New Jersey and Upstate. He would take care of his mother this way. He would prove his mettle this way. My stomach turned but the decision to reveal what I had felt right.

After *The Touring Barbarism*, I decided I was done writing about Aunt Mary, Uncle Monroe, and Cousin Pegasus, and Co. They'd received enough attention, maybe too much, and it was my fault. *My Mighty Meekness* would be a course correction, of sorts, though not for the benefit of my family. If writing the *New Yorker* article was dipping my toe in therapeutic waters, then writing the book was full institutionalization. My family's admonishments between the essay and the expanded memoir could have been the malady and their reaction to the publication of the book would either be a nasty relapse or a cure.

CHAPTER 32

The legendary editor and former science fiction writer Tonia Magnuson at Stable Home bought my manuscript only two weeks after Caroline sent it to her. She'd been a fan of the *New Yorker* article and Caroline had been discussing *The Touring Barbarism* with her throughout the past year, so once the book was ready all that was left was the formality of reading it, which she did with great interest, speed, and kindness. Tonia was a perceptive reader and an even sharper editor. She sent me global edits first, those notes that requested revisions to structure, pacing, language, and a request for additional information, and then she conducted a meticulous copy edit, correcting my spelling, challenging my facts, and improving my grammar. She fast-tracked the book and had it on the market within eight months. I guess everyone thought they could make some money from it given the forthcoming cable series, though the air date of *The Touring Barbarism* was still a full year out.

I had not heard from Raul in all that time and the figures he'd toppled at *RFN* had lost their jobs and likely careers. They'd been laying low, at the very least, as they probably planned with a crisis strategist a course of action for re-emerging in time. I imagined Raul teaching homeless kids in Thailand how to fight or maybe lounging on the beaches of Rio. He might have been climbing Mount Everest or Mount Kilimanjaro for all I knew. He could be anywhere on the planet. He could have even been dead. I'd have no way of knowing and I was pretty sure I'd never see him again, so, in a sense, he was dead. And I duly mourned.

In the two weeks leading up to publication, my memoir got more press than I'd anticipated. This was due in no small part to Caroline and Tonia's collective efforts to push Stable Home's PR department to capitalize on the anticipation for *The Touring Barbarism* and the lingering buzz surrounding the *New Yorker* article.

The New York Times said of my book, "Julian Sorrento has bore his soul and his spleen and in the process of producing an enduring work of literature sacrificed his entire family. Kin goes extinct but art remains for eons."

The LA Times called my book "exploitative," stating that I had "compromised my family for a little notoriety and money," and that "my mediocre literary endeavor was an immoral act."

On SiriusXM's Michelangelo Signorile Show, the titular host asked me how I felt about being portrayed in the media as less of a victim of my family's mistreatments and more of a perpetrator of their privacies and characters.

"I never intended for the book to make me out to be some kind of victim," I said into the giant silver mic in his cramped Midtown studio. "I only sought to tell the truth about a modern American family pressured by the demands of a capitalist society."

He cocked his head and grinned knowingly. "The struggle of the working class? Like Doug Stuart or Charles Bukowski?"

"If you like."

On the Today Show, Al Roker asked me if I had any regrets about sharing so many intimate details about my family with the world. The studio lights were bright and hot, and I recall feeling distracted and even oppressed by them.

"No, Al, not really, because it's all true."

"Even so, just because something is true doesn't mean it should be served up for public consumption, right?"

I blinked at him and was spellbound again by the lights. The cameras also began to command my attention.

"I guess that is the risk for people in a family with a writer."

People's profile on me did make me out to be a victim. "Sorrento is a meek and gentle man as his own *New Yorker* article attests. He accommodated his family to self-immolating degrees, and they took advantage of him. Ran roughshod over him. *My Mighty Meekness*, the book, is his cry for help. By documenting their lifelong travesties, Sorrento does not so much hit back as reaches out, but not to them, for it is too late for that reconnection. His hand searches for someone to pull him out of their dark milieu and lift him to a safer place. Perhaps the rescuer will be the public and their salvation for Julian might just come in the form of sales."

Time called me a "spoilsport," someone so consumed by "inadequacies and jealousies" that I just couldn't stop myself from "undermining the innocent lives of nine people who never asked to be written about, who had no interest in being in a trashy book, who never desired infamy, who never needed the spotlight shone on them. There should be charges brought against Sorrento for thrusting onto a national stage a family who are just doing the best they can through myriad financial crises and a limited education which curtails opportunities in this technocratic society."

The New Yorker re-ran excerpts from the original essay and added sections from the book. Their critic said I did the least with the opportunity they'd given me by publishing the essay. "A wiser writer would have moved on to fiction or a non-fiction book of some social value, maybe a historical book about labor unions, or a biography about an obscure artist, but not this self-regarding hack, who could only add to the heap of indictments he'd scribbled years earlier about people whose lives ought to have remained anonymous. It's therapeutic spite work disguised as a confessional autobiography and the family in question are not the only victims of the confessor's vindictiveness and sharp lack of talent. Readers will suffer, too!"

Interview Magazine conducted a vapid interview with me about my childhood role play scenarios I'd briefly referenced in the chapter about my brother. James had assumed the role of a Greek or Egyptian or Roman emperor and I would have to play his serf, and he would strip naked, and I would have to wash and dry his body with rags. They only focused on the most salacious elements but not with any psychodynamic depth. I mean, I was fifteen or sixteen at the time, so their coverage could have been more probing about James's latent, repressed homoerotic tendencies and the pedophilic properties of the encounters.

There were also reviews, interviews, and profiles in other publications, like *Vanity Fair* ("A tragedy of the author's own making"), *Rolling Stone* ("A spectacle you can't look away from, similar to a cataclysmic car accident"), *The Paris Review* ("The product of a culture that rewards TMI and self-victimization"), *The Gay & Lesbian Review* ("Problematic to the extreme, Sorrento's book poses innumerable challenges gay men will now have to work double-time to overcome"), *The Atlantic* ("It made me want to call and apologize to my own family and we have a good relationship!"), and *The Chicago Tribune* ("A reckoning with a vengeance, however ill advised."). Social media lit up for me, too, but not always in the most complimentary ways. Bookstagrammers on Instagram and BookTok influencers on Tik Tok shared their reviews and started a book club to open a dialogue about it and me to the tune of hundreds of thousands of likes and over two million views. Generally, the reviews were mixed. Many critics, and readers on Amazon and GooodReads, called the book "exploitative," "A step back for the LGBTQ community," and a "desperate grab for fame and money," though some also said I was "courageous and brave and open". I shrugged at all of it, the good and bad alike.

CHAPTER 33

Despite the stonewalling from my biological family, I was surrounded by love from my adopted brethren. On the eve of Pub Day, Edward and Kevin hosted a celebration for me, my memoir, and all the subsequent gifts it would bring. Colin, Joan, Fen, Linus, and Fanny made it their business to attend, irrespective of their busy schedules, as did myriad others, new faces and personas quizzing me about my background, knowledge of fine wines and esoteric holiday spots, favorite musicians and authors, and sexual experiences. Their incredulity notwithstanding, they toasted me, making wry jokes about joining a select club and losing all comforts associated with anonymity.

I barely ate but drank the equivalent of five meals and with the "elegant" apartment packed with guests, perhaps twenty or more, it all suddenly felt claustrophobic. One face that soothed was Tonia's, benign with a motherly glow. The publishing giant whose easy grace with words enhanced Ed's career as it would now mine. Her career began in the mid-1970s, and she'd received a fair amount of attention for being one of the only black women in the industry at the time. She had published well regarded—and socially critical—science fiction that mixed gender fluidity with race relations and queer theory, earning favorable comparisons to such equally lauded authors as Samuel R. Delany, Ursula K. LeGuin, and Octavia Butler. She'd parlayed that success into a job at Knopf as a junior editor and quickly became a full editor after only five years. She continued to write and enjoy healthy sales and solid reviews in legacy media brands, but insisted on remaining an editor, at least part time, once she had consistently sold enough copies of her books on which to subsist. She produced one a year like clockwork. Stable

Home snatched her up at her sixth book, *Manager of the Cosmos*, which won both the Hugo and the Nebula.

Being an editor, she'd once told *The Paris Review*, allowed her to "continue amplifying voices and shaping the culture". She'd felt the role provided an influence that even a bestselling novelist did not.

"You need to get ready now," said Tonia, in a relaxed purr. "Everything is going to change."

"Oh, it already has, Tonia."

I remember seeing a recent documentary about Philip Roth when he sat his parents down the night before the release of *Portnoy's Complaint* and tried to prepare them for what was to come. They'd left their son's apartment believing he was suffering delusions of grandeur. The book would almost instantly ignite the kind of national controversy and discussion reserved for a presidential scandal. Of course, that was 1969 and writers no longer enjoyed such rock star ballyhoo.

"There has already been a lot of attention paid to this one," said Edward, though I hadn't been sure if he'd referred to me or my book.

"And the money won't be bad either," said Fanny. "Took me too long to realize that this writing racket could pay off in time."

Colin then began talking about how Suliman had never been more famous than when he was in hiding. It's when no one ever saw him or heard from him that he achieved a kind of enigmatic stature. Suliman had not been in attendance as he was not ready to be public again. The effects of the attack still leaving him shaken and diminished.

"Mystery sells," said Linus. "Your publicist did a good job of selling the mystery of your family."

"Oh yes, *mystery*! Suliman's Garbo days!" quipped Fanny, prompting Edward to squeal with laughter.

"People wanting him dead certainly helped with the sales," said Kevin, who, I'd noticed, had been batting his lashes at me mockingly.

Joan, waving her pen and pad, spoke about how her fame had come

[317]

to her gradually. She said she'd published one well received book and then another and then another, until finally people started to pay attention.

"I have no idea what I did to earn the attention the world pays to me," said Fanny.

It was true. She'd written two social criticisms forty years ago and people can't stop talking about them, making documentaries about them, excerpting them.

Edward informed her that her celebrity withstood the test of time through her associations, the company she kept. You hobnob with enough famous people, you become famous yourself. Her shtick too felt timeless, and I couldn't help but tell her, which I am sure sounded condescending, or at the very least, maybe too earnest, and of course, they all giggled as if I'd just cracked a joke. Genuine expressions of gratitude and praise never went over well with this crowd.

Linus saved me by citing all the famous photos of Fanny with Warhol and Avedon and Haring and Debbie Harry and Martin Scorsese. He then called her "a regular Zelig!"

At this everyone again erupted. It was charming the way they could keep themselves and each other amused and, on their toes, serving as one another's best, most receptive audience. They were real friends and their circle had split open just enough to allow me to squeak in. And in I squeaked.

"If your fame was gradual, Joan, then mine was made of molasses," chuckled Edward. "At 82 I've never been more in the news and on bestseller lists."

"Change of agents," said Fen. "That other one wasn't doing right by you all those years."

"Well, maybe it's the times, too." Ed looked like a bashful little schoolboy, crossing his fingers over his belly with a pout. "Gay literature is all the rage right now. You know, we've really gone mainstream."

For Colin, it was the movies, he'd said. They had brought in the readers.

"If the box office and awards shows have taught us anything it's that people want Irish destitution," he added.

Also at the party were Giancarlo and Alvin. Looking at them again after all this time I realized how striking they were together. Giancarlo, a dark beauty like Joe Sansone, and Alvin, so white as if nearly translucent. The contrast of features, skin, bone structure, and ethnicity enhanced each other's aesthetic fineness. I'd wondered what kind of things they'd done to each other in bed. I became excited picturing them in flagrante delicto.

Giancarlo, who had been close to Ed all evening but eyeballing Kevin with disdain, sighed in an exasperated huff. I could tell he'd grown tired of playing spectator and had found no angle in.

Colin made small talk with Giancarlo, which seemed awkward, even studied. I am not sure anyone knew how to behave when addressing the king's favorite. Alvin sat cross-legged with perfect posture and raised eyebrows as if he'd been performing intelligence if not possessing it.

I made a crude joke about Colin's last novel, *Queens*, and even laughed at it, but no one else had. I hadn't known it was such a sore spot for Colin and of course it was the one joke no one was supposed to find funny. He'd looked at me with his crooked face and bulbous, unfocused eyes. A scowl like a cudgel. The group either looked away or right at me, impressed or disappointed, I couldn't' tell. Maybe their reactions had been a mix of both. I knew it was time to go, but I did not go. I realized I'd become drunk. I never drank as much as when I was with Edward and Kevin. I swayed and Alvin, the erotic tumbler, caught me, led me to a nearby chair and sat with me.

"You okay?" he asked.

"I guess I just need to eat a bit more."

Alvin put together a plate of olives, nuts, cheeses, sweet breads, and cured meats. I ate but still felt dizzy. Perhaps it was another panic attack. I'd had so many in the past few weeks.

Colin, merry, yet morose, began talking at an obnoxious level about the "most delicious" bartender he'd met the other night at the gay club, Elmo, an actor, of course, because they all are, with the "build of a surfer and the most handsome face, like a young Paul Newman or Alain Delon, that type of beauty with penetrating eyes and a nose like an anvil and a mouth like a Hoover, just extraordinary," and naturally this young Adonis had a girlfriend, "some Brazilian harlot".

"Anyway," ended Colin, "I defamed his country bumkin attire duly."

"Little cock-teaser," grumbled Kevin.

Colin had been talking loud enough for everyone to hear and Edward, ever decorous and tactful, nodding to placate him, or maybe he'd agreed with him. It had taken these writers decades to accumulate their wealth and status and here I was, something of a carpetbagger, an over-night success, and still so much younger than them. What right did I have to their spotlight? I then heard him saying something about lowering the bar and the dangers of personal narrative, how it sold artists without talent and presidents without experience, hoodwinking consumers and voters, alike.

Earlier in the evening Joan had pulled me aside to tell me that she'd read my memoir and wanted to make clear that I was a smart writer and that I wrote earnestly, but that my sense of structure and voice had yet to be found. She wanted me to understand that she was only being a good friend by being honest and leveling praise with critique. Obviously, she'd automatically jotted notes for her own literature as she did so. I'd thanked her and we'd toasted.

Later, Giancarlo pulled me aside and asked, "Do you really think your brother wanted to do you?" I was honored he'd read the book and excited that he'd fixated on that admission. "How depraved."

Kevin sipped his scotch and watched me like a lion studies his dinner.

"You write well, but everyone writes well, these days, what with word processing grammar guides and editors leaving their stink all over everything." Colin grunted and threw his hands up. "This is not to say that you haven't written a good book, but rather it's a solid start. And I just don't believe that your father was in the mafia! No fool would broadcast it like that. Even to his family."

"Well," I began with a dry throat, "he was a fool, I guess."

"You should be acknowledged for not doing that thing that so many new authors do, pandering to the reader, trying to be endearing and entertaining." Fanny smirked at me. "You distinguish yourself this way."

Alvin made his way over to me and pulled me away with dire seriousness to tell me that my book was not anything he would have read if he hadn't known me, but he was glad he did because I'd managed to make the absurd and the surreal feel possible. Alvin's eyebrows arched, and he looked like a devil, though one who had just given me the best compliment of the evening.

"I haven't read it yet." Kevin squinted his eyes and puckered his lips, a sudden sea bass. "You know I haven't had the capacity to read anything longer than a blurb since the election. But I'm sure it's marvelous."

I'd replayed their assessments through the night as they'd all been eager to share their views with me soon after I sat down. I hadn't minded that the reactions were mixed, the best works of art elicited such divided opinions, and Colin's later vexed conversation with Ed about the French recognition made it clear that jealousy had been afoot. I then began to wonder what Ed had seen in my work all those months ago. Why had he championed it so assuredly? Was it to get into my pants? Was he just being nice? Had he just wanted to exert power? "King Ed, The Great Maker of Make Believers." As the others joked, Edward seemed to squirm, hemming and hawing his way through his defense of my book.

"Well, you know, what I responded to was a kind of complete lack of guile." Edward's eyes bulged and rolled, and his cheeks were suddenly pink, and he drummed his fingers atop his stomach. "Julian's voice is very pure. It's not yet jaded, and he writes with a freshness that is uncommon in the MFA workshops. His book feels raw and, even, you know, that overused word, "organic," and not at all like the products they now churn out, you know? My goodness, they all seem to produce work in the same voice, somehow, don't they? It's all very unoriginal and forgettable. Julian could be our Faulkner, in time."

I smiled at Ed, but he looked nervously at me. Had he regretted giving me his imprimatur?

Beside all this ambivalence about my work, something else had been eating at me. Kevin. I could tell he was becoming impatient with me. It had been almost two years since we met and I'd yet to put out. His entitlement, my passivity. It should have happened by now. He'd groped me, cuddled with me, and I'd allowed it. I approached him, hugged him, with demonstrative sympathy. He'd smelled like alcohol and sweat.

"I can't have sex with you, and I'm sorry," I whispered measuredly into his ear. "You deserve love and passion and fulfillment, but I can't give you any of that."

When I pulled away, I saw the look on his face. Confused, but also battered. The way a long-abused or untouched person flinches when you get too close. He'd looked hurt. I'd hurt him. I was getting good at hurting people.

I began for the kitchen to get some water but stopped. It was when I thought that I had taken control and the paroxysm had passed that it really flared up and soon I was pale with sunken, dark eyes and wheezing with heaves and everyone was looking at me, and Doctor Giancarlo and Dancer Alvin looked terrified and soon so did Edward and Kevin and the rest of the coterie.

Joan, however, looked more embarrassed than alarmed, and soon returned to her automatic writing. "Julian, steady your breaths. Slow and deep."

I heard Colin make a mean joke about my untimely demise and how it would drive up profits of the memoir if I croaked on the eve of its release. Only Caroline laughed. Joan scolded both, threatening physical violence with her pen and pad. Fanny, reliably apathetic, now seemed genuinely concerned. Kevin watched with hateful eyes, and I found his glower understandable. Everyone's compassion ran thin and soon they'd made expressions of irritation, as if I'd ruined their good time.

Tonia hurried over and knelt before me, leading me by my hands back into the chair. She looked me in the eyes and breathed demonstratively, as if she were teaching me how to catch my breath and take back my wayward physiology. I nodded and mirrored her and soon I was okay. Tingling in the face and hands and tense in my jaw, but otherwise among the land of the calm and sedate, or heavily medicated.

I heard Joan groan. Caroline shrugged and everyone resumed their acidic cavorting.

"It's just nerves," said Edward from across the room. "He's about to open up his whole damn soul to the world. He's never been so vulnerable, I'm sure. It's like dropping your pants for an auditorium full of virility inspectors and wondering if your dick measures up."

Everyone chuckled and talked opera, the latest literary scandal, and the tragedies of the red states.

Tonia cringed at Edward and then smiled at me. "You're scared and I can't blame you, Julian. This is all happening faster than you thought, and who knows what the rest of the reviews will be? Who knows who will come out of the woodwork? People from your childhood or Columbia will surely pop up and level accusations on social media that will be uncomfortable. You can't really prepare for any of that."

"Are you trying to give me another panic attack, Tonia?"

"When I started writing in the late 1960s, you should have seen the hate mail I received. Thank God we didn't have email back then. Or Facebook or Twitter! I still think about the things people said all these years later. Aleksander Solzhenitsyn wrote that of all the indignities and cruelties a person can face in their life, nothing stings or stays with you quite like an insult."

"People are the worst."

"And the best. Give them a chance. Give yourself a chance. Be patient. Let the book have its life and do what it will. And then move on to the next one. And the next one after that. That's really all that matters. The work. All the rest is just noise."

Giancarlo and Alvin loitered behind Tonia during our conversation, and I could tell they were listening because they exuded displeasure with her advice. What Tonia said was sound and I'd use it, but the lesser-known guests, it had been no secret to me or anyone else in that room, had grown impatient with my "special case" treatment, as if I were an exception. Minor celebrities in my new orbit made it clear to me during the weeks leading to the book's release that I ought to stop feeling sorry for myself for catching a break, for making serious money, for having a platform that could potentially reach many. They'd reminded me of how many others hadn't, historically and currently, by dint of their identities or social class appointments or geographies. None had gone so far as Raul would have—or previously had—and tell me that I had no right to stay in the center, un-budged from the stage, the spotlight, to assert my place in a field already crowded with others of my ilk. Shut up, show some gratitude, and quit conceding to the bellyaching.

CHAPTER 34

My family had become uncharacteristically, eerily frosty. Unlike the hysterical reactions to the *New Yorker* article, their response to the book was downright silent. No one contacted me, not to congratulate me, not that I expected they would, or to denigrate me. No one even responded to my calls or texts. They froze me out. I thought about showing up at any one of their doors but decided against it for fear of providing them grounds for assault should I set foot on their properties uninvited. *My Mighty Meekness* had been released on September 1st and the first peep from my family came through a text from Sophia on November 15th inviting me to Thanksgiving dinner.

Sophia had written she would be hosting and apparently James, Luz, and Vaughan planned on coming in from Phoenix. I missed Raul. He'd make me feel less alone. Maybe the only person who still could. I worked for weeks in solitude widening the thematic focus of *The Touring Barbarism* because I'd found the much-emphasized compassion for Mary and Monroe after all. Pegasus successfully intervenes and stops his parents from paying a masochistic penance. It likely will not be considered Avant-Garde enough for the Darlington Brothers or MAX, but that's how I'd decided to end it.

I realized I'd needed space from everyone for a little while. Too many opinions and judgments had clouded me, and I could not see a way through my own thoughts, which was an alarming sensation. I worried I'd become an empty vessel ready to be filled up by the criticisms and reprimands of Raul and my family. I'd shaken free the millstones that were my family only to have walked headfirst into another weighted noose. Maybe their distance from me had been for the best.

INT. CLINT RESIDENCE — MASTER BEDDROOM — EVENING

Mary and Monroe sit on Pegasus's bed and weep.
Though they ask for his forgiveness, their
apologies are truly meant for the Bhumij and
the Kharia and the people of the world harmed
by Raytheon missiles.

                    PEGASUS
          You don't need to turn yourselves
          into slaves for my sake.

Dr. Alessandro and Joe watch from the threshold
and hid their fumes. Pegasus will not tell them
again to stay out of it. Another interference
and the whole lot of the squatters would be out
of his house. Pegasus decides that his parents
are worth saving and he chooses forgiveness. He
chooses mercy.

Long Island is a long stretch of suburb surrounded by an ocean and
a sound. Culturally, it is as vapid as Los Angeles and geographically it
promised nature, even if multiple expressways and parkways ran through
most of it. On the Long Island Railroad, I thought about Violet Scott, who'd
I'd met just the one time, but known through news reports and her films,
and I considered her punishing loneliness. I thought about Suliman Raj,
who I'd only known briefly in person and more from chatter at parties, and
I lamented his unwavering bravery. I thought about myself and my epic
insecurities. We, brief inhabitants of a rough, unstable world.

Sophia's Westbury house was a wide mid-century ranch with handsome
white brick face. Doug knew people in construction and landscaping, so the

house always looked new and expensive. Ostentatious shrubs, plants, and bushes filled the front yard, which even in late autumn promised sunshine. The walkway was blue slate, and the roof was less than a year old. Cars filled the four-car driveway, and I could hear the commotion inside from the curb. The Uber drive over from the station was quick and we passed through a small village, the kind that had multiple cafes, stores for greeting cards, and shops that sold nothing but Christmas decorations. It was late November, and the town was as ornamented as a Norman Rockwell holiday scene.

Inside, the smell of turkey, candied yams, stuffing, and biscuits hit quick and hard and rendered me a child again. I remembered my mother getting up to cook at four in morning on Thanksgiving and waking in the middle of the night to the heat of the oven and the aroma of a fresh banquet in its nascency. Such sensations promised eternal, though deceptive, comforts.

"Ma, I have it!" said Sophia. "Just take the biscuits out of the oven before they burn!"

"You don't have to get nasty!" my mother yelled back.

"I'm not getting nasty but listen to me when I say I'm okay!"

Even when they endeavored kindness their deliveries were brusque and bellicose. I closed the door and stepped toward the kitchen where Doug and Arnold were the first to see me.

Doug looked at me and nodded, "Hey."

Arnold frowned and proffered a half-nod.

My father had been talking to James at the dining room table when he spotted me and hid a scowl. Luz and Vaughan sat on the sofa in the adjoining living room, speaking closely, weirdly intimate for a mother and son, and looked at me with pale faces. My mother and Sophia stepped into the dining room from the kitchen.

When my mother saw me, she sighed and returned to the kitchen.

"Julian always shows up when we ask," said Sophia, smiling sideways, as if she'd been about to crack a mean joke at my expense, but instead gave me a hug.

Luz and Vaughan sighed collectively, as if they'd rehearsed it, and stood in unison, laboring to approach me. I watched them as I would a movie about strange behavior or maybe a piece of eccentric performance art.

"Julian, hello," said Luz, uncertain and careful.

"Hey," said Vaughan, looking like he'd been keeping a secret, possibly scared I'd share his.

We all politely kissed and hugged, though we'd all known we were only going through the diplomatic motions. We were masters of dutiful displays of dignity.

James appeared and he groaned when he saw me.

"Hi, James," I said, unable to stop myself from sounding incredulous, remembering how violently we'd left off. To James, it was nothing. Violent assaults in his world were common and nothing to apologize for. He grew up straight in Queens during a time when physical altercations between friends were as innocuous and everyday as handshakes and mom jokes.

"So," said my father, appearing in front of me as everyone else scattered, returning to their first positions, girding themselves with performative busyness. "You came, huh?"

"I'm here, so I guess so."

He wasted no time. I wasn't surprised. He'd always been all business and with each one of us the relationships had been transactional. Usually, he needed something from us, and we were meant to oblige without fuss.

A toilet flushed from the half bath down the hall and when the bathroom door opened out waddled grandpa. Angelo looked as stout as when I'd visited him in Bay Ridge all those months ago, but his skin was whiter and dryer, possibly ashier, and his bones seemed creakier. The body knew winter was coming and it duly slumped into the seasonal decline. When he saw me, he registered an artificial surprise, something that meant to convey an untold litany of assessments about poor character, selfishness, indifference. I knew too well what he thought of me so every gesture, no matter how micro, spoke volumes.

"Julian," he said, moving quicker than I'd remembered, his hands on my shoulders and around my wrist, gripping me in a kind of strange assault. "Hello, sir."

His stench was thick with Geritol, Chaps, and flatulence.

Dinner was uncomfortable, and maybe not only for me, as everyone seemed to share the same suspicion of my presence. They'd glance at me and then look away when I caught them. They'd exchange snickers and eye rolls whenever I spoke about the book or show, which was minimal, as I mostly just sat quietly and let everyone else talk. I barely felt I'd had a place at their table. After we ate, while Sophia brewed coffee and mom heated the apple and berry pies she'd baked, we all drifted to the living room to watch highlights from the MACY'S parade.

It took about two hours from my arrival at two in the afternoon for a conflict to arise, a new record for my family. I could hear Luz and my mother arguing in the dining room about "the shit she (Luz) pulled when Vaughan was a baby." My mother rehashed the awful years from Vaughan's birth to when he was about twelve, just prior to their move to Arizona, when Luz would fight ferociously with my brother about one of his conquests (she'd usually find a woman's phone number in his pants pocket or some indiscreet trick would call during dinner), and my mother would initially be pulled in to referee their melees, but once when Vaughan was about four months old Luz made the fatal mistake of threatening to run off with him to Colombia thereby preventing James or my mom or any of us from ever seeing him again. My mother made an error of equal magnitude by telling James to get a good lawyer and freeze their joint bank account to protect himself. Luz, who had been close with my mother up until then, of course, saw this as a betrayal, a line drawn in the sand, and it was an infraction for which my mother would never be forgiven.

"You are a fucking bitch, you've always been a bitch, and you're still a fucking bitch!" My mother had been shrieking, trembling with an iron pie server.

"Ma, just stop!" said James, his face desperate for peace.

"This is your mother," said Luz, red faced with clenched fists. "The same woman who threatened to have my legs broken!"

"Oh, don't be so dramatic!" said my mother, slamming the pie server down beside the array of pies on the stove. "I never threatened anybody!"

"You're this crazy Italian lady from Queens! I don't know who you know! I get followed by these scary guys after you say you're going to break my face at Easter dinner!"

"That's just an expression!" My mother threw her hands up and stood wide legged and barefoot like those Sicilian women in old Ermanno Olmi films. "I never meant it and you know that!"

"Okay," said my father, stepping between the warring women to pour a cup of coffee. "Enough. It's Thanksgiving. No more fighting. Let the old grudges go."

And just like that, as if an apoplectic blowout fueled by decades of resentments hadn't just been diffused, everyone returned to their holiday doing mundane things like cutting pie, sipping coffee, and watching celebrities on floats trundle down 6th Avenue.

Vaughan sat beside me on the sofa and started to whisper in my ear about his pursuits "back West." Had he hoped to impress me? Was this a bonding opportunity? Did he need advice? Was he trying to hurt me? Had he read Guibert?

"And see this guy," said Vaughan, showing me another photo of an older man sucking his big toe. "He's a police sergeant, former marine, and he knows my dad. It's so hot how he lets me do whatever I want to him."

"Vaughan, maybe put this away," I said, pushing his cell phone toward him, trying to turn it facedown.

"You gonna ruin his life, too?" he said, again showing me his phone, this time a Grindr interface.

I stood up and rushed for the front door to get some air.

Outside the air was cold and the crispness abated the impending panic

[330]

attack until I overheard James bragging to Doug about the number of women he'd "nailed" early on in his relationship with Luz, when she was still barely twenty.

"I was stupid and sloppy, Arnie," he said, talking with his hands like a gangster from the 40s. "I kept numbers, gave out my number. Of course, she was going to catch me. But when I met her, I was banging like six bitches from all over the city, the Bronx, Manhattan, Brooklyn, Irish, Black, Asian, Latin."

"I know, Uncle James," said Arnold. "I'm seeing these two girls, one here on the Island and another in Jersey, and they don't know about each other, but they're both fucking great pieces!"

"That's my nephew!" said James, putting Arnold in a headlock and kissing his scalp. "You're only young once, kid. Live it the fuck up."

I had been loitering behind them only a few paces and when I turned to flee their barbaric discussion, they'd heard me, and said, almost jointly, "Silence is golden, bigmouth!" and "Close your fucking ears around us!"

In the garage I ran into Doug talking with my dad and grandfather about a trunk full of "hot" TVs and Play-Stations. Doug bragged in a hushed tone about how good a deal he can make "them", and "they" should call him. The ambiguous "theys" and "thems" were mainstays in the family. Everyone around me spoke in code so as not to incriminate themselves. My father inspected the illegal merchandise and said he knew some guys who needed TVs and Play-Stations for their kids for Christmas. Grandpa claimed because he was "ancient," he hadn't known anyone who could use hot TVs or gaming systems, but Doug offered him a TV as a gift and said he'd even drive it over to his place to install it.

"There's something else," said Angelo. "There are these lowlifes in my neighborhood who are giving my friend at Carmine's, the restaurant I go to on Sundays, a hard time, and I told him I'd ask about someone taking care of them for him. He gives me a free bottle of wine and a nice cut of burrata whenever I see him, so I have to do right by him."

"Yeah, pop pop, I can send someone to help you with that," said Doug. "What are you thinking?"

"Just the legs, maybe one each, just enough to scare them and keep them off their feet a while, you know?"

"You got it," said Doug.

"You're a good man, Dougie," said my father, slapping Doug on the back of the neck and pulling him in for a kiss.

It was chilly and my nose began to run, so I sniffed. My father, grandfather, and brother-in-law turned to me, put out that I'd ruined their bonding exercise, even if it was over myriad crimes from larceny to premeditated aggravated assault, and stared with the dead eyes that attended corrupt men. The kind of eyes that have seen and sanctioned the most heinous atrocities and continued to see less dreadful affairs like christenings or communions or weddings, and always with the same dead eyes.

"Ah, fuck," said Dad.

"You gonna run your pen about this, too, you nosy twat?" asked Doug.

"You should have listened to me, Julian," said grandpa, peering into me with bloodshot eyes, dead eyes, the kind of eyes you'd expect to see on the person who finally kills you.

Dreadful, this family. I shook my head, wiped my nose, and went back inside. I'd had enough of our culture's deification of family. Family in the conventional sense was not an ideal. It was something that happens by default without any effort and no one, least of all writers and filmmakers, should exult its existence unless one took the Tolstoy approach and found its unique unhappiness.

I went to the bathroom and sat on the lip of the tub contemplating my exit strategy. If family was the thing I'd written about to much success like most contemporary writers and if it was the subject that I'd continue to exploit, then I'd have to come to view it as a piece of art or a distant memory. The return to my characters, once relatives, and stories, once bruising experiences, become smaller and more artificial, less real, like a painting by Vicuna or one of the little sculptures of Ed and Kevin and eventually something to put on a shelf and no longer live through. The characters in my book and cable series, my once and long-ago family, were "average idiots" like all average idiots who celebrate their averageness and idiocy as something noble, something authentic, something sacred in its simplicity, and good in its elemental humility. They were just as deplorable as the haughty elites except without the fame or knowledge or accomplishments or embalmed placement on people's shelves, except for when I bestowed such generosities on them in my work. And for it I was made a ghost.

After ten minutes I emerged from the bathroom and came upon my mother and father sitting next to each other on the love seat in the living room talking about the little crimes they'd committed and gotten away with.

"This stupid nitwit at the department store, she must have been new and young and didn't know her ass from her elbow," my mother began. "She didn't know the prices of anything and had no idea how to check and I was able to switch all these labels on socks and sweaters and jeans, and I got all these Christmas gifts for Dougie and Julian and Sophia for a hundred dollars less than I would have if she knew what she was doing!"

"Don't feel bad, Annalisa," said Dad.

"Oh, I don't," said Mom. "These stores are highway robbers. They got what they deserved."

"Yeah, you sound like my customers, they call me a highway robber all the time," said Dad. "Which is why I don't give a shit when I let my guys leave projects unfinished or do a shit job. They bust my balls, these people, and they get fucked in the end."

My mother saw me and gave me a coy smile. My father sighed.

"The spy! He's always right here!" said Dad. "And now that he's up there, watch out!"

Up there!

"Don't worry," I said. "I'm not working tonight."

They both laughed, but my mother's expression had been shot through with concern, as if she'd known I'd been forever marked in the family and would only be provisionally invited back in. My father's face sent a less sympathetic message. His baggy, dark eyes, pits of bloated cinder, cut through me, possibly picturing me dead, either literally or figuratively, but either way out of their lives for good.

"Alright, dessert is ready," called Sophia from the kitchen. She didn't consider our mother's three pies dessert but rather appetizers for dessert which entailed a tiramisu from a local baker originally from Naples, a box of cannoli from Arthur Avenue, and a carrot cake she'd baked herself.

My parents stood and headed for the kitchen.

My mother looked at me briefly as if to signal some unwelcome message before vanishing around the bend, following the aroma of baked goods.

I hesitated, only to take in the certainty of my decision. I'd been drawn to social work because of my family. I'd skipped childhood, thrust into the role of everyone's therapist, support coordinator, advocate, sounding board, and bank. Becoming a counselor of wayward, homeless people was a natural extension. Service had become such a deep part of me it only made sense to do it for a living. Outside of my sister's house a skinny, bedraggled boy shuffled down the street as though he were an extra on *The Walking Dead*. I was certain he'd been on drugs. He immediately reminded me of Bashir, a nineteen-year-old sex worker I had weekly sessions with who one day came to our meeting with small shards of glass in his face. He casually picked them out as we spoke, refusing medical treatment. He'd irreverently explained that "this sort of thing happens once in a while" as his johns like for him to give them oral sex while they are driving fast on the parkway. This one john had apparently crashed into a light pole and the glass Bashir picked from his face was the windshield.

In that moment, I thought about calling Dr. Nian and asking for my job back, letting go of the MAX series, leaving the Darlington Brothers to adapt the memoir themselves, and disappointing Caroline with the knowledge that there would be no new book, no follow up to the reactions of the initial memoir.

I stood up, snatched my jacket, and left. The Uber would meet me on the corner to bring me to the LIRR a few miles away. I'd be back home within an hour and working on *The Touring Barbarism* and maybe even finally begin outlining a continuation of *My Mighty Meekness*, as Caroline had been asking since we broke the 100,000 threshold of copies sold in only two and a half months. If I was indeed "up there," I would not be coming down anytime soon. I'd not need Raul's audience anymore. I'd write about what I pleased, and I'd do so without guilt, recused of all harm.

THE END

ACKNOWLEDGEMENTS

My deepest gratitude to Ioannis Pappos and Tom Cardamone for reading a quite early, and perhaps quite premature, draft of this novel in a quite different iteration, and for their generous feedback.

A thousand thanks to Daniel Pisano for his incisive edits. It is a stronger book because of his patience, time, and care.

For their unwavering support, steadfast friendship, and tireless creative guidance, thank you, Laura Schleifer, Elizabeth Isaac, Christopher Hunt, Dennis Leroy Kangalee, Brandon Zappala, Lupe Rodarte, Navanil Das, Anthony DiMieri, Samantha Desmond, and Daniel Dreifuss.

For his love, kindness, and understanding, thank you, Tommy. He's the best husband a moody, preoccupied, and self-absorbed writer could hope for.

Big love to the family for their willingness to become subjects: Mom, Lori, John, Sandy, Barry, Joey, Amanda, Myrna, Nikki, David, and Dad, whose encouragement continues though he's not here to see what it yields.

Thank you, Sven Davisson, for continuing to publish my books and for championing a legion of boundary-pushing LGBTQIA writers whose work will endure because of your patronage.

ABOUT THE AUTHOR

Brian Alessandro has written for *Interview Magazine, Newsday, PANK, Huffington Post, Galerie, Lambda Literary, The Gay & Lesbian Review, Kirkus Reviews*, and *The Florida Review*. He has recently co-adapted Edmund White's *A Boy's Own Story* into a graphic novel for Top Shelf Productions. Additionally, Brian co-edited *Fever Spores: The Queer Reclamation of William S. Burroughs*, an anthology of essays and interviews about Burroughs for Rebel Satori Press. Brian is also the co-founder and editor-in-chief of the literary journal *The New Engagement*. His first novel, *The Unmentionable Mann*, was published in 2015 by Cairn Press, and his first feature film, *Afghan Hound*, was produced by Maryea Media in 2011 and is streaming on Plex, Tubi, and Amazon. Rebel Satori Press published his second novel, *Performer Non Grata*, in 2023.

www.ingramcontent.com/pod-product-compliance
Lightning Source LLC
Chambersburg PA
CBHW030635020726
47493CB00006B/1729